Praise for *Terra*

"Prepare to be swept away by a unique and captivating fated mates romance that will enthrall you from start to finish. A fresh and imaginative take on the genre that is sure to leave you spellbound."

Judy Corry, USA Today
Bestselling Author
of Sweet Contemporary Romances

"With a Twilight feel, readers looking for a young adult urban fantasy will enjoy the hidden Elemental world of Terra. Excellent series for teen and up."

Morgan L. Busse, award-winning
author of the Ravenwood Saga,
Skyworld series, and the Nordic Wars

"Terra was a delightful surprise and kept me hungry for more. Weaving a tale of intrigue, romance, and danger, Sofia Simpson masterfully tugs on the heartstrings and crafts a tale of hope and redemption. A story to savor and an author to watch!"

Tara Johnson, Author of
To Speak His Name

Torch

Also by Sofia

Dream Weaver

An Elemental Series
Terra
Torch
Tempest

Operation Kane Novella

AN ELEMENTAL SERIES
BOOK TWO
Torch
SOFIA SIMPSON

TORCH

Original Cover by: SelfPubBookCovers.com/ RLSather
Updated Cover Designed by: EAH Creative

Editing by: Jessica Gwyn

Illustrations by: Joanna Hadzhieva

Map by: Sofia Simpson

To Charlotte, I wrote this book
with you in mind. Thank you for
loving my books so much.

p.s. I hope the kissy scenes aren't
too kissy.

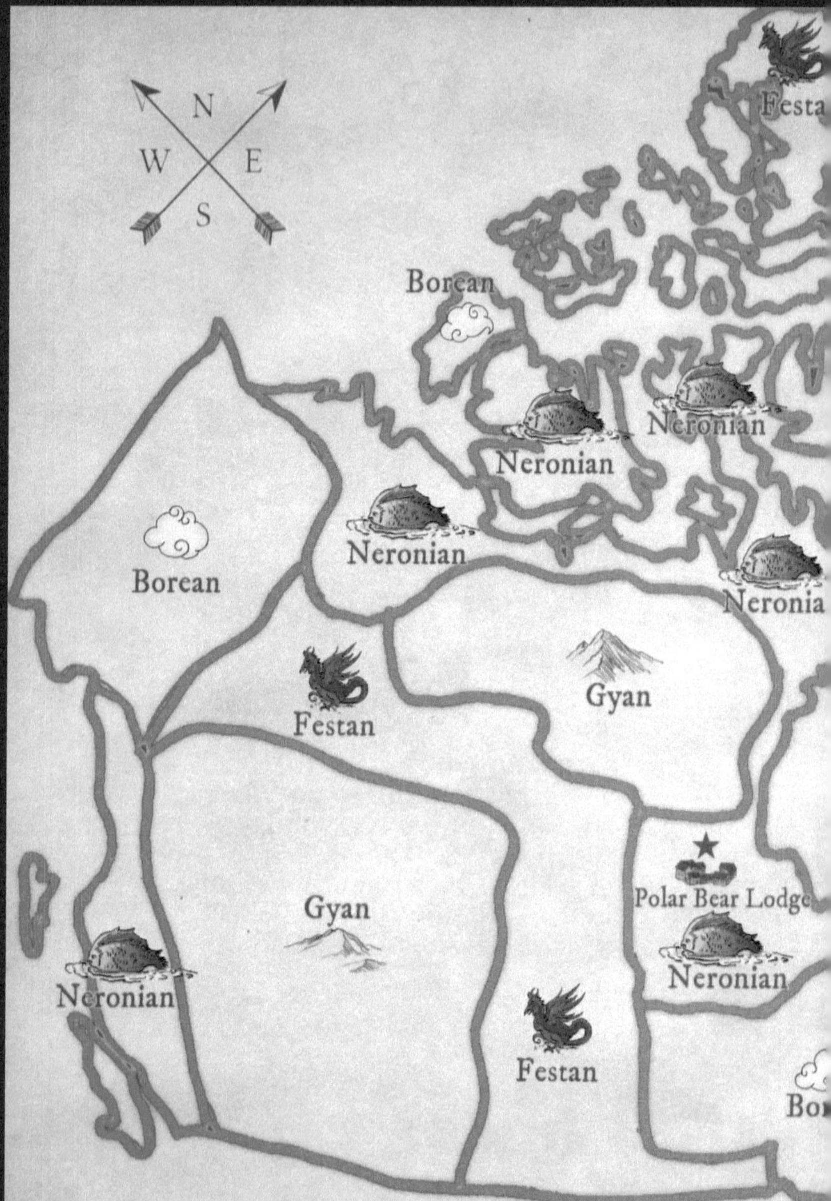

N
W
E
S
Borean
Borean
Neronian
Neronian
Neronian
Neronian
Neronian
Festan
Festan
Gyan
Gyan
Festan
Festan
Polar Bear Lodge
Neronian
Neronian
Bor
United States

Canada
Clan Territories

 Festan, Fire Elementals

 Neronian, Water Elementals

 Gyan, Earth Elementals

 Borean, Air Elementals

Vela

Linc

When the day and night are of equal length, a
warrior star who will bear the child will rise.
Under the Winter Solstice, the Hunter will emerge.
He will capture the Goat under the Northern sky
and they will produce the one who unifies.
Though their elements are diverse, through them
the Child will command them all.

Unknown
Around 1600 AD

PROLOGUE

T he man bunkers down, waiting for the Elemental Extremists to fling open the doors to the car. Clearly, his attempt to hide behind the barn has been unsuccessful.

He won't make it easy for them to kill his family.

Blinded by the lights to the two cars behind him, he tenses with anticipation. Concentrating, he reaches into the air outside the car, grabbing all the moisture he can. Zeroing in on the car's door handles, he freezes them. That should make it harder to get in.

Unless the attackers are Neronian, like him. Which is possible. He doesn't know which Elementals these are, just that they threaten him, his wife, and their unborn child.

He looks down at the love of his life, tears springing to his eyes. He reaches for her sobbing form and hugs her stomach, the child he will never get the chance to meet.

"I love you both," he says hoarsely. She knows that, but he wants her to hear it again, just the same.

She nods, choking on her sobs, gripping his arm.

"I could..." she starts to say.

"No," he says firmly. "You've done enough, and the pregnancy is precarious enough as it is."

"We don't have a choice. It's that or die," she whispers, her voice broken.

"You might have a chance to escape. If you use your element now, you will have no chance. The baby wouldn't survive either."

She whimpers.

He would do anything to live through the next few minutes with his beautiful, golden-haired wife. As he watches the figures walking up to his car, he doesn't see how he can make that happen.

His wife likely won't be spared either, not after she delivers their child into this fractured world. This group will probably kill the child...

Glass shatters, tiny slivers, like knives, explode into the air.

CHAPTER ONE

"There's someone following us."

At the sound of Linc's strained voice, I whip my head up from my book. Forehead pinched, his eyes dart back and forth from the road to the mirror.

Twisting in my seat, I see a black truck behind us. I nudge Jack, my red rust Doberman over, so I can see better out the back window. I wasn't paying attention and don't know how long the truck's been there. It's like a horse has taken up residence in my chest the way my heart is galloping. My mind races at who could be tracking our trip to the hidden Elemental community. We've taken every precaution in evading them, even going a roundabout way, making our trip much longer.

"Is it an Extremist?"

He glances over at me and says a curt, "No."

"How do you know? Who is it then?"

He hesitates, his lips a thin line. "I didn't want to tell you. I knew you'd worry. But, at our last gas stop, a couple of Borean guys caught wind that I'm a Festan."

I blow out a breath. Jack whines, sensing my anxiety. I slip my hand over his head, petting him. Wind Elementals, or

Wind Demons, as I call them, are fierce opponents. It's not a surprise they figured out Linc's element. Elementals can, when in close proximity, sense another's clan. Every clan feels different.

A cold terror climbs slowly up my windpipe. Jack whines again. "Shhh, Jack."

Linc's fingers clench the steering wheel in a white-knuckle grip. "They've been following us ever since."

"What?" I whip my body around to face him. "That last stop was over an hour ago! You should have told me." I look back again, trying to see the occupants of the truck. Because of their tinted windows, I only see an outline of two people.

My chest tightens. I can't breathe. Jack's wet nose finds my neck trying to comfort me.

Linc smacks the wheel and says, "I thought they were just making sure we left their area, but it seems like they want to make trouble."

Trouble seems to follow me wherever I go. I push Jack away. "Great," I wheeze. "Just what we need, an Elemental fight."

Taking deep breaths, I study the truck. I will them to leave us alone.

I feel Linc's gaze on me and his hand finds mine. I turn to look at him, his form swimming through my gathering tears.

Who are they?

"We'll deal with what comes. If it's trouble they want, they'll get it. But I'd rather avoid it," he says grimly.

Suddenly, the car lurches forward as the truck plows into us. My shrill scream joins the sound of crunching metal and shrieking tires. Jack yelps loudly. My head slams into the back of my seat and then whips forward. All I can do is hold on to the door. Absolute terror grips me as Linc fights to control the violent swerve of the car.

He slams the brakes, and our car fishtails madly. I try to reach back and hold on to Jack, but my hand slides off him as he's wrenched over to the other side of the car. He yelps.

Finally, our car stops, my head spinning from the crash. My breaths come quickly, and I turn my terrified gaze to Linc, praying he's okay.

Linc recovers from the crash more quickly than I do. He throws his door open, baring his teeth, hands immediately ready with twin balls of flames. I don't know what to do. I'm frozen and can hardly think.

Our car now faces the truck, but I don't see anyone in the cab. From the corner of my eye, I see Linc throwing the fireballs.

A whimper from the back seat snaps me awake. With trembling hands, I try to unbuckle my seatbelt, but can't get my hands to press the button to release the belt. Taking a deep breath, I pray, "God, help me out here." My fingers finally cooperate, and I whip the belt off. Turning around, I look over the seat to find my poor Jack laying limply on his side.

"Oh God, no." Reaching over the seat, I hold my hand over Jack's body, sensing for any injury. I can't find any from this position. He whines again and as much as it kills me, I must leave him for now. I have to help Linc. We're still in horrible danger.

Flopping back in my seat, I open my door. I scan the road for the two Wind Demons as I climb from the car.

They're nowhere to be seen.

"Vela, be careful," Linc warns me. "I don't know where they are." Linc calls out into the open air, "Come out and we can try to keep this civil."

I look over at Linc trying to get his attention, worry for Jack consuming me. He took the brunt of that crash. But Linc's busy trying to find the Boreans.

We're surrounded by forest, tall trees ominously silent of all animal and bird noises, as if they too are scared of an attack.

"Linc, Jack," I say quietly, my voice cracking.

"I know," he says gruffly. "But we can't do anything about him just yet. We have to find these guys first."

"They must be behind the truck," I say out of the corner of my mouth, stretching to peer around the back. No heads pop out at us.

"I've already lobbed two fireballs back there, but no one came out," Linc says just as quietly.

Terror strikes me in a fresh wave. Not only did these Boreans crash into our car and severely injure my dog, but now they're hunting us. I look wildly around, eyeing every tree. They could be anywhere. There's not another car on the road. This is a nightmare. *"God, help us,"* I pray silently.

"Linc, we're sitting ducks standing here on the road. Unless," I say, the idea suddenly coming to me, "they're injured and are still in the truck."

"Maybe," Linc says as he creeps over to the driver's side door.

I wait, every nerve firing warnings at me to find some kind of cover. As soon as Linc looks in the window, a windblast blows him backward, his head knocking into the cement.

I watch in horror as his head literally *bounces* off the pavement. I hear a sickening thunk, *twice*. "Linc!" I scream, tears springing to my eyes.

Linc groans and doesn't move.

Laughter fills the air, coming from both sides of me. They're hidden in the trees. I can't see where.

Horror rips through me that not only did they attack us with absolutely no provocation, but they're laughing about it. Time seems to suspend as I look over at Linc, who's still not moving.

The terror that has consumed me since I learned about the Boreans pursuing us turns into unadulterated rage. "God, help me. Give me strength," I grit out. Clenching my hands, I close my eyes and feed the anger coursing through my veins. I focus on my element and swear I feel the wind pick up. They're planning something more.

That's not happening. I won't let them.

Still standing in the middle of the road, I whip my arms up, connecting immediately to the trees on either side of me. I pinpoint where I heard the laughing. Controlling the trees' branches, I push them back to their breaking point, then let go.

The trees fling the Boreans out of their hiding places. I may have overdone it a bit, because two bodies sail through the air, landing in the middle of the road. A dark-haired guy lands on his back and another with lighter hair groans on his side. Both wheeze in pain and shock.

I look them over. *They're just teens.*

At least I'm not dealing with full-grown men. I find two roots that will work nicely as ropes on the side of the road. In a spray of dirt, I wrench them out of the ground and work them around the two writhing bodies. The roots coil quickly, pinning their arms and legs together at their sides.

I stop my efforts, allowing them just enough room to breathe. They're powerless without the use of their hands.

Running over to Linc, I wince when I see he's lying in a pool of blood but whisper a word of thanks when I see his chest rise and fall.

Thank God! He's alive.

I cradle his head and run my fingers gently over the gash on the back of his skull. My fingers are soon washed in blood. Head wounds are the worst when it comes to bleeding.

He moans and tries to move away from my probing fingers. I keep a hold of him. Concentrating on the healing power deep inside of me, I pray to do this correctly. I'm not the best healer and head injuries are tricky. But I know enough to close his wound.

Pulling up my gift, I slowly fuse the open gash. After the wound is sealed, I exhale quietly, realizing I had been holding my breath. I scan the area around Linc's injury, searching for internal bleeding. I don't sense any. Relief washes over me.

But my work isn't finished. I hold my breath again. Paying close attention to my senses, I try to tell if his brain is pushing too hard against the lining. Wishing I was a better healer, I study the area and don't think his brain is doing anything unnatural.

My heart races. I'm so relieved, a sob escapes my lips. I run my hands over his chest, arms, and legs, searching for any other wound.

He moans again.

I glare over at the two guys I've contained. Linc's rib is cracked. Nothing else seems to be broken. Infusing healing warmth into my hand, I place it over Linc's injured rib and wait until I feel it is healthy and well.

I look over at Linc's face, hoping to see his blue eyes looking back at me. He doesn't wake up. I rise from my crouched position.

I'm going to get answers, and I'm getting them now.

Controlling my anger, I speak in a low but dangerous voice, "You *hurt my boyfriend*. You crashed our car. You *almost killed my dog*. Why?"

I tighten the rope of roots. The two teens moan.

"Why?" I demand. "We did nothing to you. You find it funny to blast people down? To crash into a car? You could have killed him. You could have killed us. And yet you laugh."

Their only answers are glares.

"You will listen to me very carefully." I raise my fist covered in Linc's blood. The sight must be alarming because their eyes widen. "I'm going to count to five. You have exactly five seconds to tell me why you followed and attacked us." I narrow my eyes. "And you'd better have a good explanation for why you found it funny."

Nothing comes from my two hostages as I wait, counting silently. Their eyes drill into me angrily. If they had use of their hands, I'm sure I'd receive injuries like Linc's.

When I've finished counting and they've said nothing, I say, "Okay, let's see if you'll talk now." I squeeze the ropes, eliciting screams from them both. "Have something to tell me?" I let up the pressure slightly so they can talk.

"Fine!" the dark-haired one screams. "We just wanted some fun, is all. We knew you weren't Boreans, so we wanted to mess with you."

"Do you see him?" I scream, pointing at Linc. "He hasn't gotten up from the *fun* you had. He had better be okay, or you *will* see the full force of my rage. And you are *lucky* my dog isn't dead."

"We're sorry," the blond one blurts. "We won't mess with you guys anymore."

"Oh, I know you won't."

Walking over to a nearby tree, I call on its roots. Speeding them through the ground over to me, I wrench them up. I relish the dirt that sprays over my face, connecting immediately with my gift, making it stronger. I wrap the roots around the Boreans' ankles and pull their prone bodies toward the tree.

They both scream in terror and pain as they're dragged across the road. I order the roots to hang them upside down from a high branch.

Their screams knife through me, but I ignore their cries.

This will teach them a lesson to mess with future Elemental travelers. And it's also justice for what they did to Linc and Jack.

CHAPTER TWO

I war with myself about whether I should check on Jack or Linc first. As much as I love Jack, I need to be sure Linc is okay. Stifling a sob, I race back over to his side, praying he's at least woken up. I've done the best my subpar healing abilities allow. If he doesn't stir soon, I'll have to drag him into our car.

Dropping to my knees next to him, I turn his face toward me. His eyes are fluttering. That's a good sign.

Please, Lord, don't let him be seriously injured.

Hot anger swells, and I press my fury down where I can handle it later. I've done everything I can to those two idiotic teenagers.

Cupping Linc's cheek, my hand trembles with fear. "Linc? Linc, are you okay?"

A groan answers me. His eyes remain closed.

I tap his face gently. "Linc?"

He doesn't respond. I try not to worry; an injury like his will take time to heal. Or he could be slipping into a coma. No, that's not what's happening. He's responsive enough to groan.

I debate whether to take him to a hospital. Those places are tricky. An Elemental can benefit from traditional treatment, but when we're sick, we can accidentally lash out with our gifts.

The memory-erasing poppy seed formula has been useful in those cases.

The problem is, I don't have any.

Looking around, I'm surprised that not one car has passed since this all started. The Borean teens must have known this road is practically abandoned. It's why they smashed into us here. Glancing over at them, I ignore their shouts, but those have turned from threats to begging at this point.

They can hang there for a while longer. When we leave, I'll get them down. I scoff. I should leave them up there, so they'll fall hard when the roots let them go when I drive away.

I resist the temptation. I don't really want to kill them, but I'll let them think I'll drop them.

I hear Jack whining from the car. Leaving Linc on the road, I move to check on Jack. Racing over to the car, I look into the window to be sure Jack isn't against the door before I open it. I don't want him to fall out.

He's in the middle of the seat, his side twitching. Wrenching the door open, I crawl in, stress overwhelming me. I sob when I cradle Jack's head, my hands and mind searching for wounds.

I don't see any blood, so he must have internal injuries. A fresh flood of anger rises through me at the damage those thoughtless teens have done. I pray quickly for help in healing my beautiful dog. Running my hands over his dark, smooth coat, I immediately find one, no, two cracked ribs. I tamp down my fury and concentrate on the healing warmth in my hands. Pouring forth all my strength, I hold my hands over the first rib, slowly tracing it to be sure it's fine before I focus on the second rib.

Healing Jack so soon after Linc strips me of strength, and I hunch over, breathing hard. My head swims. I'm struggling. Hanging my head, I take a minute to breathe through my nose. My hand moves as I change position. With my senses on full alert, I feel bleeding coming from Jack's lung.

"No, no, no," I whisper hoarsely.

I need to replenish my gift from the nature around us, but I can't leave Jack. He'll die if I don't stop that bleeding.

Taking the deepest breath I can manage; I ignore my terror at losing him and push down my fatigue. I hold both hands over the bleeding and squeeze my eyes shut so I won't see the world spinning. Pouring my gift into Jack, I seal the broken veins and capillaries inside his lung.

Crying out, I slump over Jack when I finish. He softly whines and licks my face gently.

Turning my head, I look over at him. His warm brown eyes gaze at me in complete trust and I burst into tears.

"Jack? Are you okay, buddy?" I slip my limp hand onto his head, and he lays it back down to rest. With the last of my nonexistent energy, I scan his body to be sure everything else is healthy.

Thank you, God, he's okay.

I rest for a second, but know I need to get up. It's taking the last reserve of my strength to hold on to the roots suspending the Boreans. But I manage.

Linc is still out cold on the ground, and it looks like I'm the one who's going to have to get us out of here. Kissing Jack's side, I awkwardly move my legs out the open door. If I have to crawl over to the grass, I will. Once I replenish my energy, I can help Linc.

Sliding off the seat, I fall to the ground and sure enough, I can't walk. I brace myself on my hands and knees and slowly crawl over to the side of the road.

It's slow going, but once I reach it, I sink my fingers into the grass, thankful that stray bushes are close enough for my powers to reach. I pull from their leaves and roots until they go limp, and I mourn their loss.

I didn't have a choice, but immediately, I perk up.

Now able to stand, I slowly make my way over to the nearest tree. I'm still dangerously low on energy. I'll need more if I'm going to get Linc in the car.

Placing my hand on the trunk of a beautiful pine, I pull its healing energy into me. Washed with new and wonderful power, I stop taking and give back a little to the huge tree. Satisfied it'll survive my theft; I lean my head on it for a moment before walking back toward Linc.

I hope we can get out of here fast.

Which reminds me, is the car drivable? Changing directions, I go over to our gray sedan. Linc chose this car because it's so unremarkable. I shake my head as I look it over, both hands on my hips. It's definitely recognizable now. The entire fender is crumpled, and the trunk is smashed. It looks squished.

How did Jack survive that in the backseat?

Thankful he's okay, I glance over at the car to see if Jack is at least sitting up. He's not. Knowing he needs his rest, I check over each back tire. I breathe in relief. They don't look like they're obstructed. I know next to nothing about cars, but aren't axles pretty important? I hope they're not broken or damaged in any way.

I would look under the car to see, but I wouldn't know what I'm looking for, so I decide to just drive the car a few feet.

Folding myself into the driver's seat, I moan. The crash is going to catch up to me later. I can already feel my back and neck muscles stiffening.

Whiplash is no joke.

Starting the car, I say a quick prayer and press softly on the gas pedal. Mercifully, it moves a few feet. I don't hear any clunking or anything, so I brake and put the car in park.

Thank you, Lord!

I left the door open, so when I turn off the car, I hear a moan from the road where I left Linc.

I jump out of my seat and run over to him. I cradle his head and lean over him. "Linc? Linc, are you with me?

His eyes open slowly, squinting against the sun shining into them. He groans again and squeezes his eyes shut quickly.

He really needs to be in a dark place as he recovers, so I tell him, "Let's get you in the car. We'll find a hotel so you can rest. Somewhere it's dark." Wanting to hear his voice, I ask, "Are you okay? Tell me what you're feeling."

He grimaces and raises his hand up to the back of his head. "It hurts. The back of my head," he finally says.

He's not slurring his words, he's just in pain. Okay, I can deal with that. Now that I have some of my energy back, I put my hands over his wound and infuse a healing warmth into him.

He moans, but this time in satisfaction. "That's better. Now I'm just dizzy."

"That'll just take time to heal. I'm not sure how to help you with that," I say, sorry I'm not a better Gyan.

"It's okay, I'll manage."

"Come on, let's get you up." Sliding my arm behind his head, I get him into a sitting position. He leans on me heavily. His scent washes over me, and I breathe in the familiar smoke and cinnamon. "Linc, I'm so glad you're awake. I tried my best to heal your injury..." Shaking my head at my ineptitude, I finish, "But I think with a little bit of rest, you'll be fine."

He mumbles a response, but I can't understand him.

My chest swells with equal rage and sympathy that he's in this position. "Okay, I'm going to try to get you up, but I need your help. You're huge. I can't do this myself."

He grunts in acknowledgement, and I glance over at him. His eyes are squeezed shut, and his face is scrunched. Sweat dots his forehead, and I vow to get him in the car and to a dark room as quickly as possible.

I get my legs under me and squat next to him. "Okay, Linc, on the count of three, let's stand up."

"Wait. Jack? Is he okay?"

My heart squeezes at his care for my furry best friend. "He's okay. I healed a couple of broken ribs and some internal bleeding."

His eyebrows raise. "I'm impressed."

I shrug. I'm slowly going into a state of shock. I know the next time I'm alone, I'll crawl into a fetal position and cry over this. Now's not the time for that, though. "But he's still not up."

His hand finds mine on the pavement. "I'm sure he's okay. You did great, Vela."

My heart lifts in gratitude.

He goes quiet, and I see him staring at my hand. It's still covered in his blood.

"Is that yours?" he grits out. His face is set in fury, and he looks me over, trying to find my injury. "I'll kill them," he fumes.

"No," I quickly assure him. "It's your blood."

"Where are they?" He looks around slowly. I know his head wound isn't fully healed and any movement must be painful.

He soon finds their still forms hanging upside down. I'm surprised that I haven't heard their cries for mercy and help. They're quiet now. They must have seen Linc wake up and are afraid they'll be incinerated. If Linc was in any condition to do it, I'm sure he'd be tempted.

Slowly moving his gaze away from the Boreans, he asks, "The car? Is it drivable?"

Glad I already checked, I assure him, "It's good. A little crumpled, but it drives."

"Sorry I didn't help." He motions his head toward the teens, then grimaces at the movement.

"Don't even worry about it. Okay, one," I start to count down and I feel his muscles stiffening next to me as he gets ready to stand. Hoping he can, I finish counting.

In a surge, both Linc and I get to our feet. I hold on to him tight because he sways. That's to be expected. I wait until he stops rocking.

"Ready?" I ask breathlessly after a moment.

"I think so," he grits out. "Let's go."

We take a step, and he moans again. I stop in my tracks, looking him over.

"I'm okay," he rasps. "We need to keep moving."

A swell of respect for Linc pushes me on. We walk a few unsteady steps, Linc stopping often.

When we finally make it to the car, I say firmly, "You need to lie down." I know he's not going to like this, but I tell him, "You're going in the back seat."

His body stiffens. But he steps over to the side so I can open the back door.

"What about Jack?" He looks into the back and we both see Jack laying on his side.

It hurts me to say this, but I do. "I'll put him on the floorboard. He'll fit if I put his legs under the seats."

I don't have the strength to lift a hundred-pound dog and get him into the passenger seat. The floor will have to work for now.

Leaning Linc onto the side of the car, I leave him as soon as I know he won't fall over. He nods curtly, and I turn my attention to Jack.

"Come on, baby," I say to my poor dog. He looks up at me with pitiful eyes and my heart squeezes at his state. As carefully as I can, I move his front legs to the floor of the car. Bracing myself for his weight, I slip my arms underneath as much of his body as I can and slide his whole body down to the floor. I cushion his fall as best as I can and a sob slips when he whines. "Sorry, baby, sorry," I whisper.

He's landed more on his back than his side, so I contain my pity and position his back legs so they fit under the passenger seat. Then I move his front legs, curling them up because they don't stretch to fit under the driver's seat like I thought they would.

Looking him over, I run my hands over his sleek coat to be sure there aren't more injuries I might have missed. I don't sense anything, so I leave him there and move to help Linc.

"Is he okay?" Linc rasps.

"Yea, I think so." I wipe my face.

"Hey," he says softly and pulls me into a hug. He holds the back of my head to his chest, and I relax in his embrace. Just for a minute.

"You've done amazing. I can't believe you had to deal with all of this by yourself."

Sniffing, I pull away. With his caring words, I'm on the verge of a breakdown. "I'm okay, come on. We've got to get out of here."

He studies me, and I avoid his eyes. I can't look at the concern I know is there, or I'll lose it for sure.

I see him nod once, and then he tries to fold himself carefully into the car. I hold on to his middle and pull him to me a little bit, so his head won't hit the car on his way onto the seat. He makes it in, breathing heavily as he gets his legs situated.

It's awkward with him sharing his leg space with Jack, but he shouldn't be sitting up, anyway.

When he doesn't lay down, I say, "Linc, you really need to rest."

He frowns. "I am resting. I need to stay awake. I need to help."

"Stop right there," I interrupt. "You need to get well and let me take care of you for once. You need to lie down."

A burst of love fills me at the thought that I can, for the first time, take care of Linc. He's always been the one to take charge, and for the first time, I'm in that position.

Sighing heavily, he gives in and leans over to his side.

I wait until he gets himself situated; my nerves frayed with worrying about him and Jack.

Did I heal them well enough? Will they be okay? Will Linc slip into a coma? I can't let him sleep.

Instead of uselessly worrying, I put my thoughts to better use and pray. Putting one hand on Linc's leg and the other on Jack, I pray over them, "God, heal what I can't in Jack and Linc. Please Lord, help them and help me get them to a safe place."

With that, I bow my head briefly then get up, leaving my two precious friends in the back seat while I get in the driver's seat and take us away from this nightmare.

As we pull away, I drop the Boreans, suddenly enough to scare them, but gently enough so they're not injured by the fall. It's more than they deserve. I hope they learn from their punishment and never hurt another person or Elemental again.

CHAPTER THREE

I look behind me to check on Linc and Jack so frequently I'm afraid I'll add a crick in my neck to the whiplash injuries.

When I call to Linc, he answers in a soft grunt like he has for the past hour. I have to keep him awake, so he doesn't slip into a coma. That I will not allow. I think by the time we find a hotel, it will be safe to let him sleep. I'll ask mom about it, she'll know.

I need to tell my parents and Linc's what happened. But I'm trying to be quiet for my patients' sake. When we get to a hotel and get them situated, I'll be able to step out and call.

Driving as carefully as I can, I try to avoid any bumps in the road, so I don't disturb their rest. I try not to worry that I didn't heal them completely, that I missed something. Shouldn't Jack at least be up by now? I wish for the millionth time I could heal like Drew can.

Ugh.

Ok, no more worrying. Instead, I pray. I pray for their healing, for our safety, for a motel and civilization of any kind. I've been driving down this road for the past hour and still haven't seen another road or intersection.

I scream in my head and resort to begging God to bring us into a town. I'd take anything at this point.

Wait. I almost hit my head in frustration. I can look for a hotel on my phone! Pulling it out of my pocket, I slow the car to a stop and put it in park. No way am I driving and looking at my phone at the same time.

What state are we in again? Pulling up my GPS, I huff in frustration. Nothing, there's no signal. Of course not, there's probably not a cell tower within a hundred miles of here.

Last I checked with Linc, he told me we're in Iowa, the next big city is Des Moines. I try to remember if it's the state capital. Either way, I just don't want to be in a big city full of Wind Demons. It's better if we can hide out in a little human town. Elementals tend to live in groups and big cities.

Holding my phone to my chest, I beg it to give me one little bar that will allow me to search for hotels. My search spins, revealing nothing. No bars pop up.

Okay, I'm going to have to do this the old-fashioned way. Stop and get a map. But where is there a gas station around here? Checking to be sure that a car hasn't miraculously appeared on the road, I slowly get back onto the highway.

I wish I could talk to my best friend, Elia. If only I could be more like her. She always sees the positive in everything. She'd find a way to make this an adventure. That is not where my headspace is right now.

My thoughts filter back to the past few weeks when I first met Linc. He flew into my life like a blaze of fire, incinerating everything I had ever known and will ever know. He's changed my life irrevocably, and I can't be mad at him for it.

My dream of owning the best flower shop in town is caput. I won't graduate with my best friend. I already miss my parents and brothers. But again, I can't be mad at Linc.

I examine the bond in my chest that has Linc's name stamped on it. It glows fiercely, and I hold on to the warmth it feeds into my bloodstream. He makes me stronger, a better friend, daughter...bond mate. My insides light up at the thought that he'll always be a part of me.

Even those times I thought of abandoning our bond, I knew deep down he would always be there, mainly because he never stopped fighting for me. That's always been a good feeling. Even when I swore I hated it. Secretly, it thrilled me. Even thinking about it brings a smile to my face. I put up quite a good fight when it came to Linc, but then so did he. And look where that got me. Now I'm fighting for him, doing everything I can to get him somewhere safe so he can rest and recover.

A thought worms into my mind, and I can't help but examine it.

Should we really be going to this hidden place?

Have we made a huge mistake in taking this trip? I wonder at God's plan in all of this. Is He asking us to suffer this way or are we suffering because of our horrible choice to leave my home? I squirm, uncomfortable. Ever since I forgave the Festans for burning down my childhood home, I've felt such peace in my life. I certainly don't feel peace now. Is this God's way of telling me we need to turn around?

I drive, thinking that through.

We're on our way to this Elemental community so carefully hidden only a few people on earth know about it. Linc says there are more of them, but we're heading to the most established one.

That makes me feel somewhat better. The whole thing is scary, to say the least. I never considered living off the grid. I've taken advantage of every wonderful twenty-first century luxury and have enjoyed them immensely. The thought of not having a toilet with running water sends me in a tailspin rivaling the one our car did when it was rammed.

That thought reminds me to look back at Linc and Jack again. I rub my sore neck but rest it on the headrest when I turn back around. They're both resting, and I attempt to squash my worry.

God, I'm scared. Help me know I'm doing the right thing by going to this place. And, Lord, as far as Linc and Jack, you've given me this wonderful gift of healing and I don't think I used it as well as I could. Protect them, Lord, help them get better. Please!

In the far distance, I think I see a sign poking out of the trees.

Is that a town? I step on the gas, because why not? There's not a soul on the road, especially not a cop. I strain my eyes.

Hoping it's not an illusion, I grip the steering wheel and pray I don't go over a bump in my hurry to get to whatever I'm seeing.

Yes! It is a sign! I squeal despite my intention not to.

Linc grunts in question.

"We're coming into a town," I tell him, then make myself calm down. Just because I see a sign doesn't mean there's a hotel nearby. As I get near it, I see it's a sign announcing a gas station and a few restaurants. My hope deflates.

I pass another sign that announces we're traveling in Stephens State Forest. That explains the slight elevation change I've noticed.

Turning onto the new road, I scan left and right. It's a tiny town but I decide to brave asking a gas station attendant and hope to God he or she isn't another Borean. This is, unfortunately, still their territory. We don't need to run into any more of them who'll follow us for hours and attempt to kill us.

Taking a deep breath, I turn into a podunk little gas station that has one pump and a closet for a store. This place is depressing, and instantly I feel sorry for whoever works here.

I see a sad flickering light announcing it's open, and frankly, I'm surprised.

Maybe this tiny little place is like the adorable town in *Gilmore Girls,* and I've just had the displeasure of stopping at the most depressing gas station I've ever seen. I pull in along the front, park the car, and quietly open my door.

"Vela?" Linc rasps.

"Shhh, just going to talk to the attendant."

"Be careful," he mumbles.

He's still not slurring, thank God. But he's exhausted. I'm shocked he's managed to stay awake. My constant annoying wake-up calls have at least helped with that. My heart swells in sympathy for him.

"I'll be right back."

"Check to see..." he starts to say.

"If they're an Elemental, I know," I assure him.

Stepping out of the car is painful. My muscles are stiff from being in one position for a while, especially after the wreck. My neck is sore and tense, but I ignore my discomfort. I know my pain is nothing compared to Linc's and Jack's.

Walking to the store, I pull the door open and immediately see the attendant. I feel for my blood to ice in my veins if the girl is a Wind Demon.

My shoulders slump with relief when I sense nothing. She's merely a human teenager. Her hair is scraped into a messy bun on the top of her head. She's wearing a pink tank top that doesn't seem to stay on well. One strap is hanging off her shoulder, and her chest is fully on display. I guess there isn't a dress code for workers in this place. I'm sure the owner is just happy to have someone manning the register.

I look around at the sad selection of snacks and, again, I'm shocked this place is open for business.

The girl also doesn't notice me.

"Um, excuse me?" I ask.

She's leaning against the counter, eyes glued on her phone, her body moving to a beat only she can hear.

I bite my lip, trying to tamp down my frustration, but understand her indifference. If I worked here, I'd be tempted to ignore the world, too.

Waving my hand, I approach the counter.

She spots me out of the corner of her eye and stands up slowly. She doesn't bother removing her wireless earbuds. She blows out a bubble of gum and holds out her hand.

I look at her curiously. What does she want?

She glances outside, and when she sees my car isn't at the pump, she grimaces and removes one earbud. Dark slashes of makeup line her dead eyes, reflecting utter boredom and indicates that she couldn't care less about what I have to say.

I count myself lucky she's giving me her attention. "Is there a hotel nearby?"

She raises her eyebrow. "You wanna' stay here? Why?" She continues to chomp her gum.

I snort because Elia would think this girl is hilarious. Personally, I find her annoying.

I raise my eyebrow in return. "Because I'm tired and would like a place to sleep." I remind myself to not give her too much attitude. I don't need an angry human any more than an angry Elemental. Humans can pack a punch too.

She puts her earbud back in her ear, looks back at her phone and says loudly over her music, "If you can find it, there's a motel a couple miles from here." She hikes a thumb over her shoulder.

I stare at her. She completely ignores me and resumes her dance to silent music.

How am I supposed to find this place? I wave my hand at her again, irritation pinching my nerves.

She ignores me.

"For the love of..." I mutter. "Hey!" I wave my hand closer to her face.

Yanking her earbud out of her ear again, she looks up at me with an exasperated look. "What?"

"Listen, you just told me there's a motel, but how am I supposed to find it? I can't read your mind, you know." My heart rate climbs, and breath quickens when I think about Linc and Jack. I stop myself from jumping over the counter and shaking the information from her. I put my hands on my hips instead.

"Look, I don't have all day to give you directions," she spits out. Chomping on her gum, she points down the road. "It's that way."

I look in that direction through the grimy windows and see nothing but a long stretch of country road cutting through a forest of trees. I glance back at my now nemesis and see she's popped that earbud back into her ear.

Holding my breath, I study the dirty floor and count to ten. If I give into my temper, trees are going to break through the windows and make a home in this dump. I remind myself that would not be good.

When waving no longer gets her attention, I lose it. Slamming my hands on the counter, I lean into her space, staring her down. Her hair and mine pick up and blow around our faces. Looking around, I wonder what fan just turned on. Then I look down at my hands. They're crusted with Linc's blood. She stares down at my hands too, eyes wide and mouth in a horrified O.

She jumps back, holding her phone to her chest like I'm going to take it from her. I consider it. The sudden breeze goes away, and I shake off the weirdness of the moment and put the worst offending hand behind my back.

I pantomime taking earbuds out of my ears with my cleanest digits. She complies, thank God.

"I don't mean to take up your valuable time, but where exactly down that road is this hotel?"

Her eyes wide, she swallows her gum, and says in a shaking voice, "Uh, it's not far."

"Okay," I say, getting somewhere with this girl. "How do you get there?" I say slowly, so she understands me.

She does and pulls an old notebook from under the counter. After scribbling furiously in a shaky hand, she rips out a sheet of paper and shoves it at me.

Plucking it from her trembling fingers, I look at it. The directions are barely legible.

Finally. "Thank you," I say with a pained smile. That took way too much effort, and my aching body and troubled thoughts over Linc and Jack soon take over. Holding my neck, I slowly make my way to the exit and pull open the scratched glass door a little too enthusiastically. It slams against the wall. I wince and wait to see if it will shatter into a million pieces. Thankfully, it holds.

Grateful to be done, I leave and walk back to the car as quickly as my legs will take me.

These directions were hard fought to get. If this motel is somewhat acceptable, I'll take it. We don't have many options out here.

CHAPTER FOUR

I jump back in the car and throw the car into reverse, barely stopping myself from peeling out of here. Linc and Jack wouldn't appreciate a move like that.

But it would have felt really good. I hope I'm not an annoying teenager like that attendant is.

As I drive away, I comfort myself with memories of all the times I was very helpful and accommodating to anyone who asked me for directions.

I wish more than anything that I could call Elia and tell her what just happened, but the car needs to be quiet, so I reign in the impulse. Plus, my phone still has no bars.

Studying the scribbled directions, I'm halfway scared the girl might be leading me to her bored boyfriend's house. Who will be waiting for us when we get there.

Shoving that worry out of my mind, I trust my own intimidation factor enough to follow the messy directions, at one point pulling over to make out the rough letters. I open my door and pour a bottle of water over my hands, cleaning them off as best as I can. I don't need a repeat performance of what happened with that girl back there.

Getting back on the road, I make a few turns down long dirt roads and pull up to a sad excuse for a motel. I'm still hoping that the majority of the town is a tiny little wonderland to explore. I'm not holding my breath, though, as what I've seen so far is pretty dismal.

I park the car in one of the few parking spaces this place offers. Hey, it's a place to sleep. We just need a dark room. Let's hope the beds are somewhat comfortable.

Linc hasn't made a sound, and I haven't checked on him since I stopped at the gas station. I lean over the car seat and put my hand on Jack to be sure his side is still moving. It is, thankfully. Then I shake Linc's shoulder as carefully as I can.

Despite my gentle shake, he wakes up with a start and then groans when he picks his head up too fast.

"Where are we?" he finally manages when he cracks his eyes open. He groans when he lifts himself up to lean on one elbow.

"I found us a motel," I say softly, not wanting to hurt his head by talking loudly.

He nods and slowly cranes his neck to look out the back window.

"We're somewhere around Stephens State Forest, that's all I know."

His eyebrows draw down and he tilts his head. "GPS should tell you where we are."

I hold up my phone. "No bars, not even one."

"Hmmm." He looks down and deep in thought.

I hope he has some words of wisdom. I look at the motel and frown that this is the best I could do.

Apparently, he agrees it's the best option for us too when he looks up at me and says, "Let's go get checked in."

"Oh no, you're not going anywhere. You're staying right here." Alarm and disbelief zings through me.

He looks up at me through his lashes with an intent I recognize as pure stubbornness. "Oh really? We need to be sure this place isn't full of Boreans." He shifts his body until he's sitting up. He's slow going and by the time he's done, drops of sweat line his brow.

"Linc," I say, rubbing my forehead. A headache is blooming at the fight I know is ahead of me.

"Who's stopping me?" he says in a stiff voice. He blows out a breath and hangs his head, steadying himself with both hands on the car seat.

"Uh, you?" I stare him down. "You can barely move. Just let me go and see if they're any danger to us."

He lifts his head slowly and stares me back down. "You are not going without me. Don't even try."

I huff. "I'd barely have to. A breeze could blow you down right now, Linc. You need to stay here. What are you going to do if I need to defend myself? You'd be more of a hindrance than anything. Stay. Here." I pin him with my hardest look.

It doesn't work.

He opens his door and slides his legs over. "I'm coming, Vela, and that's final. I'm feeling better."

I don't believe him. But short of throwing myself bodily on him to make him stay in the car, I have no hope of him staying behind.

A sudden inspiration strikes. I rush to say, "What about Jack? We can't leave him alone."

Looking over his shoulder, he grins at me. "Nice try, Vels. He's fine where he is. Let's go."

He stands up and I have no choice but to jump out of the car and stand by his side in case he falls over. Surprised he's steady, I hover my hand behind him just in case he needs help standing.

"Like I said, I'm fine." He squints into the sun, even though it's late afternoon.

Light sensitivity is standard with a head injury like his. Again, I wish with everything I have that I could have healed him properly.

Sighing, I look at what he's studying. He seems to take in the whole depressing scene.

"I know," I say before he can say anything.

"Okay. Let's just hope the people running this place are human." He steps away from the car, and I walk at his side, intent on catching him if he collapses.

His blue eyes warm, he says with a crooked grin, "Vela. Stop hovering. I'm fine. I'd tell you if I wasn't."

"Would you really?" I ask him, studying his face for any tells of dishonesty.

"Yes, now let's go, Dr. Ashcroft." He laughs softly and reaches for my hand. Inhaling deeply, he makes his way toward the front door. Looking at his back, I suck in a breath.

"Linc, stop." I step forward and put my hand on his shoulder. The back of his shirt looks like he just stepped out of a horror movie. With all the blood drying on his neck and dripping down his back, anyone with any sense would run away screaming if they saw him. "You need to change your shirt," I say firmly.

He stops and peers back at me. "That bad?"

"Yes. Your head gushed a bucket of blood back there. It looks like someone tried chopping your head off."

He turns and walks back to the car, this time with me walking behind him to hide the horrific work of two stupid Borean teens.

It takes some careful maneuvering, but I open the crushed trunk to retrieve our suitcases. I fish through his clothes until I find a short-sleeve button down he can wear.

I turn back to him and tilt my head, looking at him. "Now, how are we going to get this shirt off you? I don't want to hurt your head."

He solves the problem easily when he grips the bottom of his t-shirt and rips it open up to his neck. Sliding it off his shoulders, I swallow when I get a look at the blood that ran down his chest, too.

I also try very hard not to notice his beautiful physique. This is not the time to drool. Especially since he's now noticed my blush and grins widely at me.

"What?" I ask, throwing up my hands. "You have a lot going on there," I gesture toward his chest, and glare at him in embarrassment when he chuckles.

"A lot going on?" he asks, his eyebrow raised cockily. He takes his forgotten shirt from my fingers and starts shrugging it on.

"Wait!" I say, running over to the back seat where we stash our cache of water bottles. I shrug off my embarrassment and say over my shoulder, "Let's get you a little cleaned up first. The blood is still visible with your shirt on."

He hums in agreement and takes his shirt back off. I try not to be too thrilled by another minute with him shirtless. A girl can appreciate a nice view, after all.

I bring back a couple of bottles of water and pick up his ruined shirt. Pouring water over the clean patches, I stand on my tiptoes and dab softly at his neck.

Blushing at his bare-chested amazingness, I ignore the butterflies taking flight in my stomach and remind myself that I'm washing *blood* off him. That needs to be my focus. His injuries. Circling him, I continue to dab at the dried blood on the back of his neck but stop when he tenses. I got too close to his injury, but he stands still, trusting me to finish without hurting him. I continue as carefully as I can.

"There," I say as I finish, studying the area that will be visible above his shirt. "We'll get the rest once we're inside. A shower will go a long way in cleaning you up."

He nods, pulls his shirt on slowly, and buttons himself up. "Okay, let's go."

We make our way slowly to the office. The guy behind the counter is about as thrilled at working here as that gas attendant had been. He's young, about my age. I'm surprised to find so many young people in this small town.

"Can I help you?" he asks in a dead voice.

At least he's being helpful. And he's human. That's a huge relief.

"We'd like one room, please." Linc asks, and my heart lurches.

I look at him, my eyebrows raised. Why are we sharing a room, I ask with my eyes?

Linc looks around and gives me a significant look.

He doesn't trust this place or the locks, apparently. I'm not thrilled with this idea, but hopefully the room has two beds.

I ask to be sure. "Do you have a room with two beds?"

The guy looks up, interest flaring in his eyes, and he flicks a glance between Linc and I. "Uh, sure we do."

"Okay, great," I say, breathing a sigh of relief.

Looking at Linc skeptically, he then asks, "Are you guys together?"

Shocked he would ask, I don't get the chance to answer because Linc says in a hard voice, "Yes." He spears him with a dark look I wouldn't want to be the recipient of.

The guy blanches and says, "Sorry, man. Didn't mean to..."

"Apparently," Linc says, still staring at him.

The guy scrambles for a key that's hanging on the side wall. He hands it to Linc and promptly looks away.

Linc gives him one more dark look, then accepts the key. Turning, he puts his hand on the small of my back, which causes me to inhale sharply. I like this protective side of Linc.

We walk to the car a little quicker. "Linc, we don't have to rush. Are you okay?" I put my hand on his arm. When he nods stiffly, my attention is immediately pulled to the back window of our car.

Jack's beautiful face is panting behind the cracked window. I cry out in relief.

"Jack!" I run over to the car and yank open the door. Jack can't get out fast enough. He practically falls out and pushes his nose into my legs. Crouching down, I hug his neck and laugh when he licks my face like I'm a cherry popsicle. "I'm so glad you're okay," I tell him and pet his sides and back, checking for any residual pain. Not sensing any, I smile up at Linc.

He's petting Jack's head and receives a couple of sloppy kisses on his hand. "Glad you're okay, buddy," he says tiredly.

I notice he doesn't get down on Jack's level, and I study Linc's face. It's strained.

"Are you really okay, Linc?"

He gives me a pained smile. "I'll be fine. I just need to rest. This is, unfortunately, the only place in miles where I can do that." He turns to walk to the back of the car. He reaches to open the mangled trunk.

"Linc!" I cry, jumping up. "You can't carry anything."

"I have to," he grits out, putting both hands on the trunk, resting for a minute. "I can't let this guy know I'm not capable of knocking his head off." He glares in the direction of the office.

"Oh, Linc," I breathe, love pouring through me at his protectiveness. I turn toward him. "I can handle myself. I'm an awesome Gyan, remember?" A memory of my hair blowing around my face suddenly leaks into my thoughts, and I shake it off, like I did when it happened. I *am* a Gyan, and I will defend myself if needed. No one would believe a backwoods creep like this guy if he told them I forced a tree branch around his throat if he tried messing with me.

Linc picks himself up off the trunk and looks at me, exhaustion crowding his eyes.

I jump at the chance to help him and deflate a little that he's too hurt to do it himself. I did the best I could to heal him, I remind myself firmly.

Finagling the trunk open, I pick up the heavier suitcase, shooting him a stern look when he tries to take it from me.

He gives in and takes the lighter one.

I smile in victory and push past him, trying not to trip over Jack. He's sticking to me like glue, but I crow internally that he's doing so much better.

"Alright you two," I tell Jack and Linc, "Let's go see what this place looks like on the inside."

Rolling the suitcase, I look for our room number, then wait a minute for Jack to do his business in the grass. Going to the correct room, the three of us start, hopefully, a trouble-free rest.

CHAPTER FIVE

We get some food from a local diner and my belly is happy to be nice and full again, even though my body is complaining with all my sore muscles. I take the pills I bought that will help that.

As it's late at this point, going on ten o'clock, I decide to get dressed for bed. I open my suitcase and stare at its contents, deciding to wear the baggiest, ugliest, darkest clothing I can find. I can't wear the little pj's I normally wear around Linc. I blush at the thought.

I go into the bathroom with my things, my thoughts full. It's strange to think I'll be sleeping in the same room as Linc.

If I examine my feelings closely, I see clearly that my primary emotion is fear. I'm afraid to sleep in the same room with him because of what could happen.

Anytime you're in a bedroom with a guy you really like, there's this elephant in the room that *you're in a room alone with a cute guy.* Things could happen that shouldn't happen until you're married and that would be a mistake.

How did he ever convince me to do this? Then I remind myself that he's only concerned for my safety and "those things" are far from his mind. He's exhausted and injured.

Those scenarios instantly fly out of my brain, and I shut the door firmly on the possibility of their return.

Besides, this is Linc. He is the consummate gentleman and would never even think about trying anything. I look down at my strange pajama pants. I should be comfortable, but I'm usually hot when I sleep and wear tanks and shorts. This will be fine, I assure myself.

He looks up when I crack open the bathroom door and walk into the room.

Linc sits on his bed, messing with his phone. He cracks a smile when he sees my outfit, and then looks back at his phone, the smile lingering.

"What's that smile for?" I ask, my hackles up.

"Nothing," he denies, a smile still in place.

"You're smiling for some reason, and I want to know why." I hold up my pillow threatening. "I'll hit you with this if you don't tell me."

He cocks his eyebrow. "That could actually hurt me in the state I'm in."

"I know."

He leans back, putting down his phone. "That's actually cruel."

"Well then, you know I'm being serious. Why were you smiling?" I hold the pillow back, like I'm ready to let it fly.

The smile returns as he looks away. He waves in my direction. "It's just that you're trying too hard."

I splutter. "Uh, excuse me! I think I chose well. These are my sleep clothes." I look down at myself, covered from head to toe. I'm already sweating.

He laughs. "Vela, every Elemental sleeps hot, even I know that. You're going to melt in that getup." He looks me up and down. "Are you sure that's you under all of that? Anyway," he drawls, looking away, "you don't have to worry."

"Worry? I'm not worried, at all," I rush to say, my throat closing in spasms of sudden nerves. I clear my throat nervously and look away.

"Vela," Linc says in a serious tone, and I drag my eyes back over to him, a blush coming over my cheeks.

He's figured me out.

"I would *never* do anything that isn't appropriate. I feel the same about waiting until marriage. I promise, you don't have to worry about me trying...anything." A soft blush comes over his cheeks, and I relax a little, knowing he's just as uncomfortable as I am.

"Not that I wouldn't be tempted," he adds, which forces a deep blush to bloom on my cheeks. "Because it's not always easy to be good," he quotes with his fingers. "But I will be. So, if you want to wear a t-shirt or something, you're perfectly safe with me."

I play with the hem of my oversized sweatshirt. "Linc, I don't know what to say. This is just a little awkward, you know? In a bad way and a good way. I mean, I'm just as tempted, believe me, so that's the bad part, but it feels a little good knowing it's just as hard for you."

He looks down and says, "How about we just turn off the lights and go to bed early? You can wear however much or little you want to get comfortable." He whooshes out a breath, and my eyes widen at his words. I mean, I know they were innocently said, but their connotation comes across loud and clear. "You know what? Never mind, I think I'm turning in now. You do," he waves his hands at me, "whatever you want to do."

I smile because it's kind of adorable seeing Linc all flushed and uncomfortable. But I don't say anything as I turn off the lights. I open the curtains a little to let in a sliver of moonlight.

My mom would have a fit if she knew we were sleeping in the same room. Well, Linc is worth her anger. He wouldn't sleep if he was worrying about my safety all night. And if I put my foot down and sleep in another room, he might even do something stupid like sleep in front of my door.

Morning comes quickly, and I kick myself for leaving the curtains cracked as the sun shines happily into our room.

Our room. That reminds me. I pop up my head and look to see if Linc's awake yet. I woke up several times in the night to check on him. Thankfully, he woke up just fine every time.

He's still asleep, and I take a minute to appreciate him sleeping. He looks so relaxed, his face smooth and free of any kind of worry.

My head suddenly spins, thinking about us. If I think he's spun my life out of orbit with his presence, then my presence has catapulted him out of the universe.

Even though he was planted in my town to spy on the Elemental Extremists, he had no idea he would find his Intended. I certainly never thought I would be lucky enough to find Linc. He's one in millions of Elementals. It's beyond rare to find your true soulmate. As Elementals, we believe that your Intended is your perfect match, a true complement to your personality. And the miraculous thing is, my parents are each other's Intendeds and found each other, too.

I study Linc's face. Something I would never do while he was awake. I appreciate the view. He really is beautiful. I hope he's as happy with me as I am with him.

It isn't just that he's perfect in every physical way. His mind is perfect, his thoughts, his very soul. It fits so well next to mine, deep inside me. I can't imagine, for one second, not having him in my life.

I look at his face and wonder about the sister he lost. He hasn't told me what happened yet, but I have a feeling whatever it was, resulted in Linc being sent away to his uncle. Linc doesn't seem to have a great relationship with his uncle or his parents. How could he when they sent him away? How could someone do that to their only child?

I think of my close-knit family and realize that I can't fathom my life without the support of my mom, dad, and brothers. They're technically sending me away too, but it's so different from Linc's situation. My family only did it because they love me and want me safe. I think Linc's parents just wanted him gone and out of sight.

Thinking of my parents squeezes my chest painfully and the reality of what we're doing crashes down on me. Leaving everything I know to stay safe in a hidden town that's in the middle of nowhere is pure craziness. But the Elemental Extremists are truly terrifying. They could find a hidden blade of grass in a football field. That's why this community we're going to exists: to hide couples like Linc and I from their murderous sight.

I shove those thoughts back; can't acknowledge them right now or I'll bury myself under a mountain of anxiety.

Memories of being back in the E.E.'s clutches, answering their questions, send a cold stab of fear that we could get caught again. Next time, we might not have my family to help us fight our way out.

We just have to be careful; I vow to myself. Stay low as we travel.

My stomach aches as I realize I don't even know where this place is or how long it will take to get there. I resolve to ask Linc for more information when he wakes, and I hope he knows more about our destination than I do. The only thing I know is that it's in the northern part of central Canada.

Linc makes a noise that sends me jumping to close the curtains. He's going to get as much rest as he can, I vow. He moans a little, and I rush over to him.

Sitting on the edge of his bed, I cradle his head to examine his injury. I just need to check to be sure nothing is wrong. Reaching out with my senses, I close my eyes to better see inside his head. I see that his brain is still not swelling. I glow with happiness at the relief I feel.

Linc's head turns in my hand, and he softly kisses my palm.

I gasp at the sensation that gives and pull my hand away from his lips in surprise.

He smiles and slowly opens his eyes to gaze sleepily at me. "Thank you," he say in a gravelly voice.

I smile down at him shyly. "For what?"

"Taking such good care of me."

I blush. "Of course."

"Everything look okay in there?"

I nod happily. "As best as I can tell. But you moaned just now. Are you still in a lot of pain?"

"Not really, just a little bit. It's a lot better than yesterday," he says at my frown. He covers my hand on the bed with his. "You did great, Vels. I'm amazed at you. You defended me better than I did you. I wish..."

I stop him. "We take care of each other, Linc. I told you, I'm not helpless, and we're a team."

"Oh, I know," he says, laughing. "I'm just glad we're on the same side. I'd hate to be your enemy."

"You were once," I whisper, shame coming over me at how I treated him when we first met. It took weeks for him to earn my trust on even the smallest level.

His eyes soften, caressing my face with his look. "Not anymore, though."

"Not anymore," I agree. Standing up, I let him take his time to wake up. I ended up just taking off my sweatshirt last night. I had a short-sleeved T-shirt on underneath it, and I'm ready to get dressed for the day.

Rifling through my clothes, I wish I had cell service so I can check the weather today. It's October and we're driving north, which means it will only get colder. In some sections of Canada, it's already snowing. I know because I checked the day before yesterday when we had service.

I try to remember what town our destination is close by but can't remember for the life of me what Linc said. We'll be traveling into Gyan territory soon, which is good, as long as no one takes offense that I'm traveling with a Festan. But then we'll be in Festan territory for a while before we cross over to Canada. As far as the Festans, Linc is sure he can smooth any ruffled feathers over my presence in his territory, like I'll do in mine.

I pray that we don't encounter any more problems and have a peaceful journey. But unfortunately, the E.E. has done a good job of inciting Elemental battles on the territorial borders to keep up animosity.

Animosity breeds distrust, and they're all about keeping us separate. That's how they make their money. By tricking Elementals in their group to heal the sick and provide fire and water services to farmers and others desperate enough to pay for Elemental gifts. I shake my head because it infuriates me that we can't just live united, like God intended all along. How did we get so far away from His perfect design?

Now it's just a seemingly unobtainable utopia. The thought of living united has always been a faraway dream. It'll only happen when the Chosen Child is born and is old enough to fulfill the prophecy and bring the clans together.

I remember the questions the E.E. asked me, and I seemed to have answered all the questions correctly. Doesn't that mean that I could be the parent of the Chosen Child? That's what they implied when they recited the prophecy to me. I've memorized it in the past few days, and I recite it in my mind now.

When the day and night are of equal length, a warrior star who will bear the child will rise. Under the Winter Solstice, the Hunter will emerge. He will capture the Goat under the Northern sky and they will produce the one who unifies. Though their elements are diverse, through them the Child will command them all.

I try to puzzle it out, sifting through the facts. My birthday is September 23rd, which is the Autumn Equinox. I was born in...wait, I don't know where I was born. I'm adopted. My real parents didn't say in their note where I was born.

My breath leaves me in a rush, and I lean over my suitcase, where I had been looking for a hair tie.

"Hey," Linc calls out in a soft voice. "Everything okay over there?"

I glance over at him and nod sharply, then turn my face away so he can't see the strain I'm sure shows.

Taking a deep breath, I pick up the clothes I'm changing into and toiletries then walk into the bathroom. I avoid looking at Linc, but I can feel his eyes on me. I step into the shower after waiting for it to heat up, then I let the tears I feel bottled up flow.

I'm adopted. How did I go my whole life without knowing that? My parents, my adoptive ones, I should say, but no, they will *always* be my parents, have supported and loved me my whole life. They will always hold the titles of mom and dad to me. They told me they didn't want me to think I wasn't as much a part of our family as my brothers. They wanted me to be old enough to handle the news and I guess at seventeen, I'm old enough. They were kind of forced to tell me, though. My mom thought she was dying and wanted to be the one to tell me before she was gone. But we saved her, miraculously, and she was able to explain a little before I had to leave.

I'm glad Linc doesn't know I'm crying. He doesn't need to worry about me. But I'm worried about me. How can I continue to handle these life-changing events without totally breaking down?

I'm just going to have to trust that God will take care of me. I've trusted Him with my life, so that's all I can do at this point. He knows my life from A to Z and it's barely begun. God knows exactly where I am and where I'm going. He won't fail me.

Finished with my shower, I dry myself off and change quickly. I emerge from the steaming bathroom, going straight to the mirror. I pick up and run a brush carefully through my wet hair. I've learned the hard way that hurrying only rips out my hard-earned long locks, so I take my time. It took years to grow out my waist-length hair.

After dabbing on some mascara and lip gloss, I go to close my suitcase and hope we're leaving today.

Linc steps into the bathroom to shower while I get ready and emerges wearing khaki pants and a t-shirt with the band's name, OneRepublic, on it. *Nice*. Not that Linc's nice, although he *is*, but the band, I meant. I'm proud that I know the band this time. I look away, hoping Linc doesn't notice my wayward mind. He smirks and says, "We need to call our parents. I don't know why I didn't think of it yesterday."

He walks past me, and I get a huge whiff of his distinctive scent that calls only to me. I inhale deeply and squeeze my eyes shut, trying to ignore the pull he has on me. "Umm, you were a bit preoccupied, Linc," I tell him, fighting the urge to pull him in for a kiss.

He seems to have the same idea, because when I open my eyes, he's inhaling deeply, too. My scent does the same thing to him that his does to me, and he's right in front of my lips, waiting for me to notice him. "Have I thanked you properly yet for the amazing way you handled our predicament yesterday?" he asks in husky voice.

I hold my breath, my eyes glued to his perfect lips. "Properly? No, I don't think so," I say breathlessly.

"Well, let's rectify that." He cups my head, pulling me the small distance to his lips.

Perfect doesn't do justice to his kisses. The way he angles his head, the firmness of his mouth, the *softness* of his lips, every indescribable feeling zings through me as he "properly" thanks me for my actions yesterday.

I inhale and wrap my arms around his neck, which he instantly takes advantage of by deepening the kiss. My stomach bottoms out with heat that quickly travels through me, and I allow myself to enjoy it for a minute before I pull away.

"Remind me to demand proper thanks every time I do anything remotely nice," I say, smiling against his lips.

His eyes are trained hungrily on mine, but I step back. "Remember what you promised yesterday, Romeo? That you'd be good."

He reaches for my waist and easily drags me back to him. "I *am* being good," he growls, and takes my lips again.

Fireworks could explode right next to me, and I wouldn't notice them with how expertly Linc teases my lips apart. I melt with how he sweeps through my mouth, sending delicious heat through me.

Somewhere in the back of my mind, I try to remember the caution I should be feeling. Something about being in a room alone...*Oh*, I remember and put my hands firmly on Linc's shoulders, reluctantly pushing him away from me and breaking our kiss.

We're both panting, and I stand still with my hands on his tense shoulders. He's holding himself back, so I say quickly, "I'm going to say one thing. It's a bad idea to be alone in a room together as perfectly healthy people. If we're going to honor God's wishes and save certain things until we're married, we need to stop now, Linc."

He looks pained as he hangs his head and nods. "You're right. I know you're right."

I step away from him, putting several steps between us. "We've been doing so well on this trip, Linc. We can't ruin our track record. My parents trust you; *I trust you*. Let's not mess this up."

He runs his hand through his hair, and says, "Okay. Let's stop doing *that*."

"Yes, no more proper thankyou's," I say, my laugh a little shaky.

"We can have them, but we'll stop before anything, you know...."

"Right," I say quickly because I know exactly what he means. Not that it will be easy. I don't want to make anything harder for us.

"So, phone call," Linc says, clapping his hands together. "We need to ask if they have a landline here." He turns around quickly, and I'm thrilled that he's able to move so much better than yesterday. He starts putting his clothes in his suitcase.

He zips it up and puts it by the door when I ask, "We're leaving?"

"Yes, of course," he says, looking at me, puzzled.

"I just want to be sure you're okay. You were badly injured, Linc. Don't push yourself."

"Vela, if I wasn't doing well, we'd have to stay another day, which your parents would not like. But I'm much better. Hasn't that been obvious?" He smiles crookedly at me, and I blush at how gorgeous he looks. His face is bright with health, his confidence has fully returned, and it looks good on him.

"Okay." I turn away. I need to stop admiring Linc. Just because we're in close proximity doesn't mean I can ogle him all the time.

He doesn't seem to mind, though. I sneak a peek at him and catch his heated look at me. This trip is fun, there's no denying it.

CHAPTER SIX

We check out quickly and are in the car before I know it. Linc's driving, he insists he's well enough to.

We're about twenty minutes into our drive when I turn my head to look at Linc. "Let's hope for no more adventures on the rest of our trip."

He snorts. "Vels, it's always an adventure with you. Crazy things follow you wherever you go. I've come to accept that."

I gasp. "That's not true!"

"Vela," he says, his voice warm. "You're trouble, woman."

"No, I'm not!" I cross my arms across my chest. I finger my scars, grounding me in who I am. *He's wrong.*

"It's okay. It's one of your many endearing qualities that I happen to find irresistible." He puts his hand on my knee and squeezes.

I lean back and think. I'm *trouble*? I don't know how I feel about this.

Not realizing I said that last part out loud, I jump when he says, "What, that I find you irresistible?"

"No, the fact that I'm trouble. I'm a completely dependable person, you know." I turn to look at him, throwing his hand off my leg.

"Completely," he agrees and smiles at me in mock innocence.

"What is that supposed to mean?" I scowl at him.

"Just that I can always depend on you to get me in some trouble or other." He laughs at my expression.

"I had *nothing* to do with those Boreans following us."

"Yet, you were present. Hence, trouble follows you wherever you go." He returns his hand to my bouncing knee. "It's okay. I love that about you. You keep things interesting."

"Linc! I did nothing to attract those Boreans' attention. It was *you* they noticed, remember? I can't be held responsible for you getting hurt like you did. Please don't put that on me!"

At my near screech, he stops smiling and looks at me seriously. "Hey, hey, that's not what I meant, Vels. I'm just teasing, I swear."

"That is not teasing material, Linc." I shove his hand off me again and look out the window. I can't look at him right now.

Linc slows the car and pulls over to the side of the road. He reaches over with both hands and gently turns my head to look at him.

I glare at him. I'm so mad, I'm not sure I can forgive him for what he just said. When I look away, he begs, "Vela, look at me."

I reluctantly turn and soften a little when I see his crestfallen expression.

"I would never put what those Boreans did on you, baby, I swear. I really was just teasing, just trying to make light of what happened."

Glancing away, I think back. He got caught up in my kidnapping, but that happened because of his involvement with the E.E. Maria had been jealous of me taking Linc's attention away from her and so told her dad about me. If not for that, I would have safely kept away from their attention. But, because of me, Linc had to reveal his role as a spy in their group. If it wasn't for me, he would still be doing an incredible thing, finding out what they're involved with and who they're targeting.

"Vela?"

His voice interrupts my thoughts. "I've ruined your life," I state. *It's true*. I have.

"No, no, you haven't, Vels. You've given my whole world meaning," he says with heat in his voice. He shifts in his seat to better face me. "If not for you, I'd be stuck in an existless existence. Believe me, when I say you have done nothing but make my life better. I was just teasing. Please believe me."

"Existless existence?" I ask with a soft smile. I lean toward him wanting to believe him.

"Completely. Vels, you bring meaning to my life. I went from having no one really caring about me to...you. That means more to me than I can possibly say." His eyes blaze as he searches my face for a sign of forgiveness.

My heart, of course, melts like goo. We're having such a charged moment that when I look in his eyes, I wonder if this is a good time to bring up his sister. He hardly mentions her. It's a painful subject, so I hesitate. But she's such a big part of his story and I don't even know her name.

"Linc?" I start, then bite my lip.

He tugs my lip away from my teeth with his thumb. "Hey stop that," he orders. "That's distracting me from my apology."

"Linc, will you tell me about your sister?" I ask softly. "You haven't even told me her name."

He leans back, looking stricken.

I just shocked him with that question. But now that it's out there, I can't take it back.

He pauses, then says, "I haven't?"

"No."

"I don't mean to not talk about her. It's just...I don't. It's too hard."

I put my hand over his and say, "I can imagine."

He looks at me and finally says, "It's Sarah. She was perfect." He stops for a minute and silence overtakes the car. He clears his throat and continues, "She was two years younger than me, and we were close. Still are. I won't ever forget her," he says, his pain-filled blue eyes burning his words into me.

"Of course, you won't, Linc," I say, unable to adequately voice my sorrow for him.

"But I've already done that by not talking about her," he says, his gaze troubled.

"No, Linc, that's not true. I understand that her loss is a very painful part of your life. It's completely natural to protect what hurts." When he doesn't say anything, I squeeze his hand, saying, "Hey, are you okay?"

His face looks defeated. He nods and stares out his window.

Wanting to comfort him, but respecting his time to mourn Sarah, I stay quiet, just keep holding his hand, rubbing circles on the top of it with my thumb. I feel helpless, so I pray for God to comfort Linc in a way I never could.

Linc's so quiet, he surprises me when he says quietly, "She was a lot like you. Not afraid of anything. That's what took her in the end."

Surprised he's ready to talk about her, I ask, "What happened to her, Linc?"

He inhales deeply, suddenly, like he just remembered to breathe. "She wanted to try anything and everything. When she was fifteen, she decided she wanted to try rock climbing." His look is so far away, I know he's there in that moment.

My stomach plummets. Please don't tell me that's how he lost her. I just look at him, hoping he won't say it.

"She wouldn't take no for an answer," he continues, shaking his head as he looks out the window. "The only thing I could do was get her lessons, so she would, at least, know how to be safe."

"Your parents?" I ask softly. Surely, they had something to say about this.

He laughs harshly. His throat swallows and he says bleakly, "They told me to be sure she didn't kill herself."

"Oh, Linc." My heart breaks for him. This sounds unrecoverable.

"Well, I failed," he said, his voice cracking. He turns his head so I can see his face, and he shuts his eyes, but not before a tear leaks out. He then hides his face from me, but his shoulders shake, and I know this I why he never talks about her. The monstrous guilt he feels is too hard, too raw to handle.

I lean over and hug him as tightly as I can. I feel his tears leak on my shoulder, and I turn to kiss his wet cheek. If I could kiss every tear away, I would, but he needs this right now.

Tears flood my eyes, and I whisper in his ear, "I'm so sorry, baby. I'm so sorry." I just hold him and try to breathe through my pain for what he's feeling. Unable to stop myself, I say, "You are loved, Lincoln Stevenson. By me, by your sister. Always. We will always love you."

His breath hitches as fresh tears attack him. I hold on silently and cry with him as I let my words sink in.

It takes a few minutes for him to settle, but eventually he leans away, scrubbing his face.

I reach into the glove box for a napkin and wordlessly hand it to him, taking one for myself, too.

"Sorry," he says as he uses the napkin to wipe away his grief. "I don't usually do this." He shakes his head.

"Hey, you can talk about her anytime you want, okay? Anytime," I promise. My heart thumps heavily in my chest at how his heart still bleeds fresh, like this is a raw wound. Then I think. If she was fifteen, he was seventeen, so this just happened last year. A surge of pity swamps me. This *is* fresh. And he's had to deal with it alone. That's not fair. I suddenly wish I could rail at his parents for leaving him by himself to deal with this trauma. They should have been the ones deterring his sister from trying something so dangerous. Instead, they put this horrible responsibility on him.

I don't say any of those things. Instead, I say, "You are incredible. And Sarah sounds pretty incredible, too. You cannot hold yourself responsible for something that could have happened to anyone. Linc, rock climbing is dangerous. One of the most dangerous things someone can do. Do not put her death on yourself. You can't."

"Except, I do," he says, looking at me with heavy eyes, full of tears again.

I start to say something, anything to derail this situation, but he continues, "Every day, I think of ways I could have changed her mind. I could have distracted her with a hundred safer activities. I should have done *something*." He clenches his fist tightly on his knee, and I know he's seconds from lighting it on fire.

"It sounds, to me, like nothing you could have said would have changed her mind, Linc. She sounds like she was very sure of herself and her decisions."

"Was." He sighs heavily and says, "I *hate* that I think of her in the past tense. I want her here. I wish more than anything that she could meet you."

Fire rushes up in his lap, and he holds out his flaming hand.

Instinct makes me lean away from him, even though his fire can't hurt me. But I rush to say, "I want that too, and one day, I will meet her. But until then, we can talk about her and keep her memory alive every day."

He sniffs and looks away. He puts his other hand over his burning one, snuffing out his fire, and I can tell he's reached his limit of sharing. He rolls down a window to let the smoke out of the car. I think now that he's talked about her, it will be incredibly difficult for him to just go on with his day. He hasn't had many chances to go through his feelings like this, I'm sure. My guess is he's going to stop talking about her and continue our trip in silence.

I hate when I'm right.

He starts the car and pulls back onto the road. His face is set like stone, and I know his opening up has closed down for now. But I hold on to the "for now" part because it's healthy to talk about things that are painful and devastating. I promise to bring Sarah up again.

But for now, we drive.

chapter seven

When it's clear that Linc wants to be left alone with his thoughts, I finally open my book. He didn't tell me to leave him alone, but I know he needs some time to process, so I try to concentrate on my story.

A while later, after reading the same sentence three times, I give up and look out the window at the forest of pines we're currently passing through. The tragedy of Linc's loss is all I can think about, and I wrack my brain, trying to come up with any way to get him out of his own head.

I jump when he says, looking at me contemplatively, "You know that was the first time you said you love me."

I look at him wordlessly, trying to catch up to the change in conversation.

"Did you know that?" he asks, his voice soft.

I shake my head. "I really haven't said it?"

"No."

"Well, I do." And I mean it, every little word.

His hand finds mine, his eyes warm. "I've already told you, but I'll tell you again. I love you, Vela. Thank you for being there for me...and loving me. Not many do."

My eyes widen. I know his parents are jerks, but surely they love him. "Linc, I'm sure people love you."

He shrugs and watches the road again while he drives. "I have an aunt with two girls I'm close to, but that's about it."

My heart drops at his words, and I'm suddenly angry. At his parents that have a perfect, wonderful son they don't take the time to know.

I squeeze his hand. "Linc, I'm sorry. For what that's worth, I'm sorry you've gone through life like this. But you don't have to anymore. I'm here, and I'll love you no matter what."

He smiles sadly at me and then returns to watching the road, the car falling back into silence.

I recall that we're an hour from Des Moines and never got a chance to call either of our parents about the attack.

Linc has the same thought because he says, "We need to call our parents. They didn't hear from us yesterday, so they're bound to be worried."

When he says, "They're bound to be worried," I know he's talking about my parents and not his and my heart sinks. I wonder if he'll ever forgive his parents for what they put on his shoulders. Or if they'll ever forgive him for his perceived failure. I hope for the sake of the family, that they're able to work through it.

"Right," I agree quickly.

He lifts his eyebrows and looks pointedly at my phone. "Well, are you going to call? We should be in range by now."

"Oh!" I pick up my phone from the console. "Right. Of course. I'll try right now." My heart picks up at the thought of talking to them and then Elia. Finally.

I go to dial my mom's number, then stop. "Should I call my mom or my dad?"

He looks at me strangely. "Either, why?"

"Well, if it's just a check in, I'd automatically call my mom. But, since we have to tell them about the attack and those Boreans, maybe it's better I call my dad."

"Either one." He shrugs.

"No, you don't understand. This is important. If I tell my dad first and my mom finds out, she will lose it. But," I continue, my words rushing together in my stress, "if I tell my mom first and my dad finds out, he'll be furious I worried her like that. He'd want to break it to her." I throw up my hands. "I don't know!"

Linc looks at me patiently saying, "I'm sure it's fine whoever you choose to call."

He clearly does not know my family. A sudden inspiration hits me. "I know! I'll call Drew. He'll know what to do."

Linc sighs. "Fine, whoever. Just call someone, please."

I dial Drew and perk up when I hear his voice. After asking him if he has a minute, I go into what happened to us. I tell him about the Borean attack, and Drew asks questions along the way, which I answer dutifully. Then I stop talking when he asks, "And why haven't you told Mom and Dad about this?"

"Drew! You know why. I called *you* first because I don't know which one to talk to first."

He sighs. "Call either one. Dad's not working today, so they're together. You'll get both of them."

"That's a great idea! I'll tell them at the same time." I flush with happiness that my dilemma is solved.

"I don't know why you're so happy to tell them all that, Vels, Mom's going to freak."

I deflate. *Right.* "I know."

"Well, get it over with. I'll handle the backlash on this end," he promises.

"You mean the kind that says you're all going on a road trip to escort me to this hidden place?"

"Yes. That backlash. I'll talk them down. I promise."

"Thanks, Drew." I hang up after a promise to keep out of trouble and dial my mom's number.

She picks up after the first ring, and I have to hold my phone away from my ear when she screeches, "Vela Marie Ashcroft! What are you thinking, not calling me for so long? I told you to call every day, several times a day, in fact, so I could be sure you're safe. And then, I don't hear from you for a day and a half, and my calls don't go through! Of course, I panic that you're dead on the side of the road somewhere!"

"Mom, put me on speakerphone, so I can tell Dad what happened, too."

"*What happened?* What do you mean you're going to tell us *what happened*?" Thankfully she does put me on speaker because I hear dad trying to calm her down.

"Vela," my dad says in a firm voice, "Why don't you explain yourself?"

Taking a deep breath, I know I'll need to go into full detail. Knowing my mom, that won't be enough. She'll grill me at the end of this conversation.

I'm, of course, right.

After explaining the whole situation three times and examining every possible outcome that could have given different results, my dad finally calms my poor mom down. I hear Drew join the conversation and he and dad talk her out of chasing us down to take me the final leg on our journey.

"How close are you to this place, Lincoln?" Mom asks in a hard voice.

Uh oh, I look over at Linc worriedly. She's using his full name. That's never good.

"Yesterday should have been the third day of a four-day trip," he answers right away.

"And yesterday was the attack, and you had to rest. So, you've only traveled two days," she says, blowing out a breath.

"Mom, I'm sure we'll be fine. Yesterday was just a fluke."

She ignores me. "Where are you guys, exactly?"

Linc answers, "We're about an hour from Des Moines."

I'm so thankful he's the one telling her. When Linc first told me we were taking a roundabout way to our destination, I had reservations. It meant traveling through Borean territory instead of directly from Gyan into Festan lands. He said it was because he wanted to be sure that no one, namely the E.E., could guess where we were headed. But now, we've had problems, and my mom is not going to like this one bit.

"What?" she screeches. "Why on Earth are you in Des Moines, Iowa? That's east of us. You're supposed to be almost in Canada by now!"

"Mrs. Ashcroft, I'm sorry, but I thought it best not to travel directly to Canada."

"You thought it best?" she bites out.

My dad's voice comes through, and I swallow. "Listen, here, young man. You never told us you were doing this. We entrusted our daughter to you and now you've put her in the very dangerous position of being in Borean territory. Explain that."

Linc glances at me and answers in a calm voice. Personally, I'm sweating for him. I hold my breath and wonder if I should jump into this conversation to defend Linc's decision. But, in a way, my dad's right. I thought Linc was being paranoid by going this longer route.

"Mr. Ashcroft, the E.E. have eyes everywhere. If they, at any point, saw me driving Vela north, they would suspect that I was taking her out of the country. I told you I kept our route secret so that if they tried to question you about Vela's whereabouts, you would be unable to answer. It's all to keep Vela safe. That *is* what you want, isn't it, sir?"

My eyes widen at Linc's brazenness, but I exhale in relief when my dad seems to agree. "Yes, it is what we want," he says resigned, but my breath tightens again when he says in a stern voice, "But don't think for one second that anything, even torture would get her mother and me to reveal our daughter's location. From now on, you will explain, in detail, your route for the day every morning and then call us in the evening and tell us how far you got. Is that clear?

Linc looks at me, considering his answer. I return his look with my mouth dropped open. How could he possibly say no to that?

Taking a deep breath, Linc answers, "Sir, I will do that on the condition that I can change the route if something comes up. But," he says, interrupting my mom's gasp of outrage, "I will let you know about any changes when we check in for our evening call."

Silence fills the car, and I breathe quietly, thinking. It makes sense, and I agree that anything could happen in our travels, so to have their blessing to change our route makes sense.

"That's fine," my dad finally says. "Now, when will you be out of cell phone range again?"

"I'm not sure. I only know that when we get to the community, we'll have to use a satellite phone to call you."

"We are aware of that; we just want to know when we cannot reach our daughter as you're traveling."

Linc pauses and then answers. "It should be about our fourth day of travel."

"You mean fifth day," Mom interjects in a hard voice. "Because you lost a day fighting and resting."

"Right," Linc agrees. "I don't see us getting much service that entire day."

I close my eyes and try to imagine what it'll be like living so far from civilization. I haven't given it much thought, but this conversation is making our future reality seem much more real.

It's all I can think about now.

What will it be like? How easy or hard is it to use a satellite phone? A million questions fly through my mind. Will we use torches and candles for lighting, or will they have some system with a battery powered light? And *toilets*, how do you use the bathroom without indoor plumbing? My nose scrunches at the image of a hole in the ground.

Linc answers a couple more of my parents' questions, but I'm too lost in my thoughts to pay attention.

Linc shakes my knee, and I tear my eyes open to see him looking at me expectantly. "Your mom's asking you something."

"Oh, sorry, Mom. What did you say?"

"I asked how you are. Are you okay? You've been through a lot taking care of Linc."

"I'm fine, Mom, promise. It wasn't anything I couldn't handle."

"I don't know Vels, I'm starting to change my mind about this whole idea."

I don't know what to say to reassure her. Because the truth is, I might get into more trouble on the road, and who knows who I'll meet in the hidden community? I also don't voice my concerns about whether we're truly meant to go there. So, I say the only thing I can, "Mom, you're going to have to trust that I can take care of myself."

She sighs heavily. "I know. But you weren't supposed to be on your own for another year. I was supposed to have one more year with you."

Her voice cracks at the end, and I wish I could reach through the phone to give her a hug. "I know Mom, I'm sorry."

"It's nowhere near your fault, baby, it's those Extremists. If I could, I would..."

I interrupt her. "Mom, remember the prayer you always tell me to pray? God, grant me the serenity to accept the things I cannot change, the courage to change the things I can, and the wisdom to know the difference?" My voice is gentle, and I send all the love I can through the phone.

I miss her so much.

She laughs softly. "When did you become the adult in this relationship?"

Dad says, "When she was five years old, honey. She was born old and wise."

We all laugh, including Linc, and I look over at him fondly.

Mom finishes the conversation with an absolute promise from me and Linc to call her at least twice a day. We hang up, and my heart breaks even more.

I sigh heavily as I look down at my phone. When am I going to feel better about this? For my sake, I hope it's soon.

CHAPTER EIGHT

"I'm sorry, Vels," Linc says, looking at me with sympathy. "You, okay?"

"Yea, I just wish I could be with her, you know? This is going to be harder than I thought, being so far away from my mom, and my dad, all of them, really."

"Of course, it is. You haven't had a chance to come to terms with living apart from your family. Give yourself permission to feel that loss."

"Yes, it is a loss, isn't it?" I say softly, looking out the window.

"But that doesn't mean for one second that we can't reach her whenever you want. Their system for satellite calls is pretty good. They only have a limited amount of time to use on their service, if I remember correctly, though. So, you won't have long conversations with her. But you'll be able to reach her if you need to."

I turn toward him. "How do you know all of this?" I knew he'd been to this place, but I wonder.

"I stayed there for a few weeks one summer. I went with my parents, who wanted to visit all the hidden groups."

"Did you go to all of them?"

"I accompanied them to a few, but not all. I mainly stayed where we're headed."

"How many sanctuaries are there?"

Linc thinks for a minute. "About ten. Usually, when a group wants to live in a different area, they form a new location. That's why there're so many."

"Linc, do you think we're doing the right thing by going to this place?"

He looks at me with his head tilted. "Why would you doubt our plan?"

I sit up straight. "It's just we haven't exactly had an easy journey so far."

He pauses and frowns, a shadow of concern showing on his face. "Vela, don't you trust me?"

I exhale roughly. "It's not about trusting *you*, it's about not fully knowing if this is God's plan."

Linc looks away, his brow furrowed. "All I know is I'm taking you to the safest place I know."

"Linc," I say carefully. "I'm just saying, maybe we should have prayed about this."

He turns to me, his expression pained. "I did pray about this. Why are you just telling me *now* that you're having second thoughts?"

"I just..." I pause, searching for the right words. "It just seemed like we had to leave so suddenly. I only want to go down the path that God is taking me down, not one I'm trailblazing on my own, out of fear and with no regard for His plan."

Linc sighs and takes my hand. "Vels, I would never take you anywhere you wouldn't be safe. But just because I feel great about going, doesn't mean you should feel the same way. I won't push you to go if you don't want to. We can figure out something else."

I search my feelings and say a prayer petitioning God to give me a sign, any sign at all. When none comes, I blow out a breath. "Just be patient with me, Linc, that's all. I'm sure now that I'm praying about it, God will tell me His will, one way or another."

Linc nods and squeezes my hand. "Of course. I'm here for you, okay? And, when we get to this community, you'll find there are many people who will support you, too. I'm sure of it," he says, his eyes hopeful.

"I can't believe there're so many couples like us."

Linc looks at me with a grin. "You thought we were the only multi-elemental couple?"

"No. Just that there are so many couples that have found their Intended. I thought it was a miracle we found each other."

"It is a miracle. A lot of these couples are just couples. They're not all bonded."

My eyebrows raise. "Really? I thought that's why they hide in these places. Because they're bonded and hiding from the E.E."

Linc shakes his head. "No. They hide because the Extremists are such lunatics, they'll find any mis-matched Elemental couple and kill them."

"Even if they're not bonded?"

"They don't stop to ask," Linc answers grimly.

"All so that the Chosen Child won't be born. Wow." I think for a minute. "They're that power hungry?"

"They're that money hungry. Remember, they make money extorting desperate Elementals who need each other's gifts. They're making millions. They don't want to lose that revenue if the territories unite, eliminating the need for the E.E.'s expensive services."

"Why is this world so greedy?" I ask, twisting in my seat. "That it would take someone like the Chosen Child fulfilling a six-hundred-year-old prophecy to bring us together? It's ridiculous."

"That's life, Vels. For centuries, there have been prejudices. Those don't just go away. The E.E. is feeding off those ingrained feelings and inflaming them."

"Like they did in Utah when I camped with my family."

"Yes. Your parents told me it only took a couple of them to get those Boreans who lived on the border enraged. It doesn't take much."

My heart sinks. "If it's that easy to incite a border battle, how will the whole world ever let go of all this animosity so we can be united, like God intended?"

"The Chosen Child has a big job ahead of himself or herself, for sure. But don't underestimate most Elementals. We all know that God wants us all to live together, in peace. It's just going to take a strong leader for it to actually happen, and that's what the Chosen Child is born to do."

"Linc, remember when we were being interrogated by the Extremists?" My heart starts to beat wildly at the thoughts threatening to spiral out of control.

"Yes, what about it?"

"I answered every question correctly. I had to lie on one of them because I was afraid of what they would do if I passed all the tests."

"I did, too."

"So, does that mean we're the parents of this Child?"

"It's a very good possibility. We check off all the boxes."

"But I could have two different Elementals for parents, which means..."

"That you could be the Chosen Child."

I nod and look at Linc worriedly. "I couldn't possibly fulfill that prophecy, Linc." I bite my lip in thought.

"Hey," he says, laughing softly. "Don't worry about that, okay? I'm sure every Elemental who could possibly be the Chosen Child worries, but I think whoever it is will have things fall into place for them."

I settle back into my seat and try to relax my stiff body. My muscles froze up at the panic I felt thinking about being the Child everyone was looking for. The one tasked with the responsibility of uniting our broken world.

Linc is quiet as he drives, leaving me alone with my thoughts.

A million of them fly through my mind. Just when I settle on one, another one flies in replacing it. Then another and another.

"It's too much," I moan.

"What?"

I turn toward Jack when he whines. I realize I've been ignoring him, and I unbuckle my seatbelt to climb over the seat. He always helps calm me down and I could really use that right about now.

Jack happily licks my face, then drapes his body over my lap. I grunt and adjust to the most comfortable position I can with a hundred-pound dog lying on me. I run my hands over his back and side, scratching his ears.

"Vela," Linc says from the front, "Tackle one thing at a time. You're going to drive yourself crazy."

"I definitely am headed in that direction," I say, and lean my head on Jack's back.

"Do I need to stop?"

"No," I say, whipping my head up. "Mom'll freak if we don't make good time today. What's the next state we're heading into?" I'm desperate to think about something tangible.

"Minnesota."

"Then we'll cross into Canada?"

"Yes. If we can get to Winnipeg today, I'll be really happy. But that's about eight hours away. We passed Des Moines an hour ago."

"Eight hours? Gosh, that's a long drive. Won't we pass into Gyan territory soon?"

"My little Gyan's been paying attention, I see."

"You better believe I want to be out of this Wind Demon territory as soon as possible."

He snorts. "I can understand that. We're going to have to stop for gas soon, so let's hope we don't run into anymore bored Borean teens."

I wholeheartedly agree.

After an uneventful rest stop and a couple hours of driving, I sigh in relief when we pass Austin. Seeing that town means we're in Minnesota and in Gyan territory. I'm grateful that every mile driven takes us further into friendlier territory.

Even though the minute we pass over the Canadian border, we'll be in Festan lands. I relish being in an area with my own kind. I breathe easier and feel lighter than I've felt in hours. I didn't realize how badly the stress had tightened my muscles until I finally relaxed.

While Jack snoozes in the back, Linc and I talk about everything under the sun and then some. We laugh at the stupidest things, and I fall a little bit more in love with him.

After an especially riveting conversation about a big sign we pass, I ask him, out of the blue, "Linc, do you think we'll get married one day?"

He laughs in surprise and says, "I certainly hope so. You *are* my Intended. Why? Are you proposing?"

My eyes widen and I stammer, "N-n-no! I'm not proposing to you."

His eyes glitter and he looks thoroughly amused. "It certainly sounds like it."

"No! I was just thinking about the way we talk. Are we going to be doing this for the rest of our lives?"

He sobers and gives me the look, the one that promises something heavy. "Vela, that's my plan. I thought about it the first time you compared yourself to a ghost and refused to face me. I knew that you were one person I would gladly chase after for the rest of my life."

Wow. My face in flames, I clear my throat and say breathlessly, "Really? It's not just because I'm your Intended?"

"Really," he says firmly. "You being bonded with me is a bonus. I couldn't possibly find anyone more perfect for me than you." Then uncertainty crosses his face. "Are you not sure?"

"About what?" My mind had suddenly gone blank at his declaration.

"About us," he says in a heavy voice. He quickly searches my face, and I don't know what to say. I mean, *I'm seventeen.* I don't know what to think about marriage. What made me ask him about this, anyway?

I pause before I reply because he deserves a well thought out answer. *Can I imagine my life without Linc?* Right now, the answer is a solid 'no'. I can't. Life feels absolutely right walking with him through this wacky world. But *I'm sev-*

enteen. The thing is, though, we have an unbreakable bond. Linc will always be a part of my life.

So, I turn to him and say, "You're my whole world, and everything in me wants to be with you."

"Please tell me there's not a 'but' coming." Linc's hands clench on the steering wheel.

"There isn't a 'but', there's an 'I'm too young to even think about a lifetime commitment.' I'm not even an adult and you're barely one. Can we take this one day at a time?"

It's not fair I've just thrown his earlier advice back at him, but it's the only thing I can say.

I allow him silence as he drives.

After several minutes, his throat bobs like he's about to say something before he stops himself. Finally, he says, "Vela, like I said, I will always want you and only you. There's no one else for me. If you need time to figure out if I'm really your match, I'll wait. But I'm telling you right now, I won't give up on you. Ever."

My heart melts, and I grab onto my seat like it's about to fly away with me in it. "Linc," I say.

"No," he interrupts. "Say nothing else. Let's just leave it at that. For now."

My breath caught in my lungs when he interrupted me, and I release it now slowly. I can't help but feel I've wounded him terribly. And, as much as I wish otherwise, I can't take back my words.

I can only hope that like I said, by taking a day at a time, one day, I'll be surer than anything I've ever known to commit my life to him permanently.

Until then, I stay quiet.

CHAPTER NINE

Hours pass as we travel through Minnesota, making small talk. Tension sits so heavily in the air, I think we could cut it with a knife. It's beyond uncomfortable, and I heavily regret my thoughtless question about marriage.

What do I say to someone who's promised his whole world, everything he is, to me, and received...what ambivalence, in return? Saying, "Let's see where this takes us?"

What kind of person am I to leave such doubt and worry for Linc?

But what else could I have said? Should I have lied to him, said I would, without a doubt, marry him?

That's *crazy.* I couldn't, possibly. I had to be honest. But come to find out, honesty hurts. I should have been more considerate of his feelings. I should have thought of a better way to say what I'm feeling: I'm scared, scared of the depth of my feelings, of the unknown, of where this growing love will take us, scared that I'm not in control.

So, we drive. He's determined to get us into Canada today, and with the light traffic, I'm sure we'll make it. I'll just have to ignore my aching heart and the stony expression on Linc's face.

He's gone from being open and honest to swapping curt answers with me.

It's excruciating. I hate it.

Helpless to do anything about this new, uncomfortable tension, I finally climb into the backseat with Jack, hoping he can help ease my agony.

It's when we get to Moorhead in Minnesota that the air changes.

Linc goes from broody to alert and focused. I instantly do the same.

"What's going on?" I ask.

"We're on the border," he answers tersely, his eyes scanning all around us.

"On the border of Minnesota and one of the Dakotas?"

"Yes," he huffs impatiently, "but also on Festan lands."

"Why are you so nervous about that? You're a Festan."

"Yea, but you're not. And border Festans are very territorial." He glances at me then away just as quickly, his look anxious.

"Yes, but I'm with you. Shouldn't that protect me?"

"You don't know Festans very well if you think that. They are more volatile than any other Elemental clan. I should know. And the ones who live on the border are the worst of us."

I ignore the bite of his words and focus on their meaning. "Linc, you're acting like they can see inside this car and know I'm not a Festan. That's impossible."

"I know that," he says in a tight voice. "But we're going to have to stop soon." He looks at the gas gage.

"We need to stop *here?* Why didn't we get gas back in Gyan territory?"

His forehead furrows, and he growls, "I wasn't thinking."

Or he was thinking too much. About what I said to him. This is my fault.

"Okay," I say in a brisk voice, trying to sound positive. "We stop for gas, and I stay in the car. I won't even go to the bathroom. We can stop on the side of the road later if we have to. I won't so much as breathe in anyone's direction." I cringe at the thought of what I just proposed. But I would do it. If it keeps us safe and takes that worried look off Linc's face.

He nods. "That's what we're going to have to do." He looks at me for the first time in hours. "You do not get out of this car for any reason."

I quickly agree.

He slows the car to take the next exit, and I hold my seats with a death grip. The only thing that could get me to leave this car would be a tornado. Linc truly has scared me. With my fear of fire, if I tick off a Festan, I'm in real trouble. Without the protection of an Intended bond to make their fire harmless, it'll be disastrous if I somehow provoke one of them.

Linc passes several gas stations slowly, studying who's at the pumps fueling up. I don't know if he can recognize a fellow Festan just by looking at them. I couldn't do that with a Gyan, but with his heat-sensing abilities, maybe he can. I decide now is not the time to ask.

He finally settles on a station and pulls in. His face is granite when he opens the door. Turning his head toward me, he gives me a look that says, 'Stay in there.' I listen loud and clear. I'm not going anywhere.

Our pump has no one near it. In fact, the only other car fueling up is three pumps away. I settle into my seat, breathing a little more comfortably. I reach for Jack, who I know needs to do his business, and wordlessly apologize to him. I can't take him out right now. We'll have to stop later on the side of the road.

I'm sitting quietly, my hands clenching in my lap, when I see in my door's rearview mirror a huge black truck pull into the gas station. I ignore it until it pulls under the same awning our car is in, stopping right next to my door.

I hold my breath and look straight ahead, not even daring to look at anyone here, fearing what Linc said. In my peripheral vision, I see a lumberjack looking guy, huge and muscled, climb down from the driver's side. He glances at me, then saunters into the gas station. Another equally large man joins him, and I study them, praying they're human.

My window is sealed shut. I sit sweating with nerves.

I look over at Linc to see if he's noticed them. He's fidgeting with the credit card machine, his back to the two guys. He doesn't see them walk into the gas station.

Linc's face appears in my window, and I jump in fright. His frustrated visage mouths at me that he has to pay inside.

Why couldn't this gas station's credit card machine work? If it did, we could have filled up and left by now.

I watch Linc walk inside, then pass the lumberjack guys as they exit the gas station. They acknowledge Linc with a nod, which he reciprocates. After they've walked by him, Linc turns back to look at me with warning in his gaze. His face flashes in fear, and I know.

Those aren't human lumberjacks. They're Festans.

CHAPTER TEN

I tremble in my seat, my breath coming in erratic bursts. Their gazes spear into me and dart between me and Jack. I don't know what to do other than avoid their eyes.

Why would they notice a random girl in a gas station lot? I have no idea. I hope they look away.

I feel them study me for an agonizing minute, then they walk to their pump to fill it up with gas. They disappear from my vision.

Jack whines, and I shush him. We cannot attract any attention.

I train my eyes on the door to the gas station, praying Linc comes out any second now. He doesn't. He must be held up inside for some reason. There's no way he would leave me here alone if he could help it.

I scream when a knock pounds on my back window. Whipping my body around, I stare in horror at the first lumberjack glaring at Jack, then me.

I freeze. What do I do? I can't roll down my window. He'll know immediately that I'm a Gyan.

"Yes?" I squeak.

He motions for me to roll my window down.

When I don't and just look at him shaking my head, he pounds on the window again.

I hear him barking at me through the window, "Your dog needs air. Open your window!"

What do I do?

My terrified gaze swings to the gas station store, praying Linc is on his way. A breath leaves me when I see him. He trains his gaze on the lumberjack, who's trying to get my attention.

I see Linc run, but at any point this guy slamming his hand on my window is going to bust the glass. Jack's barking wildly, and I'm having a hard time breathing. Hyperventilation is coming soon.

Lumberjack number two has joined the side of the first one, and they start talking, the first one gesturing angrily first at Jack then at me.

Mercifully, Linc has finally made it to the car, and I see him talking to the angry man. I see the guy's point, I really do. I should have the windows open for my dog, but I couldn't, in fear of being discovered.

The furious lumberjack yells something at Linc and shoves him hard. Linc recovers quickly and glares darkly at the offending man. His hands are at his sides, fisted and ready to answer that shove with retaliation.

This is turning into a nightmare. If two Festans start fighting, fire could follow and that would never be good in a highly flammable gas station.

But Linc stands his ground and says something to lumberjack number one. He's trying to diffuse the situation.

When lumberjack man lunges at Linc, Linc easily evades him then runs over to the driver's side door.

It seems we're fleeing the situation.

He yanks open the door and is in the car before I can blink. But, by opening the door, both Festans out there have gotten a good whiff of my Gyan self.

They swing their furious gazes at me.

"Linc," I say, my heart in my throat. "I think…"

I twist in my seat to lock my door, but before I can, one of the guys yanks open my car door and reaches for me, pulling me roughly out of the car.

I screech in fear and can't understand why I don't fight at all. I'm frozen in shock.

"Vela!" I hear Linc shout.

I'm dragged, lifted, and stuffed into the back seat of the huge truck before I can do anything. One of the guys climbs into the back with me and holds me down when I'm finally able to regain control of my body and start fighting. He throws one arm over my chest and holds my legs down with the other.

I see an enormous flash of fire, and I don't know what's happening. Is Linc using fire to try to free me? Are the Festans using it on him? Then I hear an explosion.

What's happening?! That sounded like a car.

I'm surrounded by concrete, or I'd use nature to fight my way out of this. But I give it all I have. I scream, punch, kick, and even bite when a meaty hand clamps down on my mouth. I can't get a good grip with my teeth the way he cups his hand over my mouth, but I try anyway, hoping to get lucky.

I flail and buck, trying anything to get out of his grasp. But the man's hold is like iron, and I'm absolutely useless against his mass and strength.

My captor yells at the other Festan, and I feel the truck lurch forward. We peel out of the gas station, and I see spots. I'm fighting with everything I have, but I can't breathe. The guy's hand is covering my mouth and one of my nostrils. I can barely get any air in.

My eyes stream tears, and I look at the guy begging him to let me go.

He ignores me and continues to shout at his friend to get to some bridge. I know if we make it to this bridge, I'm going to be dumped over it, and I'll be lucky to be alive when they do it.

Fear has taken such a hold on me; but I suck as much air as I can and start fighting again. But I'm not fighting. Fighting is when two opponents trade blows. All I'm doing is struggling. And it's completely useless.

Slumping, I give up for a minute, just to try and get more air. My attempt to fight back has taken a lot out of me. I'm no good to myself if I pass out. My chest is heaving, and I know I'm close to losing consciousness.

Linc will be enraged and chasing after us unless that explosion was our car. It's possible Linc has nothing to drive. These guys might have destroyed Linc's chance to save me.

Oh God, no. Is Jack alright? Please tell me he made it out. A memory of Cooper's whimpers blare in my head. He died in a fire. Please don't let Jack suffer that, too. I couldn't recover from that again.

My hopes sink. I shake my head, silently pleading with God to get me out of this situation. My captor is looking up but seems to feel that I'm not struggling anymore. He looks down at me, anger and disgust warring on his face.

I make eye contact with him, and a sob comes up from my chest, but his hand stops it from escaping. With my eyes, I beg him to let me go. Tears are coursing down my cheeks. Surely, there's some mercy in this man.

He looks away, completely disgusted. Then he says in a hard voice, "You think your tears will get you out of this? They won't. This is what your kind deserves."

What could the Gyans have done to make him hate us this much? We're on the border of Festan and Gyan land, so the answer could be just about anything. He's got a grudge with other Gyans, and I'm going to pay the price.

I cry in earnest now. Is there any hope for me? Will I die today? My breathing is getting faster, the more my terror climbs. I'm barely taking in any air now. I force myself to calm down.

Peace, Vela.

I hold my breath. What was that voice in my head? Is God talking to me? I let go of my breath slowly. Then try to regulate my breathing as calmly as I can.

I didn't imagine that voice. God is with me here in this terrifying situation. My life is in His hands.

Suddenly, the guy driving shouts curses and the truck shoots forward in speed. Is someone chasing us? Is it Linc?

Please, God, I pray, *let Linc catch up to us.*

"He found another car!" the driver shouts.

And just like that, I feel the glimmer of hope. God restored my hope, but Linc is His answer to my prayer. So, that explosion was our car. He must have stolen or begged to use someone else's.

I struggle against the arms holding me down again. I want to look out the window. I want Linc to know I'm okay.

My captor's arms had relaxed a fraction when I stopped fighting him. But they become steel bands once more.

I realize something. If I stop struggling again and this guy thinks I'm not fighting him, maybe I'll have a better chance of getting out of his hold.

So, I go limp. Then I have the brilliant idea to play like I've passed out. Then, I'll have the element of surprise, and when the time is right, I can escape. I'll jump out of this moving truck if I have to. I pray it slows down at that point, though, or I'll die in the fall.

I play it up as best as I can. I sob, which comes easily, then pretend to pass out. My eyes close, my sobs stop, and my head slumps to the side. I'm breathing normally. I pray this works.

If I was looking down at myself, I'd believe that I just fainted.

My captor must think so too, because his arms relax. I can't look at him to see if he's watching me. But I have to believe he thinks I'm passed out from my own terror.

Curses continue, and the truck speeds up. We must be flying down the road. Hopefully, we'll get the attention of a police officer and get stopped.

That thought is abandoned, when my captor shouts at the driver, "Take that side road by O'Henry's place. We'll take care of him there."

Take care of him? *What does that mean?* Kill him? Hurt him, for sure.

My heart rate climbs.

We speed down the road, and I continue to feign unconsciousness. I shout in my head, praying for God to tell Linc these guys are leading him into a trap.

Linc must know something because suddenly he rams the truck from behind. Linc is trying to make a scene while other cars are present. He knows if these guys get us alone, we're done for. Elementals never want an audience for battle skirmishes, but in this case, it's necessary.

We're safer around humans. These angry Festans could still kill us, even if there are witnesses. But then they'd have to escape the law.

The truck lurches again, this time to the side. I hear a pop from the back tire. Linc's trying to force us off the road. And I think he's disabled the truck.

Yes! Thank you, God!

My relief is short-lived when my captor says, "Let's kill her now and dump her. She's all he cares about. He won't follow when we dump her out the door."

Let's not. My thoughts go frantic.

"My tire is busted; how do you expect us to get away?" the driver spits out.

"We can get out of here and make it to O'Henry's on the rim," Psycho Lumberjack yells.

The truck is still moving, even on the flat tire, but we've slowed considerably. I could probably survive a fall at this speed. I know I would likely break something, but that's far better than dying.

I dredge up as much courage as I can and force my body to relax, despite my plan.

My captors are now arguing about how to kill me.

I'm officially in the middle of a horror movie. But, unlike the hapless victims in those, I'm going to fight back. I'm going to escape.

I take advantage of my captors' distraction and morbid argument, kick my legs viciously, and nearly crow when I break free. At my captor's surprised look, I wrench my arms free and bring his head down on my knee.

He howls in pain at a crunching noise. I ignore the flying blood, shove him off, and wrench myself up. I blindly reach for the door handle and throw myself out of the moving truck.

I take the hit to the ground, landing on my shoulder and roll with the momentum into the grass on the side of the road. Forced to take a moment to get my bearings and be sure I didn't break anything, my head spins as I lurch up and run away from the truck.

When I jumped out, the Festan slammed on the brakes, but I don't know if anyone is chasing me, yet. I don't dare to look; I scan the road ahead and see a white car with a crumpled hood, like it slammed into the truck.

"Linc!" I scream.

He's out of the car in a flash and races toward me.

I'm caught up in his arms for a second before he shoves me behind him.

He's ready with two fireballs in his hands and stands in a fighting position.

Sure enough, no one leaves the truck. It sits idle.

Linc's eyes are blazing, and I know he's prepared to answer to any Festan authority to explain why he brought out his fire. The fact that his mom is the Festan Grand Elder will probably help his case.

After what feels like ten minutes, the truck pulls out back onto the road and limps away on its flat tire.

Linc douses his fire. I didn't realize a couple of cars had pulled over with us until a woman comes up to me, touching me gently on my shoulder.

I wonder if she saw Linc's fireballs.

"Hey, are you okay?" She must not have seen Linc's fire because her big blue eyes swim with sympathy as she holds out her hands.

That's when I realize I'm swaying. The trauma of the entire situation catches up to me and I fall toward her. My entire body hurts.

I just threw myself out of a moving truck. That reality makes my knees weak.

Linc must have realized I was about to fall, because he spins and catches me in his arms.

I sob into his shirt. He holds the back of my head, and whispers into my hair, "I've got you, I've got you. Don't worry. You're safe."

I hear a crowd of people murmuring in the background.

"She fell out of that car."

"I saw that guy hit that truck *twice.*"

"Do you think she was kidnapped?"

"Someone call the police."

"Already did."

Great. Now I've got to handle a cop asking questions. I'll have to tell the police officer just part of the story. Some lunatics abducted me at a gas station. I could never share the whole truth.

This all happened because those horrible men were trying to get their revenge on a Gyan.

"Linc?"

"Yes, baby?"

"Get me out of here," I beg.

We both hear the sirens and any thought of running away flies away.

I just pray my lying skills are great. I have to remember what I'm allowed to tell them and what I'm not. With my wits at the end, that won't be easy.

CHAPTER ELEVEN

After an exhausting few hours, during which we tell the same story over and over again to the Moorhead police, who have probably never seen a kidnapping case in the entire history of their small town, they allow Linc and I to leave.

Linc holds my hand as we leave the station. Our car was burned to oblivion by the two Festans. When the cops asked how that happened, Linc told them my kidnappers threw a flash bomb in his window.

In reality, they threw fire at the gas tank.

Thankfully, Linc somehow got Jack out before the car exploded. I must have kissed Jack's face a hundred times in my relief.

It's surprising that the gas station didn't explode too, but employees and nearby residents contained the fire.

Linc had apparently asked a nearby gawker to hold on to Jack's collar while he chased after me.

As we walk away, my body is thoroughly sore, fully feeling my fall out of the truck. Thankfully, other than soreness, I seem to be fine. Miraculously, I escaped any major injuries.

I was praised to an inch of my life for my quick thinking, for pretending to pass out so I could escape more easily.

As if any of it had been easy.

Police surmised the two Festans were sex traffickers or maniacs with the intention of abusing my body.

I shudder at the thought. I'm grateful that the Festans, at least, had no intention of ever touching me. Just killing me.

My eyes are swollen from the tears I've spent on this entire ordeal. I reach up to dry them and cringe. My eyes feel puffy and swollen. I must look terrible.

If I was labeled brave, then Linc's the hero. And he really is. I never would have escaped alive without his rescue.

It turns out, he stole the car he used to chase after me and my kidnappers. He ripped the driver out of his seat just as his car pulled into the gas station and then raced off to save me.

The police forgave Linc, just as easily as the driver did, once they found out he was attempting to rescue me from kidnappers.

Linc also promised to pay for the car's damages. I only hope that the local police can find the truck and make those evil men pay for their actions by spending a few decades in jail.

"Are you really, okay?" Linc asks me gently.

I hold on to Jack's leash, which was provided by the police station because of the local leash law. Jack was apparently frantic when I was abducted and had to be taken into the gas station. It took several people to keep him from running after me, like Linc did. He's glued to my leg, and I don't think he'll pry himself away anytime soon. I'm fine with that.

I sigh and look up at Linc. He doesn't look like he's been in a death-defying car chase and saved me from crazed, bigoted kidnappers. Except for the tightness around his eyes, he looks completely normal and amazing, as always.

"I'm..." I sigh again. "I feel just like anyone would expect. I'm sore physically, but still back in that truck mentally." My breath hitches in a sob. "I thought I was going to die, Linc." I stop in my tracks, my heart beating wildly as I realize just how narrowly I missed a deadly fate.

Linc's eyes harden in promise. "I've already called my mom about those guys. The cops here might not find them, but our kind will. They will face up to what they did to you, Vels."

I nod, tears slipping down my cheeks. "That's good. It never should have happened."

He turns away, his jaw clenching. "No, it shouldn't. If I had paid attention..."

I stop him with a hand on his chest. "No, Linc, don't. Don't you dare blame yourself for this. Those men did this for their own reasons. They are responsible. *Not* you."

"Vela," he says in a pained voice, looking back at me with earnest eyes, deep and dark. "I know better than to stop in a Festan border town. I *know* what they're like. They're hotheads, all of them. I should have parked somewhere safe, walked to the gas station, and brought back a gas can."

"Linc, please. We can't live on should haves, we can only deal with what's happened. And what happened was *not your fault.*"

He looks down, his hair hiding his eyes.

I'm worn out. Worn out in my soul, worn out for fighting for my existence. But I have enough in me to drop the leash and reach up to hold Linc's face with both of my hands.

As I cradle his jaw, he seems reluctant to look at me, and when he does, my heart stutters. He has such a raw look of pain and vulnerability. My breath catches, then I say, "I don't blame you. Not at all. And I never will. You *saved my life.* I owe you everything right now."

"Vela," he breathes and reaches up to hold on to both of my wrists. "You were in horrible danger because of me. I will take responsibility because I'm not much of a man if I don't." His eyes blaze into mine. "I will protect you from here on out. You will *never* be in danger like that again. I promise you," he says in a heated voice.

"Linc," I say, softly gazing into his eyes, "You can't promise that I won't ever be in danger again." I hope he's allowing himself to believe me. "I've been lucky my whole life to never see an Elemental battle until recently. Our world is a danger every day because of lies and fear, spread by evil people, to make us all hate each other. *That,* Linc, is the reason this happened. *Not you.*"

His eyes shut, and he shakes his head, pulling my hands away from his face. "I wish I could believe that, but nothing you can say will change my mind. My own incompetency and carelessness landed you in that situation, almost got you killed. But I will do better. I will protect you. From now on."

I sigh and watch him walk away. I can't do much more than follow.

CHAPTER TWELVE

I hunch in a lumpy armchair in the corner of a motel room and look down at my phone that miraculously survived my kidnapping and subsequent fall from the truck. Reluctant to call my mom and hear her frantic reaction to my horrible experience, I also know I need the comfort that only a mom could give. I need to hear her voice and desperately wish to feel her arms wrapped around me instead of the emptiness of this cold room.

Linc is out buying a new car after his parents transferred more money into his account. It doesn't matter what he chooses, I just hope that we can get back on the road soon. He's also picking up what's left of our things from the trunk of our burned-out car. I'm not holding out much hope there'll be anything salvageable. I might have just the clothes on my back.

So, here I am, in this rundown motel, waiting for Linc to return. I should probably wait for Linc to make this call with me, but I don't want him telling my mom the same nonsense he told me at the police station.

Squaring my shoulders, I find my mom's number and the phone is dialing before I can change my mind.

"Vels?" her voice is quick to answer.

"Yeah, Mom, it's me." My voice cracks just at the sound of her voice, and I'm sobbing before I know it. I heave breaths between sobs, but that's all I can manage right now.

"Vela, what's wrong? What happened? Are you okay, baby?" Her questions fire at me, and I suck in a deep breath, trying and failing to stop my wild sobs.

"Oh my gosh, Vela, please tell me what happened to you." Her voice cracks and then she's sobbing, too.

At that moment, I miss my mom more than anything, and I can't do much more than cry into the phone.

"Mom," I barely manage. "I'm okay." Sniffing and breathing heavily, I attempt to choke down my tears. "I was...." I can't get it out. I can't. The enormity of what happened hits me just trying to say the words. I break and sobs erupt from my throat again.

My mom is barely holding it together. I can feel it when she says, "Vela, are you in a safe place?"

I keel over, holding my stomach as I try to answer her. That is not a simple question.

I'm not in a safe place. We're still in a border town and I'm terrified. We need to leave and put it and its Festan people behind us. At least I'm hidden in a motel. No one knows I'm here but Linc.

Sitting back up, I nod, then shake my head. I answer with a question, "Kind of?"

"What does that mean? How are you kind of in a safe place? That doesn't sound convincing at all."

I take deep breaths and hold the phone with my cheek on my shoulder so I can scrub my face with both hands. I hiccup and try speaking again. "So, we're in a Festan border town."

"What?! You're not supposed to stop in one of those, Vela!"

"I know, Mom, but it just happened. We stopped for gas and..."

"Stopped for gas in a *border town*?"

"Yes, and..." I force the next words out of my mouth, "Festans kidnapped me."

A pregnant silence rings in my ear.

"Mom?" I look down at my phone to see if I've lost the connection. I didn't. She's still there.

"Vela, please. Tell me what happened," she finally says in a small voice.

I take a deep, shuddering breath and everything that happened spills out of me. All the terror, the horror comes and I'm sobbing again before I finish. But I get it all out.

She listens quietly, but I catch a sob or two that she can't cover up.

"Vela," my dad's voice comes on the line. Mom must have handed the phone over to him. I didn't know he was with her. "Your mom is taking this all in. Give her a minute."

I wait while he mutes the phone, so silence blares into my ears. My sobs finally stop, and I look up quickly when my motel door opens.

Linc walks in and freezes in the doorway when he sees the state of my face and that I'm on the phone. It doesn't take him long to figure out who's on the other end of the line.

A grave mask covers his face as he closes the door behind him. He holds out his hand, asking for the phone.

I shake my head and keep it. I won't let him blame himself for this. I won't.

His eyebrows draw down and he frowns deeply. He shakes his hand, asking for the phone again.

"No," I say firmly.

"Baby," my mom's beautiful voice comes back on the line.

I turn my attention wholly to her.

"Vela, I can't tell you what your experience just made me feel. I hope to God that you never have to go through it with a child of your own. But this isn't about me. How are you? Are you injured?"

"No, I'm not injured. Well, maybe emotionally. But, physically, I'm fine."

"That's good," she sighs in relief. "Let's talk about your emotions. It's clear you don't feel safe where you are. Where's Linc? Isn't he with you?"

"He's here." I look up at him, and his eyes are throwing daggers, wordlessly demanding I hand him the phone, his hand still extended.

He won't stop until he talks to my mom. He's got this stubborn look in his eyes, so I say, "He actually wants to talk to you."

"I think that's best. Hand him the phone, baby."

When he takes the phone, I get up off the bed and walk into the bathroom. I don't want to hear his guilt.

I'm feeling too raw, too *much* to take on his sense of responsibility, too.

Jack follows me as I shut us into the bathroom and turn on the exhaust fan. I can hear the hum of Linc's voice, but can't make out what he's saying.

I drum my fingers together as I sit on the commode. Jack pushes his nose into my hands. I rub his neck and then decide to wash off the river of tears I cried.

Standing up, I walk over to the sink and look up into the mirror. I gasp. I haven't looked at myself since the incident. My image frightens me.

My eyes are red, my face pink from crying. I try not to be shocked at the haunted look in my eyes. They look dead and nothing like what I'm used to.

I've always had a serious look to me, but never have I looked so broken and utterly devastated. But that's what I am, a victim of a horrific crime. A sob climbs through my throat, and I look away, not wanting to see what crying looks like on me.

I bend over the sink, holding onto the edges. My hair falls into my face, and I allow it to curtain me in. I allow myself to grieve. Mourn what happened, what might have happened to me. I've never been so close to death before. Even when I fought in two Elemental battles, never once did I think I was actually going to die. Maria had me in a chokehold, and even then, I didn't think death was coming for me.

I whip my head up and force myself to look in the mirror. I hiccup at my reflection, watching tears trail down my face. It makes me cry even harder. I refuse to look away though. I need to see this. I will not hide from my fears, my grief, my pain. I feel like if I look away, I'll never recover. I'll carry this around forever and it feels very important I deal with this now.

Jack whines and nudges my leg, but I don't break my stare. I sob and memorize what this experience has done to me, both physically and mentally. I want to remember what victory over this kind of pain looks like. But I also need to remember what the pain has done to me. Seeing it in its rawest, most real form will be forever seared into my mind.

God, will I get over this? Are you here?

Scripture comes into my mind. *Rest and know I am with you.*

Awe fills me, a peace inside stretching into my heart. I feel Him, His presence is here, right now with me in this motel bathroom, and my eyes fill up again, but this time with tears of gratitude. My fingers clench on the sink edges, and I revel in the rightness that fills me.

It amazes me how God always knows where I'm at and gives me just what I need.

I jump when a knock sounds on the bathroom door.

"Vela? Your dad wants to talk to you."

"Ok, give me a minute," I say. I haven't torn my eyes away from my image. I take one last look and then take a deep breath.

Thank you, Father. Pure love fills me with how much I appreciate my God, who is always there when I need Him the most.

I turn on the faucet and splash cold water on my face. It shocks me but feels good.

Grabbing a towel, I dab my face and breathe into it for a minute. A powerful thing happened just now, owning my pain. God helped me rise above it and conquer a little bit of it. I know I have a lot more healing to do. But I've started the process, and that's the important thing.

Jack barks at me, sick of being ignored. I take a minute to kneel and put my face into his neck, breathing in his scent. He tries to lick me, but I don't give him a chance, wrapping my arms around his neck instead. He whines and I laugh softly.

"Okay, buddy, go for it," I say, and lean back.

He takes immediate advantage and must taste the remnants of salt from my tears. He soon finds proof all over my cheeks and neck. He tries to wash the tears I missed, as much as I'll let him.

"Okay, okay, that's enough," I finally say, pulling away from his reach.

Standing up, I face the door and make myself open it. I needed a few more minutes to prepare myself, but don't want to keep my mom and dad waiting too long.

Stepping into the room, I see Linc sitting hunched over on the bed. He's holding the phone, and I look at him curiously. He's either ignoring me or is just so lost in his thoughts he hasn't noticed me yet.

I walk over and stand in front of him. He jumps like I've startled him and hands me my phone, turning his head away.

Accepting it, I lean over to see he's scowling. Maybe I should have listened to the conversation.

"Mom? I'm here," I say, settling next to Linc on the edge of the bed.

"Honey, it sounds like Linc has things all settled. He's got a car and you guys should be able to leave."

I jump up and spin to face Linc. "You did? You got a car? Let's go!"

Holding the phone to my ear, I run over to the door, ready to yank it open and get the heck out of here.

Linc jumps up and runs over, slamming his hand on the door before I can open it. "Wait," he says, "we need to talk."

"Yes, honey, you both need to talk," my mom agrees.

I furrow my brow in confusion. "What? You got a car; we can leave now."

Linc's scowl deepens even more, and it's really alarming me now.

"What?" I ask. "Why can't we leave yet?"

"Baby," my mom says to me, and I give her my attention. "We think it's best that you leave at night when you're less likely to be seen. You know, out of sight, out of mind."

Linc must hear what she's saying, because he nods.

"Mom," I say, my voice raising. "I *need* to get out of here. You don't understand."

"No," Mom says in a pained voice, "You don't understand. There are hundreds more Festans in that town, like those two horrible men, and all of them hate you. Linc is just trying to protect you. Leave at night. Get to your car and drive back into Gyan territory then."

"But when we cross the border into Canada, it's still Festan territory," I say in a small voice. I know I can't escape from Festan lands completely, and my muscles stiffen as terror fills me so I can barely move.

"Linc has that covered," Mom explains in a calming voice. "His parents have a contact up there who knows the situation and has agreed to escort you both until you make it to the hidden community. He'll help protect you."

Relief floods my chest, and I start to breathe normally again. "Really?" I look over at Linc and he nods again, his eyes sad.

I end the call with my mom, promising her I'll be safe and follow her instructions implicitly when we leave. "What's wrong?" I ask Linc.

His face hardens, and he says, "I've planned this trip well. You shouldn't have to worry about our route, and if you have, that means I've failed you."

"Failed me? No! You haven't! Not at all."

His face closes off, and he turns to the door, saying, "I'm going to get us dinner. Please stay inside."

He leaves, and I'm faced with a closed door instead of the person I want to reassure. His sense of altruism is going to be his undoing one day. I turn away from the door and fall down on the bed.

There is one person I still need to call. I smile at the thought of her cheerful and upbeat voice.

I dial Elia's number and fall back on the bed when I hear her answer.

"Vels?" Elia screeches into the phone. "I haven't heard from you in *days*. That's just downright painful, sister."

"Hey friend. Wow, I didn't realize how much I needed to hear your voice right now."

"Is Linc already driving you crazy?"

I shake my head because, *yes*, he is driving me crazy but not in the way she thinks. "LeeLee, there have been a couple of problems along the way," I say instead.

"Dish it, tell me everything."

So, I do. I launch into an explanation of the Borean attack and the kidnapping. I surprise myself by getting through it without crying this time. I'm quite proud I could say it all without breaking down into a sobbing mess. My bathroom chat with God helped me more than I realized.

"Vels," Elia finally said, "that's more than a couple *of problems*. You have been through the fire, not once, but twice!"

"Yeah, it feels that way, for sure."

"Are you okay? How are you holding up? How is *Linc* doing?"

"I'm hanging in there. Prayer is my saving grace right now. It's really the only thing holding me together. And Linc..." I pause, "is angry."

"Angry? At you?"

"Yes? No? I don't know. Well, he was angry at me for telling him something insensitive, but, no, I think now he's mostly angry at himself. He says he failed me by letting me get kidnapped."

"Failed you? How's that possible? He literally saved you, Vels. How did he get to that point?"

"I honestly don't know." I sigh deeply. "He can barely look at me. And, after our fight, I don't know how to reach him."

"What fight? You fought over being saved from a kidnapping?"

"No, it was before that. I may have said the stupidest thing ever."

"You? Ha! I don't believe it. You are the most empathetic person I've ever met."

"Not this time, LeeLee," I say, grimacing as I remember my blunder.

"Okay, what could you have possibly said to upset him that badly?"

"Well, I guess he could have moved past it by now, but we never did make up from it, so we still have to resolve it."

"What's this terrible thing you said? I still can't believe it was that bad."

I take a deep breath. "I might have asked him if we would get married one day."

Silence fills the phone, and I cringe. I can picture her expression. Her mouth is in an 'O' and I've struck her speechless. I give her a minute.

"Vels, that's...that's...wow," she finally says. "What did he say?"

"What do you think he said? He said, yes, that he has no doubt whatsoever in his mind that he wants to marry me and head off into the sunset, together forever."

"And then you couldn't say it back?" she asks in a sympathetic voice.

She knows me too well. "Right."

"He does realize you're seventeen years old, and he's only a year older, right?"

"That's exactly what I said!" Then I deflate. "He didn't really take it well."

"Hmmm. Maybe he needs a chance to think about this before you bombard him with it again."

"I never want to bring it up again! Now, he's devastated that I was taken. I've damaged him permanently."

"No, Vela, don't go there. He's a strong, capable man. He'll be fine. And you will talk to him about the marriage thing. Just give him, and yourself some time."

"Yeah, maybe. I just don't know how to act around him anymore."

"What do you mean?"

"Well, it's so awkward now. Do I pretend I never said anything, and we go on our trip like before? We got to such a wonderful place before this all happened. He actually opened up to me about his sister."

Elia inhales sharply. "He did?"

"Yes." But before I can say anything more, I hear Linc at the door. "I've gotta go, LeeLee. Pray for me, k?"

"You know I will. Love you."

I say, "I love you, too," and hang up just when Linc walks in. He barely looks at me and then absently pats Jack's head when he goes to say hello.

My trusty sidekick has the right idea. I should greet Linc, too.

I put the phone down and stand up, taking the takeout containers from his hands. He gives me a small smile, and I smile back, thinking this is more promising than I expected.

"So, what did you get?" I take a peek and see he got slices of pizza with various toppings. They look delicious and my stomach growls. I realize it's been hours since I last ate. I bring the containers to the bed and sit them next to me. "Which one do you want?"

He shrugs.

My heart sinks and I pat the bed. "Come sit, let's at least eat."

"At least?" he asks, his eyebrows raised, expression hard.

Uh oh. This sounds like he's spoiling for a fight. I don't bite.

"Yes, eat. You know the act where you put food into your mouth and chew?" I pull my lips into a smile.

He looks at me a little too long and then huffs and sits on the bed. He reluctantly pulls a container over to him and reaches in for a slice.

I jump off the bed and say, "Let me feed Jack first. He looks like he's going to eat me if I don't."

When I reach for the door, I nearly jump out of my skin as Linc yells at me and runs over to the door, forcing it closed.

"What do you think you're doing? You can't go out there," he fumes at me.

"I'm going to get Jack's food out of the car." My face pales. *Oh.* How did I forget?

"The car? You mean the new one I just got that doesn't have Jack's food in it?" he growls. "Or did you mean the car that blew up? You know the one that I could have saved if I had just gotten the situation under control or even *prevented*? That one, Vela?" His voice rises until he's practically shouting at me. His eyes are shooting daggers, and I lean back, suddenly a little afraid.

He's never gotten this mad at me before, and I don't really know what to do. All I can do is shake my head. "I forgot," I whisper.

"Forgot?" he seethes. "How could you possibly have forgotten, Vela?"

Everything hits me again at his words. I burst into tears and hide my face in my hands. My shoulders shake, and I try to turn toward the bed so I can sink my weak legs on to it. I can hardly hold myself up.

Before I can go anywhere, Linc's hands land on my shoulders, and he blows out a breath. "Vela, I'm sorry. Baby, I'm sorry."

At his words, my tears come faster. I had managed to forget, for two seconds, what happened to me today, but Linc very clearly brought it back again.

He pulls me to him and tucks me into his chest, cocooning me in his arms. I melt into his solid warmth, and it comforts me. Clearly, I'm the only one comforted though, as Linc's body is tense, held rigid and tight. I can feel his heart pounding.

This ordeal has been a lot to handle, and Linc and I clearly have different coping mechanisms, and that's okay. I just don't want to be on the receiving end of his anger when he finally lets it vent.

So, I say that to him in a shaky voice, "Please, just don't take this out on me."

He sighs into my hair and says softly, squeezing me closer, "I won't. I'm sorry. I'm just so mad at myself. You've fought off two groups of attackers, and I should have been the one to do that. Not you, never you."

He suddenly pushes me away, and I stumble, even though I can tell he tried to be gentle. He spins around and bellows out a cry of fury so loud it shocks me.

But he's not done. He faces a blank wall, and he pulls his fist back and punches the wall as hard as he can.

I scream. What is he doing? I look on in horror as he continues to beat the wall with both fists now. He successfully punches three holes in the wall, destroying the plaster.

When he finally stops, he leans his head against the wall, his breaths hard and heavy.

I stand in shock, frozen to my spot on the threadbare carpet.

His head stays bowed for a while, but then he looks up at the damage.

"Linc?" I ask in a small voice. "Please tell me you're done."

He turns to me, still breathing hard. He looks calm enough, but I'm not sure if I trust he's okay after all that rage. Has he lost it?

He sees the fear in my eyes and the sight seems to calm him. His eyes soften and he looks away, putting his bleeding hands on his hips.

"I'm sorry," he breathes. "That was completely unacceptable." He shakes his head and lunges toward the door.

Before I know what I'm doing, I reach for his arm. "Linc, wait. Let's talk about this. Don't run away."

"We need to leave in about a half hour," he says in a hoarse voice. He avoids my gaze. "And I have to pay for these damages."

"Okay, we can do that, but talk to me, please."

He whirls toward me, "Don't you see, Vela? I can't look at you without remembering the terror I felt when I thought I'd lost you. I have to... have to get away, to get some air. Give me half an hour. Please?"

I nod. That's all I can do. Give him time. And while he's out, I'll pray. I can do that, too.

After one last tortured gaze at my face, he heads out and I find myself staring at a closed door again.

CHAPTER THIRTEEN

I wait the half hour and submit to a very disgruntled human employee coming into the room to inspect Linc's damages. The man quotes us an amount I'm sure is way over the cost of repair, but Linc pays it, no questions asked.

Once that's taken care of, we carefully head to the car and drive away, very, very happy to leave that little town behind.

Linc wants to drive through the night all the way into Canada, about a four-hour drive. We left at about 8:30, so I expect we'll make it to the Canadian border at about 12:30 in the morning.

Unsurprisingly, the air in the car is still heavy with tension. Linc refuses to even look at me, and I'm feeling alone in the car.

It's miserable riding along in tense silence, but I refuse to sleep, because I'm waiting for an opportunity to talk. The day and entire experience have caught up with me in full force and, frankly, I'm shocked I haven't already passed out.

Adrenaline can do funny things to a person, and I allow it to fuel my body with unnatural energy.

Hours into our wordless drive, I'm about to lose my mind. When I try to turn on the music, Linc stops me, and I snap.

"I need some music! You can't stop me!" I attack the radio, desperate to find a song, any song.

"What's the matter with you?" Linc's still not looking at me, but he screws up his face like I've officially lost it.

Maybe I have, but I don't care. I can't stand this quiet for another second.

Turning toward him, I shout, "Linc, you're shutting me out! You say you can't look at me because you almost lost me, but what do you call this?"

"What? What am I doing?" He finally turns toward me.

"You're losing me, Linc! That's what you're doing. How can I make it clearer?" I cringe inwardly at his stricken look, but I have to say this now. "Yes, we've just endured a horrific experience, one that could break us. But do we need to punish each other for it? Can't we heal together?"

He looks at me silently, his jaw working.

"Can't we move on from this and come out stronger on the other side? Isn't that what couples do as they go through life together?"

Now it's Linc's turn to explode. "Oh, the life you're not sure you want to live with me? That life, Vela? Why should I bother when I'm just going to lose you, anyway?"

His chest heaves, and his eyes look so wounded, I want to crawl in his lap and soothe his pain away. But now is not the time. He's trying to pay attention to the road, and to me, and I'm tempted to tell him to pull over so we can have this conversation safely.

But all I can do is look at him with my heart in my throat. Me and my stupid, careless words. Why did I ever ask him about marriage? Why couldn't I just leave that well enough alone?

But then a heat-filled resolve fills me. I'm sick of feeling guilty for asking an innocent question.

"Linc, you have to understand how utterly unfair you're being. I cannot imagine my life without you in it. Just because we're each other's Intendeds, does not guarantee a happily ever after. But guess what? We've had it so far, and we're going to have to be like any other couple in history and wait for my answer to your eventual proposal. You want an answer now? Well, you're going to have to wait for it. We have an entire relationship to experience before you should ever even think of asking it. So, pull up your big boy pants and stop pouting about what I said. Stop making me feel guilty for a question I playfully asked."

His turbulent eyes study me for a long moment, then he nods and replies, "You're right. I already said I'd wait for you. So, I guess that's where we're at, then? Take it one day at a time, with no promises?" His knuckles turn white as he grips the steering wheel.

This feels suspiciously like a test, and I hold my breath as I contemplate my response. I take the plunge and answer with what my instincts are screaming at me to say, "I promise to be the best girlfriend you've ever had. I love you, Lincoln Stevenson. I don't see that ever changing. But, until I get that question, your proposal someday, you're going to have to be happy with that."

At my words, a smile spreads across his face and my heart thumps in relief at seeing it.

"I can do that."

I look on in confusion as he slows down the car and pulls over. I didn't expect him to be happy with that last comment.

"In fact," he says with a determined set to his mouth as he turns to look at me, "I can do even better than that."

My head spins with how fast he's gone from being icy and mad to downright pleasant.

Linc opens his door and steps out of the car. I watch through the front windshield as he walks around the car and comes over to my door.

He opens it and pulls me to my feet.

My legs wobble and with wide eyes, I say, "Linc, what on earth..."

His eyes are determined, completely centered on mine. "You've given me no other choice. Remember, you asked for it." He grins. "Well, kind of."

I look at him, wondering where this can be going.

When he drops to one knee, everything freezes. My heart, my head, my eyes, I don't even blink as I realize what he's doing. What he's about to do.

"Vela," he says, looking up at me as he grabs one of my hands. "I know what I want more than anything. And it's standing right in front of me. I want to make you mine. Before anything else happens on this crazy road trip and life of ours, I want to do the one thing that I've wanted to do since you first dodged me. Marry me, Vela. Marry me in the next town, or the next, you tell me."

Linc's eyes are blazing with love, fire, and everything he's saying.

I can barely move, I'm so shocked. Never would I have thought my conversation getting him off the ledge of his own blame would lead to this ledge.

"Vela? Did you hear me? You can hear me, right? You're not in too complete of shock?" His eyes have a twinkle I'm happy to see but crushed, too.

I've barely nodded when he says, "Good. Because I'm serious. I want to marry you, Vela Ashcroft." His eyes are now a deep blue and trained on mine.

Panicked, my eyes switch between both of his before I look up at the night sky. Unable to comprehend my life right now,

I suddenly have the craziest urge to laugh. So, I do. I laugh so hard, I keel over, and Linc has to put both hands on my waist to steady me.

Linc's words barely reach me. "Vela? Vela, are you okay?"

Sucking in lungfuls of fresh, clean air, I wipe my streaming eyes and look down at Linc, who still hasn't gotten up.

I hear him say under his breath, "I've broken her. I've officially made her lose it." He looks down at the ground.

Getting a grip on myself, I say softly, "No, no you haven't." I nudge his chin up to look at me.

When he finally raises his gaze to mine, I can only do one thing. I sink to my knees with him in the grass, under the moonlight, with Jack yipping, wondering what the heck we're doing.

Ignoring Jack, I rest my forehead against Linc's and breathe in his miraculous, wonderful scent and pray he'll forgive me for doing the only thing I can do right now.

I'm already holding one of his hands, so I reach for his other one. I entwine my fingers with his and look deep into his eyes.

"Linc, I'm begging you. I'm literally begging you on my knees right now to do one thing for me."

"Anything, Vels, you should know that." His eyes are soft and a little sad. I swear he knows what I'm about to say.

Swallowing, I kiss him softly and then ask my question. "Wait for me?" I whisper against his lips. "I can't say yes to you right now. Only because," I lean back to stare into the endless expanse of sky, watching this letdown right now. I pray an angel or two is watching out for me, for us. I return my gaze to his. "I don't think I legally can, for one thing."

When he starts to say something, I put my finger on his lips and wait till he stops trying to talk.

"Also, my family would literally kill me, and probably you, if I agree to marry you when I'm only seventeen years old. So, Linc, I'm asking you. Will you please wait for me? To be older, to be wiser? For the day when I know I can answer you with my whole heart and soul and not leave a single thing behind?"

Looking lovingly at his face, I wait with bated breath. I pray the sense of regret I'm feeling now doesn't linger. It's only temporary, I remind myself.

One day...

He studies me for a minute, his face serious. I think my heart is going to explode right out of my chest if it beats any faster.

Will he agree? Will he wait for me?

I glimpse a flash of pain that crosses his face. "I'll agree," he finally says, and my heart lifts. "On one condition."

I nod wildly. I'll do anything. Anything so I don't see that pain flash in his eyes again.

"Be my girl. Promise you'll be that."

I lean my forehead back on his, knowing I can answer that with my whole heart. "I've always been your girl, Linc. That won't change."

He leans back to look at me, grinning a little. "Even when you hated the sight of me?"

I huff a laugh. "I never hated you, Linc. I was terrified of you. It just looked like hate. It never was."

"Yeah, I guess Festans have always brought change in your life." He brings my hand to his lips and kisses my knuckles softly. Then he pulls my arm to his mouth, kissing my burn scars gently and oh so tenderly.

"If you count burning down my home and then stealing my heart, then yeah."

His eyes light up. I didn't realize how dead they'd gotten. "Have I though? Stolen your heart?"

"Yes," I answer, looking at him with all the love in my eyes.

He returns my gaze with one of his own, before he says, "Good." Then he kisses my lips with a tenderness that makes my heart crack open. Why couldn't I just say 'yes' to his proposal? Would it have killed my family if I had? Romeo and Juliet did it despite their family's lack of approval.

And look where that got them. That's not exactly the ending I want for us.

I pull away and rub my nose against his. I kiss his top lip, then the side of his mouth, then the other. I continue until I've peppered his face with soft kisses.

My stomach heats with each kiss I give, and I'm about to go up in flames. When I lean back to look at his face, he's not far behind me.

His eyes burn into mine, and I take a deep breath to cool the emotions fanned by his look.

"Those are promises," I say breathlessly.

"Promises of what?" His voice is gravelly and husky enough to send a thrill through me.

"Until I can give you the answer you're looking for, I promise to be yours, and only yours."

In response, he leans in and presses his lips firmly to mine. But it's when he deepens the kiss that I melt. He explores and shows me exactly what he thinks of my promises.

His strong arms wrap around my back, pulling me to him. I revel at being as close to him as I've ever been. The presence of the strong planes of his chest so near teases my senses, and I suddenly long to explore.

I let my hands graze his shoulders, his biceps, and then move toward his delicious chest, appreciating every contour.

"Vela," Linc breaks our kiss and purrs a warning, "Stop that or I might not be so well behaved."

I pull back suddenly, my chest heaving and look at him, my eyes burning to see his face.

We both stand up and Linc takes a few steps away.

He's right. I've gotten too carried away.

Linc turns around and says, "If you're not going to marry me right now, we need to slow down. I'm afraid we'll lose control, and I don't think either of us wants that to happen until we're actually married."

I nod, agreeing, albeit reluctantly, to cool things down.

"So, unless you've changed your mind, and we're getting married tonight, we need to stop doing that."

I look up at him in exasperation. "You're telling me we can't kiss until I agree to marry you?"

"No. I'm telling you, we can't do *that*," he points back to where we were kneeling, "until I know that you're mine, completely."

I look away and try to pretend that I don't regret my answer. I *wish* I could say yes, but something held me back. I just knew it wouldn't be the best thing for me or for Linc.

I'll need to trust myself, my instincts, right now. That's all I can do.

"Okay," I say, sighing heavily. "I can't change my mind about your proposal, but I'll be better at controlling myself."

He nods curtly, and we return to the car. Because of our little excursion, our ETA is now 1:30 a.m.

The mood in the car for this leg of the journey is much more enjoyable. We fill the time with music. We talk and he makes me laugh until my belly hurts. I only catch him looking at me longingly once.

I didn't give him the answer he wants this time, but I think he understands. I can only hope.

Chapter Fourteen

"Linc, what happened to our clothes? Was anything salvageable?" I ask when we have two hours to go on this road trip from Hades.

His eyebrows raise and he looks at me with a fondness I don't deserve. "I cannot believe this is the first time I'm hearing this question."

"Hey, there's been a lot on my mind, okay? Give me a break."

And there it is again, a shadow in his eyes before it's quickly gone. "I know you have."

I don't know if he's referring to my fighting off the Boreans, escaping a kidnapping, or refusing his proposal. All of them send a spear of pain into my chest.

I put my hand on my heart to contain the ache and say, "It's okay, though! I survived, we survived, Jack survived. Isn't that what really matters?" When I reach back with my hand to pat Jack's smooth head, I catch Linc grimace. "Hey, that *is* what matters, right? Come on, Linc, let's try to put this horrific road trip from our minds and look ahead."

He nods silently, looking as if he bears the weight of the world on his shoulders.

I ignore the urge to reassure him again that nothing was his fault. But he wouldn't appreciate that, and I respect him too much to go there. He's made it perfectly clear how he feels. He's only going to blame himself.

One poor wall in Moorhead, Minnesota, can attest to those feelings.

I don't intend to repeat that experience, so I say brightly, "Well, do I have anything to wear at all?"

"A few things," he says. "I'll have to take you shopping before we get to the community."

"Is it called anything besides the community?" I'm suddenly curious and perk up at the shopping comment. That sounds like fun.

"They all have different names. I think this one's called The Polar Bear Lodge."

"What? Why that name? Oh, dear God, don't tell me it's overrun with polar bears."

He grimaces and raises one shoulder. "Well, not exactly. But they are the closest place to the polar bear capital of the world."

"How close, Linc?" I'm clenching my seat so hard my knuckles are white. I've heard terrifying stories of polar bears. They aren't the cute little white bears that drink soft drinks. They can be vicious and have actually been known to eat humans.

"Don't worry, Vels," he laughs. "I don't think they've ever seen one. They're probably two hundred miles from that place."

"Well, then, that's a terrible name," I grumble as I settle back into my seat.

"Noted. I'll tell the leaders you feel that way."

"Please do. Now, let's talk about a more pleasant topic. Like shopping." My whole being lifts at the notion, then crashes almost at the same time.

"Wait! Please tell me my shirt that says, 'Flowers are my happy place,' survived! And my little white dress?"

His forehead furrows, and he says in a regretful tone, "I don't know about the shirt. But," he brightens, "your dress survived. Amazingly enough, despite the fire and water. I love that dress."

I look over at him, humor warming my cheeks. "I wore that dress the day you tracked me down at school."

"The stairwell," he says in a hushed voice. "I love that place. Maybe I should have proposed to you there."

My stomach sinks. But his gaze is playful. He doesn't look upset. *Still.* "That's not funny, Linc."

"Hey, I don't want to tiptoe around my proposal, Vela. It's part of our story. Let's not ignore it."

"I like that," I say, smiling. "It *is* part of our story. How do you do that?" I ask in sudden awe at his attitude toward the one question every guy dreads getting the answer to. And my answer was *no.* How is he smiling right now?

"Do what?" He lifts his eyebrow.

"You know, take things in stride the way you do?"

He runs his hand through his hair. "I don't always, Vela. You know that."

I think back to his blowup in the hotel room and agree. "I don't mean that. I mean my answer to your proposal," I say softly. I can't look at him. I don't want to see any more pain cross his face.

"Hey," he says. "Look at me."

When I do, he reaches for my hand and says, "Maybe because I have the craziest of hopes that you *will* say yes. One day. And I love you enough that I'm okay with waiting for that."

When I gape at him with what I'm sure is a love-sick puppy look, he continues, "You said you'd be my girl. And that's the next best thing. I'll take it. For now."

"I really do love you," I say and mean it.

"I think you know I love you, too."

I squeeze his hand, and we continue driving into the night in a comfortable silence, each alone in our own thoughts for a while.

I break the silence when I see a sign for Emerson.

"Isn't that the checkpoint for Canada?"

"Yeah," Linc says with a surprised smile. "How'd you know?"

"There were signs we passed that told me. And I might have looked it up on the map. I kind of need to see where we're at and where we're going. It helps with..."

I try to think of how to explain the helplessness I felt after the Borean attack, when I didn't know where we were, and I was alone to take care of Linc and Jack.

Linc stops my mental gymnastics with a wave of his hand. "I get it. I haven't exactly been the best at explaining the logistics of this trip."

"I understand, though. You didn't expect any problems." And I really did understand.

"Actually, I did know." He frowns. "My uncle and I saw many a prejudiced Elemental in our travels. My uncle explained where to expect problems. And he was always right."

This time I frown. "It's not right. All this hatred and fighting."

"I agree. But we can't change people's minds with our two measly selves. It's going to take an act of God to do that."

"Or the Chosen Child."

He nodded. "Yep, or that.

Changing the subject, I ask, "Are we going shopping in Canada or in the U.S.?"

"I don't know," Linc says, oblivious to my torment. Or maybe he isn't, because he puts his hand on my knee and squeezes reassuringly. "It doesn't matter to me."

"Which place has the biggest mall?" I say, forcing a smile up at him.

"That answer has to be the U.S. I don't know of any country with more places to shop than us."

I laugh because it's true. "You know, I think Italy and France would take great offense to that statement. Hey!" I say suddenly, a new thought hits my brain. "Am I going to develop a Canadian accent? Or will I need to learn French?"

He chuckles. "You're thinking of Quebec and that's way over on the east coast. We're going to central Canada. So, no, you won't have to learn French. At least, I don't think so."

"But the accent is a given?" Then I mimic a Canadian accent as best as I can. "I mean, we will be Canadians, *you know, eh?*"

He laughs and rumples my hair, like Kane used to do all the time. "*Oh, fer sure.*"

"Hey, stop it!" I laugh and swat his hand away. But my heart is in my throat because I'm missing my family again.

Linc must notice my sudden frown because he asks, "Are you okay? Where'd you go?"

"Sorry," I sigh. "Just thinking of one of my brothers. Do you think they'll visit us?"

"Of course, I do. Your family is nothing like mine. Well, my parents, anyway. Sarah would have visited us in a heartbeat."

And now his face is downcast. We both sit missing our siblings, but for much different reasons.

I nearly jump out of my seat when my phone rings. "Who in the world is calling me?" I fumble with my cell to see who it is. My mouth goes slack with surprise as Elia's name pops up.

"Hello?" I try not to worry that something is wrong.

"Vels! Isn't Earth the most beautiful, wonderful place you've ever been to?"

I giggle. "Compared to Mars and Pluto? Yes, Earth is the best."

"Yes, it is," Elia breathes dreamily.

I can picture her right now, spinning around the room in circles. I'm already getting dizzy thinking about it.

"What has you so euphoric, LeeLee?"

"Kane," she sighs into the phone.

My eyebrows shoot up in surprise. "My brother? Has he finally done away with the silly notion you're too young for him?"

"Oh, I'm sure he still feels that way. But today, he was utterly dashing when he helped me pick up my books."

"Where did this happen?" I can't picture Kane happening by Elia's house, so I really am curious where they bumped into each other.

"I was coming out of the Center, and I dropped my books. He, like the gallant gentleman he is, helped me pick them up, then gave me a ride home in his horse-drawn carriage."

"Horse-drawn carriage?" I ask dryly.

"Well, that's what it felt like. He even did the thing from *Pride and Prejudice* where he helped me in the car, holding my hand until I got into my seat. It might as well have been a carriage." She sighs heavily and I sigh with her.

"That *is* romantic," I say. I'm proud of my big brother. I know, without a doubt, that he has a thing for my bestie, and if I could change his mind about their age difference,

I would. But he's staunch in his belief that he can't have anything to do with her right now. Sadly, at seventeen, she's too young for him. I haven't even gotten him to *admit* he likes her. But the signs are clear.

Like this one.

"Don't worry, Elia, he'll come around."

"Oh," she chirps, "he already is. I can feel him weakening the older I get. Every day that passes is just one day closer to us being together."

"I agree. But until then, you hang in there, bestie."

"Oh, I will. But I might have to turn to more drastic measures."

At her serious tone, I instantly start worrying. Whenever she sounds like that, I should worry. "Elia," I draw out her name. "What are you planning?"

"Oh, I might be planning a little thing called Operation Jealousy."

I laugh, unable to help myself. "Operation Jealousy? Who are you going to rope into doing this scheme of yours?"

"Hey!" she screeches. "Who says I have to rope anyone into anything? Man, Vela, you wound me."

Surprise grips me. "Sorry, LeeLee, I didn't mean you can't get another guy to like you. I just always thought you only have eyes for my brother."

"I do only have eyes for your brother, but that doesn't mean guys don't have eyes for me," she says in defense.

"Of course, but please, you're keeping me in suspense! Who is going to take part in Operation Jealousy with you?"

She pauses. Then says in a breezy voice, "Evan may have asked me out."

"What? Elia, no!"

Linc looks over at me with a questioning look, and I wave him away. Evan is the last person I want to remind Linc of right now. But it looks like I'll have to. I must talk Elia out of this insanity.

"You realize Evan is one slavering piece of meat and is only looking to destroy your reputation."

Elia laughs. *She laughs.* "I know. That's why I said yes to him."

I'm speechless. I hit my head and say in a controlled voice, "How does that make any kind of sense, Elia?"

"Well," she says in a serious tone, "Kane already knows Evan is a total player. I'm hoping that when Kane finds about the date, his protective instincts will flare up, and Operation Jealousy will be a raging success." She finishes proudly and waits for me to comment.

I almost can't comment because I have no words. Then plenty come forth. "Elia, you are not safe with that guy. He is all hands and no brains."

Linc shifts in his seat.

"You don't think I can take care of myself?" she asks.

"No! I don't. You are tiny, and I'm worried he'll take total advantage of that!"

"Hmm, maybe Kane will too," she muses. "Maybe I should let it slip in the rumor mill at the Center that we have plans, and I can start Operation Jealousy without going on an actual date."

"Listen, Elia," I try to say, but she's not listening.

"And, when Kane comes to confront me, I'll just have to bat my eyes and say I'm just waiting for the right guy and maybe that's Evan," she continues in a sing-song voice.

I rub my forehead. I am officially getting a full-blown headache listening to this.

"And then, when Kane tries to tell me I shouldn't go out with Evan, I'll just have to say, 'What else am I supposed to do on a Friday night?'"

I grunt, because once Elia gets on a roll, there's no stopping her.

"Which is when he'll say, 'Go out with me instead!'" She finishes with a flourish, and I can hear her spinning around now, and I have to put a stop to this.

"Elia," I say loudly. "Listen to me. This is what's going to happen. Well, two things could happen. One, Kane hears about your date and does nothing, because you are not dating him, and he doesn't have any right to say *anything*. And then you'll have to go on a date with the most ridiculous guy in existence.

"Two, Kane gets involved and confronts *Evan* and not you. Then Kane'll have to give Evan a bloody nose to convince him to drop the date. Do you really want either of these options?"

I know my brother. He would absolutely lose it when he hears Elia is going on a date with the world's biggest flirt. But what he'd do about it is really anyone's guess.

Elia really does squeal, and I hold my phone away from my ear. "Ooo, ooo, option two, option two!"

"Elia! You really want my brother to get arrested for punching a minor in the nose?"

I can hear her literally deflate. "No," she says. "Vela, I have to do something, though. Please give me advice."

This is better. "Okay, I'm not saying the date idea is a total bust. Just don't go on a date with Evan, please. Pick a safer, nicer guy and make sure Kane hears about it."

"Yes. That's what I'll do," her voice resumes its chipper and happy state. "Operation Jealousy is back in effect! Just without Evan."

"Yes," I breathe in relief. "Without Evan."

We hang up soon after, me promising to call her every day until I lose service and her promising to break off her date with Evan.

Linc's voice fills the car. "So, Evan again?"

"Not for me this time," I blurt. "It's Elia. She has a hare-brained scheme to get my brother jealous and wants to use Evan in her plan."

He grunts and I leave it at that. I don't want to bring up Evan any more than I have to. Linc apparently agrees because the subject is dropped.

CHAPTER FIFTEEN

We finally make it to the Canadian border, and I could scream in delirious happiness. It's 1:45 a.m., and I haven't been this tired in a long time.

I got a couple hours of sleep, but it's not nearly enough.

Linc produces paperwork his uncle and parents bought, giving us different names and information.

I look at my new passport that says I'm nineteen, and my name is Julie Hadlowe. I've seen this before, and I test the name out in my mind over and over in case I'm questioned.

It turns out I am. The Canadian officer looks into the car at me and immediately asks me my name and age. When I repeat the correct information, he studies my face, then stands up and examines my passport at every angle.

I want to ask Linc what he thinks the officer is doing, but I don't dare say anything. For one thing, he's human, so that's good. I don't want to accidentally say something I shouldn't, so I stay quiet and pray he believes our counterfeits.

The officer finally hands my passport over to Linc, then accepts his. He doesn't seem to question Linc's like he did mine, and I breathe easier when he waves us on.

"So, what's the plan? Where do we go from here?" I ask once we drive away. Now that we're in Canada, I feel like the hardest part is behind us.

"We meet my parents' contact. We'll stay at his house, and he'll help get us to the community."

"The Polar Bear Lodge," I mutter, still distrustful of the name and the actual existence of nearby polar bears. "How hard is it to get to this place?"

"It's not that easy. It's a little out of the way." He looks sideways at me, and I tense.

"Define 'a little,' please," I say, my stomach tightening with nerves. Linc's never been one to exaggerate, and if he says it's out of the way, it really is.

He cringes. "We have to do a little off-roading to get there."

"Again, please define 'a little.'"

"Okay, so don't panic, but we'll have to be flown in as close as we can and then go on four wheelers directly to the Lodge."

"Where exactly are we going? To the North Pole?"

Linc breaks out in a laugh. "Vela, you are not the type to be afraid of a little challenge. Really, I'm surprised at you."

He turns his amused eyes at me, and I look at him with a wide-eyed expression.

"You're *surprised* that *I'm* surprised that we have to be flown in close to my new home, then take ATVs even further? Really?"

He has the decency to look a little chagrined. "I guess I should have mentioned it."

"Yes, you should have." I huff and turn to look out the window. Then I jerk up, crying, "My parents! They will never be okay with this."

Linc's expression sobers quickly. "For your safety, they'll be fine with it."

"What happens if the E.E. finds us out there? How are we going to escape?"

Linc looks at me with an exasperated look. "They will never find us out in the middle of nowhere, Vela."

I fold my arms over my chest and huff in exasperation. "I should have thought this through better. The chance to shop at a mall has become impossible."

I'm given a fond look when Linc says, "I'm sure they have ways to do online shopping, Vels."

"That's not the same as trying things on," I grumble.

Linc's been driving on bigger roads, so when he slows down to take an exit, I take notice of where we are.

We enter a small town.

Linc checks his phone several times, and I watch as he enters an address into his GPS.

"Linc, isn't it awfully late to be meeting someone? It's almost two in the morning."

His face has turned grave. "It's better this way. This is Festan territory, and we need to keep you hidden. This is the perfect time."

I sit and think about that seriously. As bad as I feel about someone getting out of bed to welcome us, I appreciate whoever it is. I never want to meet another angry Festan as long as I live.

After following the GPS's directions down several roads, we end up in a nice neighborhood, which comes as no surprise. If this is Linc's parents' contact, I'm sure whoever we're meeting is well off.

We end up at a two-story home that is dark except for the front door light. It beckons me to go inside, and I'm so happy for the chance to rest in a safe place. I could kiss whoever comes out to take us in.

But when a big, burly man comes out after Linc texts, I quickly change my mind.

The man is Andre the Giant, but a couple of inches shorter. I'm completely intimidated. I couldn't get my arms around him if I tried.

"That's Andy," Linc says as he opens his door and I snort. "What?" he asks.

"I just compared him in my mind to Andre the Giant, and his name is Andy. It's funny."

"Oh," he laughs. "That is funny. I thought you were just getting delirious."

"I'm close. Don't count that out yet." I unfold my tired body and climb out of the car, before pulling open the back-door and putting a leash on Jack.

Andy approaches me, and I shrink back and keep looking up until I reach his face. "Hi," I say, shyly. "I'm..."

"Vela, yes, I know. It's nice to meet you." He has a cultured voice, and it completely takes me back. I expected a heavy, gravelly voice, and this is so unexpected. I just look at him with wide eyes. He offers me his hand, and I watch as my hand gets lost in his much bigger one. Standing near him, I feel a hot flush, which clearly tells me he's a Festan.

After shaking my hand gently, he turns to Linc. "Linc, it's nice to meet you." He looks warmly at Linc and shakes his hand much more briskly than he did mine.

"Sir, it's nice to meet you, too. Thank you for helping us. As you know, Vela can't be seen here."

"I know," Andy says gravely. "Come inside. Can I get anything out of the car?"

Linc frowns. "There's not much because of the fire. I can get it."

"That's unfortunate," Andy says, and he looks at me curiously. "You have quite the story. I hope I can hear it sometime."

"I think I can do that," I say in a small voice. It's not really something I want to relive, but this man is doing a lot to keep me safe, so I can manage telling him what his clan did.

I try not to hold all Festans in that low esteem. I know from bitter experience that the actions of a few can destroy faith in the whole. I don't want to allow myself to fall into that hole again. I force the bitter pill of anger and resentment down. I'll need to give this to God, but later, in the safety of my bed.

Thinking of a bed, I ask, "Sir, are you sure you have room for us?"

He booms a laugh and says as he leads the way to his home, "I think I can find a bed or two for you. Don't worry, I've got plenty of room."

I blush at the thought of one bed between Linc and me, exchanging a shy glance with Linc. He had the same thought because there's a half smile on his face.

I follow Andy into his enormous home, hoping for an easy couple of days for a change.

CHAPTER SIXTEEN

I wake up the next afternoon fully clothed. Once Andy showed me to my room, I fell into my bed. I was too tired to do much besides crawl under the covers. It's gotten chillier at night the further north we've gone, and the minute I step out of bed, I go to find a warm shower.

But I don't know what's Linc done with the little bit of clothing I have left, so I go to find him first.

It's 1:00 in the afternoon, but that doesn't mean Linc is up. We didn't get to sleep until 2, so he could be in bed.

Still, I need my clothes, so I tiptoe around the second floor and listen at closed doors to hear if Linc is snoring in any of them. When I hear nothing, I make an executive decision to peek into the rooms.

I open a couple of empty guest rooms first. On my third try, I find Linc. Except he's not sleeping. I gasp in surprise when I open the door and find him changing.

I slam the door shut and lean against the wall next to it, covering my mouth with my hands in mortification. The image of him pulling his pants down is burned into my mind. I can only be thankful that he wasn't naked. Just half naked. I close my eyes at that surprising image and run down the hall before he can come out and question why I didn't knock.

"Vela!" Linc shouts down the hall I'm fleeing. "Vela, wait!"

I ignore him and find my door, dashing in and quickly locking it behind me.

"Vela," Linc complains in a deep voice after he tries to open my door. "Open the door, please."

I shake my head mutely, hand still clamped over my mouth, not trusting myself to speak.

"Vela, it's okay. That was bound to happen at some point on this trip. Please don't be embarrassed." His voice sounds amused, but I'm mortified.

He thinks *I'm* embarrassed? What about him? He's the one found pulling his pants down.

"Okay," he says after I refuse to answer him. "Look, I'll be downstairs when you're ready to come down. But it's okay, really." He laughs softly and leaves, to my utter relief.

How am I going to face him now? And that he finds it funny is ridiculous. This is *not* funny.

As pleasant as it was seeing him shirtless, I'm not sure I can look him in the face again.

I sit on my bed and pace around my room for an hour before Jack's whining finally catches my attention. Only for Jack do I agree to leave the room so he can go to the bathroom outside. Tiptoeing into the hallway, I look down both ways to be sure no one is around. When I see the coast is clear, I allow Jack to lead me downstairs. He seems to instinctively know where to go. He probably remembers his way from last night, but in my sleep-deprived mind, I can barely remember how I got to bed.

I wonder if Andy has a wife and kids somewhere around here, because in my earlier exploration, I found only generically decorated rooms and nothing with anyone's personal stamp on it.

I find no trace of life as I step off the last stair, but I do hear Linc's distinctive laugh. At that, I whisper to Jack sharply, then apologize to my poor dog when he looks up at me, soulfully, as if he's wondering why he can't just go out like all the other dogs.

"I can't see Linc right now, I just can't," I whisper to Jack and look around for the front door. I'm guessing Linc is in the kitchen with Andy, so maybe the front door is safe?

As I go the opposite direction of Linc's voice, I find myself in another hallway with open doors this time. I pass a library, a study and finally, I see the front door.

Just as I'm reaching for the handle, I scream when I hear a voice behind me, "Hiding from me, are we?"

I spin around. "Linc! You scared me!"

"As you did me," he said with a crooked smile and a stupid twinkle in his eye.

"No, I mean now. You scared me now." I blush fiercely.

"Ah, yes. And I meant from, uh, before. You scared me."

I blush ten shades of red before I blurt, "You didn't seem scared at all."

"No? What did I seem like to you?" He cocks his head.

Coughing, I step back, trying to ignore the barrage of images pouring into my head at the moment. I see it all, despite my attempts not to. I try to remember if he seemed remotely scared. No, I wouldn't say I saw any hint of that emotion at all.

"Surprised, maybe, but definitely not scared. Why would you be scared? Are we not in a safe house?" I look around with new eyes.

"Vela," Linc laughs, reaching for my hand. "We're in a very safe house. The safest. I'm just teasing you. It's impossible not to." He squeezes my hand and my face flames even more, but I'm not sure how.

"I'm sorry, Linc, I'm really sorry to barge into your room like I did," I implore him with my eyes to believe me. "I thought you were still asleep. I didn't have any idea…"

He chuckles and pulls me to his chest, where I promptly bury my hot face.

Linc's deep voice rumbles in my ear when he says, "Come on, come see Andy, he's got breakfast for us."

My nose just notices the delicious smell permeating the room. *Bacon. Oh heaven.* "Yum, let's go," I say as my mouth salivates. "Oh wait, Jack really needs to go out."

We step away from each other and Linc motions to Jack to follow him. It's wise for him to go outside with Jack. I shouldn't be seen outside. It doesn't take long. Poor Jack really needed to go.

When he comes back inside, Linc takes me by the hand and leads me to the blessed kitchen where I can feed my raging stomach.

Andy greets us with a warm smile, and I smile back at him. He's garbed in an apron that doesn't do a very good job of covering his front. He's just too big for apron industry standard sizes. But the red checkered print really does try.

He's standing in one of the largest kitchens I've ever seen. Its vaulted ceilings make the white kitchen with warm brown cabinets appear even more spacious. A huge island with a white marble countertop dominates the space and holds the biggest sink I've ever seen. I wonder if he has such a big sink and kitchen to accommodate his huge size. His entire house looks like it's meant to fit his large frame. Again, I wonder, is there a Mrs. Andy or little Andy's running around?

"Hungry?" Andy asks, making me jump from my ruminations.

"Too hungry," I acknowledge with an embarrassed grin. I'm surprised my stomach isn't announcing its emptiness to the world.

"Well, that's good, because I made enough for ten people, so eat up," Andy replies with a smile.

"Let me feed Jack first. I'd feel guilty if he had to watch us eat with no food of his own."

After serving Jack a pile of dog food Andy had been kind enough to buy, I don't have any problem dishing up some egg casserole, then putting a pile of bacon on my plate. Snatching a piece of toast, I sit down at the kitchen table, and I don't do anything for several minutes but eat as I satisfy my appetite.

When I look up, I see Linc has done the same, and Andy is looking at us both with an amused expression.

"Did you not feed yourselves yesterday?"

Linc shakes his head and says around a mouthful of food, "We ate dinner, but we were both so," he looks at me with a pointed expression before he finishes, "upset about what happened, we didn't have much of an appetite. And I really needed to get Vela out of that place, so we didn't stop anywhere. Not that anything would have been open, anyway."

I nod in agreement, but just being reminded about the kidnapping and Linc's blowup makes the food in my mouth turn to ash. My stomach refuses to accept any more when I half-heartedly try to take another bite. So, I put my fork down and look out the window.

Andy's voice is gentle when he asks, "Vela, I understand what you experienced was terrifying. But would you mind telling me about what attracted the Festans' notice?"

I swallow thickly, tears suddenly springing up at his kind tone. It would have almost been easier if he adopted a more clinical tone, not the fatherly one I would dearly love to hear from my own father.

"Um, well, we were trying very hard not to draw any attention when I was in the car with Jack. The windows were all the way up, so the Festans couldn't sense my element. And," I blink away tears at the frightening memory of the Festans' angry faces. I say in a quiet voice, "They took offense at Jack being shut in a car with no AC or open windows. They kept telling me to put my window down for him, but I couldn't, because if I did, they'd know what I am."

"I tried diffusing the situation," Linc adds in a dark voice, "but they were two hot heads looking for a fight. The minute I opened my car door to get us out of there, they figured out Vels was a Gyan." Linc's arm flexes as he grips his fork tightly, and I know he's having as hard a time as I am. He looks out into the distance, and I put my hand on his arm to comfort him.

I need his comfort just as much, and when I squeeze his arm, it relaxes a little, which in turn relaxes me. Jack, too, notices my anguish and pushes his nose against my knee.

"That's all you need to say. I can get the details from Linc, if that's better for you," Andy says. "I just needed to know what sparked the flame, if you will. We don't want to repeat the experience, by any means."

I nod gratefully and get up to put my half-full plate in the sink, first trying to find the garbage so I can throw out what I couldn't finish. I look around helplessly because in this kitchen I don't see any sign of a garbage can.

"Here, let me," Andy offers, to my relief. He opens a non-descript cabinet, and it magically produces a garbage can.

"Nifty," I say shyly, my battered feelings easing some. Curiosity overwhelms me, so I ask, "Is there a Mrs. Andy anywhere? Do you have a family?"

He flushes, which is a strange sight. He looks embarrassed, and I regret my thoughtless question. Andy's the manliest man I've ever seen, and his show of vulnerability pulls at my heart strings. "No," he says, shaking his shaggy head. "I haven't found anyone to take me on. Not yet, anyway." He gestures toward his large chest, "I'm a lot to accept. I know that. No one's been brave enough to try."

I smile up at him and can't help but think that any woman would be lucky to have this man in her corner, backing her up in any area of life. I just know that I'm going to love having this giant man in my own life. I mean, the man cooks! That's a huge plus. I can tell he's a very good egg, and I like him immensely. "I'm sure there's a line of ladies who are hoping they're lucky enough to catch your eye. I'm sure whoever you choose will be thrilled to be in their shoes."

He smiles at me, and I know I've made a friend.

"So," Andy says, rubbing his hands together, "Do you want to see the route we're taking to get to the Polar Bear?"

"Oh, okay. Sure," I say.

Andy brings us to an area of the house I've already seen, and we walk down the front hallway and go into what looks like a study.

It's a cozy room, but again, with high ceilings. I'm sure Andy doesn't feel cramped in this room. He's over six and a half feet tall, if I had to guess, and I'm sure the standard eight feet is too close for comfort.

Windows bring cheerful light into the room, and Andy goes right to the large oak desk that sits proudly in the center of the office.

"What do you do for a living, Andy?" I ask.

"I'm a contractor. I mostly build homes, but I've had a hand in building some commercial buildings, too," he answers proudly.

I can easily see him with tools in his hand building anything he sets his mind to.

He motions for us to come around his desk to look at something. "So, come look at this map. I've highlighted in blue how we're getting to the Polar Bear, but I've also highlighted how to get to the other communities in other colors. You might need to find them."

I immediately notice the lack of roads on this map. I understood this place is in the middle of nowhere, but the enormity of it being inaccessible by road leaves me reeling.

God? Is this the place you want me to go? I hope to get an answer soon, because before I know it, we'll be there, and it won't be so easy to go home.

"Can we leave at first light?" Linc asks. "I'd like to get there as soon as possible. For Vela's sake."

Before Andy can answer, I ask a question of my own, "I know we're in Festan land now, but will we pass through any other clans' territories on the way?" I try to contain a worried expression. I've had enough attacks from other clans to last me a lifetime.

"We'll be passing through Borean and Neronian territories, ending up in a Neronian clan's land. We'll fly over the Boreans, but we'll end up in Neronian's land. There's quite a bit of lakes and rivers up in northern Manitoba, so they thrive there. But don't worry," Andy reassures me when he notices my alarm. "There are hardly any souls out there. Canada is not like the U.S. There are a lot more places to hide than what you're used to."

I breathe in relief and try to imagine living in the middle of no-man's-land. I can't, yet. But that'll change soon.

"So, when do we leave?" Linc asks again.

This time I stay quiet so Andy can answer.

"I understand you have some shopping to do?" Andy asks, eyeing me.

I nod eagerly, ready to do something normal that doesn't involve fighting for our lives.

Andy laughs at my excitement and says, "Well, if you go forty minutes out of town, you'll be in Gyan territory. I think it's best you shop there, as your clan isn't as aggressive as Festans can be. They have a pretty excellent collection of shops you can have fun in. But remember, don't go too crazy. We'll have to cart what you bring on four wheelers at one point. So, try to keep your shopping to a minimum, just buy the necessities. Once you're in the community, there will be young ladies your age who I'm sure will be happy to share their clothes with you. They often have to do that living so far off the grid."

"Off the grid," I breathe. "It's hard to imagine." Suddenly struck with a new thought, I ask, "Wait, how are we going to get Jack to this place? Where I go, he goes." I say this firmly because there's no way I'm making this trip without my best friend.

Andy's faces scrunches in thought. "He'll fly with us to Churchill and after that we'll take ATVs over the tundra. I've seen dogs strapped to the backs of those before. When we're going slower, he can run beside us. Then, we'll hit a lot of water and bogs, making the ATVs impossible to ride over all of that. So, Jack'll join us in a Sherpa."

"What's a Sherpa?"

His face lights up. "I have a friend who hires out the use of his Sherpa to go over water and land. Its tires inflate and deflate at will, depending on the terrain."

"There are swamps in northern Manitoba?" I pictured mountain ranges and trees as far as the eye could see. Not bogs.

"I'm afraid so, yes. In the winter months, they'll be iced over, and we can go over them on ATVs, but for now they'll be impossible to get through without the use of an all-terrain vehicle."

I'm cowed at what we'll have to do to reach this place. "What's it like living in the middle of nowhere?"

"Be prepared to be amazed at their ingenuity out there," Andy says with an encouraging smile. "What they can do with a battery is pretty amazing."

"Like a double A?" I ask.

"No," Linc says, laughing. "A really big one that they attach to generators."

"They have generators out there?" My mouth hangs open in surprise. My dad has a generator, and that thing is a beast.

"You'll have to ask them how they did it, but yes, they're well equipped to live completely on their own. We'll be bringing extra gas cans with us to help the community feed their generators. It'll be our contribution to the place."

I nod in amazement and suddenly can't wait to see this place for myself. "Are we leaving soon?"

"As soon as you're ready. Go do your shopping today, and we'll leave first thing in the morning."

My heart skips in excitement, and I turn to look at Linc, who seems just as pumped as I am.

"You ready?" he asks, suddenly serious.

"For shopping? Always."

"No," he says, taking my elbow and bringing me closer.

"Ahem," Andy coughs, looking between Linc and I. "I have some things to take care of. If you need anything, just find me."

Linc looks relieved, and I eye him curiously, eyebrows raised in question. "What is it?"

He leans toward me to speak quietly as Andy leaves the room. "You've expressed concern about going to this place, and I want to be sure that you're sure. It's just been the two of us, and by tomorrow you'll be in a completely new place that's very different from anything you've ever experienced." His eyes study mine.

"I'm not completely sure. I don't know how I could ever be okay with upending my life this way and leaving all I've ever known. It's scary. But, on the other hand, I'm kind of excited," I confess. "Until I get a clear answer from God, I'm treating this as an adventure. I'll be experiencing all new things and living in a place that sounds beautiful and safe."

"Safe is the operative word," Linc says reflectively, looking away.

"Hey, I trust you, and you say this is the safest place for me, so I have no reason to doubt it."

He turns, his face determined. "It will be. They've had no issues and let's hope we won't change that by joining them."

"Well, if we're going to find me something to wear, let's go. But first let me call my mom and let her know we made it safely. I already texted her, but I want her to know we're okay."

Linc agrees, and I retreat to my room to call my parents. I can't wait to get started on our day, but I promised mom I'd call her every day. As soon as I'm done, I'm going shopping. And I intend to enjoy every minute.

CHAPTER SEVENTEEN

Mom can tell I'm in a hurry to start some shopping therapy, so we wrap our conversation up quickly. I make a quick call to Elia to get a status update on Operation Jealousy, and when I find nothing new, we hang up.

Knocking on his door this time, I find Linc in his room. After getting directions from Andy and leaving Jack in his care, we head out.

I'm fidgeting in my seat when Linc chuckles and puts his hand on my leg. "Don't worry, we'll get there, Vels."

"Do you think we're going far enough in Gyan land for you to have no problems?"

"I'm comfortable enough with it. Border towns tend to be the testiest when it comes to tempers, but I'm sure it'll be fine."

I sigh. "I hope so."

We make good time, and I squeal in delight when I see a decently sized mall. My hungry eyes look over all the shops, and I'm close to giddy when I see some of my favorites.

I pull Linc in one direction, then another, when I realize he also needs clothes and shoes.

"So, we can use your parent's credit card for everything we need?" I ask after hitting several stores. "You're sure your parents won't mind?"

"They won't even notice," he says, snorting. "But if they did, they've approved a shopping trip for both of us."

"Why me?" I ask as I hand over a bag to Linc when he reaches for it. *Such a gentleman.* My heart warms at his gesture and at his parents' generosity.

"Vela, you're my Intended. That's as good as married in their eyes."

My eyebrows fly up. "Really? Wow," I say, my heart beating erratically.

Linc eyes my expression, and I try to hide my unease. "Hey," he says affectionately, "My parents are just old school when it comes to finding your Intended. Don't be nervous, please."

"I'm not" I lie quickly, then cringe when he looks at me knowingly. I roll my shoulders to relax my tense muscles. "Is that why you were so relentless in pursuing us?"

"Pursuing *you*," he says, his dark eyes looking at me with an intensity that makes me stop breathing.

I stop walking and put my hand on his chest, feeling it beat strong and sure beneath my palm. It thrills my senses that it beats only for me. I want him to know I might have turned down his official marriage proposal, but my heart beats only for him.

"You know how I feel," I say, stepping close to him.

"I do," he agrees in a deep voice, his scent suddenly making my head swim with its deliciousness.

"I was a little behind you when it comes to us, but I'm caught up now. I'm committed."

"Not completely," he disagrees, sadness flashing across his eyes.

"For what it's worth, I'm completely yours. I don't need a ring to show that."

"I know. But I'd like to put one on, soon," he says relentlessly.

I'm tempted to just give in. Give him what he wants and say I'll marry him. But my parents' faces flash through my mind. And, as much as Linc's parents consider me their daughter, my parents won't be as understanding.

"Remember what I asked?" I breathe, leaning in for a gentle kiss. Speaking against his supremely kissable lips, I say, "Wait for me?"

Frustration leaks through his careful expression. It's gone before I can say anything, and then it's replaced with a look of patience, so sweetly worn on his face, I love him more in that moment than ever before.

I wrap my arms around his neck, coming in for a better kiss. I don't care that we're in the middle of a busy mall. That anyone can watch our display, I just want to seal what we just agreed on with a promise.

So, I angle my head for better access. I move my lips against his and gasp when he suddenly pulls me tightly against him. He takes advantage of my gasp and deepens the kiss.

I melt. Something about that drives me wild. I find his kiss the most delicious taste I've ever experienced.

Breaking away from me, Linc pulls back and puts his forehead against mine, breathing heavily. "Vela," he moans. "You are going to drive me to my grave."

"I hope as a happy man," I say, giggling.

He leans in for a peck and steps back quickly, as if to prevent himself from coming back for more. "The happiest."

Encouraged that he seems to have let go of the marriage question, I pull back and walk away from him, putting a little sway in my hips.

I say over my shoulder, "As long as you're happy, I am."

He laughs and runs to me, grabbing me from behind, swinging me around. "You need to stop torturing me, Vela Ashcroft."

"Never. Not till the day I die," I say, laughing. "And even then, I want to torture you with my memory."

"Now, that's a definite possibility. But let's not talk about dying just yet."

"Why? You brought it up."

"Only that you're killing me with your provocative ways."

"What better way to live?" I ask.

"The best," he says and then grabs my hand, pulling me back to our shopping spree.

I happily allow him and think this is the best day I've had in a long time.

We shop for a couple more hours, and I happily hold on to the few bags Linc allows me to carry.

"Will we be able to carry all this to The Polar Bear?"

"We should. I'm a very good packer. I'll teach you my tricks," he says, his eyes twinkling.

"Oh, you will, huh? What if I can teach you more than you can teach me?"

"We'll see about that."

We leave the mall unscathed and with no issues from the Gyans we sensed. They give Linc a wide berth and glare at me in disbelief, but they leave us alone.

We make it back to Andy's house by dinnertime, and Linc makes me run into the house with empty hands. He doesn't want to take any chances that any Festan might sense me from hundreds of feet away.

I don't argue and do as he says, thankfully with no issues.

We eat a satisfying meal with Andy, who cooked a pot roast all day. It melts in my mouth and is one of the best meals I've had in a while. Eating takeout every day is not what it's cracked up to be, and I've sorely missed my mom's homemade dinners.

"So, Andy, how did you come to be in the loop with these hidden communities?" I ask after I push my plate away, rubbing my overfull stomach.

"Well, that's an interesting story," he says, wiping his mouth with his napkin.

"Oh, really? Do tell," I insist.

He doesn't need any encouragement from me. "I was on a bit of a sabbatical out in the middle of nowhere when I got a little too close to The Polar Bear." He laughs as he remembers and I find myself smiling with him, not even knowing the story yet. But I could imagine a huge man like Andy accidentally finding a hidden community like that, raising some suspicions.

"I was on my own, or so I thought," he says, raising his eyebrows, "when I found a trail that branched off mine, and I thought it was a little strange. "It was a little more than a deer path. It was well used. So, being the curious sort, I followed it."

"Where were you exactly?" Linc asks with eager eyes.

Andy starts off in a tone that suggests I sit back and enjoy a good story. So, I do.

"It was May of last year when I was flown into Churchill, in the northern part of Manitoba. I made sure to go in May, because Churchill is known as the Polar Bear Capital of the World and the polar bears migrate there between July and November. I'd prefer no nasty surprises."

I cringe. It's October and we're heading to this place in the peak of polar bear season.

"I'm going at a great pace when I come across a small lake. I figure that's why the path was there, so the deer can get to water. As I approach the water's edge to refill my canteen, I see the remnants of an old campsite. Again, I'm the curious sort, so I wondered who would be camping out in the middle of this vast open place."

"Basically, who is as crazy as you for being out there?" Linc asks with a grin.

Andy answers with one of his own and says, "Right. Exactly. When I do my long trek hikes, I rarely see signs of any other humans. I enjoy being one with nature, if you may, so imagine my surprise at finding this campsite. I'd been hiking for days at this point and was nowhere near any settlement. And then, when I examined it further, I saw the existence of several old campfires near the one I found."

Andy's eyes are as wide as walnuts while he recounts his tale. His surprise is still evident, and it makes his story come to life.

"So, I walk on, thinking to myself, maybe there's an indigenous people who live off the grid. I wanted to find out if I was right."

"Indigenous, like Native Americans..uh, Native Canadians?" I ask, holding my breath. This story has me captivated.

"Yes. That was my thought. So, I kept going, even though I had planned to turn back after spending the night at the lake. I wanted to see a unique culture. I thought that would be wonderful to see."

I nod. It would be.

"So, I kept going. I found more trails, and I followed the more used ones. Eventually, I found a settlement. But instead of a camp of native people, I found The Polar Bear Lodge. They are a well-established group, with log cabins and buildings. They were just as surprised to see me as I was them. I could immediately sense all the different elements present when they came out to greet me, and I was shocked, to say the least.

"Usually when someone stumbles into their community, they immediately administer the memory-erasing poppy-seed formula, so the interloper forgets ever seeing it. But I convinced them to leave me be. That I could be a valuable resource to them if they allowed me to remember. I think it's a wonderful community, and if I didn't have my responsibilities here, I'd happily live there."

"How did you convince them? I know they're extremely protective of their secret location," Linc asks.

Andy's face turns red. "There may have been a bit of a scuffle, and I was left alone long enough to give a rather convincing argument against administering the formula."

I laugh. "I can only imagine how many people it would take to bring you down."

He looks chagrined. "It wouldn't be easy," he admits. "I can hold my own."

"Absolutely," I giggle.

"So, anyway," he says, straightening. "They allowed me to stay for a while and help them improve their buildings. They have impressive capabilities. Many of them are quality builders, but with my expertise, we added a much-needed meeting room. It was fun," he said, his eyes merry. "I'm looking forward to returning tomorrow. It's so nice to have so many of us living and working together in harmony. I even injured my head while I was there, and a wonderful Gyan woman healed me right up. She was amazing." His face lights up at the thought of this woman.

"Now I understand why you're so eager to go back." I say knowingly.

He chuckles, rubbing his reddening face. "I'm sure I don't know what you're talking about."

"Right," I say dryly. I'm so happy he found someone who caught his eye. She must be quite a woman and I can't wait to meet her. "What's her name?"

"Hannah," he says promptly. "She's pretty amazing."

"You keep saying that," Linc says, cocking his eyebrow.

"Did I?" he asks, his face reddening further.

Feeling bad for teasing this mountain of a man, I change the subject. "What time will we head out in the morning?"

"The plane leaves at 5 a.m.," he answers, and I drop my fork.

"That means we'll have to leave here at..."

"4:00."

"Okay, so on that note, I'm going to bed," I announce. I'm still sore from the ordeal in the Festan town and after a day on my feet and shopping, I'm ready to sleep like the dead. Especially in a comfortable bed before finishing our journey to this mysterious compound.

Andy and Linc both get up when I do and, after cleaning up, we promptly say goodnight.

Despite being exhausted, I find myself staring up at the ceiling when I lie down, my mind reeling at what I'll find tomorrow. Again, I wonder if it's God's will that I go to this remote place.

Restless, I reach for my phone and open my Bible app, needing God's word right now. The last passage I read shines up at me. It's in Matthew, and Jesus is teaching his disciples how to pray.

I read:

"Our Father in Heaven, hallowed be your name. Your kingdom come, your will be done, on earth as it is in heaven. Give us this day our daily bread, and forgive us our debts, as we also have forgiven our debtors. And lead us not into temptation, but deliver us from evil."

My heart cries out, *Let your will be done, Father, not mine. Let me know if this is your plan. I want to follow your plan for my life, not mine. Do, not what we think is right, but what you will for me. My life is yours, Father. Take it and use it.*

At that thought, I'm washed with a gentle warmth that can only come from God. It takes my breath away. I know in that moment, God is giving me His blessing to go to this place, and I revel in it. Tears leak from my eyes, and I roll over to cuddle with Jack, closing my eyes with a smile on my face.

My last thought before sleep claims me is, *Thank you, Lord. Please take us there safely.*

CHAPTER EIGHTEEN

After waking up at the extremely early hour of 3 a.m., we make quick work of stuffing our new clothes in duffle bags that Andy gives us. Those are apparently much easier to pack on a four-wheeler than a suitcase.

After a hurried breakfast, we make our way to a small airport, and I eye the airplane that's supposed to carry us to Churchill. I'm extremely nervous for several reasons. It's October, and that means it's polar bear season. Also, this plane is the smallest one I've ever flown in. It's a Cessna and only seats four people. I try to bolster my confidence that this tiny plane could get us anywhere, let alone four hours in flight.

My look of distrust must prompt the pilot to take pity on me and give me actual numbers in reassurance. He tells me that the Cessna can go over 1,000 miles on one trip and our destination is only 700 miles, so we're well within range.

"Can't we take a train or something?" I ask Andy when the pilot walks away.

"That is an option, but Elementals usually fly in because we need to cross Borean territory and land in Neronian. We don't want any problems, and it's just safer flying over it than riding through it."

I nod morosely. He's absolutely right. Linc takes my hand and squeezes it encouragingly. He smiles, and I squeeze his hand in appreciation for his comfort.

It's a good thing I'm not claustrophobic because by the time we all squeeze into the small plane with Andy and Jack, I'm cramped like a sardine. Frankly, I'm shocked Andy fits into the seat next to the pilot. Linc, Jack, and I are in the back.

With nothing to do but pray for safety and good weather, I lean my head back, and after an uneventful takeoff, we begin this final leg of our journey.

I sleep for a couple of hours. When I wake, Andy and Linc are in the middle of a heated conversation about the merits of two football teams.

My mind wanders as they argue, but soon my attention goes to Jack, who's getting antsy flying for so long. Thankful I thought to buy some, I fish in my backpack for medicine to calm his nerves. After helping Jack eat the pill encased in a treat, I pet him to soothe his rattled nerves.

He calms after the medicine takes effect, and I lean back in my seat when he falls asleep. Images start crowding my mind. After trying and spectacularly failing at blocking memories of my kidnapping, I turn to the guys and ask, "How much farther?"

After checking his watch, Andy says, "We're making great time. I'd say we'll be there in an hour and a half."

The time passes even more quickly when I join in the conversation and I jump when the pilot announces, "We'll be landing in about ten minutes."

My leg bounces, and I fidget in my seat. I'm more than ready to start my new life.

"Who's providing the four-wheelers?" Linc asks Andy.

"The Polar Bear has a contract with a company in Churchill. They tell this company that they are a group of adventurous hunters. We'll use their account," Andy answers.

"How long will it take to get to The Polar Bear?" I ask. Two hundred miles suddenly sounds like a really long distance.

"Well, it might surprise you that four-wheelers can go up to 45 miles an hour. If we find some good trails, we'll eat up the distance pretty quickly. But most likely it'll take us about four hours to meet up with the Sherpa."

It surprises me. "Wait, will I be driving my own four-wheeler?"

"Do you want to?" Andy asks.

"Not really. I've never even ridden one before. I can't imagine going through the woods on rough trails, completely on my own."

"Well, then you can either ride with Linc or me," Andy says with a kind smile.

I look at Linc and blush as I picture myself pressed close to him for four hours.

But when I try to imagine clinging to Andy like that, I shudder. No, I'll be going with Linc. For sure.

Linc seems to have the same image and seeing his mouth twitch goes right through me in a flash of heat.

I warn him with my eyes to stop it. To my relief, he does and looks away, a mischievous grin on his face.

I cough and say, "I guess I'll go with Linc."

"I understand," Andy says graciously.

Before I know it, we're landing. I try not to let fear seize me at landing in Neronian territory.

"Andy, will there be Neronians when we land?"

"Yes," he says gravely, "but they're used to seeing all kinds of Elementals come through. This town is a sort of by-way. We won't shock them. Don't worry."

Somewhat appeased, I climb stiffly out of the small airplane and bless it for carrying us here safely. I hold on to Jack's leash tightly, worried he'll want to wander after being cooped up for so long.

"Glad to be on the ground again?" Linc guesses.

"Yes," I say exuberantly. "I could kiss the ground right now."

But, instead of giving into the urge, I turn and thank the pilot profusely for delivering us safely.

He smiles at me knowingly, as if he's seen many like me before, distrusting the small plane.

I turn and look at Churchill, Manitoba. One thing I can say about this place is that it's cold, with a capital C. I blow on my hands and could kiss Linc when he hands me a pair of thick gloves.

"I didn't know it would be this chilly," he says with a grimace, looking around. "Andy gave us these gloves."

Linc is already wearing his, and I quickly follow suit.

I join Linc in examining our surroundings. The land is beautiful in its simplicity. It's not mountainous, but rather flat. I don't know what I expected, but I guess it was a plethora of mountains. And there's an immense body of water on our right. When I ask, I find out it's called the Hudson Bay. Bay doesn't do it justice. It looks big enough to be an ocean.

Andy directs Linc and me off the small runway and towards a Jeep Explorer. We've been expected, apparently, and I appreciate Andy more and more for arranging all of this.

I get Jack inside the SUV and, after throwing our bags in the back, we make our way to the four-wheeler rental place.

A small white building greets us when we arrive, and we head in for the next part of our adventure.

A small older woman with a halo of wild, curly gray hair greets us. "Oh, hey there, come inside. Why don't ya, eh?"

I smile widely at her. She's brimming with energy, this one, and I instantly like her.

"You all here for some huntin' are ya?" she asks us, looking Linc up and down and examining me even more skeptically. "You, I remember," she tells Andy with a frank grin, craning her head up to look up at him.

Yes, Andy would be hard to forget. I smile.

"I'm taking them on the hunt of their lives," he says confidently. "Isn't that, right?" he asks Linc and me.

I nod with fervor, and Linc does the same. Then I wonder how we're going to explain the lack of rifles.

I don't have to worry about that for long because when we go to retrieve our bags, I notice a long skinny one Andy brought I didn't think about before. It's a canvas bag with several pockets on the front. And I realize that's the rifle bag.

The woman coos over Jack for a good minute, then briskly walks us to a small warehouse, which houses our rides. Looking over the twenty or so ATVs stored here, I learn her name is Fran. She lovingly runs her hand over each four-wheeler she passes, like they're her pets. I stick to her side, wanting more of her unending energy to pass to me.

She takes my appreciation in stride, and when she brings me over to a four-wheeler; I shake my head at her.

"Oh, I'm not driving one," I tell her sheepishly. I'm sure a seasoned hunter is not afraid to drive one of these behemoths, so I explain, "I'd rather just be a passenger."

She looks at me with sympathy and then says with a cackle, "Well, whoever you'll be with will be in for one fun ride!

Personally, I'd go with the big 'un, but that one's pretty respectable, too," nodding her chin at Linc.

My mouth could catch flies at her comment, and it only makes her laugh harder. "Don't take the fun out of my little life out here. I get my kicks when I can get 'em, don't cha' know," she says in her Canadian accent, and I giggle with her.

She's amazing, and I absolutely love her. She's human, which is a shame, because she'd make a spectacular Elemental. Despite that, she's still wonderful, and I tell her that.

"Oh, honey, don't butter me up. Save that for that young 'un who's eyeing you like you're a steak slathered with butter."

She slaps me on my shoulder, and it kicks me out of my awed reverence. I look over at Linc, who's quietly laughing, and narrow my eyes at him.

"Watch it," I tell him, and it only makes him chuckle harder.

The guys check out their ATVs, and I notice the four large gas cans on the floor. We can't go a hundred and fifty miles on one tank. But I know any extra will go to the Polar Bear for their generators. Then I wonder which four-wheeler we're going to strap Jack on. I see that they both have a rack on the back, but with our bags, gas cans, and Jack, I'm not sure how it will all fit. Andy sees my inspection and says something quietly to Fran.

She turns to a cabinet and retrieves a strap system.

"This'll keep that beauty safe on there," she assures, nodding her chin at Jack.

I watch with fascination as Andy attaches the end to one of the ATVs. When he's finished, it looks like a mish mash of crisscrossed straps, but Andy says, "Don't worry. Once he's in this thing, he's not going anywhere."

Nodding, I then strap our duffle bags to the other four-wheeler, while the guys attach the gas cans under the racks. It's a good thing we packed light, because after adding three duffle bags and the rifle bag, it's going to be a tight fit for me behind Linc. I picture the scenario again and my face flames at the thought. I turn around and see that Linc is right behind me.

I jump and narrow my eyes at him.

"Ready?" he asks in a deep voice.

I gird up for a long ride behind him, and say, "As I'll ever be."

"It'll be great."

I look up at him warily. "What will?" I'm not sure if he's talking about the ride with me closely pressed against his back or this place we're making our way to.

"All of it," he answers with a crooked grin. "Can I have one of your promises?" he asks in a low voice.

"What do you want me to promise?"

"You know," he says and tips my chin up.

Oh. "Umm, sure," I say and tilt my head to give him better access.

He softly kisses me, and I die a little bit in his arms. He's not making this trip any easier by starting this now.

Pulling away, he looks down at me and studies my face.

Looking up at him in a daze, my eyes slitted open, I cling to him and wonder what he's thinking.

He soon tells me, "Whatever happens there, just don't change, k'?"

I open my eyes. "Why would I do that?"

"Experiences like this have a way of changing people. You're going to be having plenty of new ones, and I want you to be exactly as you are right now."

I smile, easily promising. "I promise. Or do you need another way of showing my promise than with my words?"

"I'll take both," he says and presses his lips firmly to mine, making me practically forget my name.

"Anh, anh, anh, none of that now," Fran says in a teasing voice. "Plenty of time for that when you get there, don't you know?"

I break away, embarrassed that I forgot we had an audience.

Linc looks only too proud of himself and says back to her, "Oh, I plan on it."

"Ok, enough of that," I say. My face flaming, I look over our vehicle for the next four hours. "Maybe we should be praying over these things to get us to where we need to go."

"Yes, let's switch the conversation to praying, if that makes you feel better," Fran mocks.

"Hey, you practically dared me to throw myself at him!" I cry.

"What I'd do and what you should do are two different things, young lady," Fran responds with a big grin. "You have a life to live. I've lived mine, practically. But I'm not dead, yet," she says, wagging her finger at me.

It's like we've known each other for years the way we're bantering. I laugh, and she does, too.

"Well, neither am I. So, I guess we should switch places, then?" I ask, still standing in Linc's arms.

"Hey, hey, don't I get a say in this?" Linc asks, his eyes wide.

"No!" we both shout and even Andy joins us in laughing.

Still giggling, I call Jack to me and bring him over to Andy and his four-wheeler. I let him sniff it over, and after a few minutes of encouraging words, I try to get him to jump on. He's not having any of that, however, and I step back, frowning.

"Let's just pick him up and put him on there," Linc suggests. "He's not going to get used to this anytime soon. We're going to have to desensitize him quickly, I'm afraid."

I reluctantly agree, my heart clenching at his whine when we pick him up. The guys lay a blanket on the rack they're setting Jack on. They work together to get his limbs in the straps, and I coo in his face, praising him for his bravery. He wiggles around, but settles after a few minutes, looking at me with soulful eyes.

"I'm sorry buddy," I say. "If you could run 45 miles an hour, you wouldn't need to be on here. We'll let you off when we go slower," I promise him.

Once Jack is settled behind Andy, I climb onto the other four-wheeler, getting myself as comfortable as I can, wondering how Linc will fit on the small piece of seat in front of me. I mourn my poor bottom; it's going to be sore for days after today.

Linc hands me a helmet, and I put it halfway on so I can still hear conversations and look up at him.

"Is this how you got to the..." I stop myself before I say The Polar Bear. I look at Fran, whose back is to us, but I'm sure she's listening with her curious ears. "Hunting camp, too?" I finish lamely.

"Yep," Linc says, giving me a warning look.

Sure enough, Fran whips around and asks, "You've been out here before?" She looks at Linc with shrewd eyes.

"I was a bit younger, but yes," Linc answers.

Studying him, she finally says, "I do remember you; you were with your parents?"

Linc nods and his face changes. Anytime his parents are mentioned it's like he shuts down and closes himself off.

My heart beats painfully for him. I haven't even met them, and I'm terrified of them. If Linc reacts this way, I'm not sure I'll fare much better. I wonder how they'd treat me. I wonder how they treat *him* for him to respond like this every time they're mentioned.

"Well, it's good to have you back. We don't get many repeat customers out here. But I'm good with a face, and I'm shocked I didn't pin you at first. The years have a way of turning a boy into a man, though." She looks him over, and I can't hide my smile when he cringes at her frank perusal.

"Hey!" I cry, "He's mine, you can't have him!"

Linc looks at me with his eyebrows in his hairline and that only makes me die laughing.

"He wishes that I'd be interested," Fran says with a snort, and all four of us chuckle.

I suddenly feel bad for any older gentlemen who comes through here. They're probably accosted within an inch of their lives. I wonder if she's married and still acts this way. I snort. I certainly hope not.

"Well, if you're done laughing at me, young lady, you'd all best be on your way. You have a trip to take. Make use of the light, eh?"

I nod and try to make room for Linc on the seat. He slides on, settling himself in. I wrap my arms around him and am immediately enveloped in his delicious smoky and cinnamon scent that's there because of me.

I love this closeness and wish we were traveling longer than four hours. An eternity wouldn't be long enough.

Right before Linc fires up the engine, I tap him on the shoulder, asking him to wait for a moment. When he nods, I jump off and run over to Fran, who's at the door of the garage waiting to close it up after we leave.

Not asking for permission, she'd probably be snarky at me if I did, I wrap my arms around her and squeeze tight.

"Hey, you're snuffing the light out of me, don't you know," she complains, but squeezes me back, patting my back.

"I've only just met you, and I'm going to miss you," I tell her when I pull back.

She blushes and says, "Oh, you're just joshing with me. None of that. You go on your little adventure, and I'll see you when you get back, eh?"

I look back at Andy, wondering what to tell her when she doesn't see me back for a while, but his engine is fired up and he can't hear our conversation. He told me in the plane that his friend who owns the Sherpa has buddies that will get these ATVs back to this sprightly old woman.

I keep it simple and just nod and say, "Of course, but still. You're a treat. Have a great day."

Her eyes twinkle merrily, and she says, "Oh, you betcha'."

Letting go of her, I make my way back to Linc, who's started our ATV up as well, and I climb on.

I rest my head on the back of his shoulder and pray we don't have any more unexpected adventures on this last long day of travel.

Knowing we're in Neronian land, we can only wait and see.

CHAPTER NINETEEN

I feel like we leave in a blaze of glory, or anticipation at least, and after getting adjusted to the bumps and jiggles that come with riding this thing, I settle in and enjoy holding tight to my Intended.

Jack seems to be loving his little situation. I laugh when I see his tongue lolling out of his mouth, catching mouthfuls of fresh air. He's always loved sticking his head out the window when we ride in a car, and I guess this isn't much different.

All my worries being pressed up close and personal to Linc fly out into the wind as we go. Even though we're traveling through mostly flat land, I'm concentrating more on holding on than my intimate proximity to Linc.

It's all I can do to keep a tight grip around Linc's middle and keep from falling off.

We soon leave the little town behind us and venture into the wilds of Canada. Looking around, I can't believe how different this place is from my imagination. I had pictured in my mind this place covered in trees, but Andy explained in the plane that it's all flat and rocky tundra. Trees can't really grow out here. The farther inland we get, the more trees we'll see.

I'm surprised when we pass by a gray stone fort. Since this town is right on the Hudson Bay, they must have taken advantage of a military standing at some point in the past. I wonder if it's still functional. But, when we pass by, I notice the old fashioned cannons and realize it's just for show.

I would love to tour the place, but obviously there's no time for that.

So, we zoom by it, and I busy myself imagining what life must have been like a hundred years ago living in such a remote place.

I'll get a first-hand look at such a life soon, I remind myself. Excitement that I'll be in my new home soon zings through me.

But, first, we have to get there.

We travel for two hours and finally make it to a wooded area. The trees aren't thick as thieves like Colorado forests, but they're close enough that we're skirting around them.

I'm so thankful for my gloves and helmet because if the wind touched any part of my skin, I would have experienced frostbite.

Hours pass as I marvel at the wonderland of bright green pines. We even catch glimpses of pheasants and foxes as we pass their homes.

Andy holds up his hand at a clearing, and Linc slows down our four-wheeler. We stop for a short half hour before we're off again after re-attaching Jack to his harness. We don't even make a fire; Andy says it's to make good time.

I've seen no one the entire ride, and it's a little disconcerting. I remind myself that's a good thing because anyone encountered likely would have been Neronian since we're in their territory.

But it still takes some getting used to.

So, we travel on, taking the flattest route, and as the day goes by, I'm more and more thankful I'm riding behind a warm Festan. His heat radiates to me, and I cling to his warmth gladly.

Andy said during our stop that it's about fifty degrees, which is respectably cold for me. But add the wind and riding through it, it feels colder. Colorado winters get much colder than this, but I've never been one for cold weather. He also said we're traveling two hundred miles south, which makes me feel reasonably better than if it were north, with even colder temperatures.

I also feel bad for Jack to endure this cold without a dog jacket, so when we make a quick stop for a bathroom break, I find a sweater from Linc's bag. We unstrap Jack and let him go to the bathroom and sniff around for a bit. Then we pick him up and put him back on the rack, wrapping the sweater around him under the harness.

I must have a less-than-pleased look on my face when I get back on the ATV because Linc takes mercy on me.

"The ride is boring, I know," he says. "Here, connect your phone to my earphones. Music will help." He gives me half a smile.

I should have thought about buying a pair of wired earbuds when we went shopping. Being without music in my ears when I'm going about my day is just about going to kill me.

I accept Linc's gift gratefully, syncing them to my phone. Andy promised there are generators that will be able to charge my phone. Not that I'll get any service out here, but at least I'll be able to listen to music I've already downloaded.

As we get back on the small trail we've been following for a while, I think about what I know about cell phone service.

Apparently, and fascinating enough, to make calls, we'll have to use an actual satellite to get a signal.

It's wild to think about, but they have a phone that connects to a satellite somewhere, way out in space, in order to make calls. From what I've heard, though, it's a pricey service. Understandably so.

As much as I mourn the loss of calling my parents or Elia anytime I want, I console myself with the thought that I'll be able to reach them at all. I'm calling this technology a space phone.

Our new life will be much different, that's to say the least. Preferring to spend time in our beautiful garden most days, I was never one to be on my phone all the time, but I did use it several times a day.

We stop again, and I'm sure we've made great time so far.

Andy takes off his helmet, holds it under his arm, and blows out a breath into the crisp, cold air. "We'll be going a bit slower on the next trail, so if you're sure Jack will stay with us, he can get off and run."

I cheer for Jack, and we promptly get him out of his seat. He bounds around us, sniffing the place for anything and everything.

After watching Jack for a minute, Andy says, "I'm thrilled we haven't been forced to make any stops."

I warily ask, "Why would we have been *forced* to stop?"

Andy shrugs and soon changes the topic. It leaves me feeling uneasy.

My imagination goes wild, speculating about what he could have meant.

Andy takes mercy on me when he sees my worry. He explains, "I've come across Neronian hunters before, so I'm glad it hasn't happened on this trip." He looks at me soberly.

"Vela, if we have to, we'll fight. I'm going to do everything I can to keep you safe."

Linc comes behind me and puts his hands on my shoulders. "Make that two of us," he says in a hard voice.

I try not to panic and attempt to calm myself down by taking deep breaths. Finally, I say, "I can't worry about what-ifs. I won't do it." I firmly put my worries where they belong, in the back of my mind, and nod briskly. "Are we ready to go?"

When Linc and Andy both nod, we climb back on our rides and begin moving again.

I see why Andy says this trail will be slower going. The trees are denser now, and it takes some maneuvering to avoid the beautiful pines. Jack happily follows us, and my heart lifts seeing his exuberant bounds easily keep up with us.

I try not to think about what Andy said about the Neronians and just enjoy the beauty of God's land all around us. I know I'm practically squeezing Linc to death in my stress, so instead of running through my worries, I take them to prayer.

God, I don't even know what to pray except please protect us. I just want to get somewhere safe. I'm tired of fighting, God. Please, please protect us.

And at that, I quiet my mind and relax my death grip on Linc. I think about how far we've gone and how many more hours we have to go. I look at my watch. We left around 10 a.m. and it's 1 p.m. now. We're making good time, so that means we should have about an hour to go, depending on our speed.

Excitement replaces my anxiety, and I squirm in my seat. It has grown even less comfortable as we travel, and no amount of moving relieves the pain I knew to expect.

Linc reaches for my leg, squeezing it in sympathy. He puts his hand quickly back on the handlebars, but I squeeze him back in affection. He knows I'm sore, and he's sorry for it, even though it's not his fault. He's driving as carefully as he can.

We're following along behind Andy when he suddenly stops. I peer around Linc's shoulder to see what made our leader pause.

What I see halts my breath.

Three figures block the trail. My stomach plummets. I look at Linc through my helmet. His gaze is trained on the unexpected roadblock, and I sweat. His body has gone brick hard under my hands.

I look back at the three people, but they're not close enough for me to tell if they're Elementals.

Jack catches up to us, and I jump off when he immediately starts barking.

Linc and I run over to him and grab him by the collar. I'm close enough now to feel these aren't humans. My blood starts to race, indicating they're Neronians.

Andy's helmet is off, and he asks them politely, "Is there a problem?" You'd have to be an idiot not to hear the warning in his voice.

They are idiots, I realize when one says, "You're not welcome here. Turn around."

I'm about to let Jack loose when Andy says, "We're just passing through. We don't want any problems."

"What business would two Festans and a Gyan have in our lands?" the leader asks in a hard voice.

"No business, just pleasure," Andy responds calmly.

The leader and the other two look at us skeptically. "We've seen different Elementals pass through here before. They never seem to leave."

Andy ignores his implication that other Elementals are staying somewhere in the area. "We mean you no harm. We're just passing through," he repeats.

"If you don't turn around and leave, we'll be forced to take measures to ensure you do," the leader says cryptically.

At that, Andy responds with fire. He blows it toward the feet of the three Neronians, making them stumble back in alarm.

We have seconds before they put it out easily. Linc reinforces the fire around the three and soon a circle of fire surrounds the Neronians when the branches and leaves catch ablaze.

Andy bellows, "Get back on your ATVs! Let's go!"

I can only call Jack to me as we jump back. Thankfully, he follows us as we skirt the circle of fire and leave as fast as we can. I pray we've seen the last of the Neronians in this area.

CHAPTER TWENTY

I slam my helmet back on and Linc does, too, so I can't communicate like I want. I just hold for dear life and keep my eyes on Jack, praying he can keep up with us.

We can't go full speed, because of the trail, but we're going pretty fast. I look back. Jack has no problem keeping up.

I crane my head behind and see smoke where the flames were. Water is pretty effective against fire, and they've controlled the blaze. Do they have ATVs, too? Or are they on foot? Are there more of them somewhere?

I look ahead of us and try to see if there are any more Elementals on the trail or hiding in the trees. I don't see any and breathe in relief.

Just when I think we've made it far enough to be safe, a spear of ice flies from behind, nearly hitting my face. Linc swerves left to avoid it.

He cuts to the right and the left, driving in a zig-zag pattern. He's trying to make us a harder target. I see his wisdom, but when I look behind me, I can't see anyone, so I don't know where they're firing from.

Linc looks back at me, and I can barely hear him asking me where they are. I shake my head and yell back, "I don't know. I can't see them!"

He nods grimly and continues his erratic driving, and I see Andy's doing the same. I look back frantically for Jack. He's keeping up with us, but I don't know how much longer before he exhausts himself. And would they attack him, too?

Ice shards fly around us, but Linc's doing a great job of making it hard for them to hit us.

When I hear a yelp, I whip my head around and see Jack on the ground.

I yank on Linc's arm roughly, screaming at him to stop. He does, reluctantly, and as soon as it's safe enough, I jump off, running back to Jack.

I lean over him, protecting him with my body, and I look around wildly to see where to direct my attack. We're not in a concrete jungle this time. We're in my element, and I plan on making full use of my powers.

I see a head peer around a tree and a hand aimed at me and Jack. Before he can fire any ice at me and my injured dog, I command the bushes around the Neronian to wrap him up in an impenetrable cocoon.

After I ensure that Neronian isn't going anywhere, I gasp and rear back when I see an ice spear hurtling toward me. I freeze in fear. Before I can react, a flame of fire envelopes the ice weapon, melting it completely.

I look up at Linc gratefully, but he's already turning around, looking for more attackers.

He soon finds them, and he hurls fire balls to his right.

I see a Neronian in a tree, aiming at Linc and with a growl, I take the branches and slam a second attacker to the ground.

Reluctant to leave Jack, I pull roots from the ground so fast, they come up in an explosion of dirt. I instantly wrap them around the moaning Neronian, rendering him completely useless. He swears at me, which I ignore and look around for who else is attacking us.

Too late, I notice it's just Linc and I. Andy must not have seen us stop.

Linc is locked in a struggle with a Neronian who's trying to spray water. If Linc gets wet out in this weather, he'll freeze to death. This guy knows that, and he's trying his best to get Linc in his spray. Linc is blowing a huge firestorm at the guy, dissolving the stream of water into steam.

I'm about to go help him when my head is yanked back viciously. I can't move when an arm comes around my neck, choking the air out of me.

With one arm, I struggle to get free, but my other is directed toward the ground. I find a root quickly and bring it up behind the Neronian so they can't see my attack. When I feel it's level with their head, I whack my attacker with it, and I'm instantly released.

I whip around, sucking in air and treat my root like a bat. I use it to hit the woman viciously in the head again. She drops to the ground, unconscious.

Jack is coming to his feet, and I can only stand guard in front of him, checking to see how Linc is faring against his lethal rain shower.

The man Linc is fighting screams when Linc throws a fireball at him, burning his face. He drops in a heap, screaming at his burns, holding his face in his hands.

I cringe at his cries, even though the man asked for it going up against a Festan.

Linc comes to my side when more Neronians materialize out of the trees, despite our efforts to get free of this place.

I stand back-to-back with Linc, with Jack at our side, growling menacingly as four, no, five Neronians surround us.

"We asked nicely for you to leave. Now, it looks like you won't be leaving at all," one man says with a sneer.

All the Neronians hold their hands up, and I know we're only an ice spear away from dying right now. One can be sharp enough to pierce the chest, but if we're hit with those by all five water elementals, we'd be speared to death.

I swallow thickly and hold up my hands, trying to come up with a way to incapacitate all of them at once.

As I wrack my brain, the man then says, "You might be able to take one of us down at a time, but if you try, the rest of us will be sure to kill you slowly. You might as well give up."

"Even if we do, you'll still kill us," Linc growls.

The man nods. "Probably."

Before I can blink, a blast of fire from behind them takes three down in a heap of cries and whimpers. Linc and I react, leaping at the one closest to me, punching him in the face. I reach for the closest branch and pull it around the man's hand, wrenching it behind him until I hear a crack. He goes down screaming, cradling his arm.

I turn and lurch to the side when an ice spear grazes my cheek. I bring two saplings near this Neronian and crash them into him. Jack takes advantage of his prone state when he jumps on him, biting down hard on his leg. The man screams hoarsely, and I turn away to see what else I can do.

Suddenly, I'm thrown to the ground, hit in the chest by an ice bomb. My breaths come in shallowly, and I pat my chest to be sure I'm not impaled. I got lucky because it just knocked me down. My chest hurts like fire but is fine.

I lurch to my feet, and when I look around for whoever threw the bomb, I'm hit again, this time in the head.

Falling to the ground in a dizzy heap, I groan into the earth and pray I can get up. I try to shake my head clear, but it's too painful. I only groan. Holding my head, I look up, blood pouring from a cut above my eye.

My beautiful dog takes a running leap at my assailant and takes her down easily. I look away when he viciously bites her chest. Screams soon follow, but I can't feel bad for her, because she almost killed me.

I can't do much more than look on as Linc and Andy finish off the rest of the Neronians.

They soon lay in lumps in every direction. There must have been ten or more of them. But I know there are still plenty more, and I'm unable to do much in my state.

Linc, too, is limping, and Andy looks to be favoring his arm.

"Are you guys, okay?" I ask when they make their way over to me.

Linc leans down and takes a look at my head, frowning deeply. "We have to get you to a Gyan."

I barely nod, only because even that hurts. "Are you guys, okay?" I repeat.

Andy nods and looks grimly around. "We need to leave here. We probably have another hour to go, and we'll be safe."

I see his wisdom in not naming our destination. Any Neronians conscious enough to hear him don't need to know about our secret community.

"Come on," Linc says to me, gently pulling me to my feet. He puts his arm under mine, and he helps me to our ATV that's still idling.

"Jack," I say weakly, pulling us to a stop.

"He's here, don't worry. We'll strap him to Andy's rack, and we can go."

Linc helps me move my leg over the seat and then sits in front of me. He reaches for my limp arms and pulls them around his torso, helping me cling on to him.

I watch in dazed amazement as Andy picks Jack up and gets him in his harness, but he works quickly.

Before I know it, we're off and away from this place.

It's hard to feel anything but pain, but I grip my Intended as best as I can.

Linc holds on to my arms by tucking them under his armpits. It's awkward, but it helps me stay on. I'm so weak, I can only be thankful for the help.

He navigates the path as carefully as he can, but the bumps are unavoidable, and I moan when he hits an especially big one.

I do everything I can to stay conscious, but I feel sleep calling to me. With a head wound, I'm perfectly aware that's the last thing I should do, but it's hard to avoid the lull of rest.

I grow weaker the longer we travel, but I hang on. Linc seems to feel my body weakening because he slows down even more. So much so that Andy drops back till we're side-by-side to check on me.

What he sees must make him concerned, because I hear him yell, "If she can't stay on, you'll have to put her in front of you. We're almost to the Sherpa. Then she can ride in there with us."

Linc stops the four-wheeler and repositions me to be in front, holding me in place.

It's a tight squeeze, but I soon appreciate the change. My head falls back to rest on his shoulder and soon darkness takes over my vision before I'm out completely.

CHAPTER TWENTY-ONE

My eyes slowly open to a blur of colors. I squint, trying to get my bearings. The vision clears a little and I gape in utter confusion at what looks like a painting.

Did I end up in a museum? Or did I die and go to heaven? Because the image I'm looking at is a perfect rendition of a glorious garden. Bright colors dominate the space, but its glory sooths and wakes me at the same time.

I wonder how it got on the ceiling, and when I look around, I notice the flowers and vibrant green vines trail down the walls, too. The logs that make up the walls don't detract from the scene. In fact, it adds to the beauty.

It seems I'm in a very colorful room.

Just then, I hear a whine that causes me to rouse completely.

"Jack?" My voice scrapes from my dry throat.

His beautiful, wet nose pushes into my hand that rests on the blanket covering me. His body crowds mine, and I realize he's lying right next to me.

"Oh! She's awake!" a sweet voice squeaks.

Jack leaves me to jump off the bed and rushes to a chatter of voices that fill the room.

I turn my head, which, to my utter relief, doesn't hurt. I see three little girls bouncing their way to me, and I'm hit with a maelstrom of feelings.

A rush of adrenaline, meaning a Gyan comes near. My blood races, which to my terror means a Neronian. Then when I heat up, it can only mean a Festan is close by.

The only explanation is that these three adorable faces beaming smiles at me are all different elements.

I lurch back, unable to help myself. A thought sits at the edge of my awareness that I'm in a safe place, but after everything I've gone through, I can only feel terror at knowing Festan and Neronian children are looking at me, very curiously, I might add.

"Are you okay, now?" the sweet voice asks. I identify the speaker as the Gyan girl. She has brown hair, with long, soft curls that makes her one of the cutest children I've ever seen. With a smattering of bold freckles across her nose and cheeks, they only highlight her youthful face.

She puts a soft, small hand on my head and closes her eyes.

I feel a resulting warmth, and I realize she's trying to heal me. I smile, put my hand on hers and say, "I'm fine. You don't need to do that." I marvel at her gift. She's going to be a strong healer one day. She reminds me of my brother Drew, who I suddenly miss terribly. He, too, had been gifted as a child.

"Oh good," she chirps, her big brown eyes sparkling at me. Then she turns to her friends, the Festan and Neronian. "See, I told you, she'd be as good as new. She just had ta' wake up."

Jack, refusing to be ignored, utters a long whine, to which all the girls respond to. They fawn and coo over him, to his utter delight.

After giving Jack his proper attention, the Gyan child turns back to me, pride all over her face.

"Did *you* heal me?" I ask with awe.

Jack jumps onto my queen-sized bed and resumes his place next to me. I rest my hand on his back, relishing his presence. But where's Linc? I wonder.

"Oh, no!" she says, smiling a gap-toothed smile. "That was my mom. That reminds me," she says and bounces away, leaving me with the Neronian and Festan children.

I'm in the secret community. I realize belatedly. I woke up to such a strange vision, it was hard to remember what happened and where I might be. I must have been carried to the Sherpa and ridden here in it. I squash down the disappointment that I don't remember that experience.

I ask the two remaining girls, "Are you two friends?"

The Festan is a blonde, with her hair in two long braids. She looks at the other girl, a red-haired cutie. They raise both their eyebrows, and they look at each other, confused. "Yes," the Festan girl says slowly, "Of course, we are. Why wouldn't we be?" She looks at me with such innocence, my heart nearly explodes with emotion.

Tears spring to my eyes instantly and twin looks of alarm comes over them.

"What's wrong? Are you hurt again?" the Neronian girl asks, fear dominating her face.

I shake my head, unable to express my overwhelming feelings. To think that these three girls are all friends just goes to show that we can, all of us Elementals, live together and it's *beautiful*.

Tears stream down my face, and I swipe at them furiously, because they only upset the two girls.

"I'm okay," I assure them, showing them by sitting up. "I'm just really glad to see you all. I didn't know if I'd make it," I say, deciding to be completely honest.

A woman bursts into the room, with Andy at her heels, and I try to contain my disappointment that Linc's not with them.

"Oh, honey, you're awake!" the pretty brown-haired woman cries. She rushes toward my bed, looks at my wet cheeks and asks me, "Are you alright? Are you hurting any-where?"

I wipe my wet cheeks and shake my head, "I'm fine."

"May I check you?"

"Of course," I say.

The woman looks just like the little girl who tried to heal me. Or the girl looks just like her. This must be the little girl's mother, the healer. She asks me to lie back down, and when I do, she ghosts her hands over my entire body, concentrating on my chest and head.

Those are the two places the Neronians hit me with their ice bombs, so I appreciate her diligence in making sure I'm well.

But I am, truly.

When she finishes, she looks over my burn scars on my arms with a touch of sympathy then flashes me a bright smile. "You're good as new. Welcome to The Polar Bear Lodge."

The little brown-haired Gyan peeks around her mother, I assume, and sure enough says, "See, I told ya' Momma. She's fine." She looks curiously at my arms, but keeps her questions to herself.

I smile at her because she's just so cute and sweet. "She did a very good job of healing me."

The woman smiles fondly at her daughter, saying, "Yes, Greta, she's fine now. You did well."

Greta's chest swells with pride, and she looks proudly at her two little friends, showing off her success.

We all laugh, and I say to Greta and her mother, "Thank you very much."

I then look up at Andy and say, "And thank you, Andy, for getting me and Linc here." But then I ask, "He's here, too, right?"

Andy is quick to respond. "Yes, of course. He sat with you for hours, but the leaders needed to talk to him, so he stepped out not too long ago."

I stamp down the crush of disappointment he wasn't here when I woke up because it's obvious he tried to be.

"Would you like to get up?" the woman asks.

I nod shyly at having an audience and sit up, swinging my legs over the edge of the bed.

"What's your name?" I ask the woman. "And yours, too, of course!" I say to the girls.

"Oh, I'm sorry," the pretty woman says quickly. "I was just so pleased to see you awake. I'm Hannah."

I smile widely at her when she says her name. I can't help it. "Please tell me you named Greta her name because of yours."

She gives me a confused look, and I explain. "You know, Hansel and Gretel?"

Hannah laughs loudly and then looks at me with wonder in her eyes. "I never once thought of that, but now that you say it, I can see how it sounds intentional. I did not, unfortunately, have that epiphany when I named her. It's a happy accident."

I laugh too, and then take a peek at Andy, who's looking at Hannah with stars in his eyes. Only when she's not looking at him, of course.

So, this is the infamous Hannah. I can easily see why Andy would lose his head for her. She's gorgeous, with her generous smile and sparkling eyes. I wonder if she's a widow or something because she has Greta. And I don't think Andy would be interested in a married woman.

It's none of my business, I tell myself firmly. She's wonderful and I tell her so.

"Oh, thank you, sweetheart. I take that compliment in high esteem. I've heard a lot about you. All of us have been dying to meet you!"

When I think of all the other people in this community I'm about to meet, a rush of nervousness grips me.

What if they don't like me? Or think I'm standoffish? I really don't want to make a bad impression. So, I smile and say, "I can't wait to meet everyone." I run my hands through my hair, shocked when I don't run into any tangles.

I look down at myself and see that any dirt on my arms has been wiped off, too.

"You cleaned me up?" I ask, shy to have been worked on like this and not know it.

Hannah says with a smile, "It's the least we could do. I only took your jacket and gloves off. They're over there on the chair."

"Momma?" Greta asks, "Can Alisha, Betsy, and I go to the river and pick the last of the wildflowers? I just know we'll have a bonfire tonight with new people here. We always do. And we want to make necklaces like the big kids."

What necklaces?

Alisha and Betsy hold their hands in supplication, like a prayer, as they turn pleading eyes to Hannah. Who could resist those faces?

Hannah doesn't because she says, "Of course, but don't stay long. It looks like we might get an afternoon shower."

They all happily agree and skip out of the room. I smile at them as they leave.

"Are you ready to leave this room, young lady?" Hannah asks me, and I nod eagerly. I stand up and follow her and Jack trails after me, like he always does.

I kiss his head, and he washes my face, obviously happy to see me awake. I hope the journey here didn't traumatize him too much.

Standing up, I take stock of how I feel. I'm perfect, really. I marvel at Hannah's talent for healing.

"There's lots of people your age," Hannah says as we walk toward the door. "So, you should fit right in here."

Before we leave the beautiful room, I ask, "Who painted the ceiling and walls?"

She stops and answers with a fond smile, "Oh, that's Grace. She doesn't talk much, you'll see. But she expresses herself beautifully with artwork. This room is our clinic, and she tried to make it as cheerful as possible."

"Well, she did an amazing job," I tell her truthfully. I'll make sure to tell Grace this, too, when I meet her.

"We don't want to overwhelm you, sweetheart, so there are just a few of us in the house. When you feel comfortable, I'll take you on a tour of the town to meet everyone."

I nod gratefully, and even though she said there were a few people waiting to meet me, it still takes me by surprise to find them. We come out of the room and into a small communal space where they stand.

They all turn to look at me, and I freeze. I don't know why I'm suddenly scared, but after running into Boreans, Festans, and Neronians on the way here and all that happened, meeting more of them in one room just throws me off. I freeze awkwardly, eyes darting for the exits. This is not my best first impression, I know, so I smooth my hands on my pants, taking care of my sweating palms and straighten, ready as I'll ever be to meet them.

Like Hannah said, there are five people waiting in the common space. They're seated in handmade wooden chairs with colorful cushions in the living room or standing in the warm kitchen. It's awash with cheerful light shining through a small window hung with bright white curtains.

They're all my age, by the looks of it, and I absorb the sensations coming to me. They represent every element. Before it makes me panic, I force myself to calm down. They're not here to hurt me.

In fact, one girl with dark ebony skin and springy black hair in cute-looking pigtails comes up to me, introducing herself. "Hi! I'm Tonya." Her wide smile puts me more at ease, even though she's a Borean. "Welcome to The Polar Bear, even though we have yet to see one here." Her big smile charms me, and I shake her hand, happy to meet someone my age and to hear they haven't seen any polar bears.

A blonde girl, this time a Festan, approaches and says, "I'm Jennifer. We're glad to have you." I return her shake, noticing her warm hand immediately.

A brunette Neronian, named Claudette, and a blonde Gyan, named Alice, also welcome me. A big handsome guy with chocolate brown skin, bright blue eyes and a mop of shoulder-length dreads grabs my attention next. He captures my hand and says, "Welcome to our lodge. We're happy to have another Gyan with us."

I smile shyly at him. "And you are?"

He smiles warmly and says, "I'm Anthony. You could say I'm the town jester."

The girls all laugh and I don't know what to think.

Tonya giggles and says, putting her hand on Anthony's arm, "If you're the town jester, then I'm Hillary Clinton."

He looks at her with wide eyes. "Hey, you really could be a world leader. I don't know if I'm offended or not."

"Hillary Clinton? Really, Anthony? Our political views are about as different as can be."

"Anyway," Tonya says to me with smiling eyes, "he's not the funny man of the group, he's the most serious person I've ever met. He's the deep thinker of us."

Tonya sinks to her haunches and pets Jack, asking, "And who is this adorable creature?" This surprises me because Jack usually intimidates before he charms.

I put my hand on his neck. "This is Jack. He's my sidekick. Where I go, he goes."

She nods and says to him, "It's very nice to meet you, Jack."

Jumping up, she and the rest all look at me with different degrees of curiosity. I'm sure my face is fire red at this point. I don't really like being the center of attention, so I smile and say simply, "It's nice to meet all of you. I'm really happy to be here."

"We heard you had a hard time getting here," Tonya says, reminding me of my recent horrors.

I nod grimly and say, "Yes, we hit a few problems on the way."

"A few?" Claudette asks, scoffing, her hands on her hips. "I hear even Jack needed to be healed when you guys made it here."

Since she's Neronian, it surprises me when she says, "Those brutes nearly killed you! I wish I was there. I would have given them a few ice spears of my own." She looks away, fuming, and my eyebrows climb into my hairline. I'm so shocked, my mouth is left open in an O, when someone says, "She's going to have to get used to us. *Let's leave her be.*"

I don't know who said it, but I'm grateful. I've never known such equanimity among Elementals and it's overwhelming. My heart is pumping a wild rhythm, and I'm finding myself surreptitiously taking small breaths.

Jack, always sensing my distress, nudges me, and I hold him to me, thankful for his solid presence.

"Come on everyone, let's let Hannah do her magic, and we'll see you later, Vela," Tonya says, and I give her a weak smile.

They all look at me like they understand my turmoil, as if they've seen it before. Then they file out the front door that looks suspiciously like a Hobbit door.

I notice it and other things about the house for the first time. Like the two pictures above the fireplace that are perfect silhouettes of Hannah and Greta, but look exactly like Bilbo Baggins's mantle pictures in the film.

Or the chest by the door that could hold a sword, map and Bilbo's mithril.

I look up at Hannah's kind smile, and her eyes twinkle at me merrily, like she's enjoying my dawning understanding of her fascination with the Middle World.

"You obviously love *The Hobbit*," I say lamely, unable to think of a witty way of putting it.

"I do," she answers, her hands folded primly in front of her. "Well, I should say we do. Greta and I are Hobbit-crazy. If we could, we'd wear our hairy feet shoes wherever we went, but we got tired of being laughed at. So, now we just put them on for kicks and giggles around here. Greta hasn't seen the movies yet, but we've read the books, and she loves hearing the stories."

At my wide-eyed look, she just laughs and motions me toward the kitchen. "Come, you must be starved." She turns to wink at me. "It's Elevensies."

I giggle and just then notice my hollowed-out stomach, begging it not to embarrass me and grumble too loud. Thankfully, it obeys.

"I'd really like to see Linc," I say, everything screaming at me to check that he's well before I take care of my stomach.

Hannah turns from her job of making me a sandwich, assuring me, "He's great, wonderful, actually. All the girls are raving over how he spent hours watching over you, waiting for you to wake up. Well, he and Jack there. They're both devoted to you."

At the thought of girls being in raptures over my Intended, my insides twinge, and I hope, for the first time, I won't have competition for Linc's attention. But the thought of him spending hours at my bedside banishes that worry, and I smile at the image.

"He really is something, isn't he?" I manage to say without smiling too dumbly.

"He is to you, hmmm?" Hannah asks knowingly, her eyes warm.

"Yes," I admit and decide to tell her, "He's my Intended."

Her face lights up and she gushes, "Oh, the girls are just going to die over your story! You must tell us how you met at the bonfire!"

I reach for a sandwich, because they're just sitting there all innocent-like and my empty stomach is demanding I take one. "Bonfire?" I ask around my first glorious bite.

An explosion of flavor takes over my mouth, and I moan in complete bliss. I look over the biscuit-like bread and vow to find out how to make such delicious food. I can't decide which I like more, the homemade bread or the seasoned meat. They're both that good. I take a piece of meat out of my sandwich and hand it to Jack, who literally swallows it without chewing.

"You're wasting it, eating it like that," I tell him.

"I have fed him, believe it or not," Hannah tells me, and I thank her profusely.

"Good! Now I don't have to share," I say happily. "This is the best sandwich I've ever eaten." I look at her in awe. She's not only an amazing healer, but an excellent cook as well. No wonder Andy is so smitten. With their cooking skills combined, they'd make one power couple. "It's delicious, but not like anything I've eaten." I wonder what the meat is. The closest comparison I can make is deer meat.

"Thank you," she says, blushing. "It's caribou. I try to slice it super thin when we have sandwiches."

"Wow! I've never had caribou, but I would think it would taste like deer meat, which I've had, and it's never tasted like this." It's true, the deer meat I've had is a lot gamier, while this tastes like heaven on bread. And the bread! It's soft and rich. I wonder how they get their hands on flour way out here.

"Oh, well, just a bit of this and that," she says, blushing more deeply.

I take pity on her discomfort and ask again about the bonfires. "Yes," she says, perking up, "we don't have much in the way of entertainment around here, so we have a huge bonfire at least once a week where we tell stories, dance, and listen to music under the stars, all kinds of fun things. We'd look for any excuse to have one. You and Linc are an excellent reason to celebrate, so we're having one tonight."

"Wow, really? Sounds fun," I say, trying to imagine it. But then I ask, "How many people live here?"

"Oh, you and Linc make a nice round 50 of us," she answers, and I nod, thinking.

I'm going to meet most of them today, so I shore up my courage. I only hope I'm able to remember all their names.

"Are there other Intended couples here?"

She nods. "One. Shireen and Gary were lucky enough to find each other."

I'm surprised only one other couple has the Intended bond. A sudden pang hits me, and I hope Linc is with me during the introductions we're about to have. I've come to love having him around, and I can't imagine doing it without him.

I fidget with my shirt when I think. If I ask to wait for him, what would that make me look like? I'm too dependent on my Intended? That I can't do anything hard on my own?

Stuffing down my insecurities, I ask before I can chicken out, "Is there anyway Linc and I can do the whole meet and greet together?"

Her eyes warm, she puts her hand on my arm. "Oh, honey, of course. When I first came here, I couldn't have managed without my Tom next to me. I completely understand."

Looking around, I only see signs of Hannah and Greta's shoes by the front door. No man's shoes. And I certainly couldn't see Andy pining for a married woman.

"Tom?" I ask tentatively, afraid to bring up a bad subject.

Her face falls and my heart plummets. I've upset her and wish I could take my question back immediately.

"We lost him two years ago," she says, looking down, setting down the sandwich she had just picked up. Brushing her hands off, she looks up with a determined smile. "It's not easy, but Greta and I, we manage."

"I'm sorry to bring up a painful subject." My heart means every word.

She looks at me with an understanding I can't imagine having. "We miss him. Every day, we miss him, but God gives us strength. And peace, too. I just had to ask for it."

"Ask for peace?" I'm not sure I've ever asked for that. I've asked for God to take away my problems, but to ask for peace through them? Never.

She nods serenely. "God doesn't always take away the storms of life. He wants us to ask him to walk on the waves with us. That's when we find peace."

"I remember that story," I say. "Peter walked on the water, but then he..."

"Sunk when he took his eyes off the true prize," she finishes softly. She looks away in the distance. "How often I've done that. I start off with such great faith to ask such a question like 'help me walk on water.' Then, halfway to Jesus, I get distracted by the pounding waves and wind and sink. Just like Peter."

I nod. This trip was the hardest thing I've ever done. I felt like I handled it the best as I could. But never once did I ask God to give me peace to get through it. I suffered, and I asked for comfort, but really, I relied on my own two hands and feet to get me here. I can now see it was God who did the work. We did not make it here by our own efforts.

"I understand," I tell this woman I've come to love within minutes of meeting her. "I have a feeling you can teach me a lot."

"Oh honey," she says, laughing, "We can teach each other. How about that? Now, how about we find Linc, and you can both meet these wild and wacky people I get to live life with? You're going to love them, well, most of them."

I had turned away from the kitchen, but at her last words, I turn back around. "Any warnings now would be greatly appreciated."

She puts her hand on my shoulder and turns me back around. "Now, that ruins the fun of it. Come on, let's get our jackets and go."

And with that, I move to leave this haven of comfort, not sure I'm ready. I inhale and pray quickly, *Peace, Lord, please.*

A smile lights my face. *See, Lord, I can learn.*

CHAPTER TWENTY-TWO

The minute I open the adorable Hobbit door, I feel like I've entered Bilbo and Frodo's world.

I immediately step into a plethora of bushes on both sides of a stone walkway. There's a short fence that hems it in prettily, and I half expect to see a sign on it saying, *No admittance except for party business.*

When I don't, I'm not too upset because everything else I see eclipses my wandering mind.

I command Jack to stay next to me as I walk into this charming place and push my way out through the swinging gate.

A town of old-time log buildings stands proudly before me, and I swallow at how long these buildings must have taken to build. A huge structure draws my eyes at the end of the dirt road that has Andy's fingers stamped all over it. It's not only a size he would appreciate, but it also has a similar design to his house.

This must be the town hall he mentioned building. It's the size of a two-story house and frankly, I'm shocked it's here in the middle of nowhere. I admire the bold lines and the details, too. Fleurs des lis dip and swirl in the arches at the corners of the roof and my heart swells in pride that I know the architect of such a building.

Parked next to it is a huge black monstrosity of a vehicle. It's got enormous wheels that look a little deflated, and I turn questioning eyes to Hannah.

"That's the Sherpa that brought you here," she says with twinkling eyes.

My eyes must show my surprise because I could not have imagined a vehicle to be that big and hidden in this place. It looks like a tank with its steel sides, but with huge tires. "What's wrong with its wheels?"

"Oh, that's just how they look, depending on what they're driving over. They deflate, I think, when they go over hard ground."

"Andy's friend owns that thing?"

She nods.

Thinking of the man must have summoned him, because, just then, Andy comes around a corner with two older men and one younger. When I get a good look at the younger man, I nearly stop in my tracks.

One of the most beautiful guys I've ever seen strides toward Hannah and me. Immediately, I compare him to Linc. I can't help it. Where Linc is dark, this guy is light. He has blonde highlights in his golden-brown hair that are so perfect you would think it came from a box. I can't see the color of his eyes, but they're trained on me, and I squirm under his intense look. He instantly reminds me of Thor, the god of thunder.

Not allowing him to cow me into turning away, I, instead, force my gaze to stay on his. His eyebrow raises, like he's amused. It's then that I look at Andy and his two friends. Andy's rushing toward us. I wonder what his hurry is.

Andy's face is lit up, and I can't help but smile in return, but I know who's causing that smile. He surprises me, though, when he reaches us. He pulls me in for a hug, nearly crushing me in his exuberance. He's talking, but I only hear muffled words since I'm smushed against his chest.

I hear laughter when he yips and jumps away from me.

"He bit me!" Andy cries, holding his backside.

I'm not surprised. Jack does not like people hugging me, except Linc. Jack is crowding us, staying close to me. He looks up at everyone as if to say, 'who's next?'

"Andy, man, you were suffocating the poor girl!" Thor-Lookalike says with a wide smile.

I swallow. That smile only makes this guy better looking. I look away, noting that Jack is guarding my side and eyeing the newcomer warily. Jack has been fine around Andy before, probably because he's a Festan, like Linc. I guess there are just too many new people around right now, and Jack felt the newcomers were threatening.

"You should have seen that hug from my angle," the guy says, his *brown* eyes dancing. "Your arms were flailing around, begging someone to save you. So, your dog did," he said, looking at me like it's just the two of us standing here.

I jump when Hannah says, "The big guys never know their own strength. You okay, Vela?"

I tear my eyes away from Thor and say, "Umm, yeah, I'm okay. I didn't realize my arms were moving at all." I shut up before I can embarrass myself further.

"Vela, let me introduce the leaders of our little community," Hannah says, her hand gesturing to the two older gentlemen. "This is Rick and Gary."

Rick, the bald man of the two, says good-naturedly, "Welcome to the Polar Bear." In a graver tone, he says, "We were fully apprised of your journey here. So sorry to hear you had so many unpleasant encounters."

The new guy is eyeing me, and I'm trying not to squirm under his perusal. My attention swings to the other man, Gary, when he says, "We don't get many tiffs with the Neronians. We're so far inland."

"They seem to have suspicions we're here, unfortunately," Rick states gravely. "Let's hope they don't get too curious and attempt to come find us."

We all nod. Contemplating another fight with the water elementals silences everyone.

"So, you're Vela," Thor Man says, obviously changing the subject.

I blush, nod, and then look down. I don't know why I'm blushing, and it frustrates me. I hide my face with my hair, hoping no one's noticed.

"Vela here is looking for Linc. Does anyone know where he is?" Hannah asks.

I whip my head up at the question.

Andy's face scrunches up, and he looks toward the building I think is the Town Hall then scrutinizes Gary and Rick. "I think he's still at the Hall. You guys know what's holding him up?"

When they both shake their heads, Andy says, "Maybe they're not done questioning him about the attack."

Hannah asks the question I'm thinking myself. "Why don't they ask you? You were there, too."

"They did ask me. Gary and Rick were part of the group who talked to us both about it, but some others must have had more to discuss with him. Maybe some Festan business?"

I nod. As the Grand Elder's son, he would know the current state of things in their clan.

"Oh okay," Hannah says. "Vela and I were just going to do a tour of the town. So, let us go so we can get started."

"I can give her the tour if she wants, Hannah," Thor Guy offers. I find it very odd no one's introduced us yet. I shift on my feet, uncomfortable.

"Oh. Vela, would you prefer someone your age showing you around?" Hannah asks, seemingly ignorant of my inner turmoil.

He just looks at me with an amused smirk, like this awkward moment is funny.

My eyes are wide when I look at Hannah, panic stumbling through me. She cannot leave me alone with this guy. Thankfully, she successfully deciphers my look and says, "Rayne, thank you. That's sweet. But girls like to stick together. I think I can manage."

We all turn our heads when we hear someone calling Hannah's name frantically.

A young girl, who looks to be thirteen, runs over to Hannah, asking breathlessly, "Please come. Momma's not feeling right. She thinks something's wrong."

Hannah straightens from her relaxed pose, alert now. "I'll be right there, Ruth."

She turns to me and says, "Sorry, Vela. I have to go. It looks like Rayne here will have to be your guide, after all." Looking at me with sympathy, she rushes off and leaves me alone with not Thor... Rayne, apparently.

"By the way, that's my name. Rayne," he says, holding out his large hand. He's a big guy too, easily six foot, three inches tall.

He's a Borean, I belatedly realize, but there's something else coming from him that pauses my hand on the way to shake his. Not only does my blood ice like a Borean cold wind, but it rushes through me, too, as if a Neronian were near. Is he both a Neronian and a Borean?

I've never felt two elements coming from one person before, and my face registers my shock because Rayne starts laughing.

"Wow! I'm her first!" he crows, holding his arms up. He turns around, pumping his arms like there's a crowd watching.

I look at him and step back in shock, not only because of his words, but because he's right, he is the first mixed Elemental I've ever met. Jack barks at him, unsure of this strange new person's actions. I rest my hand on his head to calm him.

Rayne's words draw a small audience, and he happily relates his experience, or rather, mine.

"I'm half Borean and half Neronian, at your service." He bows toward me with a flourish of his arms.

I laugh. I can't help it. At that graceless moment, I see Linc walking toward us.

I shriek and run toward him, not caring that I'm making a complete spectacle of myself. Jack follows, barking happily. Linc laughs, bracing himself when I throw myself into his arms. Utter relief floods me. He's really okay.

Linc grips me and swings us around, making my feet fly out from under me. I giggle as I fly through the air.

I bask knowing that we made it. We fought, struggled, and suffered an enormous amount to get here to this sanctuary. I take this moment to just let myself be, enjoying the relief that pours through me at finally reaching our destination, our refuge.

Thankfully, Linc puts me down and stops twirling. I drop my head onto his chest, trying to get the world to stop spinning. I grip his shirt, looking up at him with all the love I feel.

His eyes are shining with a happiness I haven't seen in a long time. I say, "You did it, Lincoln Stevenson. You got us here. Congratulations, oh triumphant warrior."

He pushes hair away from my face and says, "You're the warrior Vela Ashcroft. And we did it together. With God's help."

I nod. Indeed. "He did help, didn't He? We'd be dead if it weren't for His intervention."

"That's right," he says, and glancing over my shoulder, he picks me up again and does a half spin so we're facing the crowd that went from a small group to a much larger one during our little display.

Linc releases me, tucking his arm around my waist. With his free arm he gestures and announces, like the leader he is, "Hi folks, I'm Linc Stevenson and this beautiful girl here is my Intended, Vela Ashcroft. We're happy to make it to your fine community and look forward to meeting all of you."

A resounding cheer sounds from the group, and I happily gaze up at Linc, with what I'm sure is a look of pure adoration. Then Rayne catches my notice when, instead of cheering at Linc's announcement, he folds his arms across his chest and settles his eyes with distaste on Linc.

I dismiss it, because we don't need a welcome from Rayne, even though I technically got one personally. It's Linc he doesn't seem to like. Why, I have no idea. It's not as if they've even met.

When Linc starts walking toward the group to meet everyone, I can't help but wonder if he's going to like Rayne. I have a terrible suspicion they won't get along. I shove my suspicion to the back of my mind and enjoy meeting each new face with my Intended solidly by my side.

I met a couple of them at Hannah's, but Linc hasn't yet, so I introduce the two whose names I can remember. I'm thoroughly proud of myself for not forgetting their names, because I'm notorious for the opposite. Ask me tomorrow, though, and it'll be a sad story because I won't remember half of them.

Linc and I soon become separated, but when I look over at him, he's conversing easily with Rick. They seem to be having a lively conversation, and I stop for a minute to absorb the many, many sensations I've been feeling. Being in the middle of a group of this many mixed Elementals is overwhelming.

I blow out a breath and try to discern the different gift combinations. Since I'm near so many people, I'm not sure which person is causing which sensation. It's going to take some getting used to, that's for sure.

"Vela!" I hear my name being called, and I look down the street at Tonya, walking toward me. She wasn't with the welcome crowd, I'm calling them, and is just now joining us. "Hey, you," she says when she reaches me, looking fondly at the others.

"Hey back at you," I say, knowing I'm much more at ease now than when she first met me at Hannah's. I smile at her, and her eyes brighten.

"You've officially become one of us, I hear," she says with a wide smile.

"Oh, I have? Was there a test or something?"

She laughs. "Kind of. We pride ourselves when we're the first one with two elements that a new person notices. Rayne told me he was your first." A secret light enters her eyes, and I want to ask her what she's thinking, but that would be far too presumptuous since we've just met.

"He was," I confirm. "How did I not notice when I was with you earlier?" Because now I can identify that she's not only a Borean, but a Gyan.

"I don't know," she answers, her eyes glancing away in thought. "Maybe because you're a Gyan, you didn't notice my latent gift right away?"

"Latent?"

"Yeah, they haven't explained it to you yet, but I can give you the condensed version. You don't get your second gift until you turn eighteen. And it's not as strong as your primary gift, either. Just so you know."

"Wow, two gifts. That must be pretty cool."

I stuff down the twinge that I'll never know. But then maybe I will. I don't know who my true parents are. That revelation stops my breath for a second.

She doesn't register my internal stress, and says, "Oh, it is. You wouldn't believe the fun I've had learning about my new powers. I especially love fighting with my new Gyan abilities. Nature can pack a punch!"

I wince at that, not wanting to be reminded of my recent altercations.

"Sorry. I can see that you're uncomfortable. Let's change the subject."

"No, it's okay. I'm just a little sensitive about that topic right now. Give me time. I'll be alright."

"Well, if you ever want to talk about any of it, I'm your girl."

I smile gratefully at her, liking her even more with that offer. "Thanks. Wait, did you say you guys fight around here? Do the Neronians know about this place?" I try to calm down my spiked adrenaline at the thought.

"No, thank God. We have mock battles to practice fighting with our element. If they ever do find us, we'll be ready," she promises, a fierce light entering her eyes.

"I don't doubt it," I say, then look around. "You know, I don't know where I'll be staying. Do you?"

"Oh! I don't know. Let's find Hannah, she'll know."

"She got called away," I say, bummed she had to leave.

"Hmmm, well, we can always find her later and ask."

I agree and secretly hope I'll be staying with Hannah and Greta. I was instantly comfortable in her Tolkien home, and I'd be thrilled if I can bunk up with her and her cute little girl.

I feel a tap on my shoulde,r and before I turn around, I immediately sense a Neronian Borean behind me. Turning around, I'm not surprised to see Rayne smiling lazily at me.

"Ready for that tour now? You got a little distracted," he asks, his gaze flicking to Linc then back to me.

I notice Tonya stiffen at Rayne's presence, and I look over at her, but she's looking everywhere except at him.

"Well, I guess. But I'd like Linc to come, too. And Tonya, do you want to join us?"

She shakes her head with an apologetic look to her eyes. "Sorry, but I have something I have to finish. I'll see you later." She gives Rayne a meaningful look and walks away.

"Well," Rayne says after following Tonya's exit with his eyes and rubbing his hands together, "Should we get started?"

"I'd like Linc to come with us," I remind him, then wonder why he keeps forgetting that.

"Maybe I'm trying to get you all to myself," he says, his eyes trained on me.

My stomach drops at his bold words. "Well, I'd really like my boyfriend to be included, if you don't mind."

"What the lady wants, the lady gets," he says in a smooth voice.

"Thank you," I say, not sure what else to say.

"Sorry, Vela," Linc says, walking briskly up. "I didn't know that conversation was going to take so long." He looks Rayne over, and I can see him tense.

Maybe it's because Rayne doesn't have the friendliest of looks on his face. In fact, it's as if he's issuing a challenge.

"I was just trying to give this loveliest of ladies here a tour. But we were held up by you." He emphasizes his words about me by giving me a warm look and a smile. But when Ryane talks about Linc, he turns cold eyes to my Intended.

Trying to diffuse the suddenly tense mood, I turn to Linc, looping my arm with his. I never thought I'd be the hold-onto-my-boyfriend's-arm kind of girl. But I guess in this situation, I need to be.

"Uh, Linc, this is Rayne. He's half Neronian and half Borean," I rush to say, unsure how to de-escalate this uncomfortable moment.

Rayne accepts Linc's handshake, and both their eyes tighten. Their knuckles turn white with a much tighter squeeze than a normal handshake.

After a long moment, they unclasp their hands, and Linc says, "It's nice to meet you, Rayne, was it? Like the weather?"

Rayne gives a half laugh, staring Linc down, then says, "I'll let you figure that out."

With that, he turns and walks away, then looks behind, motioning for us to follow.

We do but before we go, Linc gives me a look, like, what's with this guy? I shrug and follow behind Rayne, who starts talking about whose house we are passing, but the names mean little to me.

Trying not to notice Rayne's very fit physique, I turn to Linc and whisper, "Has this place changed much since you've been here?"

Linc's eyes are hard as they're trained on Rayne, but they soften when he turns to me. "Just that big building over there. Everything else looks pretty much the same. Maybe a few new houses. I'm not sure."

As we walk, I see the crowd that gathered is dispersing and going about their duties, including Festans who light lanterns that are hooked on poles with a flare of fire from their hand. I nudge Linc to look at the display of using gifts so openly.

He nods at me, and we go on. The lanterns are charming in their dark ironwork and have been spread around to ward off the falling darkness.

We continue to follow Rayne as he talks about the merits of this small town, and I can only hope that one day I'll feel as much a part of it as Rayne obviously does.

CHAPTER TWENTY-THREE

Speed-walking down the street, Rayne announces, "Let's take advantage of the light so I can show you the basics." We rush to keep up with him, but Linc is not as enthusiastic. He huffs a sigh and reluctantly follows.

Rayne points out a building that surprises me. It's a greenhouse. "We can't grow anything in the ground out here, since it's all sand, so we use this to grow our vegetables."

I marvel at the different way of life out here as he then continues to rattle off the houses and their occupants.

"You'll meet everyone at the bonfire," Rayne says when he finally notices my clueless looks at the names of the townsfolk.

At the mention of the bonfire, I suddenly find myself desperately in need of a shower to wash off our adventures.

"Does every house have water?" I ask, dreading this question. If I can't take a shower again, I will literally cry.

"Yep. Each house here has a small generator that fuels their water pump to supply the faucets, toilets, and showers. The supply is limited, but every house has access."

I slump in relief, not realizing how stressed I was when I asked him the question in the first place.

He turns and continues the tour. "We have about twenty homes built and just last year, Andy came and convinced us we needed a Town Hall."

"How does that huge place have electricity? I doubt a small generator can power a building of that size," I ask.

"Well, we've snuck in a much bigger generator for that. All our homes are hooked up to it. It's right over there. It fills up that entire house."

He points to a small building that I thought was a house, and I wonder for the life of me how they got a generator that size to this remote place.

"How on earth did you get it here?" I ask, unable to imagine his answer.

I'm shocked when he says, "They flew it in, hanging from a helicopter on cables. It was a big job, especially keeping this place private. Andy helped with that, too."

"It sounds like he's been a big help around here," I comment.

Rayne stops and says with his eyebrow raised, "Yes, it'll be nice if he decides to move here. We could use some capable guys. Lately, we've only been getting lazy good for nothings."

He looks directly at Linc, who I feel tense under my arms, since I'm still holding onto him.

"That's too bad," Linc says in a flat tone.

Rayne smiles and says, "Yeah, it really is."

They stare each other down, and I'm about to jump to get their attention away from each other.

"Vela! Sorry I left," Hannah gushes, walking up to us briskly. "It turned out to be nothing, thank God."

I hadn't even noticed her approaching. I'd been too focused on the drama in front of me, but I've never been happier to see her.

"Hannah! I'm so glad you're back!" I know I'm being over the top, but I let go of Linc's arm, and pull Hannah to the side.

"Things aren't going so well over here," I whisper to her.

She peers around my shoulder and sees Linc and Rayne standing apart, not talking to each other, both in stiff postures.

"I can see that," she says. "That's too bad. Rayne is kind of the town favorite. Usually, what he says goes with the young people."

"Well, he basically just told Linc he's useless and wishes Andy would move here."

"Did he really?" she asks with a frown. "Hmmm. Well, he's right about Andy, anyway. He's been wonderful, especially convincing us to build the Town Hall over there. He turned it into a piece of art, really," she says, looking over at the building in question.

I watch carefully for signs she might return Andy's affection when she mentions him. Other than a fond look, which could pertain to the beautiful building or the man himself, I come up with nothing. But with the recent loss of her husband, she must not be ready for someone new in her life.

"Well, let's hope they warm up to each other," she says and pats Jack's head as he comes to say hello.

Glancing over at Linc, I see he's started talking to someone else while Rayne is off to the side. Rayne turns to look at me, and when he sees that I'm looking in his direction, he walks over to Hannah and me.

"Vela, I have to run off," he says. "There's somewhere I have to be. I hope my tour was satisfactory, and that you'll let me show you more of this place another time," he says with a charming smile.

I would never have guessed he has a darker side to him with that smile. But I saw it in full action with Linc and I warily say, "Sure, that'll be great."

When he leaves, I take the opportunity to ask Hannah a question that's been burning in me to ask. "I'm afraid I'll be assigned to live in a house I'm not comfortable with," I say as I glance at Rayne walking away. I need to avoid living in his house, if possible. "Can I live with you and Greta? If I had my choice, I'd love to bunk up with you guys."

She turns rounded eyes to me and says, "Vela, are you sure you don't want to live with someone your own age? I don't want you to make this decision without you meeting everyone."

I tell her firmly, "I'm sure. You're a Gyan like me, and I could do to improve my healing skills, if you'll teach me."

"I'd love to teach you, sweetie, but..."

"Just please think about it. Your house is amazing. Plus, I'm a huge Hobbit and Lord of the Rings fan. So, I can totally add my fandom to your house shenanigans."

"Shenanigans," she says, laughing. "I like that. Yes, we do have those."

"And if you can teach me how to cook like you do, that would be a total bonus."

"Well, alright," she says, putting her hand on my shoulder. "I'll ask if you can live with me and Greta. But Linc'll have to live somewhere else."

"Oh, I understand. Linc will, too."

"I will what?" Linc asks, walking up to our conversation.

"You'd understand needing to stay in a different house than me," I tell him.

"Would I, though?" he asks me, but I know he's teasing with the smirk on his face.

I'm glad to see he's back to his normal self without the presence of Rayne. "Linc, stop it. Hannah doesn't know you yet. Please tell her you're kidding."

Linc dutifully turns to Hannah, who's watching our interaction with an amused expression. "I am kidding. I'd love to live in the same house as Vela, but as she has yet to accept my proposal of marriage, I will have to let her live somewhere else, for now."

Hannah's eyebrows shoot to her hairline. "Really? You guys must tell that story at the bonfire, too!"

"What other stories are we telling here?" Linc asks as he rubs his chin. "Because I distinctly remember telling you I'm not a kiss and tell kind of guy."

I swat his arm, and Hannah's giggles tell me she knows he's kidding. "That's not what she's talking about, and you know it," I say to him. "She just wants to know how we met."

"Oh! Yes, that is quite the story. One you'll have to wait to hear at the bonfire, which I'm hearing is the go-to event."

Hannah giggles. "It's the only event, you mean."

I ask her, "Will there really be one tonight? Just because of us?"

"Yes, but don't worry. As I said before, we make any excuse to have one."

At that confirmation of an infamous bonfire occurring tonight, where apparently Linc and I will take center stage telling our story, I notice that the sky is getting darker.

"Wow, it gets dark early around here," I say, watching the sun descend in a glory of orange and red. It couldn't be 6:00 yet.

"I'm afraid in the winter months, the days get much shorter in these parts. All the more time to enjoy a good party at the bonfire!" Hannahs says with a big smile.

I hear my name called and turn to see Jennifer jogging over to me.

She's only slightly out of breath when she reaches us. "Hey! You must be Linc."

Linc looks slightly surprised to be addressed by someone he's never met. He rebounds quickly, however, saying, "Last time I checked. And who might you be?"

She blushes slightly. For what, I have no idea. It's a perfectly innocent question.

"I'm Jennifer Carlson, sorry. I didn't mean to throw you off." She averts her eyes, and her blush just gets redder and redder.

I've always wondered what Linc is like around girls of his own element. I'm getting a front-row seat. I can see he's just as desired by Festans as Gyans. I think of Maria and shudder. I certainly hope Jennifer is nothing like my former Gyan acquaintance.

Linc glances over at me and stuffs his hands in his pockets. He says politely, "No, not at all. It's nice to meet you."

"Well, I was just wondering. I mean, *we* were wondering if we could show you guys something."

I look behind her to be sure, but she's alone, like I thought. "We?" I ask.

I didn't think it was possible, but she blushes even harder. She stammers, "Th, there's a group of us waiting down by the lake. I, I, I was sent to come get you."

Linc looks at me, asking with his eyes if I want to go. Thinking it might be fun, I nod. "Okay," he says, then looks over at Hannah, "I mean, if that's alright with you. We appreciate your tour. Do you mind if we head off?"

"No, no, no!" Hannah gushes. "Of course not! You two go enjoy yourselves. I'll see you at the bonfire later unless you guys get hungry beforehand. If so, just come find me. I'll be happy to feed you."

I impulsively give her a hug. "Thank you, Hannah," I say in her hair.

She's surprised at first, then hugs me back, laughing. I have a feeling she does a lot of that. She enjoys life and it shows in the laugh creases around her eyes.

I lean away from her. "Not only for the tour, but for healing me and taking me in."

"You're living with Hannah?" Jennifer asks, her eyes wide with surprise.

Hannah answers for me, "She sure is. It looks like I have a new apprentice!"

Excitement wells up inside me at the thought of all she can teach me. She reminds me a lot of my mom and at that thought, I gasp and turn to Linc. "We need to get a hold of my mom! She needs to know we made it."

Linc rests his hand on my shoulder. "It's already taken care of. I called from the space phone," he says, using air quotes for the name I gave their satellite phone.

"Wait, did you tell her I was hurt again?" Anxiety pinches my stomach. My poor mom's going to get an ulcer at this rate.

His expression falls a little. "I had to, Vels. But I knew you'd be fine when I talked to her."

"Okay, can we call her again? So, I can talk to her?"

"Absolutely." His eyes hold that promise in them, and I'm going to hold him at his word.

"Can we go now?" Jennifer asks, moving from foot to foot. "We're losing light."

We are, the light is fading. So Linc and I say goodbye to Hannah and follow Jennifer away from the buildings.

Jack barks and happily comes with us.

Linc laces his fingers in mine, and I smile up at him. I appreciate my view. His face against the setting sun will be imprinted on my mind for a long time. It's one of those moments you just never forget. Purple skies interspersed with streaks of orange and red make a stunning backdrop for Linc's handsome face.

"I love you," I lean in and whisper as we start down a trail snaking through the trees.

"Oh, yeah?" he asks, smiling. "Why are you whispering it to me? Shouldn't you be, I don't know, shouting it from the rooftops?" He swings our hands up and down playfully.

"So, is that what it takes to be your girlfriend?" I shoot back. "I have to stand on a roof and tell the whole world you're mine?"

"Preferably. I have high standards for my girl."

I look at the back of Jennifer's head bobbing up and down as she walks down the trail that I can now see is leading to water in the distance. I think about the telltale signs that she was flustered around Linc and what they mean. I was in high school long enough to know those signs point to the fact she finds Linc attractive.

"I might have to," I muse.

He looks at me in surprise. "Really?" he coughs out a laugh. "You would do that?"

"Maybe. Ask me again once we meet everyone," I say cryptically.

He smirks and looks ahead at the crowd of young people our age that are milling around a lake.

When Rayne calls my name and walks toward us, I feel Linc's hand tighten on mine. I'm pretty sure it's pure reflex, because when I glance at him, he is not happy. He's got a look in his eye as Rayne walks over. The kind that screams dislike.

When I look at the guy, I can't blame Linc's hackles for rising. His little flirty comment earlier did not go unnoticed by my Intended. And Rayne's good looks are criminal. The jury's out on whether he uses them as a crutch to get him in good graces with everyone and actually has zero personality. I guess we'll find out.

Jack, too, pushes against my leg, unsure of Rayne's approach.

"Vela! Good. Now that you're here, we can get started."

I'm surprised when Rayne grabs my other hand and pulls me, and subsequently Linc, toward the lake's edge. Linc doesn't let go of my hand and, by the feel of it, he won't, unless someone takes a crowbar to it. He's squeezing the bones together and I shake it, giving him a look that he's squeezing too hard.

"Sorry," he mumbles, but he doesn't let go, just releases some of the pressure.

Rayne keeps hold of my hand for a moment longer than necessary. We've been standing next to the lake for a good twenty seconds. There's no reason to hold my hand at this point. He finally lets go and announces to about fifteen teenagers and young adults, "Okay, our new recruits need to have their grand welcome. Everyone, this is Vela Ashcroft and...what's your name again?"

Rayne looks at Linc expectantly and for a second, I'm not sure he is going to respond, before he grits out, "Linc."

"Okay, Linc with no last name, welcome!" Rayne turns to the group, and I spot my new friends, Claudette, Alice, Anthony, Jennifer, and Tonya, standing in front. They all smile at me encouragingly. "Now, as we all know, if there are any new *unmarried* additions to our little community, we acknowledge them publicly."

It's right then that I spot the girls are wearing purple flower necklaces and the guys have yellow ones. I wonder why.

Rayne continues, "Now, as Vela and Linc are not yet married, they will both be wearing the necklace that states you're single. So, come Vela and accept your necklace."

When Tonya holds out a necklace made of beautiful purple wildflowers, I can only stare at it. I'm too shocked to do anything but numbly try to step forward.

But when Linc feels my body swaying to take a step, he pulls me back against him. That's when I feel his body radiating heat, and it's like he's turning to stone.

I half expect him to erupt in flames right now. He's glaring at Rayne like he promises to incinerate him where he stands.

Rayne looks at Linc innocently. "Is there a problem?"

Is he serious? Maybe he doesn't know we have an Intended bond. But he heard Linc announce it not twenty minutes ago.

"She is not wearing *that*," Linc growls. He holds me to him.

"Are you two married?" Rayne asks with a challenge in his eyes.

Linc growls again.

"Okay, I'll take that as a no, so again, what's the problem?" Rayne asks with a smile.

Linc takes a deep breath through his nose. "She is my Intended. She is *not* available."

Rayne looks up at the sky, apparently contemplating Linc's answer. "Well, where I come from, which is here, by the way, that doesn't mean you're engaged. It just means you might be *one day*."

"She. Is. Not. Available," Linc spits out. "And neither am I."

At that, he spins and pulls me away from the furiously whispering crowd.

I hear Rayne laughing behind us and I look over my shoulder at him incredulously.

Does he have a death wish?

Insistently, Linc turns me forward and says under his breath, "I'm going to kill him."

I know Linc needs a minute to cool off before I try talking to him. He's angry again, angry like he was in the hotel room. Frankly, it worries me to see him like this, and I pray God will help him calm down. I pray for him to be able to ignore the teens' presumptions and laugh it off, secure in knowing that he is the one for me.

He continues to mumble. It's to himself, but it's loud enough I can hear. "Stupid, archaic, backwoods place. What are we in, the Renaissance?"

He's pulling me along, and I can barely keep up. It's when I trip over a root that I complain, "Linc, slow down, please."

He stops suddenly and turns me to him. "Please don't wear that necklace." His eyes are wounded, and my heart bleeds for him. If I had said yes to his proposal, this would not be an issue at all.

"Linc, what is your deal with these necklaces? It's purely innocent, and you're making this seem like I'm choosing someone else. I won't wear it, so calm down, please."

He turns away, putting his hands on his hips.

"What is it, Linc?" I ask softly, putting my hand on his arm.

He hesitates, before he says, "They know, Vela." He half turns his body so he can look at me, his face open and vulnerable. "They know we're not engaged, so that makes you fair game in their minds. Do you know what that does to me?"

"Yet," I say firmly.

"What do you mean?"

"We're not engaged yet. I want to be eighteen before I make that decision, Linc. You said you'd wait until then. Please don't go back on your word."

"Tell that to Thor over there," he grumbles.

I laugh softly, thinking it funny he's given him the same name I did. I throw my arms around his neck. "He could look like Adonis himself, and that won't help his chances."

His body softens a little in my arms. He rests his hands on my waist, and I say against his neck, "Who could compete with you, hmmm?"

He leans back, saying lowly, "They'll try. *He'll* try." His blue eyes are twin blazing sapphires as he glares in the direction of the lake.

"Who's *he*?" I ask, smiling.

"That ringleader, Adonis, was it?" He cracks a smile at me

I laugh, happy he's smiling again. "No, I never said he was Adonis. I said even Adonis couldn't tempt me away from you."

He looks away, his eyes troubled again. "I can't explain this feeling I have with him. I don't trust him, and I especially don't like the way he looks at you."

"How does he look at me?" I say, doubting his words.

He returns his gaze to me, his eyes hard. "Like you're a sirloin steak. I swear," he breathes and leans in to bury his face in my hair, breathing deeply. "If he even so much as looks in your direction like that again..."

This time, I lean back and say firmly, "You will do nothing, because you have *nothing* to worry about. Stop letting his attention bother you. Just trust in our bond."

He looks at me like he's unsure, then leans in, but stops right in front of my lips.

I stop breathing.

"I love that feeling right when I'm about to kiss you," he whispers, his breath against my lips.

Speaking is impossible with this anticipation of the kiss I need at this point.

He continues to torture me when he says, "Our bond makes everything heightened. It's not just a kiss. It's an experience. It's like," he pauses for a moment. "I will die if I can't kiss you. It's so addictive."

"Linc, you're killing me slowly right now. Please kiss me."

"Not before you promise."

"I've promised not to wear that stupid necklace!" I grab his jacket and pull him toward me to stop my suffering.

"No," he says, resisting my pull. "Promise me, these lips will always be mine." At my desperate look, he moans and finally, finally, presses his glorious lips to mine.

I lose myself in this, in his kiss, and it's not too much later when I realize. I never did make that promise.

CHAPTER TWENTY-FOUR

Hannah, Greta, Jack, and I leave the house for the bonfire with Hannah holding the food she whipped up for tonight. It smells amazing. I didn't get the chance to eat much earlier, and I'm starved.

Instead of eating, I finally had the chance to clean myself up and change clothes after Linc brought me back to the Hobbit house.

As we walk along the dimly lit paths, I ask the question that's been bugging me, "What's the story on the flower necklaces? How did that all start?"

Greta starts to answer but Hannah restrains her by putting her hand over her daughter's mouth. "Let me tell this one, oh little one. When the group first started at this location, there were about five of them. And, as word spread, others came, some by twos and threes, sometimes by the dozens. Rick came up with wearing flower necklaces because of the nature of the flower. They're here today and gone tomorrow, which is how we think about ourselves. We could be discovered at any time by the Extremists and so, while we're enjoying life, why not celebrate the state of being unmarried? That way, when you find someone who's wearing a necklace, you know they are a possibility, someone to share life with you, eventually marry, and maybe even have a child. And that would further your line if you're gone tomorrow."

"Huh," I say noncommittally. I'm not sure how I feel about this gone tomorrow mentality, so I nod my head like I'm agreeing with it.

Hannah looks at me knowingly, like she can read my thoughts. "I know it's a little old-timey, but it creates a fun atmosphere around here and the kids especially love it."

"It's not so fun for me," I grouse. "Linc about had a conniption fit when they tried to give me one."

"He'll hopefully come to understand that it's really innocent."

I shrug, because I highly doubt he'll ever be okay with me taking part. Even though it feels kind of nice to know he loves me enough to be jealous, he needs to control himself and trust me.

"Will you be wearing one tonight, Momma?" Greta asks, and my heart breaks at Hannah's crestfallen expression.

"No, honey. Not tonight, I'm not ready. I'm still married in my heart, princess."

"To Daddy?" Greta asks.

"Yes," Hannah answers softly, and I wonder what happened that she lost her husband so young.

"How long has this place been here?" I ask, trying to change the sad mood.

Hannah screws her face up in thought and says, "About twenty years? Give or take a year or two, I think about that long."

Greta cheerfully starts filling me in on everything I need to know about tonight's activities. "We start by telling stories," she says in a serious, but adorable tone. She's wearing her highly symbolic flower necklace. "And everyone takes a turn telling a story we already know or one they make up. But my favorite are the stories about The Chosen Child."

"Oh, really? You guys have stories about that?"

Greta nods and says, "No one knows anything about who it could be, so I love the stories people make up of who they think it is. It could even be me," she says proudly.

I squirm, uncomfortable with this topic. "Oh, is that so?" I say instead.

"Uh huh, I'll get my second gift when I'm big, so I could be the Chosen Child."

"My Tom was a Festan," Hannah says in a soft voice. "So, she'll get that gift later."

I marvel at that. Little Greta is exactly the kind of child Linc and I would have. "How do you know which gift will be primary when you have a multi-elemental child?"

"You don't," Hannah says as we walk the darkened path.

I can't help but notice the magic this place offers. It's like visiting America in colonial days with the dark houses and oil lamps lighting up the corners and windows. Families join us in walking to the bonfire, and I love watching the multi-elemental children scampering around.

"You wait until they show their first signs as a baby or toddler," she explains.

"That must be fun waiting to see which gift comes first," I say, eyeing a little boy Greta's age concentrating on his hand before it erupts in flame. He glances over at Greta, who rolls her eyes at his achievement. I smile when he scowls and sticks his tongue at her, running away.

Hannah smiles and ruffles Greta's hair. "It made for some interesting bets between Tom and I, that's for sure."

"Do you think you'll ever marry again, Hannah?"

She looks out into the distance and sighs. "Maybe one day. But that's not today or any time soon."

I nod. I can't possibly imagine planning to spend your life with someone, only to lose them when your time together has barely begun.

At the lull in conversation, Greta rambles about her favorite parts of the bonfire. I listen while admiring my surroundings. In the chilly evening air, torches intermingle with the lamps swinging from posts as both dot the streets. With the stars twinkling above, it makes for a beautiful view and a wondrous feeling comes over me of being alive.

A Festan walks ahead of us, his hand alight with his own torch of fire, lighting his way. I could watch Elementals using their gifts all day.

The bonfire roars on the outskirts of the town, but it's so big, I can easily see it from where we are. Jack stays by my side as we walk closer, and I dig my gloves out of my pockets to put them on. I'm pretty sure Jack would come back if I allowed him to explore around the bonfire. But, since I'm still unsure of how he will handle this new environment, I choose not to take the chance just yet.

I nod my head in greeting to others who are walking with us, scanning faces to see if Linc has made his way to the evening entertainment.

I don't see him yet, so I return my attention to what Greta is now saying, "I told her the kittens would be fine. The momma did a great job of birthing them."

I smile down at her. "How old are you, Greta?"

I'm sure she's going to say ten or older, but she surprises me and says proudly, "Eight. But my birthday is in two weeks."

"You sure are something, little lady," I praise and laugh when she stands straighter.

"Thanks," she chirps.

"She's older than her years," Hannah interjects. "But most of the kids around here are. They have to grow up fast to keep up with our way of life."

"I would think it would do the opposite," I say. "It's like this place is suspended in time."

Hannah grimaces. "You would think so, but life is not easy around here. We work hard, and the kids all help a lot. They have more responsibilities that most other kids in more populated areas have."

As we walk, I see a small dark-haired girl, who looks to be my age, step out of one of the houses, but as soon as she sees me, shrinks back and rushes inside.

I look at her closed door curiously. Everyone else here has been so welcoming that it's odd to see this reaction.

Hannah sighs. "That was Grace. She's...not very social, I'm afraid."

"Is she scared of me?"

Hannah shrugs. "I'm not sure. She's like that with every-one, really. All you see of Grace are her paintings."

It's then that I notice the side of her small house. There are a couple of torches near her home, which light up a breath-taking scene. A mural of a gorgeous old-time wooden ship brilliantly shines. I can't help but stop to admire it. It's sail-ing in aquamarine water, but it's the beautiful long-haired mermaids watching it pass by with looks of longing on their faces that strikes me. The story she's telling is so compelling. I imagine the mermaids wishing for lives they can't have or that their loves are sailing away.

"Where does she get the paint?" I ask, burning with cu-riosity about the girl.

Hannah answers, "She makes most of it. She has to have a few ingredients from town, but when she gets them, she hoards them like jewels."

"I hope to talk with her one day," I say. "Her paintings really draw you in."

"I'm sure you will. Maybe at the bonfire, she likes to hide in a crowd, but you might catch her."

We've approached the bonfire now, and I stop to take it all in. It's like they used an entire tree to fuel the huge fire that roars in the middle of a field. Crude makeshift tables are set up with food and my stomach growls.

Hannah excuses herself to add her dish to the large buffet. Greta is literally bouncing in her shoes and looking longingly in the direction of a group of kids.

I tell her, "Go ahead, you can leave me. I'll be fine."

Her face lights up in relief, and I smile as she scampers off. I stand under the blanket of stars and draw a deep breath. Every story I know about these illustrious beacons is time stamped on my mind. I remember where I learned about the constellations, who introduced me to their wild adventures, and how old I was when I first heard their timeless tales. I was in California at our first house. My dad told me all their stories, and I started learning them when I was six.

They are as a part of my childhood as my brothers or Elia. I love their impossible love stories and tragedies. Some, I had to learn when I was older, for their stories revolved around love affairs and the tragic results of such torrid relationships.

A voice that makes my heart jump wildly whispers in my ear, interrupting my thoughts, "We can make one of those constellations ours, if you want."

Jack barks in welcome of Linc's presence.

I step back and lean my head on Linc's shoulder, scanning the skies for which ones I would want to claim.

"That sounds nice," I say, sighing. Linc wraps his warm arms around my middle, and I rest my hands on his. "Which one can I have?" I ask playfully.

"Whichever you want. Take your pick."

I look up at him and say, "You know, most of them are already claimed and have stories of their own."

"Oh yeah? Tell me one then."

"You mean, you don't know them?"

"It's one part of my education that's lacking. Teach me, Vela."

I take a deep breath and scan the endless expanse to pick which one to tell him first. "Okay. You do know there are salacious stories up there?"

"Oh, this I have to hear," Linc says with a laugh.

"For instance, the constellations Ursa Major and Ursa Minor were the result of Zeus cheating on his wife, Hera, with the nymph, Callisto."

"Salacious is right. Continue."

"When she learned of her husband's affair, Hera, in a jealous rage, turned Callisto into a bear. Later, as a bear, Callisto came upon her son Arcas who, not knowing she was his mother, began to hunt her. To protect his son from killing his own mother, Zeus turned Arcas into a bear too and flung them both into the night sky. Ursa Major is the mother bear and Ursa Minor, the son."

"Point out the mother to me."

I settle more snugly into his chest, and he holds me easily. I point up. "Do you see The Big Dipper?"

He looks up and then scans left and right. "I think so. Is that it?"

He points correctly. I say, "Okay, the ladle and cup are her back." I trace the sky with my pointer finger. "See her head and legs below the cup?"

Linc laughs. "No, but I'll take your word for it."

We're quiet for a moment before he says, "You know, I can always find The Big Dipper but not the little one." I feel him tip his head up so he can study the stars.

"There's a trick to finding the Little Dipper," I say in all-knowing tone.

"Really? Care to share?"

"Well, that depends."

"On what?" Linc turns his attention from the stars to me.

"If you'll dance with me." I look up at him.

"Right now?" He looks slightly terrified.

"No, silly, when the music starts. Will you?"

He squeezes my middle and says, "You keep telling stories to me, and I'll think about it. Now, how do you find The Little Dipper?"

Now that I have his hesitant promise, I look back up at the stars. "Okay, so trace the bottom two stars in The Big Dipper across the sky to the Polaris star, or the North Star. It's the brightest star in the sky. That's how you'll find The Little Dipper. It's the first star in the ladle."

Linc's eyes follow my guide, and his eyes light up. "Is The Little Dipper upside down?"

"Yes!"

"Ha! I found it! I can't believe it. I've never been able to find it before. I just never expected it to be upside down."

"You did good, Stevenson," I say proudly.

"Tell me another story," he breathes in my ear, so close his lips graze my skin.

I shiver and a flood of heat fills my belly, especially with his hands holding me. "Okay," I say breathlessly. Looking up at the sky, I see a story he would like.

"This is a first for me," I wiggle excitedly. "I've always seen pictures of this constellation, but never in person. I guess this is the right month to see it."

Linc looks around the sky. "What? Which one? There's a million up there."

"So, there was a woman named Queen Cassiopeia who claimed she was more beautiful than even the sea nymphs. Poseidon wanted to punish her for such a statement, so he sent a sea monster named Cletus to attack her kingdom."

"Pride is a mighty downfall," Linc says, nuzzling my neck.

I giggle and lean away from his ticklish lips. "Yes, it is. So, she ties her daughter, Princess Andromeda, to a rock in the sea as an offering to the monster."

"*She's* the monster!"

I nod. "Don't worry. Perseus the Hero rescues her, and she later marries him."

"That's a good story."

"But her constellation is right there," I say, pointing up to the northern sky. "It looks like a W and is higher than The Big Dipper. In fact, they're opposite of one another. The story goes that as a punishment for her actions, she suffers the indignity of being upside down for half the year, clinging to her throne so she doesn't fall off as she circles around the North Celestial Pole. That's when she's an M."

By this time, the music has started. I hear a guitar, a violin, and a harmonica. I spin in Linc's arms and bury my face in his jacket. I inhale deeply his smoky cinnamon scent and savor it. I say when my senses are swimming, "It's your turn. Dance with me. I told you two stories; you owe me two dances."

He groans. "There's no one dancing yet. We can't be the only ones, Vela."

I look up at him in surprise. "Are you reneging on our deal?"

He pauses. Then says with a heavy sigh, "I don't really dance. I prefer to just listen to the music."

"Really? How can you ignore the beat in the music? I can't," I say, smiling up at him. "I love where it takes me. I love dancing to its story."

"It's story?" Linc's eyes twinkle.

"The words of the music," I explain. "They tell the song's story."

"And which is better the music or the lyrics?"

"They are one and the same. They play together in a beautiful tangle of words and sounds. I love them both. I couldn't choose if I tried."

"Hmmm, I never thought of that. You are an exceptionally observant girl, Vela." He looks at me, tracing my features with his eyes.

He looks distracted, so I have a thought. I sway in his arms. Just side to side, nothing that will scare him too much.

Linc's face instantly goes from dazed to alert as he reluctantly follows my movement. "What are you doing?"

I smile widely. "Dancing. It's nice, isn't it?"

"This is not dancing. And you're leading. You are not supposed to be leading." His eyes dart from me to the people around us.

"Linc, hey, hey, it's alright." I stop moving. "Dancing doesn't have to be a complicated thing. It can just be...swaying. I'll take anything at this point. I just want an excuse to be close to you."

His eyes warm, and when I move to leave his arms, he tightens his grip on me. "No. Please don't leave. I can do this. Just don't ask for too much more. I like being close to you, too."

"Lincoln Stevenson, I've never seen you scared of anything. Are you intimidated by dancing?"

He turns his head. "My mom tried to force me to learn ballroom dancing, but I hated it. I quit after the first lesson."

"This isn't ballroom dancing."

"I know. But I just never thought I could dance. So, I don't."

At this point, he's joined in my swaying again. Delighted, I lay my face on his chest. Thinking I could stay this way forever, I've suddenly become a huge fan of bonfires.

In my happiness in the moment, I'm surprised when I hear the entire crowd suddenly erupt in whistling and singing together. Picking my head up, I notice the sky and my breath catches. A flare of bright green light whisps across the starry expanse. It dances across in a constant movement, like it's rushing off to a destination only it knows about. Linc and I stop moving, both transfixed at the sight.

"Those are the Northern Lights, aren't they?" Linc asks, his voice in awe.

I can only nod as I watch them fluctuate across the sky in a blaze of greens and hot pinks. The longer I watch, the brighter and more magnificent the colors become. I can't pull my eyes away from them. It's like watching a miracle. They constantly move, never stopping, and I'm suddenly thrilled to be witnessing this. Cameras could never do this sight justice.

I dimly wonder why everyone is either whistling or singing.

Hannah walks up to me and puts her hand on my shoulder. "This is a tradition the tribes taught us a while ago," she explains.

Without taking my eyes off the lights, I ask, "The tribes?"

"Tradition?" Linc joins in, without tearing his eyes off the scene either.

She laughs. "You see, the indigenous people meet with us every once in a while. They're the only ones who know we live out here. They have a folklore that if you whistle or sing while the Northern Lights display themselves, you can bring down the lights to dance around you. They believe," she says wistfully, "that your ancestors or loved ones that have died are visiting you."

I tear my eyes away from the sky and give her a sympathetic look.

She shrugs. "I've tried every time they show up, but so far, it's never happened to me. Or anyone here, for that matter. But we still do it." She softly smiles at everyone, then watches the sky, her arms crossed over her chest.

"Though," she continues, her face turned up to the brilliant display, "They also believe if the lights come down around you and you've done bad things or are a bad person then bad spirits will start haunting you and do terrible things to you." She huffs a laugh. "It's a way to keep the children on good behavior. As often as we get the lights here, it's a good deterrent for them to misbehave. Some of the older ones, too, believe it, so I guess it's a good deterrent for all of us."

She falls silent, enjoying the show as much as Linc and I. I lay my head on his shoulder and a feeling comes over of suddenly being very glad I'm here to enjoy this. As much as I wondered if God really wanted me to come here, this almost confirms my belief that I am meant to be here. Linc and I are destined to be in this moment.

The whistles and singing fall silent and before I can enjoy the stillness of the night with the magnificent lights moving above us, a voice booms, "Okay, folks, it's time to start the night off! Now, we have two new residents who we'd really like to get to know tonight. Wouldn't it be great to hear how they got here and for all our young ladies, how they met?"

I groan, which Linc covers with a quick kiss. He reluctantly pulls his attention off the sky and says, "It's show time." And then he turns us to face the crowd now forming in front of us.

I guess I don't have much choice.

CHAPTER TWENTY-FIVE

Against the backdrop of the brilliant, moving sky, Linc stands tall and says to the man who spoke up, "We'd love to, Frank."

Linc holds my hand, and I hope desperately that I don't have to be the one to tell the story. I try to school my features into a calm expression, but I'm begging him to be the storyteller. So, when Linc turns to face the crowd and stands like he's preparing to speak, I breathe a sigh of relief. People settle on the ground around us and turn expectant faces in our direction.

Linc leans over me, whispering, "Let's tell this together."

My heart jumps in fear, but it calms when he says, "Like we're having a conversation."

"Okay, maybe I can do that. Just don't expect a fancy story or anything," I whisper back.

"Deal."

When everyone's settled, Linc starts by saying, "I met this beautiful woman next to me, purely by accident. I was in the right place at the right time."

Awe's and oooh's sound from the crowd and encouraged, Linc continues, "But, for some reason, she didn't want anything to do with me. It was like she hated me immediately." He looks down at me, smiling, and I know he's forgiven me for how I treated him, but my heart clenches anyway.

"It wasn't that I hated him," I rush to defend myself. "I just had a problem with Festans and since he is one, it was really hard for me to accept our bond."

When the crowd gasps at that, I realize Linc hasn't mentioned that part yet. So, he jumps in, "The moment we met, we realized we are each other's Intended. Which explains why I pursued her so relentlessly."

It's then that I notice Rayne walk up to the outskirts of the crowd and lean against a table. If he's heard our story so far, I don't know, but he doesn't look very interested.

Linc goes on describing his pursuit of me and my evasions, during which I make sure to interject a few explanations of my actions. It feels more like a journal entry telling our story than anything else. I laugh when everyone cheers that Linc finally convinced me to give him a chance after our duel in my backyard.

"It was the fireflies that convinced me," I say.

"Lightning bugs," Linc corrects, and I laugh softly.

Linc continues, and the mood gets sober when they hear how I was hunted by the Extremists and captured.

Rayne's face becomes grimmer at this news, and I glance away, determined to stop noticing his reactions.

I can understand the mood changing. The Extremists are the entire reason this community exists. Every one of these people is targeted by that terrible group.

When Linc's story lulls, someone calls out, "Tell us the prophecy again."

I tell it to them, and an even more somber mood falls over the group. "When the day and night are of equal length, a warrior star who will bear the child will rise. Under the Winter Solstice, the Hunter will emerge. He will capture the Goat under the Northern Sky. They will produce the one who will unify. Though their elements are diverse, through them, the Child will command them all."

I don't share that my birthday falls on the Autumn Equinox, when the day and night are of equal length. Or that it's when the Capricorn, or the Sea Goat, shows up in the sky in the Northern hemisphere, making part of the prophecy very real to me.

It's hard enough to explain all this to myself, let alone a bunch of strangers that are hanging onto my every word.

"Who do you think the Hunter is?" someone asks.

Linc's forehead furrows, and he stands, thinking. I answer, "I think the Hunter is Orion. But what he has to do with any of this is beyond me."

My gaze snags on Tonya, who I realize asked the question. She says, "The only thing we know about Orion is that he boasted he could kill any animal. So, one of the goddesses sends the Scorpion, or Scorpio, to kill him, which it does."

"Oh, right," I say. "Zeus puts them both in the sky to warn humans about the folly of pride and boasting." I mull over that for a minute. It's like someone hears my thoughts because they ask, "Aren't Scorpios an astrological sign?"

"Who are known to be passionate and fiercely assertive," Linc says, his eyes widening. He looks at me suddenly, and I wish we were alone, because he seems to be communicating something to me.

"If the Scorpion kills the Hunter, then how can the Hunter catch the Goat?" someone asks.

Linc waves his arms, calming down the sudden tense mood. "This is just mythology we're talking about. None of this is really true."

"Isn't our prophecy true, though?" Greta asks.

"Yes, we believe it is," Linc accedes.

"Then how come the other stories aren't true?" Greta asks with fear in her eyes.

I jump in, "It's not that those stories aren't true, it's just we have to look at the facts. Sometime in December, which is the Winter Solstice, our prophecy says the Hunter, which is Orion, will find a Capricorn, or the Goat, and they will be the parents of The Chosen Child. Who those people are, we don't know, just that their elements will be different."

"I could be the Chosen Child!" one of Greta's friends, Alisha cries out.

"Or me!" Betsy says indignantly.

Soon, a chorus of little kids' voices start clamoring they could be the Chosen Child. I throw my hands up, giving up on controlling this hot topic.

Tonya takes mercy on me and comes to where Linc and I stand. "Look everyone, let's give them a break. Now, let's really celebrate Vela and Linc by starting the dancing!"

I breathe a sigh of relief, and when I glance at Linc, he's doing the same thing. I laugh, saying, "That was fun!"

"If you call that fun, I don't think I can be your boyfriend. I thought we were about to have a child-sized riot." His half smile tells me otherwise, so I step into his arms, while people around us scatter and find partners for the promised dancing.

"You, sir, owe me two dances." I say to him coyly as I finger the buttons of his shirt.

"Hey, I think your math is wrong. I'm pretty sure I did one of those dances already."

"Well," I back away from him, "if you'd rather I find someone else to dance with, then that's your prerogative." I look around.

He grabs me by my middle and pulls me toward him. He says with a growl close to my turned cheek, "Are you trying to get me jealous, Ashcroft?"

"Yes," I say definitively. To my delight, instead of being reprimanded, he starts swaying us.

We're not Fred Astaire and Ginger Rogers or anything, but I'm pretty proud of dancing with one of the most good-looking guys here. Linc's got me flush against him. It's wonderful.

I'm resting my head on his shoulder when I spot Rayne talking to a small girl covered head-to-toe in black. No, I realize it's not a girl, it's Grace. She's got a hoodie covering her dark hair, and she's stepping away from Rayne.

I don't blame her. Rayne makes me want to run, too.

As I watch, she downright flees their conversation, and he's left scowling in her direction. I swear I saw a look of fear in her eyes, and I wonder.

Linc pulls me away from him and takes a peek at my face. He glances in the direction I'm looking in, and his body stiffens.

"See something interesting?" he says coolly.

"Someone," I answer offhandedly, still wondering why Rayne would frighten the poor girl so much.

I'm looking for Grace in the crowd when Linc drawls, "When you stop drooling, I can ask you something."

I turn to look into Linc's stormy eyes. What I find there is not surprising. His jealousy betrays him completely. So, I say with all sincerity, "I just noticed a peculiar interaction, is all. It just happened to involve *him.*"

"I don't like him," Linc mutters.

"I can tell. Now, what were you going to ask me?"

His dark expression lightens a little as he looks at me contemplatively. "I want to take you on a picnic. Just the two of us."

I smile widely. "That sounds nice! But don't you think we should get to know people around here first before spending time alone?"

"As far as I'm concerned, they can wait to get to know us. We worked hard to get here, and now I just want to enjoy some time with you alone, in relative safety. You game for that?"

I throw my arms around his neck. "Yes! I'd love that. When do you want to go?"

"Let's go tomorrow when the sun is at its warmest, so noon."

"It's a date." I lean in to peck his lips. "It's nice to have you back."

"Where'd I go?" Amusement touches his eyes. He knows what I'm talking about.

I humor him. "Oh, to that cave over there when you tried to club me on the head, throw me over your shoulder and claim me."

His lips quirk. "I do take what I want, don't I?"

This time I smile. "A little. Not that I don't like you fighting for me, but it's a little much sometimes. I like having you back to your normal self."

"I'll get back to myself when other guys stop looking at you like you're available," he says, but he's looking over my shoulder, so I turn to look.

Rayne holds a drink up to his mouth, hiding his expression, but he's definitely watching us, namely, me. A flush goes through me, and I bristle at his obvious disregard for my relationship with Linc. He lowers his cup and smiles as he looks pointedly at Linc.

I feel a tap on my shoulder. I look up and see Anthony standing next to us, offering me his hand.

"May I have this dance?" he asks with a sweet smile. His blue eyes sparkle with a hopeful gaze.

Linc's body goes rock hard under my hands while he glares at poor Anthony. Linc ignores the question and turns me around so my back faces the poor guy.

"Linc!" I whisper furiously. "You can't do that."

"I just did," he says, his arms now steel bands trapping me to him.

"Linc," I say again and look back to see Anthony still standing there with a confused look on his face. "You can't do this. It's an innocent dance. I'm not wearing the stupid necklace, so it's nothing more than a dance. You're being *rude*."

"Yea, but he *is* wearing the necklace, so the answer is no." He steps away from Anthony until we're a few yards from him, but Anthony's hurt expression clutches my heart.

"Look, you're going to have to trust that I won't throw myself at any available guy who asks me to dance. So, stop being a caveman, and let me dance with the guy." I say all of this as I look deep into his eyes.

I see him relent before I feel his body catching up to his decision. He lets me go, and I kiss him before I leave. I step away. I go to find Anthony in the crowd, but he's now disappeared.

I'm stepping in between dancing couples when I hear a deep voice behind me. "Lost your bloodhound?"

I turn to see Rayne, his hands in his pockets, looking very much like a magazine model I once saw. I step back at his question and say curtly, "No, I didn't. I was just looking for…"

"Anthony?" His eyebrow lifts. He points behind me, and I see that Anthony has found another dance partner. When I look back at Rayne, he shrugs. "Looks like you lost your chance."

"Oh." I search for Linc in the crowd.

"But I'd like to dance with you. If you'll have me?" he asks, a lazy smile on his perfectly situated lips. His hand is up, and I consider the ramifications if I accept this dance.

"I think no," I tell him and turn away.

Before I walk off, he says behind me, "That was quite rude."

I whip my head at him and narrow my eyes.

"You were going to accept Anthony's dance, but your bloodhound wouldn't let you."

"And?"

"Is there something so wrong with my asking you to dance?" His brown eyes look so different than Anthony's did. His are practically challenging me to say no again. He's right, in a way. I was rude in not accepting his dance. My only reason was Linc's objection. I look around again and don't see Linc, so I reluctantly accept Rayne's hand. I'm pulled into the steps of an unfamiliar dance.

I concentrate on not stepping on his toes when Rayne says, "Relax, let me lead. It'll be easier if you do."

I stiffen and turn my embarrassed frown away. "I'm not used to dancing like this." He's turned us a couple of times, and when he turns again, I stumble into him.

Rayne steadies me by putting his hands on my waist. He laughs softly. "You don't have to trust me as a person, Vela, just as a dance partner. Now, relax and let me lead."

I decide to stop trying to guess his moves and just follow him. We make a few more turns with this new mindset, and I soon find that I'm enjoying myself.

Looking up at him with a smile, I nearly stop when I see his frown. He says, "You shouldn't be afraid to dance with someone, you know."

"I'm not afraid," I say quickly, scanning the crowd for Linc's form. "I'm just trying to be respectful of my Intended."

"It looks to me like you're trying to hide this dance from him. You didn't see him around, so you agreed to dance with me."

His words strike truth, but I argue, "I'm not hiding anything. I'm just trying not to be rude, like I was to Anthony."

"I don't think it was you who was rude," he says in a low tone. He's looking to the left of me, and when I turn to see who he's looking at, I go rigid in his arms.

Linc is standing next to Gary, but he's not paying any attention to what the man is saying, his furious eyes are trained on Rayne and me.

"Maybe we better stop," I say, suddenly worried for Rayne.

"A girl can't have an innocent dance? What kind of relationship are you in anyway?" Rayne challenges.

"You've obviously never met your Intended. If you did, you'd understand Linc's feelings."

Rayne's been holding me with relaxed arms, but at my statement, he tightens his grip. He doesn't say anything for a moment, but he also doesn't stop our dance. "Maybe you're right," he says, his deep voice thrumming into me. "It's a chance in a million that I'd meet her living out here," he says with a bitter note in his voice.

At his words, I can't help but look up at him in sympathy. I'm sure my words hurt his feelings. I meant what I said, but now I'm regretting it.

"I'm sorry," I say. It's then that I notice his scent. It's completely different than Linc's. It's woodsy and musky at the same time. I hate that I keep comparing him to Linc, but I can't seem to help myself. And anything that smells like the earth calls to me. At that thought, I stop dancing.

Rayne looks at me curiously but says nothing.

I can't do anything but say, "I'm sorry. I've got to go."

I don't want to run to Linc and explain why I danced with someone he so obviously dislikes. He looks too angry to have a civil conversation with me now, anyway.

And I'm too keyed up after what Rayne said to me to stay. Am I too easily led? Don't I have a voice of my own anymore? I file those questions for later and push away from him and Linc, walking off in the opposite direction. I find Jack lying down next to the makeshift dance floor and call him to me.

Rubbing my hand on Jack's head for comfort, I scan the crowd for Hannah. I breathe a sigh of relief when I see her dancing with Andy. As happy as I am to see them spending time together, I still approach her. "I'm really sorry to interrupt, but..."

At the look on my face, she stops dancing and takes my hand, asking, "Oh, honey, is everything alright?"

She searches my eyes, and I put on a brave face and ask, "Is your house locked? Or can I just go on in? I'm ready to call it a night."

Hannah looks behind me and quickly interprets what's happening between Rayne and Linc. They stand still, glaring at each other, like two lions squaring off in a fight.

"I'm sorry," Hannah says. "Are you sure you just want to go?"

I nod firmly and look away from the standoff. "I'm sure. But I don't want to interrupt your evening. I just wanted to be sure the front door wasn't locked."

"What? The Hobbit House? Never," she says, smiling, and I appreciate her attempt at humor.

"Okay, well then, good night."

"Vela, just sleep in Greta's bed tonight since we have to keep the clinic room open. She'll sleep with me till we figure out the beds."

I nod and then flee because that's all my confused mind is capable of right now.

CHAPTER TWENTY-SIX

I lie on Greta's bed staring up at her star-covered ceiling. The painted night sky is whimsical, and I'm sure it's another of Grace's works. I'm starting to recognize her style, and I hope I can meet and get to know the elusive artist soon.

I think back on what Rayne said to me and am bothered to realize that his words have gotten under my skin.

What he doesn't know is how hard I fought against allowing Linc into my heart. I didn't even give him a chance to talk to me until he cornered me in the stairwell. And that was full well knowing he was my Intended.

I bury my head in Jack's side, breathing his unique scent in. He's always been a comfort to me, one I sorely need right now.

Who does Rayne think he is making me question a relationship I've fully embraced? My relationship is *none* of his business, anyway.

I lie back on my pillow, idly rubbing Jack's side as I fume. I think about Linc's actions at the bonfire for a moment, examining them from every angle. He was jealous and protective, but was he overbearing?

He was certainly rude to Anthony, but he came around after I talked to him. And when he saw Rayne and I dancing, he didn't charge up and pull us apart. He restrained himself.

Barely.

I'm suddenly sorry I didn't resolve things with him before I left the bonfire. In a panic, I fled the scene when I should have faced it.

God, when will I learn to trust my Intended and not allow anyone to break us apart?

'I'll talk to him tomorrow,' I resolve firmly and throw an arm over Jack while I close my eyes to attempt some sleep.

I wake up to a beautiful morning and the smell of fresh bread. There's no better smell in the world, in my opinion, and it gives me hope that my day will be better than yesterday.

Bright sunlight streams through Greta's window, and I stretch, saying a quick prayer that I can resolve things easily with Linc.

"Are you awake?" Greta asks, poking her head into the room.

"Greta!" Hannah admonishes from somewhere in the house. "Leave her be."

Her little face scrunches up in a frown and she whispers to me, "Can I come in? I've been waiting *forever* for you and Jack to wake up."

Suddenly, I'm aware that we've taken over her room, and she probably wants to change. I swing my legs over the bed and jump up, scooping up my clothes.

"I'm so sorry Greta. I'll give you your room back in just a second."

She steps through the doorway and laughs when Jack approaches and licks her face enthusiastically. "I don't need my room back. I just wanted you ta' wake up. I've always wanted an older siss'ther," she says, her gap-toothed answer making me giggle. "Are we siss'thers now that you're living here?"

Her hopeful eyes shine up at me, and I can't help but smile back at her. "Of course, we are. I've never been an older sister before. I've always been the baby."

Greta takes my acceptance as permission to come further into the room. She runs in and jumps on the bed, folding her legs under her. "Really? You have an older siss'ther?"

"No," I say with a sad smile. I miss my brothers terribly. "Two older brothers, Kane and Drew. They're awesome. They've given me lots of good examples of how to have a younger sister. What do you want to do first?"

She flashes me a huge smile, then looks at my arms I've crossed over my chest, a look of curiosity coming over her. "What happened to your arms?"

Her innocent question brings up the old scars inside of me, but I swallow them down. I've defeated those with God's help. "I was burned in a fire when I was younger."

Her eyes scrunch up in a cute way. "Why just your arms?"

My heart squeezes. "Because I reached into the fire to save my Cooper. But, I didn't...he didn't..." And suddenly I can't finish, tears crowding my eyes. I look away.

"I'm sorry," she says softly. Then in her wise, 8-year-old way changes the subject. "Well, first thing is you haf' ta' see the grotto. It's a cave that we explore a lot. And then there's the trails. I need to make sure you know the right ones and where they go. And there's a family of foxes I wanna' show you. They won't let us get too close, though. I have a great tree we can climb so you can see their den."

That gets her started on the litter of kittens she witnessed being birthed, and I wipe my eyes and look at her with wonder. Here's a little girl born off the grid, and she's just like any child would be. It's like she has no idea there's this gigantic world out there. She's perfectly happy being here.

My stomach decides to make a statement, growling noisily. Greta laughs and says, "Momma made breakfast ages ago. She left a plate for you."

When I turn to leave the room, I hear Greta bounce off the bed and suddenly I feel her little hand in mine.

She smiles up at me and I return it, so happy to find myself in this home. I'm going to be fine here.

A peace comes over me, and I thank God for putting me in such a warm and loving environment. Any lingering worry that I shouldn't have come vanishes.

I let go of her hand and walk contentedly to the front door to let Jack out. I go with him to the back of the house and as he does his business, I think about Linc. If I can succumb so easily to Greta's charms, I'm sure Linc will too. I'll find him and hopefully, he'll come on this little excursion with Greta and me today.

Jack and I walk back into the house and find Hannah in the kitchen, washing dishes. When my eyes watch the running water, Hannah laughs and says, "You didn't believe me when I said we have all the normal conveniences?"

"I'm amazed at it, is all. I was yesterday, too, when I took a shower."

"Well, it's not endless, that's for sure. We can run out if we're not careful."

"So, no long showers. Got it," I say. "By the way, how do the toilets work around here?"

Her face brightens. "Oh, yes! Gary was a plumber in the states, and here he was a magician in figuring out how to make all the homes have working toilets. The flush happens with gravity!"

At my confused look, she continues, "You see, we get the water from the lake. The pump for the toilet is at the top of a hill, and pipes connect to all the toilets in the community. When we flush, it prompts the water to run down the hill, bringing water back into the toilets."

"And the showers? How do they work?"

"For those, we use a combination of the lake water and a reservoir for each home that catches rainwater. As long as the generator is working, we have warm water for showers, but it's limited. I know it's not what you're used to." She looks down and grief flashes across her face. "I had to adjust to this kind of thing myself."

Sympathetically, I change the subject. "I hear there's breakfast?"

She nods and turns to the counter, picking up a plate with a towel over it. "Figured you'd be hungry. Did you get a chance to eat last night?"

"No, I left before I could."

Her face registers sympathy, and she hands me a wooden plate. "Oh, and here's a plate for Jack, too." She sets a plate full of meat scraps on the floor that Jack soon devours.

"Oh, Hannah, thank you. His dog food was bound to run out."

"I figured. It's fine. The good news is we have plenty of game around here that he'll love."

When I study my plate, Hannah says, "It's pretty neat, huh? We can get handy when we need to be. One of the men make the plates, cups, and bowls out of wood.

I can only nod in awe, and she says, "Well, eat up. I heard Greta making all kinds of plans for you. Sounds like you'll need the energy." She smiles softly as she looks fondly at Greta, who's sitting next to me.

"The bread smells heavenly," I say, breathing deeply. Like the sandwich I had before, it's a biscuit of some kind. I look over her kitchen and see a griddle and one burner that's hooked up to a big battery, but no stove. I guess it would be impossible to get a heavy stove out here.

"So that's how you make bread without an oven! Where do you get the flour?" I ask.

"Believe it or not, we grow as much as we can out here. If we need more, we run into town and get the staples we either need or run out of," she says and then motions for me to eat.

Not needing any more encouragement, I tuck into my food while Hannah and Greta chat. When Hannah goes over her day with her daughter, I ask, "Does everyone here have jobs to do? Or do you just stay busy keeping up with your own chores? I'm assuming you have cows or goats for milk. And I saw your hen house out back for eggs."

I need to find out what my place in this community will be as we move forward.

Hannah answers, folding her arms, leaning against the table. "Yes, to all of that. There's a family that raises the goats we managed to bring back, and they take care of the milk. We've all learned how to make cheese and butter if we want those. A cow would be a tall order to get out here, so goat milk, cheese, and butter it is. And, as far as jobs are concerned, we all have our roles here. I'm the healer, but if I need help, there are a few Gyans who can assist me. A few of the guys are usually busy building or fixing something or other. Then we have the ones who make chairs, plates, and things for around the house. We decided to buy utensils instead of trying to make them, but I guess we could if someone tried."

I realize my fork is metal, so they do bring some things in from the outside world to make their lives somewhat easier.

"Everyone has something they contribute to the town. It's been nice not to have to worry about money," she says.

"I guess there's no reason to have that here, is there? But then, how do you pay when you go to buy staples?"

"When people move here, they agree to pool their resources. There are enough of us now that we can live off what we have. We have investments, too, that grow our money. There are people who live in the states that help us manage them."

"Wow, this really is a utopian society," I say in awe at all this tenacious group has accomplished.

Hannah smiles. "It really is. It's the cost of living safely from the E.E."

"What brought you here, Hannah?" I ask, not able to keep my questions to myself.

Her face takes on a faraway look. "My Tom is a, I mean, was," she frowns at that, but continues, "a Festan, as you know. He's the one who knew about this place where we could be together without fear of the Extremists." She hangs her head. "They're so bloodthirsty. Chasing after every couple they think could become the Chosen's parents."

"What happened to your husband?" I finally ask the question I've had since I met her. I ask her as gently as possible.

She looks down, her face sad. "He was crushed by a felled tree. His injuries were so severe, he died quickly. I couldn't save him," she whispers.

My stomach clenches. "Hannah, I'm so sorry."

"We can't save everyone," she says in a resigned voice, and I know she's talking about her Gyan abilities.

At her words, I suddenly remember my mom because that's something she has said in the past. I jump up from the table. "I'm so sorry, Hannah. I don't mean to leave so suddenly, but I have to call my mom! I can't believe I forgot until now. She must think the worst."

Jack runs after me when I race to the door, my heart thumping wildly. My family doesn't know that I've woken up. Tearing the door open, I'm surprised to feel Greta's hand clasp mine.

"I'll take you to Linc. I know where he's staying," she promises, a serious light in her eyes. I squeeze her hand and allow her to tug me to the right when we get to the path.

As we run, I wonder how long it'll take me to understand the layout of this place. Hopefully, not long.

We make it a few houses down, and Greta knocks briskly on the door. It opens to Rick, his head shiny in the sun.

"Hi Vela, Greta," he says pleasantly. "Here for Linc?"

"Yes, but also for you," I say, biting my lip. Jack presses against my leg.

When he waits for me to explain, I rush to say, "It's very important that I call my mom. Can I use the space phone, I mean, the satellite phone?"

He nods grimly, an understanding look coming into his eyes. "We only get ten minutes a month with our plan, so it's really only used for emergencies. Linc already used about four minutes with his last call. You can call her, but it needs to be brief."

"What happens if I go over the ten minutes?"

His frown is deeper when he answers, "Then we pay extra for every other minute we use."

"I promise it'll be brief. I just know she needs to hear my voice, to know that I'm okay."

Before he can answer, Linc fills the doorway, dressed and ready for the day. I drink in the sight of him. It looks like he just took a shower, his wet hair dripping slightly onto his shirt collar.

A little wary, I say, breathlessly, "Hey."

"Did I hear you're going to call your mom?" His eyes show he's holding back a little, but he understands that I need to call my family. He's here for me one hundred percent.

I nod and smile gratefully at Rick.

"She's welcome to use the phone, but I told her about the time limit," Rick says.

From what I know about how the town pools together their resources to live out here, I wince at what they're paying for this extravagance. I guess it's not an extravagance as much as a necessity. I'm sure a lot of the people here want to keep in touch with their loved ones.

"I will, I promise." I say and accept Linc's outstretched hand.

"I'll show her where it is," Linc says and my heart swells that he doesn't sound angry with me.

I look at him, puzzled. But with both my hands taken, I'm led away by Linc and Greta. Greta promptly starts chirping away, telling Linc about the day she's planned for us.

He listens with his head leaned in her direction, and she talks around me, still holding tightly to my hand.

Jack follows us, but he's looking in every direction like he wants to explore. I'm going to have to let him loose eventually.

I listen to Linc and Greta in silence and can't help but be excited about talking to my mom. I quell the anxiety I feel when I think of how much she's probably been worrying, but I can do nothing about that. I feel bad that she's been kept waiting for news.

We make it to another small house. This time, Linc knocks on the door.

I wonder when I'm going to get the chance to talk to Linc about my dance with Rayne.

A door opens and interrupts my thoughts. A red-haired woman with a stern expression looks at us questioningly. Of course, I cannot remember her name.

"Shireen," Linc says, and I'm proud of him for his good memory. "We're here to use the satellite phone. Rick said it was okay."

When he says her name, I recall that she's one half of the other couple that are bonded.

She frowns but opens the door, allowing us to enter. "Gary is in the back. You can ask him."

"Is it okay if my dog comes in, too?" I ask.

She frowns down at Jack and shakes her head. "No. I'm cleaning the floors and don't want him to track in dirt."

I reluctantly command him to lie down on the front doorstep, hoping nothing will entice him to disobey me and wander away.

I walk into the house, glancing at our host. Her behavior is abrupt, but not necessarily rude. I try to tell myself that as she ignores us and goes about her day, stepping into the kitchen.

I glance at her, and she frowns at me again. I wonder what I've done to upset her.

She answers my unspoken question when she barks out, "Gary, the newcomers here want to use the phone, but as we all need to use it, too, I don't see why they get the right to it, being as they just got here."

After my surprise at her obvious antagonism, my attention is drawn to Gary, who walks toward us after rising from a chair at the end of the house.

"Now Shireen, don't get your hackles up. That's why they need the phone, because they just got here, and their loved ones need to know they made it. We all got that opportunity when we arrived."

She nods, reluctantly by the looks of it, and resumes sweeping the floor in hard, hurried strokes.

I stamp down the urge to defend myself, as Gary already did that. I can tell that the use of the phone is a touchy subject for some.

"Sorry," Gary says after glancing at Shireen. "It's just a very expensive service, so we need to keep the plan as cheap as possible. We pay monthly and try to keep the minutes down, if we can."

"That's understandable," I say and Linc nods in agreement.

I wonder if it's only the bond that keeps Gary tethered to Shireen. She seems to be hard to love.

I tighten my hold on Greta's hand. Linc had let go of mine when we walked in. But for some reason Greta held onto me, and I look down at her.

She's looking at Shireen with trepidation, like she's wary of the woman. I guess I would be too at her age.

Greta pulls me down to whisper in my ear, "She's my teacher."

I stand back up, a little surprised because Shireen hasn't even acknowledged Greta.

Gary returns with the phone, and I'm surprised that it appears to be a standard, current phone model.

"Oh, you don't need a fancy phone to hook up to a satellite?" I ask.

Gary shakes his head. He holds out another device. "No, we can connect to this with our phone, making calling pretty easy."

I'm grateful when I realize I know how to use this phone. I take it and look around for a place to talk to my mom privately.

Gary reads me easily. "Go into the bedroom. You can have privacy there."

Thanking him, I glance down at the phone, wondering if I need to do something special to make it connect to the other device.

"Just keep them together. It'll do the job," Gary explains.

Taking both with me, I close myself in the bedroom and quickly dial my mom's number.

She answers on the first ring with a breathless voice. "Hello?"

"Hi Mom," I say and force tears away. There's no time for those.

"Vela? Vela baby, you're, okay? Oh, thank God," she says, her voice cracking.

"Mom, I have to be very, very quick, I just wanted you to know I'm okay, and I love you so much. Tell everyone I miss them, and I'll call when they allow me to use the phone again."

"Allow you? Why do you have to be allowed to use the phone?"

She sounds indignant, and I rush to explain, "They only have ten minutes a month for everyone, so I understand."

She's silent for a moment, but then says hurriedly, "Well, if I don't have much time left, I should tell you that Kane knocked out some kid named Evan the other day."

"What?" I screech. "He did?"

"Apparently, Elia was supposed to go out with the guy and Kane heard some not so good things about him. So, he went down to the school to talk to the poor kid. It got ugly."

I groan. Holding my head, I say, "That's because he tried talking to a moron. Is Kane in trouble?"

As much as I'm afraid that Kane got arrested for hitting a minor, I'm secretly thrilled he made this move. It shows a lot about his true feelings for my best friend. She must be ecstatic. Unless Kane got arrested.

"No," Mom answers, and I breathe in relief. "It was after school, so no one saw it, and apparently Evan isn't pressing charges."

"Kane got lucky then."

Gary pokes his head into the room, motioning toward his watch.

"Mom, I'm out of time. Please keep Kane from doing anything stupid like that again, okay?"

"And be sure you do the same," she says. "I love you, sweetheart. Please take care of yourself. Give my love to Linc."

"I will. I love you too."

We hang up, and I wonder how many minutes I was on the phone, hoping it wasn't too many.

I come out of the room, and when I see Linc, I go to him, wrapping my arms around his middle, my heart cracking, knowing I probably won't talk to my mom again for months now.

"You, okay?" Linc asks, holding me.

"It's not easy to say goodbye," I say on his shoulder.

He squeezes me in response, and I feel Greta wrapping her little arms around me, too. Tears slip from my eyes at this new life I've found myself in, but not everything I'm feeling is sorrow. I'm full of emotions that I can't name. Part anticipation, fear, the unknowns of my future, and then there's the sorrow for leaving my family behind.

Not wanting to intrude on Gary's time, I untangle from the embrace and ruffle Greta's hair. "Thank you for the hug."

"That's what siss'thers do," she says with her bright eyes blinking up at me. "Right?"

"Yes, absolutely."

I thank Gary and then Shireen, who grudgingly gives me a nod goodbye, telling Greta, "I'll see you tomorrow, young lady."

"Yes, ma'am," Greta answers politely. She grabs my hand again, and we step outside, this time allowing Greta to lead us away. "Are you coming with us today?" she asks Linc, craning her neck to look him in the eyes.

"Yes, we have a date, remember?" I say, glad to see Jack stayed put. He follows us down the street.

Linc stops and shakes his head, looking at me. "I can't today. Rick asked me to help him with something. I don't want to tell him no when he's allowing me to live with him."

I deflate a little but nod. "I understand."

He looks at Greta and asks her, "Do you mind if I talk to Vela for a minute? I'll bring her right back."

My stomach drops. But I know it's better we get our discussion about last night out of the way. I let go of Greta, and she waits on the street while Linc takes me over to stand under a tree.

He faces me and then looks away before he finds my eyes again. "Look, I'm not going to say I'm necessarily happy about last night, but the worst part was not being able to talk with you about it. You made that choice for both of us when you left."

"You were just so mad."

"Of course, I was mad, Vela. I know a predator when I see one. Rayne has no compunction at all for targeting the one person who means more to me than anyone in the whole world." He searches my eyes. "Why did you run away?"

My shoulders slump. I honestly don't have a good reason, other than fear of an argument. When I think of it that way, it seems incredibly immature.

"I don't know. I was scared, I guess," I mumble, looking down.

"Of him?" he growls, his hands turning into fists.

"No!" I assure him, bringing my head up. "Of you, what you'd say and do."

"Vela," Linc breathes and looks away. "You don't ever have to be afraid to talk to me. Trust me when I say I trust *you*. It's *him* I don't trust. Not for a second."

"You know there aren't exactly a lot of places I can hide from the guy, Linc. This place is too small. I'm going to run into him, often."

"I know that," he says, stuffing his hands into his pockets. "I'm just telling you; I know what he's doing. He's going to try to get you to second guess our relationship. Don't allow that to happen, okay?"

"I won't. I wish I could spend the day with you." I reach for him, holding onto his jacket, trying not to be too disappointed.

"I do too, but I have to do this thing with Rick. I gave him my word."

"That's one of the things I love about you," I tell him before I wrap my arms around his waist.

"Oh, yeah? What's that?"

"That your word actually means something."

He squeezes me and then lets me go. "I think your little shadow is getting antsy."

I look in Greta's direction and see her practically bouncing on her toes. She's looking in our direction, waiting as patiently as a soon-to-be nine-year-old can.

I laugh. "Yes, she is. But she can wait one more second."

"For what?" he asks, but his eyes say that he knows the answer.

"For me to kiss my Intended," I say before I pull his head down to meet me for a kiss.

I feel so many emotions at this moment. His trust does something to me, and as he kisses me, I return it, trying to show him he means everything to me. That he doesn't need to worry about losing me. Ever.

We pull away, and I leave him under the tree. I feel him watching me. As I walk away, I hear a chirp close by. I look up and my mouth drops open as a gorgeous gray and white bird flies right up to me and, to my complete surprise, lands on my shoulder. It blinks at me and chirps prettily.

"Hello," I say, being careful not to move. I don't know what else I can say to it.

"Ooooo, what a pretty bird!" Greta exclaims. "It's a Whiskey Jack. How did you get it on your shoulder?"

I have no idea, so I shake my head. But she laughs and says, "They're not afraid of humans at all, but I've not heard of one actually sitting on someone's shoulder before!"

Suddenly I know exactly why I have such a wild, beautiful bird on my shoulder. I look back and see Linc smiling widely at me, with his hand outstretched in my direction.

I smile brilliantly at him, and a resolve fills me to put Rayne in his place next time I see him. Because he can't have me, if that's what he wants.

I'm already taken.

CHAPTER TWENTY-SEVEN

I laugh as Greta pulls me along, talking a mile a minute. Jack happily bounds along in front of us, sniffing to his heart's content. I'm sure he's thrilled to finally have the freedom to run.

After a few minutes, I'm sure that by the time we get to the grotto, I will have learned of every fox kit, martin kit, lynx kit, squirrel kit, and any other kit that has been born under her watchful eye.

She seems fascinated with the concept of birth. She's not sure how babies are made just yet, but her mom says that this knowledge will come in good time.

"Will you tell me, Vela?" she asks, her eyes blinking up at me, innocently.

"Oh, no, you're not dragging me into this," I laugh and say with all certainty. "That's for your mom and only your mom to tell you."

"Oh, all right," she says, grumpily, her shoulders slumping. "But I don't know what the big deal is."

I snort because, of course, she thinks that.

Greta says we're halfway to the grotto, when after passing another trail, she stops and holds up her hand so she can listen. "I think someone's coming," she explains.

As we wait to see who's out here, I whistle for Jack to come back. He's gotten to where I can't see him around the bend in the trail.

When I see who's coming, however, I immediately turn to go back to Hannah's.

"Vela, wait," Greta calls out. "It's just Rayne. Let's see if he wants to come with us."

It's not only Rayne who comes off the trail, but my new friends, too. Anthony, Jennifer, Tonya, Alice, and Claudette are all smiles when they see me. Us girls give each other half hugs in greeting.

Jack returns and sniffs everyone thoroughly, eliciting oohs from the girls, but his wariness of Anthony and Rayne is obvious.

"You're not Festans. They're his favorites," I say and shrug.

Both Anthony and Rayne edge away from him slowly.

"What are you guys doing out here?" I ask.

"Don't the rifles give us away?" Anthony says with a big grin.

I blush. "Oh. I didn't see them strapped to your backs," I say, embarrassed not to have noticed. All I've been aware of since I've seen them is Rayne's quiet, intense stare.

"Where are you guys headed to?" Tonya asks in a cheery voice.

"The grotto," Greta says proudly. "Then I'm taking her everywhere else, too."

"Well, if one of us takes our hunt back home, the rest of us can join you," Tonya says, eyeing her hunting companions.

A chorus of "I'm not it," fills the air and Anthony slumps when he realizes he's the last one to say it.

"I guess that's me then," he says, dejected. He gathers squirrels and another animal that I don't have the name for but looks like a quail, from his friends.

When I look at it curiously, Anthony says helpfully, "Grouse, we call it a road chicken cause they're so easy to catch. You can literally pick it up off the ground without chasing it."

"Wow. So, no deer today?"

He gives me a funny look, only to say, "There aren't any deer that live here. Only caribou and moose. And we didn't see any of those today."

"Really?"

"And we don't have rabbits, hogs or possums here either, like in southern Manitoba."

I feel my eyebrows raise in surprise, and I nod. I look around and say, "Well, you sure you guys want to take the time showing me around when you've been hunting all morning?"

"Personally, I want to see your face when you see the grotto for the first time," Tonya says, linking her arm to mine.

I'm uncomfortably aware of the still silent Rayne following us as Greta leads the way. I peek behind to look at him, but he's studying the ground. At least he's stopped watching me.

Jack is glued to my side, and I wonder if it's Rayne's presence that's making him uneasy. The hair on his back is standing up.

"Hey, this is great. It's much better than soap making with my mom," Claudette pipes up.

"You guys make your own soap?" I ask.

"How else can we get clean?" Greta asks with wide eyes, and I wish I wasn't so ignorant of off-the-grid living.

"Believe it or not, the bonfire ashes are an ingredient in our soaps," Tonya says proudly.

I look back at Rayne and catch him glancing at me, then quickly looking away. Is that why he smelled so much like the forest when I danced with him? Because of his soap?

"Really? That can't be the only ingredient." I say with a good amount of awe at their way of life.

"Oh no, we use animal fat, too," Alice says.

When I crinkle my nose, they all laugh.

"My favorite is the kind with pine needles and pinecones," Greta says.

I realize that's what Rayne smelled like, evergreens and smoke.

"We're here," Greta calls out in a singsong voice.

When we walk up to a rock wall, I look around and wonder where the grotto could be hiding.

"Where is it?" I ask, giving up.

"The entrance is camouflaged," Claudette says and walks right up to the wall and...disappears.

My eyes widen, and Greta's peal of laughter has me shaking my head in wonder. "How on Earth?" I walk to where she vanished and find a cleft in the face of the wall. A person would have to turn sideways to fit, but it's an entrance to something.

"Cool." Excitement climbs in me, and I edge myself in not knowing what to expect. Jack barks at me, and I come back out and tell him to go in ahead of me. He's not thrilled, but at my direct command he enters, his nose to the ground as he sniffs for danger.

"Hey, wait for me," Greta complains, and I wait for her to catch up.

I peer inside and see nothing but black. "Greta, how am I supposed to see anything?"

"You don't." She giggles. "Just take a few steps and it gets lighter. I promise."

Deciding to trust her, I blindly walk a few steps. After a moment, I notice a slight light in the distance. I keep my hands on the walls on either side of me. I can hear Jack's sniffing, so if he's not scared, I won't be. I make my way toward the light and soon regain my sight. The tunnel opens up into a cavernous room. When I hear water, I look around and see a pool off to the side.

The place is stunning. It feels like we've stepped back in time. The textured stone walls drop off to a pool of water whose music lulls me from the water dripping from the ceiling down the walls.

Jack investigates every nook and cranny of the place, and it eases my worry that there could be an animal lurking about.

Awe fills my voice when I say, "It's beautiful. It's absolutely beautiful." My voice echoes around, and I laugh, then laugh harder when it bounces off the walls.

Soon, everyone's filed in, and I sit down just admiring the light. Sunlight is filtering in from somewhere and it quietly highlights the beauty of the place. It's the size of my living room back home and its coziness oozes into me, releasing tense muscles.

"During the summer, you'll want to swim in that water," Rayne says to the right of me.

I flinch, startled. I hadn't even noticed that he had joined me. Everyone sits around and someone passes out granola and dried meat. Chatting fills the air, and I watch Greta go over to the water and splash it at Alice, who's sitting the closest. She shrieks and splashes her back, but they soon stop. The threat of being wet is not appealing in this chilly weather.

"What do you think?" Rayne asks. He's sitting with his leg propped up, utterly at ease in his kingdom.

"I like it," I say and look away. I can't be comfortable around him knowing how Linc feels. But I remind myself that Rayne's only ever been nice to me.

He studies me from the side, but I refuse to look at him. He continues until finally, I ask, "What?" when I'm tired of being examined.

"Just wondering what you're really thinking."

I whip my head to look at him and ask before I can stop my mouth, "Why would you ask me that?"

He draws his finger in the dirt on the cave floor idly and says, "Just trying to test your reaction."

"You're testing all right," I say, then smack my lips shut.

"You know, for a girl who's just gotten here, you're awfully comfortable telling me how you really feel."

"Is that what you want?" I ask, my temper slipping like water out of a glass. "To know my true feelings?"

"Always," he says, an amused look coming into his eyes at my show of anger.

"I don't like guys who dig where they're not wanted. You don't know me. I don't know you. Let's keep it that way, okay?" At that, I get up, brushing off my pants.

"I'm ready to go back," I announce to the group.

"Awe, so soon?" Greta asks, her mournful eyes, making me feel bad.

"Yes, I'm sorry."

After some grumbling, everyone else picks themselves off the floor of the cave, and we make our way outside.

"But I haven't shown you the foxes' den," Greta whispers to me.

I bend down and whisper in her ear, "Let's do that with just the two of us, okay?"

She agrees and takes my hand, leading the way back to the community.

Completely ignoring Rayne, I call Jack to me and walk with Greta, hoping that my words were enough to get Rayne to back off.

Because as much as I hate to think it, he's interested. But he can't be in me. He's going to have to pick another girl.

CHAPTER TWENTY-EIGHT

I listen to everyone talking around me as we walk back to the community and am amazed at their knowledge of living off the land. Greta tells us she's going to go find her friends, so she runs ahead of us on the trail.

I'm taking in as much as I can when Claudette suddenly squeals, "Ooooo! I have an idea! We can go through Vela's clothes!"

When I look at her strangely, Tonya laughs and says, "We have so few chances to see different clothes here that we share everything. But's it a take and give situation. If Claudette takes a shirt, she gives you one of hers. That way, you don't end up with fewer clothes. Does that sound okay? Do you mind us pawing through your stuff?"

I think about it for a second. I really like the new clothes I bought, but when I look at their hopeful faces, I can't possibly tell them no. I hear a snort behind me, and I turn to glare at Rayne, who looks at me with a knowing grin, somehow aware that I secretly hate this.

I mean, who would want to trade brand new clothes I handpicked for more worn-out ones? But I'll do it. It's the least I can do for this community that's taking me in.

Turning back around, I answer, "Just as long as I get to keep some of what I brought," which sends a bevy of excitement through the three girls.

"Wait, are all the girls in our community going to do this?" If that happens, I won't have anything left. I didn't bring that much.

"No," Tonya answers. "Don't worry, just us. It's first come, first serve around here. And we were the first to ask. But if you ever see someone wearing something you love, just ask them to consider a trade."

I look around at the majesty of the pines, maples, and oaks around me and think that this is one drawback of living in such a beautiful place. Non-existent shopping access. But Jack is loving it. He's finally relaxed in Rayne's presence and he's exploring off to the side.

"Have you guys always lived out here?" I ask.

Tonya answers first. "I came here when I was two, so this place is all I remember."

Claudette, Alice, and Jennifer all say they were born here, and my mouth hangs open in shock.

"So, you guys have never had a cell phone?" I ask.

They all shake their heads.

Even though I know they live in the middle of nowhere, it's still a surprise to me. Our generation is known for being addicted to the things.

"We've seen the satellite phone before. Does that count?" Jennifer asks. She opens up her palm and holds a ball of fire, playing with it, running it up and down her fingers.

I inhale sharply.

"What?" she asks.

"You can't go around in my hometown doing that," I explain, thinking I'm going to have to get used to this way of life.

She laughs. "Yea, I can imagine. Humans would probably pass out."

"You do not know how hard it is keeping our powers from their eyes."

We all sober.

"I can imagine. I've never known any other way of life, so I really don't know. But, welcome to freedom, Vela," she says sweetly.

"Thanks. But you guys have no idea what you're missing. People our age in the real world live and breathe their phones."

I go on to tell them the different apps that are popular and how great internet shopping is, which they've heard of before, but never done.

I then offer, "I'm told I can charge my phone here; you guys can look at what apps I have that don't require Wi-Fi."

They nod with polite smiles. It's Tonya who says, "I'd love that."

"We've heard about these apps, but I honestly love my life here. I wouldn't want to change it for anything," Claudette says, her brown eyes sparkling.

Tonya shakes her head, disagreeing. "Imagine what you could do to reach an audience, though. In the right hands, it could change lives."

I smile softly. "Many feel that way. That's why there are hundreds if not thousands of apps trying to get your attention. It's exhausting. Once you guys start these games, you'll be hooked. You'll be fighting for my phone."

"I would think you'd love that," Rayne's deep voice interrupts us, surprising me.

I turn narrowed eyes at him. "And why is that?"

"People vying for your attention. You seem to enjoy people trying to catch your eye," he says with a calculating grin.

He's baiting me, but I won't let him get to me in front of the others.

Tonya, however, gasps and smacks his arm. "Rayne, you're being rude. What's your problem?"

I stay quiet and listen because I'm interested in knowing the answer, too.

"Just an observation," he says, shrugging.

My chest burns with all the insults I want to fling at him, but I hold them back. I *will* be the more civilized one here.

"It's not meant to be an insult, though," he says and continues to walk ahead of us, throwing over his shoulder, "I like a girl who knows what she likes and isn't afraid to show it."

I snap, calling out to him, "I don't like attention, Rayne. What gave you that idea? In fact, nothing could be more opposite."

He stops and turns to look at me, one eyebrow raised. "And I also like a girl with a temper. It shows personality." He smirks at me and then turns again to walk away.

I stop and watch him go. I'm left spluttering at his retreating back. "I could hit him. I really could," I say, completely out of words.

"He's usually right, though," Alice says thoughtfully looking at him as he saunters away. Her blonde curly hair floats around her face and the sunlight hitting her head makes it look like a halo.

Her words only send a fresh spear of anger through me.

"Well, he's wrong," I say with gritted teeth. "I hate attention."

Jack barks madly at something at the base of a tree. I yell at him to stop, and when he doesn't, just digs into the ground,

I go over to him and give a yank to his collar for him to move away from the tree.

"But you do have a temper," Tonya says with a knowing glint in her eye, watching me chastise Jack.

"It's okay if you like Rayne, Vela," Claudette says quietly with a smile. "We're all resigned to everyone having a crush on him. None of us hold much hope of getting him."

Today, she's wearing her long brown hair in two braids wrapped around her head and it's quite pretty.

I huff. "Why don't you think you can get his high and mighty's attention?" I ask. "You're beautiful."

I look all of them over. They're all beautiful. Alice looks like a Madonna with her angelic face. Jennifer is tall and stately and has a grace I could only beg for. Claudette has a sweetness I haven't seen in many people. And Tonya is gorgeous with her smooth skin and clear, bright, intelligent eyes.

Claudette blushes, but it's Alice who answers. She smirks. "He's known all of us too long to take any of us seriously. We've always thought it would take a newcomer to get his attention." She looks at me frankly. "And we were right. You came, and he hasn't taken his eyes off you since."

Jennifer and Claudette both nod.

I look at Tonya with a gaping mouth. "Please talk some sense into these three!"

She shrugs and says in a clipped tone, "They're not wrong. You can understand why any girl would find him attractive."

"It's not that! He is unquestionably beautiful, but that doesn't mean you guys aren't good enough to snag him. You're all giving up too easily. And he's not interested in me, anyway. Didn't you just hear him insulting me?"

They all snort and turn to walk down the trail.

"Vela, you're not naïve enough to truly believe that are you?" Tonya says over her shoulder.

I follow them, calling Jack to come with us. "Yes?"

"Then you are naïve. He's flirting with you. And you're the one who grew up in civilization? We can even tell you that much, and we live in the middle of nowhere."

"Well, I'm not on the market. I think I've made that clear."

"Not clear enough," Jennifer says in a brisk tone. "You're going to have to try harder to get his attention off you."

"What? How do I do that?"

Tonya stops and turns, saying with her arms crossed, "That's not the right way to do this, she has to act completely disinterested to give him the hint."

"But then, he'll try harder to get her attention," Claudette disagrees, shaking her head. "That's not good, either."

I throw my hands in the air. "I give up. I can't win for trying."

"You could give up," Tonya says with a grim set to her mouth. "Just give in. Be his. Why not? He's pretty great."

I study her face because surely, she's kidding. She has a pained look, but then it's gone, she hides it quickly.

I suddenly understand. She likes him more than any of the others. Where they believe they have crushes on the guy, she actually might be in love with him.

Looking at her with a new light, I say, "You forget that I have an Intended. There's no comparison. Don't worry about me. I won't fall for his charms, considerable though they may be."

"Well, since we won't ever know how that feels, having an Intended, we'll have to take your word for it," Tonya says in a flat voice.

That seems to silence any other comments because we walk back to town in a still quiet.

When we arrive, I notice Linc right away talking on the street with Andy. I approach them with a big smile, happy to see someone smiling back at me after the pained silence I just endured with my new girlfriends.

"Hey beautiful," Linc says, wrapping an arm around my waist and tugging me toward him.

"Hi yourself," I say and then say bye to the girls after they wave at me, walking toward their homes.

As I wave at them, my eye catches on someone on top of a roof, leaning over, reaching their hand out. There's a hammer on the ground, and there's no way he'll reach it from where he is. Then, to my surprise, I see the hammer levitate up to his hand.

"What in the world?" I say, my mouth gaping. I point to the hammer that is slowly rising to the roof.

"Oh, yeah, I've seen things all over town where people are using their gifts in plain sight." Linc's eyebrows climb, and his expression is as awed as mine. "I forgot about this from the last time I was here."

"It's really a beautiful sight, isn't it?" Andy asks. He flicks his hand open and watches fire dance on his fingers, laughing. "I forget I can use my gift freely here."

Linc turns back to me, his arm still wrapped around my waist. "How did your day go?"

"The grotto is unbelievable. You have to see it. It's a marvel of nature."

He flashes a grin at me. "I will."

I was half afraid Linc would be furious seeing Rayne coming off the trail before us, but he's acting like nothing's bothering him. I'm happy to see him smile.

"Unfortunately, I haven't had the pleasure of seeing it," Andy says, closing his fist, snuffing out his fire in a trail of smoke.

"Oh?"

He gestures at himself. "I wouldn't really fit."

"Ah," I say, then say to Linc, who's looking at us in confusion, "There's like a secret entrance. It's kind of small."

"Kind of?" Andy snorts. "That's an understatement."

"Yeah, I had to go in sideways to get there," I say with a sympathetic look at Andy. "I can go back and take pictures on my phone if you want."

"That would be nice, thank you, Vela," Andy says. "Now, if I'm not mistaken, I understand we're all having dinner together at Hannah's."

A light enters his eyes at the statement, and I secretly smile. "Oh, really? That sounds great!"

Linc says, "Yes, she asked me earlier to come, and I was just telling Andy about it."

"There's not a lot that can compete with Hannah's home-cooked meal," Andy says, rubbing his hands together, his face set in a wide smile.

"Your food is pretty comparable, Andy. Don't sell yourself short."

Linc nods in agreement.

"Well, I'll see you two lovebirds later," Andy says, then turns to leave.

I turn in Linc's arms and say with awe, "This place is amazing. I wish we could live like this everywhere."

"Yes, it would be nice if humans knew and were accepting of our gifts."

"What happens if a human wanders in here and sees things like that? Do they have the poppy-seed formula?"

"I would think so. You can grow poppies in cold weather, and they'll bloom in the spring. I'm sure they've grown some. You couldn't have a community like this without them."

I nod, then wrap my arms around his middle. "So, what's the rest of your day like? Did you finish your thing with Rick?"

He kisses me on the forehead and says, "I did. It was just a little carpentry work."

My eyebrows raise. "I didn't know you knew how to do carpentry. Color me impressed."

He laughs. "Don't be too impressed. I'm a novice at best. Rick taught me a lot today, actually."

I snuggle into his chest and say, "Well, you constantly surprise me with your many talents, Lincoln Stevenson."

"I aim to impress, my lady."

"Lady?" I complain, frowning at him.

"Hey, stop that," he says, running a finger down the creases of my forehead. "Or you'll get stuck like that."

"I'm not a lady. You're making me sound old."

"I'm sorry. What should I say, my girl?"

"Yes," I say, smiling. "My girl, I like that."

"I do, too."

"What now? What should we do today?"

"I don't know," he says, letting me go so he can swing our clasped hands between us as we walk. "Let's just see where the day leads us?" He looks around like he's deciding which way to go.

"A fly by the seat of your pants guy, too? Wow, I'm a lucky girl."

As we walk along, Linc stops and turns to me suddenly. "Hey, I just thought of what I wanted to talk to you about at the bonfire."

"Oh, yeah?"

"You know when everyone was talking about the Chosen Child? I had a thought about the Scorpion and the Scorpio's part of the prophecy."

"Oh, yeah, you had a look like you wanted to tell me something."

"Yes. So, Scorpions are known to be passionate in nature and very assertive."

"Yes, so?" I say, not knowing where this is going.

"Well, the Scorpion is what kills Orion, right?"

"Yes, and?" I wave my hand impatiently.

"So, they remind me of the E.E. Who wants this prophecy to die more than anyone else?"

"The Extremists."

"Yes. So, if they kill the Hunter before he ever finds the Goat, the Child will never be born."

"Linc, we don't know if all that is right. What if we're wrong?"

"It's our best guess."

"Yes. But, the Scorpion, or the E.E. could kill the Hunter after he has the Chosen Child, if what you're saying is true."

He nods. "True. I think it's possible."

"Linc, we can't worry about a prophecy that's unfulfilled for six hundred years."

"It could pertain to us, Vela."

I shake my head. "No. We're not going there. I'm not ready for that, Linc."

I start walking, and Linc jogs to catch up to me. "Okay, Vels. We won't talk about it."

Seeing something up ahead, I have an idea. "Let's go over there."

"Okay," Linc easily agrees, and he follows when I pull him over to the other side of the street.

I'm hoping I'm right and that Grace will be painting there like she was yesterday. I have a hunch when she gets the creative urge to paint, it takes over her completely, not allowing any breaks until she's finished.

There's a skip in my step in my excitement. I've wanted to meet her since I first saw the garden she painted inside the clinic.

"Where are you pulling me?" Linc asks, curiosity leaking into his voice.

"There's someone I want to meet," I say and then stop when I see her. Sure enough, Grace is sitting on the ground, adding detail to the leaves of a vibrant blooming flower. It stands dominant in a field of flowers blowing in the wind. The flowers are a blend of bright red, orange and yellow in a sea of green leaves. They're mesmerizing.

"That's her," I whisper to Linc, afraid to spook her. I point my finger at Jack to stay by my side.

"Who is that?" Linc says and I shush him, covering his mouth with my hand.

Thankfully, she doesn't hear him. She's completely engrossed in her work, and I watch, fascinated. She adds texture here and there and there's a dynamic element to the flowers like I've never seen before. I love her work, and I vow to do this introduction right.

I shift on my feet and wonder about the best way to initiate a conversation.

"What are we doing?" Linc whispers close to my ear.

"We're trying to meet her," I say just as quietly.

"We are? Then why aren't we talking to her?" he asks still in a low voice.

"Not yet. I'm thinking how," I continue to whisper.

She's so skittish that any wrong move on our part could terrify her. I don't want to do that. And, for some reason, I find it's important I do this right. Like we're meant to be friends.

"Vela?" he whispers.

"Shhhh."

He clamps his mouth shut, and he looks at me in amusement.

"Okay, this is what we're going to do," I whisper. I lead him away to where I can pitch my idea.

After I tell him my plan, he says uncertainly, "Okay. If you say so. You really want to meet this girl?"

"Yes," I say with certainty.

"Then let's do it."

"Just follow my lead, okay? We may have to improvise."

His answer is walking toward where Grace sits. My heart warms that Linc is willing to do this with me. He's always been like this. Easily goes with the flow and adapts to any situation.

We walk carefully so Grace can't hear our steps. I hope I don't scare her to death with this plan of mine.

When we've reached her, I say loudly, "This painting is incredible. The colors and the scene are so realistic, but more beautiful than anything I've ever seen." I'm not lying when I say this, and I hope she can hear the sincerity in my voice.

Grace jumps when she hears us. She scrambles up, but before she can run away, Linc says as he studies her work, "You're right. It's inspiring and visually perfect. I wouldn't have picked any other color combination than this."

Grace peers at us over her shoulder, her paintbrush poised. Her face is frozen in fear, but it slowly morphs to wariness the more we talk.

I continue to study the painting, glancing at Grace, but looking away quickly. "Yes, it's like we're standing in the middle of the most perfect field of flowers. I feel like I'm there, don't you?" I ask Linc.

He nods vigorously and says, "I wish I could see a place like this in my lifetime."

"I think the flowers are..." I look at Grace this time, asking her, "Poppies, right? That's what this flower is?"

She nods slowly. I see her relax a fraction, and I count that as a huge win.

"See," I tell Linc. "it's a version of poppy we've never seen. We've only known the red ones, but these must be the kind that grow here with more oranges and yellows. I'd love to see a field like this myself." I sigh loudly. "Maybe one day."

Grace is silent, but she stays, just watching us.

I squeeze Linc's hand and continue. "I wonder if these flowers bloom in the summer." I tilt my head at the painting as I look it over carefully. I scrunch my face in thought and put my finger to my lips and wait.

In the corner of my eye, I see Grace start to say something, then stop herself just as quickly.

I say to Linc, "The way the light reflects on the flowers, it looks like a warm season, but I could be wrong."

He stares intently at the painting, and I cheer at him silently when he catches on to what I'm doing. He says, "I'm not sure I agree. I think it could be any season. How can you tell what the light does in each season?"

This time Grace squeaks, "Spring."

When we turn to look at her, she covers her mouth like she can't believe she said something, her eyes wide.

"Oh?" I say, giving her an encouraging smile.

Her eyes dart between Linc's and mine. Linc thankfully stays quiet, and we wait because I'm hoping she says more.

In the silence, she slowly lowers her hands and says in a whisper, "We just planted them but the poppies bloom in the spring."

My brows raise and I say, looking back at the painting, "Huh. I thought so. I'm a Gyan, and I can tell that the light you use in this painting looks like late spring or early summer."

She nods quickly and then squeezes her hands together, looking away as a pink blush covers her cheeks.

"I'm Vela. Vela Ashcroft. I haven't met you yet, but I've admired your paintings around town." I tell her gently. I don't hold my hand out, not wanting to push too hard.

She has a gentle look about her. Long black hair frames her pale oval face. Her skin is like porcelain, it's so smooth. Her big doe eyes look at me, then dart away, as she nods her head, like she's greeting me that way.

I motion toward Linc and say in a quiet voice, "This is Linc. We came together, which I'm sure you know. He's my Intended."

Her eyebrows fly up, and she looks at us both with her mouth open. "Really?" she breathes.

I smile at her and say, "It was a surprise to us, too." I squeeze Linc's hand in remembrance and he smiles softly at me as he nods.

"Wow, I wish I could meet mine," Grace whispers, and a yearning look fills her eyes.

My heart twists because there's hardly any chance she'll find her Intended, but I nod anyway. "You never know. He could walk in here at any time."

She nods and then looks at the ground, studying her shoes.

I think this is probably the extent of the conversation we're going to have with her today. I don't want to push her too much with conversation, so I say, "Well, it was really nice meeting you. I hope to talk to you again. I'd love to hear more about your inspiration behind your paintings."

"Me too," Linc says.

She blushes scarlet at Linc's words, and I tug him away. "Until next time. I'll come find you."

She nods timidly and turns back to her work, glancing at us over her shoulder.

I take one last look at her, smiling, and walk away with Linc.

"Let's go back to Hannah's. I'm going to see if I can help with dinner," I say.

Linc turns toward the Hobbit House immediately and I sigh happily. That went better than I expected. There's a skip is in my step as we walk home.

CHAPTER TWENTY-NINE

When we arrive at Hannah's, I'm not sure if I should knock or just go in. It's technically my home now, so I could just open the door, but I hesitate.

Linc stands with me on the doorstep and says quietly, "I understand. I feel the same way about Rick's."

I end up knocking and when I don't hear any response, I open the rounded door, stepping in warily.

"Hello?" I call out.

Hearing voices in the clinic, I realize she must be treating a sick patient and hasn't heard us.

Giving her and her patient privacy, I go into the kitchen, Linc following close behind. Jack makes himself comfortable in the living area.

Wondering where Greta is, I walk up to the wooden counter and see some half-sliced zucchinis.

"I'm not sure what else Hannah's cooking, but you can go relax while I cut these up for her," I tell Linc, getting right to work after washing my hands.

Instead of leaving, he leans against the counter, watching me slice the vegetables.

"I thought you and Greta had a day planned. What happened?"

Rayne happened. But I don't say that. Instead, I shrug and say, "We've got plenty of time to explore around here."

I glance at him and can tell he doesn't believe me.

"The Vela I know wouldn't promise a little girl to spend a whole day with her, then cut it down to an hour or two."

I sigh and stop cutting. I might as well tell him the truth. I just don't want to admit that Rayne got under my skin.

"Rayne was there. We ran into him and several others on the trail, and they decided to go to the grotto with us," I say quietly as I resume cutting.

He pauses. "And?"

"And he was being a bit insufferable, so I asked to come home early."

I see Linc stiffen his stance. "What do you mean insufferable?"

"He thinks..." I stop and collect my thoughts before continuing, "He thinks he knows me. Which he doesn't. At all. I didn't want to spend the day with him. I promised a day with Greta."

He nods and looks away, his jaw working. "I see."

"What? What do you see, Linc?" I ask, putting my knife down, frustration welling up. I don't want to be blamed for this tension.

He looks at me with a frank expression. "Only that he's continuing to make his move."

I blow out a breath I didn't know I was holding. I finish my chopping and rub my hands together, searching the cabinets for a bowl.

"I don't know why he's interested," I mutter. When I find what I'm looking for, I scoop up the vegetables and drop them in.

"I do," Linc says quietly.

I look at Linc and say, "I don't want to fight about this."

"Neither do I," he says, then moves to hold my arms. "In fact, let's promise to never have a fight with Rayne's name in it again."

I nod, agreeing easily. I take a deep breath. "Sounds perfect." I lean in and rest my head on his chest, relishing his solid presence and thankful he didn't turn ugly with jealousy. This is growth in our relationship.

We break apart when Hannah emerges from the clinic with a heavily pregnant woman. I'm suddenly very happy I gave them privacy when I came in. I might have peeked into a very embarrassing situation during her exam.

"Oh, hi guys!" Hannah says, with a big smile. She motions her hand toward the pregnant woman, who's holding her back like it's the only thing keeping her from falling over. "This is Sally. Sally, this is Vela and Linc, our new residents. Sally is, as you can see, about to have a baby. Any day now."

Sally smiles tiredly and says, "It's nice to meet you. I can't wait to finally deliver this little person. I can't walk, sit, sleep, or move in any comfortable position. If I have to carry him or her much longer, I'm afraid I won't be able to breathe." She waddles to the door and says over her shoulder, "Hopefully, I'll be letting you know soon that the time has come, Hannah. Just don't get mad if it's three in the morning."

"I'll be waiting to hear. Anytime, Sally. Remember, when the contractions come five minutes apart consistently, that means it's time. But have Ruth come get me if you need anything."

Sally nods tiredly and leaves the house, waddling slowly.

Hannah follows her and closes the door, then leans her back on it. She wears a tired and worried expression.

"Is everything alright?" I ask.

"I hope so," she answers and walks slowly over to us. "She should have had the baby by now. She's pretty overdue." Hannah studies her hands, and my heart goes out to her. It's obvious how much she cares about her patients.

"You can't start her labor?" I don't know anything about Gyans helping in labor and delivery.

"No," she breathes. "I wish. I would do it right now."

"Is there anything you can give her to prompt labor?" I ask, suddenly worried about a woman I just met.

Hannah grimaces. "I can, but I prefer not to. It's best for things to happen naturally. But they don't always happen the way you want them to." She rubs her forehead.

"What can you give her to start labor?"

"Well, I can give her red raspberry leaf tea, but it can overstimulate the uterus and be dangerous for the baby. For now, I've been walking with her every day. Exercise is the best way to speed things up." She sighs heavily, then walks into the kitchen and sees the cut-up zucchini.

"Did you finish these for me?" she asks, with wonder in her eyes.

"Yes," I say, embarrassed. "I came home to see if I could help you with dinner."

"That's so nice. Thank you, Vela. It's going to be great having help around here," she says and turns to the cabinet to fish out a large canister of flour.

"I'm going to start the bread. How does bread on a stick sound?" she asks us over her shoulder.

"What?" Linc and I both ask.

She laughs. "The name literally tells you what it is," she says, finding a cup and measuring out flour into a bowl. "It's kind of like a breadstick but wrapped around an actual stick. Pick out the green branches, though, or they'll burn too fast. The bread is delicious."

Linc's face registers surprise, and I'm sure mine does, too. "Sounds wonderful," I say.

"Where do you cook it?" Linc asks, looking around.

I've already noticed the absence of an oven, so I wait to hear Hannah's answer.

"Over a fire," she says matter-of-factly.

"Huh, that's creative," I say, looking over at the fireplace. She has a fire going, and I try to imagine cooking bread over it. "Andy's coming too, right?"

"Yes," she says, brightening. "I thought this could be a late welcome dinner for all of you."

"How well do you know Andy?" I ask, fishing for clues about a possible romance.

Linc looks at me with his head tilted and eyes knowing.

I give him a look that says, 'Let me do this.'

"Oh, I guess I know him better than most," she answers. "He had a head injury the last time he was here that required multiple healings. He spent quite a bit of time in the clinic." She mixes sugar and yeast into the flour.

"He's really great," I say lamely, hoping I'm not being too obvious. I've come to care for the big guy and wish him the best. Hannah is obviously one of those. They'd be great together.

Hannah glances at me, and I keep my face smooth so it doesn't look like I'm trying too hard.

"He is," she agrees easily.

"What can I do to help?"

"Well, in a minute, I'll have to knead this dough for about ten minutes, which can get tiresome. You can take over for me halfway through. Does that sound okay?"

"Sure! I'll watch how you do it because I've never kneaded bread before."

"Oh, a novice! Sounds good."

While she gets the counter ready for the next step by dusting flour on it, I turn to Linc and say, "Thank you for your help talking to Grace."

He smiles warmly at me and says, "Of course."

"You spoke to Grace today?" Hannah asks, her eyes wide. She smacks the dough onto the floured surface, and I watch as she punches it with her one fist, then the other. She folds the dough over only to repeat the first step. "How on earth did you get her to talk to you?"

"Vela had a plan," Linc said with raised eyebrows, emphasizing the last word.

"Oh? And what was that?"

"I didn't approach her directly," I say, getting warmed up to the conversation. "We kind of snuck up behind her and then started complimenting her painting. The one she's doing now, the field of poppies."

At Hannah's encouraging nod, I continue, "Linc and I got into a discussion about it, and I figured she'd talk about her work, which is what happened." I shrug.

"Well, you are one of the lucky ones. There are people who've been here a year who she hasn't spoken to yet," Hannah says, getting out of breath with her exertion of kneading the dough.

"Can I try?" I ask.

"It hasn't been five minutes yet," she says with surprise.

"That's okay. It looks fun. I'd like to try it," I offer, itching to get my fingers doughy.

"Okay, I won't argue," she says, and washes her hands off in the sink.

"Best you don't argue with her," Linc says with a grin.

Hannah laughs. "You sound like you've crashed and burned already, trying to do just that."

Linc nods and says, eyeing me with fondness, "Yea, but I enjoyed it. It's fun getting her riled up."

I swat his arm as I pass by him to approach the counter. "I knew you enjoyed getting me mad. Careful, or I'll show you a version of my temper you won't think is so cute." I pull my hair back into a messy bun.

Linc laughs at me. "Now this I have to see."

I look at him with outrage and start punching the dough, trying to do it exactly like Hannah. Folding over the dough, I punch it again and again.

Apparently, I look like I'm taking out a bad day on the dough because Linc says after a minute, "Are you imagining my face in there?"

Blowing my hair out of my eyes, I look up at him and say, "What gave you that impression?"

He holds out his hands, warding me off. "Nothing, nothing at all."

"It's actually therapeutic," I say as I attack the bread. "I'm enjoying this," I tell both Linc and Hannah.

So much of my life now is out of my control. Kneading this bread feels like the one thing I can do for myself. I pour my emotions into the action, missing my family, my home, my best friend, my school. I pull back a little so I can do this for several more minutes.

"Wow, I'm just glad it's the bread and not me," Linc says.

I look up at him, stopping for a second. "I'm not mad at you, Linc. This isn't about you. I just miss... everything, everyone."

I resume my work and find I feel better for my efforts.

Hannah walks up behind me, putting a hand on my shoulder. "I understand what you're feeling. Don't think you're alone. We're all in your boat here."

I look back at her and smile softly, grateful for her words. "I'm so glad I know you, Hannah."

"Oh, honey," she says, giving me a half hug, "I'm happy to know you, too. And we'll only get to know each other better and better."

"I'm looking forward to learning more about healing," I say as I continue to knead, this time being a little gentler, pacing myself so I can keep going.

"You can start following me around anytime. I figured you'd want to get acclimated first."

"Yes, it's been nice. The grotto we saw today is lovely. I can get started anytime helping you, though. Will Sally mind if I watch during the labor?"

Her eyebrows lift and she says, "I'll ask her. I don't think she'll mind. When you've had a baby already, you lose all sense of propriety. I'm sure she'd be happy with extra hands helping. You can assist me."

I'm nervous at the thought of having actual responsibilities during the birth of a baby, but I inhale deeply and nod, accepting the challenge.

I look at Linc, who's staring at me with wide eyes. When Hannah walks out of the kitchen to tend the fire, he walks up to me and says quietly, "Are you sure about this, Vela? Labor is an intense thing."

I continue to knead the dough and say quietly, "I'm sure. I am a little nervous, though. But I'd like to know what to do in that situation."

"Okay," he says warily, but looks impressed. "There's not a chance I'd ever want to be in your shoes."

I grin. Men quake at the thought of labor. Always have, always will.

A frantic knock sounds on the door. "Hannah?" someone calls from outside.

Hannah rushes to the door and pulls it open.

A bleeding Rayne is held up by Anthony and another guy I haven't met who's as big as a linebacker.

Blood drips from Rayne's forehead and onto the floor.

"Oh no," I say, thinking this night has just taken a turn for the worse.

CHAPTER THIRTY

I wash my hands off in the sink quickly and pick up a towel to bring over to Rayne.

"No, Vela. I'll get towels. You put that towel over the dough. We're still going to need dinner when this is done," Hannah instructs, ever practical.

She's all business as she guides the three guys to the clinic, and I hear Linc mutter under his breath, "Can't get away from this guy."

I give him a frustrated look and follow the group into the clinic room.

"What happened?" Hannah asks briskly.

"We were mock fighting with staffs, and mine hit his head pretty bad," No-name guy says in a deep voice.

"Yea, it was hard. Knocked him out cold," Anthony says with an impressed look at Rayne, who's now lying on the bed, his head resting on towels.

"He roused a few seconds later, but we had to help him walk here," No-name guy says.

"Thank you, Leon. He'll be fine. But head injuries are tricky. Please tell his parents he's going to have to stay the night here where I can keep an eye on him."

He nods, flicking a glance in my direction, and backs away from the bed.

"Now, you guys, please give Vela and I room to work."

They both look at Rayne but leave, as asked.

"You need me, Hannah?"

She looks at me. "You wanted to be my assistant, right? Well, assist me."

I snap to attention and snag a few more towels off the small table by the door and bring them to her.

She says, "Let's get some of the blood out of the way, so I can see what the damage is."

Rayne's eyes have been fluttering this entire time, like he's trying to keep them open, but having a hard time.

Standing by the bed, I move so I can press on the bleeding with half of my towels, mopping up the rest of the blood with the other half. It's a good thing blood doesn't make me queasy, or I'd be sick.

Hannah leaves the room while I work then returns with a bowl of water, which I use to clean Rayne up as best as I can.

He's quiet the entire time, not even uttering a moan when I press on his wound. I worry that he's more injured than Hannah realizes.

"Hannah?" I say urgently.

"I'm coming," she says. "Just wanted to wash my hands." Nodding at me to make room, she slips next to me and lays her hands on the source of the bleeding. She closes her eyes.

I hold my breath, not wanting to make a sound while she senses his injury. I say a prayer that he'll be fine. I really hate head wounds. They're so unpredictable. Concussions can have serious lasting effects, not to mention the threat of a coma when he falls asleep.

Finally, she opens her eyes. "I've sealed his wound. I can't sense any swelling on the brain. Vela, do you have any experience with head wounds?"

I look directly at her, my mind filling with the horror of Linc's injury from just a few days ago. "Yes, I do."

"Can you check behind me to see if there's anything I've missed?" Hannah straightens up slowly. She must have lost a ton of energy healing him. She moves out of the way so I can replace her. "I'll be right back. I'm just going to wash my hands."

I step up and lay my hand gently on Rayne's forehead. His eyes slit open, and he cracks a small smile when he sees me. He starts to talk.

I stop him by putting my hand on his lips. "Shh, shh. Don't speak just yet."

He obeys but watches me, his eyes wider open now.

Like Hannah, I close my eyes and reach my senses toward his injury. It's gone, Hannah's done a good job of sealing it. I look toward the lining of his brain, starting at one point, and follow it around his whole head. I sigh in relief when I don't sense any swelling.

"Am I going to live?" Rayne's scratchy voice asks.

I open my eyes to find him staring at me with a fondness I don't deserve. I've been pretty terrible to him.

It seems to be a habit of mine to treat guys badly who like me. It's not very nice of me, and I'm not proud of myself.

"Yeah," I say softly. "You're going to be okay. But Hannah and I will have to take turns waking you up all night. That's the penalty for being too rough on yourself."

"Hey," he protests, "It was Leon who was too rough with me. I'm the victim here."

I smile. "Yes, but I've seen those mock fights. You weren't being rough on him for you to get a hit like that?"

He smirks. "Maybe." His brown eyes sparkle at me, and I lift my head to escape them.

Only to see Linc in the doorway, frowning deeply.

"Linc," I say, but before I can say anything more, he turns and leaves.

"I'll be right back." I chase after him, catching up when he's at the door. I grab his shirt sleeve to stop him from storming out. He stays, just barely. "Hey, where are you going? We were having dinner together, remember?"

Hannah's in the kitchen, drying her hands off with a towel. She eyes us warily and leaves, giving us privacy.

Linc flicks his stormy eyes at Hannah, quickly retreating, then looks at me. "If I stay for dinner, you can be sure that guy will get another head injury."

"Linc, you can't really leave. This dinner is for you, me, and Andy." I put a hand on his arm and it's flaming hot.

"I am. I'm not staying in the same house as that guy. I can't watch him with you, Vela." His eyes reflect a pain that I want to erase immediately.

"What can I do?" I ask, helpless to stop this train wreck.

"Not be yourself."

"What do you mean?"

"Be as unpleasant as possible. For me." He cracks a small smile and leans in to kiss me softly. "I hope you understand."

In a small way, I do. I hate it, though. I watch him leave, the door closing softly behind him. It might as well have been slammed shut, the way my heart hurts. I sigh heavily and rub Jack's head, grateful he followed me around as I went from room to room.

He stays with me as I return to the clinic. I wish Linc had stayed, too. I do not want to be alone with Rayne. Linc makes me feel safe where Rayne leaves me flustered.

Rayne's lying just as before. Hannah's leaning over him, both hands on his head.

I know I need to help care for Rayne, but I'm stuck in an impossible position. Linc wants me to have nothing to do with Rayne, yet I have to care for him as a patient.

Hannah straightens and turns to glance at me. "Did I hear Linc leave?" She studies me with a knowing look.

"Yes. It looks like he won't be staying for dinner after all." I look down, trying to swallow my disappointment.

"I'm sorry to hear that," Hannah says, brushing her hands off on her pants. "Well, it looks like it will be just us, Andy, and Rayne, if he's up for dinner."

Rayne sits up, his hand rubbing over his head, saying, "Hannah, your gift never ceases to amaze me. I feel good."

"Is the pain gone?" she asks.

"It's there a little bit, but it's fine," he answers, swinging his legs over the bed.

"Oh, no, you don't," Hannah says, picking his legs up, putting them back onto the bed. "You don't get to leave yet. You need to rest. You've just had a concussion. When dinner is ready, I'll check on you and see if you're ready to get up to join us."

Rayne lays back down, a frown marring his perfect face. How does someone look beautiful when they're frowning?

I shake my head and ask, "Hannah, is there anything I can do?"

She turns. "Do you mind putting these towels in a bowl of water in the back? I'd like them to soak. Maybe we can salvage them from being too stained."

"Sure," I say and gather the towels that have been discarded on the floor. I stand up with my arms full and ask Rayne, "Can you pick your head up? I need that towel."

He complies, then moans when I take the towel off the pillow.

"What's wrong? Are you in pain again?" Worry slices through me I missed something.

He grimaces and says, "A little. Maybe you can give me some of your healing mojo?"

"Of course." I drop the towels on the floor and lean over him. Before I place my hands on his head, I look into his eyes, looking for weird dilation or an unfocused gaze.

He looks at me with eyes that seem clear and healthy.

"Hmm," I say, looking at him uncertainly. If he says he's in pain, though, who am I to argue? I place my hands on his head and close my eyes, sending in warmth meant to soothe and heal.

Jack leans into my leg, loving when I use my gift. How he can sense it, I don't know. It's his doggy superpower, I guess.

After a minute of healing, I open my eyes and ask, "Is that better? Did it help?"

"Definitely," he says, with a rather devious smile.

I wonder why and then brush it off as Rayne being Rayne.

"Okay, let's let him rest while we get supper ready," Hannah says. She picks up the towels I dropped and leaves the room.

"As long as you're okay?" I ask Rayne before leaving.

He closes his eyes in response and folds his hands on his chest. "Never better," he says with a smile still on his face.

I shake my head at him and leave the room, closing the door softly behind me.

When I return to the kitchen, I see Hannah placing a piece of meat on a wooden cutting board.

"Well, I think he's all set. He seems okay," I say as I join Hannah in the kitchen.

"Yes, he's fine. He's had a head injury before, so I'm thankful he didn't have any further complications this time." She sighs. "They're so rough on each other."

"We practice fighting, too, back home. But, with our gifts and not staffs. I'd like to learn."

"I'm sure someone will be happy to help you," she says in a dry voice.

I look at her. "You mean Rayne?" I ask in a low voice so he can't hear us talking.

She looks at me and nods. Rubbing spices and herbs into the meat, she says, "You've attracted quite a bit of attention around here, his especially."

I frown. "I know. I'm trying to tell him not to bother with me, but he's refusing to take a hint."

She laughs. "And he won't either. I've never seen a more single-minded guy in my entire life. What Rayne wants; he usually gets."

"Well, it won't happen with me. And you don't know Linc yet," I say, then lower my voice again. "Linc is going crazy about this. Any advice for me?"

She smirks. "I heard his advice for you. Take it. The only way to discourage this is being as unpleasant as possible."

"That won't make for a very nice evening tonight, though."

"You don't worry about Andy and me. You worry about yourself and keeping your Intended happy."

I sigh. "I wish Linc was coming tonight."

"I can understand that." She takes a deep breath and looks over her seasoned meat that's been thoroughly rubbed in. "Now, let's take this tenderloin to the fire. Once it's done, the bread should be ready to cook."

"I didn't think you had deer out here."

"We don't. We do, however, have caribou and moose. Those are our primary food sources. That and the road chickens."

I laugh. "I heard about those. Are they really that easy to catch?"

"Yes. The story we like to tell is they're the quail God sent from heaven to the Israelites when they were wandering the desert. They literally won't even run away when you walk up to them."

"Wow." I follow her over to the fireplace and see a grilling rack propped up that I hadn't noticed before.

"They make for good eating," she says.

When I kneel and look into the fireplace, I can see there are stone pieces jutting out to support the grill rack. Placing the rack on the stone pieces, she pokes the burning wood with a stick until she's happy with the flame.

She carefully places the meat on the rack, situating it off the flames as best as she can.

"You're cooking it with indirect heat?"

She looks at me with surprise. "You know your grilling jargon."

"I watch my dad grill a lot. Or I did." I frown when I realize that I don't know when I'll see him again.

"Well, you're right. I don't want it to burn, so I cook it as off the flame as I can."

I nod and then sit back on my haunches and take a moment to watch the fire dancing around. I sigh heavily.

"You okay, Vela?" Hannah asks me gently, putting her hand on my shoulder.

I look at her and say, "I'm just a little overwhelmed. My life has been so chaotic lately, to say the least. And," I rub my face. "I miss my family and my best friend. I miss my way of life. Thank God I have Jack here...and Linc."

I rub Jack's coat as he sits next to me. "He's more of a therapy dog than just a pet, you know?"

She nods and pets Jack's head, too. He instantly smells the meat on her fingers and enthusiastically licks them. "Can I ask you something?" Her voice is gentle.

"Sure," I say, looking at her curiously.

She flicks her eyes down at my arms and ask, "Who is Cooper?"

At his name, my heart lurches. It's never easy remembering what happened to my precious dog. "My best friend, well, my dog, from years ago."

Her eyes mist over with tears. She inhales deeply. "Greta told me you lost him to a fire?"

I drop my gaze, studying the fire. "Yes," I whisper. "I tried to save him, but," I say with difficulty. "He wouldn't jump over the fire."

She squeezes my arm and says, "I'm so sorry, Vela. That sounds like a tragedy you're still hurting over. Probably always will."

I nod, unable to talk around the tears in my throat.

She nods her head succinctly. "Linc and you will be fine," she encourages. "Rayne is a roadblock. You just have to figure out how to get around him."

I appreciate her changing the subject. I swallow my tears, pushing them down and laugh softly. "If Linc had his way, he'd go through him."

She rubs her moist hands on her pants after Jack's attention. "It'll be interesting watching them practice fighting with their gifts. Rayne is a Borean and Neronian, and Linc is a Festan. It's hard to say who'd come out on top."

"Wait, when do the mock fights happen?"

She stands up, and I follow her as she walks back to the kitchen. "Most every day. The kids especially like to learn their skills. The ones who receive their latent gifts really love to hone their newfound powers."

"That sounds amazing. I can't imagine getting a whole new gift."

She looks at me before she peeks under the towel at the bread. "It's kind of like a party when someone gets their latent element around here. This looks about ready." She uncovers the bowl and reaches in to retrieve the risen dough.

"A party? Like a bonfire? You guys do that whenever a latent gift emerges?" I watch in fascination as she takes a wooden rolling pin and rolls out the dough into a rectangle.

"Sure, it's a cause for celebration." She takes a knife and cuts the rectangle piece of dough into strips. "It's one step closer to being the Chosen Child. We have great hopes one of our kids will be the Child who will free our world from being divided. We wouldn't have to hide out here. If the Chosen Child comes, we could live freely anywhere we want, without fear of being discovered."

"Aren't you afraid of the E.E. trying to kill the Chosen Child? That's one way of stopping him or her from uniting us all."

She puts her knife down and says soberly, "Every day I worry about that. It's just so important, though, to conquer the current system. We're not meant to live divided, Vela. Our community shows you just how amazing our world would be if we lived together in peace and harmony. But, if Greta ever emerges as the Child, she'll be well protected."

"What do you mean?"

She picks up green sticks and starts wrapping dough around them. "We train ourselves every day so that if the time comes, if one of our children is our leader, our community will be his or her first defenders. We've all signed up to protect the Child with our lives. I would do that and more for Greta if it's her."

I take a moment to let that sink in. "That's incredible. Everyone here is willing to do that?"

Her eyebrows rise. "Yes. We're all deeply invested in protecting our future."

I lean back and process that for a minute. Do they expect Linc and me to join in this bodyguard detail?

Uneasy, I change the subject. "Where is Greta, by the way? Will she be home soon?"

"She'd better be. I let her go over to Betsy's house. She, Alisha, and Greta are as thick as thieves. They're all the same age and love each other to death."

"I still find it amazing that children and people with different elements all live happily together. It's so different at home. We only know Gyans there. Linc, when he came, threw everyone through a loop. But he handled it amazingly well."

"That doesn't surprise me," she says as she continues to loop long strips of dough around the branches. "He seems like he can take on any challenge."

"He did and he does." I think about Rayne lying in the next room. Will Linc manage to control his jealousy and temper with Rayne challenging it every five seconds?

I'm terrified at what it will look like if he can't.

CHAPTER THIRTY-ONE

By the time Hannah wraps about ten branches with dough, I can't wait to try this new culinary treat.

"Well, that about does it for dinner. I wonder when Andy will get here," she says, washing her hands in the sink.

A knock sounds on the front door and I go to open it. Andy fills the doorway, looking eager and hopeful. When he sees it's me, he slumps a little and says, "Oh, hi, Vela."

I smile. "Hi Andy! Please come in." I don't take any offense that he'd rather have been greeted by Hannah.

He ducks as he steps inside, narrowly missing the top of the rounded door frame.

"Andy, hello," Hannah says warmly. "Here, let me take your coat."

He brightens when he sees her, hands her his coat and then looks around. "Where's Greta? She's usually bouncing around somewhere whenever I come."

"She's due home any second now. Greta knows what'll happen if I have to fish her out of Betsy's house again."

He smiles fondly and then sniffs. "It smells delicious in here. Is that venison cooking?" He leans over to inspect the meat. I wonder why every male I've ever met finds it fascinating to discuss every piece of meat they encounter.

"You guessed it," Hannah says. "Please sit. It will take a while to cook, and we have to wait for Greta, anyway."

"Did I hear Andy?" Rayne asks, leaning against the doorway of the clinic.

"You did," Andy says, getting up. "I didn't know you were here." He turns toward Hannah. "I thought Linc was joining us for dinner."

She grimaces. "He was, but he realized he had other plans," she says, glancing at me.

Rayne turns away. It looks suspiciously like he's hiding a smile.

I give Hannah a grateful nod and say to Andy, "Rayne has a head injury. He has to stay the night so we can be sure he's okay. That's why he's here."

"Awe, yes, the hourly wake-up calls," Andy says, not noticing or commenting on the sudden tension in the room. A fondness comes into his eyes as he looks at Hannah. He turns to say to Rayne, "I've been in your shoes, my friend."

Rayne asks Hannah, "Is it okay if I leave my bed now? I've rested like you asked. I thought I could join you guys for some company, like a good boy."

Hannah laughs. "Oh Rayne, you're welcome to join us. You know my rules are healing first, fun second. But, yes, I think you can leave the sickbed for a while. But I'm keeping a sharp eye on you."

He salutes her. "Yes, ma'am."

We all go to find seats and just as I'm about to choose one, Rayne appears next to me. He sits down on the loveseat, and I almost abandon joining him when I see Hannah.

She sits down in one of the other chairs and Andy takes the other one. If I don't sit next to Rayne, I'll be sitting on the floor. Now, I know I'm supposed to be rude, but can I be that rude? Also, there's no possible way she and Andy can fit on this small couch together.

When I sit down, however, I find this is an even cozier situation than I'd expected. Rayne's lounging in his seat, not leaving me much room at all. I squeeze to the left as far as I can, so I avoid any contact. But it doesn't do much good. My thigh is pressed against his and I shift uncomfortably.

Jack settles on the floor next to my legs and stares at Rayne like he's waiting for any wrong move.

"I have a feeling he doesn't like me much," Rayne says, looking down at Jack.

"He doesn't like most men," I say.

"He seems to like Andy well enough."

"Andy is a Festan. Festans have an unusual way with animals. You knew that, right?" I ask.

He nods and settles further into his seat, laying his arm on the back of the pillow behind my head. It feels like an embrace.

I try to move over. Jack growls lowly.

Rayne removes his arm, smiling. "He'll get used to me."

"Will he? You seem to think you know my dog really well."

Silence fills the room.

I fidget in my seat, uncomfortable with Rayne's proximity, and he smirks. I squeeze my hands together, placing them in my lap.

"It smells good in here, Hannah." Rayne says conversationally.

"Thank you, Rayne. I still have to cook up the zucchini, but it'll be ready soon."

"Is that the caribou they hunted yesterday?" he asks.

"It is. They gave me a nice cut for my welcome dinner...uhhh, I mean, dinner."

Rayne gives her a confused look, and she reluctantly explains, "This was supposed to be a welcome dinner for Linc, Vela, and Andy." She looks away like she's embarrassed.

I fume. It's not her fault we can't have a welcome dinner. It's Rayne's presence that's done that.

"And Linc had other plans?" Rayne asks too innocently.

I know he's poking the bear with this question. He saw Linc get angry and leave so I say tightly, "Something came up, and he had to go."

Rayne smiles widely. "That's too bad."

I turn my head so he can't see the fury I'm sure is shooting from my eyes. He just makes me so mad with everything he says.

Hannah clears her throat. "Yes, it is. Now, Andy, is there any news today?"

"Actually, there is. We had a couple of guys come in from the hidden community in the west. I think they said it's called Saddleback."

"Yes, I met them before I got whacked in the head," Rayne says, leaning forward. "That's a ways away. It must have taken days to get here."

Andy nods. "It did. They said they were nervous coming this far east. Too close to polar bear country for them."

"I thought you said this place has never seen a polar bear before," I ask Andy, nervous. I've heard polar bears are vicious man eaters. I have no desire to ever go near one.

"As far as I know they haven't...Rayne and Hannah? Am I still correct?"

Rayne shifts to the left, which moves his body even closer to me. His side sits warmly against mine and I stiffen, uncomfortable. "Uhh, actually Andy, there was a sighting of a hybrid polar bear recently."

Hannah turns worried eyes to Andy. "Should I not allow Greta to go exploring? I'm terrified she'd stumble into it."

"Into what?" I ask, trying to move further to the left, but there's simply no room.

"Into a grolar bear," Rayne says in a somber voice.

"A what?"

Andy leans forward, his eyes gleaming. "Are those real? I heard about them but didn't believe they exist."

Rayne answers in as serious of a tone as I've ever heard from him, "It's a bear that's a mix between grizzly and polar bear. It looks like a white grizzly, it's called a grolar bear, but some call it a pizzly, too."

"And you've seen one of these things?" I ask in a shrill voice. What kind of place have I found myself in?

Rayne shakes his head. "No, I haven't, but some of the guys were hunting about ten miles from here and they saw one."

Ten miles was way too close to this monster bear. I've already had nightmares about man-eating polar bears. Now grolar bears are being added to them.

Greta bursts through the door, panting. "Sorry Momma! I lost track of time. Those kittens Betsy has are so cute!" She skids to a stop in front of us, looking us all over. "Where's Linc? I thought he was coming. And what's Rayne doing here?" It's at this point she notices the blood on his shirt and says knowingly to him, "Training got 'ya again?"

He nods.

"Linc had to go...unexpectedly. So, it's Rayne with us tonight," Hannah says.

"Oh, okay. Well, let me wash up." She leaves as quickly as she came.

"Where are the travelers staying, Andy?" Hannahs asks.

"I believe they're at Rick's house," he answers.

I'm glad Linc has some new company to keep his mind off me being here with Rayne.

"Makes sense since he's single," Rayne says. "He has the most room to put people up."

Hannah gets up to check the meat. "I think I'm going to cook those zucchinis now." Before she walks away, she asks me, "Do you mind grabbing some more firewood for me? It's out back."

Andy gets up. "Let me get that for you, Vela."

Needing fresh air, I say, "No, it's fine Andy. I don't mind."

Popping up, I slip on my jacket and go out the front door to get the firewood, only too happy to leave Rayne's presence.

Once outside, I lean my back on the door and take a deep breath of cold fresh air. Blowing it out slowly, I study the stars, remembering with a smile Linc's offer to name a constellation for me.

I'm bumped when someone tries to open the door. Stepping away, I look to see who's coming outside.

I frown when I see Rayne.

"Am I really that bad?" he asks, smirking, as usual getting right to the point.

I turn and start walking around the house to find where the wood is stored. "Sorry, it's just, you're a lot you know?"

He follows me, keeping up easily.

I spin around. "Hey, you're supposed to be injured. You need to take it easy."

He stuffs his hands in his pockets and cocks his head. "I'm a lot, but you're still concerned for me? That's an improvement. I'll take it."

I study him for a minute. "Take what? My sympathy? My good esteem? Well, you have the former, but as for the latter, that's questionable."

"Why?" He shrugs. "You can't think good of me? I haven't done anything horrible enough to give you such a bad opinion. Have I?"

I sigh heavily and rub my forehead. He's right. He hasn't done anything that terrible, except for his flagrant disregard for Linc and refusing to take no for an answer.

"Look, you're just making my life very complicated right now."

"Why? Because I don't buy all that crap about an Intended bond and how it trumps everything?" He gestures toward himself. "I think I have as good of a chance of catching someone's attention as anyone. I don't need a bond to do that."

I stare at him. "The fact that you say that means you don't have the first clue how special an Intended bond is. It completely takes over you."

He takes a couple of steps toward me. "And you immediately ran into his arms when you first met him? Is that what I'm hearing?"

I shake my head.

"I thought so. Because from what I heard at the bonfire from your own lips, 'You weren't sure about him.' What did he do to get your attention so completely? Tell me because I'm willing to make that same effort. Ga! I already did that. What am I talking about?" He turns, giving me his back as he puts his hands on his hips and shakes his head.

"What do you mean?" I think back to my interactions with him. What grand gesture has he made? I come up with no answers.

He turns and pins a look at me. "I'm here tonight, aren't I?"

"You're here? Yes, you're here. I still don't understand."

He scoffs. "I'm going to have to spell it out to you, aren't I?"

I look around, wondering what he could possibly be talking about. Then his words hit me. *He's here. Tonight.*

I point at his head. "Did you get yourself injured on purpose?" I screech.

He claps. "And she gets it! Congratulations, Vela Ashcroft."

Putting my hands on my head, I look at him in amazement. "You really got a concussion so you could be in the clinic where I live?"

He laughs. "Well, Leon wasn't supposed to hit me *that* hard. But, yeah, I couldn't figure out a way to get your attention, so I got injured. Besides, I know how great of a healer Hannah is, so I knew I'd be fine."

I splutter, completely thrown off. "You are the worst...the most insufferable...I can't believe you." Spinning around, I stomp to the back of the house and start slamming pieces of wood into my arms. I mutter under my breath, "I have never met such an idiot in all my days. I never will either, I'm sure."

"I hope you're saying all good things there, Vela," Rayne says, following me to the stack of firewood and collecting his own pile, too.

I snap a look at him. "Hardly."

"After all, I did go through quite a bit of pain to get here." He looks at me from the side of his eye. "I hope it was worth it."

I almost drop my load but manage to say with gritted teeth, "That is the stupidest thing I've ever heard of. You don't manipulate a healing so you can talk to a girl, Rayne."

"Why not?" He looks at me with a true question in his eyes.

I huff and stomp off, a few branches falling off my pile in my haste to leave. I don't answer.

He catches up to me, easily keeping hold of his load. "Vela, I'm serious. Why not do what I did? It worked, didn't it? I got you alone."

"You forget one very important detail," I say, seething. "You've made me furious with your revelation. That does not earn you brownie points."

"Oh, so I need to score brownie points to get your attention? I have to plaster you with compliments and sweet nothings? Why can't a guy just be himself?"

I stop and breathe in slowly through my nose. "I'm not saying you can't be yourself. But you worried Hannah and *me*. This whole thing is *insane*."

He smiles. "Well, that's also a plus. You were worried about me. If you hated me, you'd be glad I was hurt."

"No, I wouldn't! What kind of person do you think I am, Rayne? I don't wish harm on anyone, even on people I don't like."

"So, you're saying you didn't try to beat the snot out of those Neronians who attacked you on your way out here?"

"That's not the same thing at all."

"It is. You happily put them out of their misery for a few hours when you knocked them out."

"That's where you're wrong. I wasn't happy about it. I had to do what I had to do to survive."

"That's what I'm doing, too." He growls, taking a step toward me. His eyes reflect the moonlight, and I start walking again before I notice more.

"You're not surviving by trying to get my attention, Rayne. You're playing with fire."

"But I am surviving." He speeds up to walk ahead of me, then turns and stops.

I hold on to my firewood tightly, so I don't drop my load as I stop suddenly, too.

"I can't conquer the world, Vela, stuck in this backwoods little place. Because of my two gifts, I'll be hunted my entire life if I try to go out into the world. All I have is to make a life for myself as best I can. I want the kind of thing most everyone else has found out here. Love. And, so far, no one has caught my eye, until you."

The wind picks up and starts blowing my hair around.

"So, you can believe for my survival, my sanity, I'm going to attempt to get your attention. If you don't like it, I'm sorry, but I have to try. And if I'm playing with fire, I literally will do that. I'm not afraid of a Festan. What I am afraid of is going through life not going after something, someone, I want. Don't hate me for that. Please." His eyes spear into me, and I know if he wasn't holding onto a pile of firewood, he'd be trying to hold me right now.

I've never been so thankful for firewood because I don't know what I would do if he did try.

His words have splintered and destroyed all my previous thoughts about Rayne. I understand him a little better now, at least.

I clear my throat. "I don't know what you want me to say."

His throat works before he says, "I don't want you to say anything. Just know where I stand."

"You can't hurt Linc. No matter what you think about Intended bonds. He's off limits."

"I can't promise that," he says in a deep voice.

"You have to. That's non-negotiable. If you hurt him, you hurt me. We're connected, remember?"

He pauses. "Fine. I don't want to purposely hurt you. I'll agree. But that all goes away when we're on the training field."

"As long as it's for training. No life-or-death situations with Linc."

"Agreed."

We walk back in tense silence. I glance at Rayne, and he does the same, except he has a smile.

What will this negotiation look like in the near future? I shake my head at him, not sure what I just agreed to.

CHAPTER THIRTY-TWO

Despite missing Linc, the dinner goes smoothly. I absolutely love the bread on a stick and wish Linc could have tried it.

"They're better than s'mores," I tell Hannah as I pull a soft piece of bread off the stick.

Greta giggles. "What are...s'mores?" she asks, her face scrunched up adorably, reaching her stick into the fire to cook another breadstick.

Rayne waits for the answer, too, his eyes curious.

"Oh, man. S'mores are amazing. Please tell me you guys have tried chocolate."

Rayne and Greta both nod, and I breathe a sigh of relief.

"I don't know how I would have explained that to you if you hadn't. S'mores are basically two sweet pieces of crackers with melted chocolate and a roasted marshmallow in between. You roast the marshmallow over the fire until it's hot and golden. So, it's a delicious, gooey mess."

"Marsh-what?" Greta asks.

I hit my forehead. "Okay, next time you guys get staples in town, ask for a bag of marshmallows too. It's a soft, white piece of candy, I guess, that are little cubes. You can just eat them by themselves or with chocolate in between two graham crackers."

Rayne shakes his head and laughs. "It sounds complicated."

"Oh, Momma, I wanna' try one!" Greta cries.

"You will, princess, one day." She looks at Andy, who's gazing at her with affection. He looks away, his cheeks a little pink at being caught.

I hide a smile.

Once we polish off dinner, Andy excuses himself to leave, but it's clear he doesn't want to go.

"I've signed up for an early hunting detail," he explains. "I should get some rest. It's already ten o'clock."

"Sure," Hannah says. "Thank you for coming, Andy."

"Thank you for having me," he responds warmly.

Once he leaves, she, Greta, and I clean up the kitchen and plates. Hannah shoos Rayne to the clinic, which he reluctantly enters after glancing back at me.

Hannah turns to me. "You don't have to help me wake him every hour, Vela. I can do it. I've done it lots of time on my own."

"No," I say quickly. "I'm here to help. How about I take the first half of the night, you do the second? I'll wake him up on the hour for four hours, then I'll get a solid four hours of sleep. Same with you."

Her eyes flash with relief. "Thank you, Vela. If you're sure?"

"I'm sure."

"Okay, well, we're off to bed. I'll set my alarm for 3 a.m. Thank you, Vela." She turns with Greta, and they go into her room and close the door.

I walk into Greta's room and grab my phone. I've been able to charge it on a battery since I've gotten here, so I set the alarm for every hour until 2 a.m. After making sure it's on, I promptly fall asleep.

The alarm dutifully wakes me up with its blaring, and I swing my legs off the bed and pad over to the clinic, the socks on my feet protecting me from the cold floor.

I find Rayne still awake and lying with one arm under his head. He's looking out the window at the moon shining through.

"Why aren't you sleeping?" I ask softly from the doorway.

He turns to look at me and cracks a smile. "I don't know. I was just thinking."

I lean on the doorframe. "You've been thinking for the past hour?"

He regards me silently. "Yes."

"Okay, well, you need your rest. So, it's time for sleep."

He smirks, his trademark look. "Are you telling me it's time to go to bed like a good boy?"

I snort. "You are no good boy Rayne, so no."

He picks himself up and leans on his elbow. "You don't think I'm a good guy, is that it?"

"Is that it? Rayne, you've been pretty relentless since I got here. How am I supposed to respond to that?"

He swings out of bed and walks over to me. I retreat several steps into the hallway. He follows and takes me by the elbow, bringing me back to the clinic. My heart kicks up speed.

"I just want a chance like anyone else. Can you do that, Vela? Let me prove to you I'm worthy."

Breathless at how close he is to me, I say, "It's not that you're not worthy, Rayne, it's just my heart is..."

"Taken, I know. Believe me, I know." His eyes flash in frustration and he turns his head.

"Linc isn't just anyone, Rayne. He's everything to me."

He faces me. "Give me a chance, Vela. Let me show you I'm a good guy, too. Let me be your friend."

"I'd like a friend, but nothing else. I've already got the only boyfriend I want," I say firmly.

His eyes become determined, and he straightens and takes a step forward.

He's too close.

I try to step back, but he makes me stumble with one word. "Stop."

I look at him incredulously.

"Don't tell me you're not affected by me, Vela. You feel something, I'm sure of it. We both do." His brown eyes darken dangerously.

I catch my breath and this time I do step back. "I don't feel anything."

"Liar."

I turn and stomp out of the room. "Wake yourself up," I seethe.

"You'll be back," he calls after me.

"Only because you're my patient," I call back.

I stumble into my room and put my hand on my pounding chest as I lean back on the closed door. He does affect me. I hate thinking that, but it's true. His brutal honesty is arresting. I can't help but admire him for it.

But I won't wake him up for any reason other than as a nurse to her patient. I just pray my heart catches up to that idea.

CHAPTER THIRTY-THREE

A couple of days go by in a quiet way. My new girl-friends come by and raid my precious store of clothes. Thankfully, I only have to say goodbye to three shirts and the ones I receive in return are cuter than I expected. Greta and I have our special day. We had to wait until her school day was over, which gave me time to follow Hannah around and meet more of the community.

Linc is busy learning the art of carpentry from Rick. I love to see him covered in sawdust. There's something about seeing him with his sleeves rolled up and covered with wood shavings that's undeniably attractive. He laughs at me for saying so, but I don't care.

I've run into Rayne a few times. But it's been when I'm alone or with Hannah. Other than a few flirtatious comments, he's been relatively safe to be around. I say 'safe' because ever since he declared his intentions, I've been wary, but strangely much more understanding. I'm worried that if he really tries to win me over, I'll be susceptible.

I don't want to be susceptible. I'm gorgeously happy with Linc. And what my betrayal would do to Linc, I shudder to think about.

This morning, Jack and I are walking with Hannah to check on Sally.

"I know you're worried about her," I say to Hannah, laying my hand on her arm. "Do you think it's time to induce her labor?"

Her face is set in worry. "I really don't want to unless it's the last option. But it looks like it's going that way, unfortunately."

Shireen calls from her doorway, "Hannah! Can you come by?"

Hannah stops. "I'm sorry Shireen, I can't right now. I'll come by later if that's okay?"

Shireen grimaces and grumbles, "If that's how it has to be." She gives Jack a dirty look and walks inside.

"It is." Hannah walks away and I follow, wondering what that was about.

"She has pain in her joints. She likes me to heal her aches and pains on a regular basis," she whispers.

I shake my head. "Between Rayne manipulating the healing system to Shireen abusing it, I don't know how you handle it all, Hannah."

She sighs. She was not happy when I told her that Rayne had purposely gotten himself injured in an attempt to get my attention. I haven't told her about the wake-up call conversation—I'm keeping that one to myself.

"It's all part of the job, I guess," she says. "I tell you what, though, Rayne is a piece of work. I'm going to have a talk with him about his little act of romance. Honestly, I've never heard of such a thing."

I scoff. "Believe me, neither have I, and I've lived in a Gyan community. He blew my mind."

We're passing the training grounds where young and old alike are paired off to practice. I see Rayne right away spinning a staff and bringing it down to connect with Leon's staff. They move in what looks like a choreographed dance, both turning in fluid movements, meeting strike for strike.

In the middle of a spin, Rayne locks eyes with me and winks. He completes his move, his body turning in a complicated motion that would make my head spin. Twirling his staff in the air, he brings it back down on Leon's with a hard whack.

His shirt does nothing to hide his very nice build, and I blush and look away, continuing to walk.

Hannah looks sideways at me, softly laughing. "Oh, girl. I would not want to be in your shoes. How did Linc take Rayne's attempt to woo you, by the way?"

I cringe. "I haven't told him. I literally can't. If Linc knew I bargained with Rayne to keep his hands off him, he'd be livid. There's no way he'd take that news well."

"And if he knew the lengths Rayne went to, I'm sure he'd hate that, too."

"Honestly, I think he suspects it. He's dropped a few comments that he's not sure Rayne was even injured."

We reach Sally's door and Hannah knocks. "He was definitely injured. Didn't he see the blood?"

I nod as the door opens. Ruth breathes a sigh of relief when she sees us. "Oh, thank God," she says, pulling us inside.

"Can Jack come in, too?" I ask. "He'll be good. I'll have him stay right by the door."

She nods quickly and takes our coats, laying them on a bench by the door.

Sally calls from the back of the house. "Please tell me that's Hannah!"

"It is, Mom," Ruth calls back.

I order Jack to lay down, which he does promptly.

Hannah and I walk into a room where Sally lies in what looks to be an uncomfortable position. Really, every position she's in looks unbearable. That baby needs to come out.

"Okay, Sally, let's hope there's some dilation today. That's the news we need."

Ruth helps her mom sit up and move into a position to be checked.

Hannah leaves to wash her hands and comes back into the room. She kneels and looks under Sally's blanket. After a moment of tense silence, she straightens with a grave face.

Sally's face falls and she groans. "Still nothing?"

Hannah wipes her hands off with a towel and turns to Sally and Ruth. "It's time to take the next step. Your baby can't get much bigger or I'm afraid he or she'll get stuck in the birth canal."

Sally turns her head, her face pinched in worry. "Can we wait for Jim to come home?"

"Of course. Vela and I will come back tonight. I'll give you a tea that will help induce contractions." Hannah says this in a brisk and business-like tone, but I can see this news distresses her, too.

"It's safe?" Sally asks.

"Safe enough. I'll be sure to give you the right amount. We're going to do this with much prayer, Sally."

Sally nods tiredly and rests her head on Ruth's shoulder when she leans in to hug her mom's side.

We leave Sally's and I'm a bundle of nerves in anticipation of tonight. I say prayer after prayer under my breath as I walk with Hannah back to the Hobbit house. She must be doing the same, because I see her mouth moving from the side of my eye.

We're passing the training grounds again when I see Linc stroll up to the group, still practicing with staffs.

"Hannah, wait." I put my hand on her arm.

When Linc asks to join the training, my hand tightens on Hannah's arm. I look at Rayne, who's looking at Linc with glee.

"Oh no," I say quietly. *Does Linc know how to even use those? Rayne will destroy him.*

Hannah puts her hand on mine.

Someone throws Linc a staff, which he catches easily. He turns it around with both hands and then, to my complete surprise, spins it around his head like he knows exactly what he's doing with it.

"I think he's going to be just fine," Hannah says in admiration.

I watch when he walks right up to Rayne. He gestures to him and says something I wish I could hear.

Whatever Linc says causes Rayne to throw his head back and laugh. Linc's back is to me, but I can still see the tense lines of his body at Rayne's amusement.

I can't take my eyes off the scene before me. Even Jack is watching from my side. Everyone seems to know a good match is about to start because the other sparring stops, and everyone moves to watch Linc and Rayne.

Linc's face is set in angry lines. I can only hope his emotions won't get the better of him during the fight. Anger can either aid you or completely hinder you.

Rayne's face, in contrast, is completely different. He's enjoying himself or is about to.

They move, circling one another. Both are holding their staffs, two-handed, ready for anything. Rayne is first to attack, bringing his staff down hard on Linc's. Linc, in a move that shows hours of practice, throws Rayne's staff up and away, spinning around him, only to bring his weapon down, almost cracking Rayne's head open.

Rayne blocks the move from behind, but just barely. His face has changed to a more calculated one. He spins to face Linc and gives him a respectful nod then jousts his weapon into Linc's stomach.

Linc smacks Rayne's staff away almost lazily. Then, there's a flurry of moves that I can barely keep track of. They both attack and defend in a mix of turns and spins.

I'm in complete awe of them both, but especially of Linc. Where did he learn how to fight with a staff? What I'm witnessing is hours and hours of specialized training. Rayne, I can understand, he was born here. But Linc? His parents must have had a hand in teaching him this skill.

Because that's what this is. A show of pure skill. They're both sweating and breathing heavily at this point. Both their arms bulge with muscle and I can't decide who looks in better shape for this.

While I thought Rayne and Leon's practice looked like a dance, what Linc and Rayne are doing is something far more dangerous, deadly even.

After a few more complicated moves, they're face to face. Linc says something to Rayne, which contorts his face into fury. He pushes Linc back hard and he almost goes down.

Linc keeps to his feet though, and with a roar, lunges back to Rayne. Linc spins his staff above his head, then bringing it ferociously down towards Rayne's arm.

I cry out, thinking he's going to break Rayne's arm, but he manages to block the move. They meet, and Linc pushes his staff down as Rayne pushes his up. It's a force of will and strength. Linc has the upper hand, in my opinion, as he's pushing down. He's using both his arms to rid Rayne of his staff. But Rayne holds on, planting his feet to resist the momentum.

They both grunt in exertion, and I hold my breath at what's going to happen.

"Give up!" Linc yells in Rayne's face. I know Linc is referring to more than just this sparring match.

"You know that's not going to happen," Rayne seeths.

Linc sweeps his foot under Rayne's and they both go down. Linc is quickly on top of Rayne, pushing his staff into Rayne's neck.

"I win. And believe me when I say, I always will," Linc says in Rayne's face.

When it's clear Rayne won't be able to get up without Linc allowing him to, the crowd starts clapping, turning, and whispering to each other.

They part when Linc gets up and throws his staff to the ground next to Rayne's head. He walks away without a backwards glance.

I'm not sure if he knew I was watching. It was like it was his personal mission to throw Rayne down.

I turn stunned eyes to Hannah, who looks as impressed as I'm sure I do. "Oh, honey. Now I do wish I were in your shoes."

We both watch Linc walk back away with a resolute look on his face.

"Do you think he saw you?" Hannah asks.

"I really don't know. He was amazing though, wasn't he?" I breathe as I watch him move in long, confident steps. I look on in pure admiration at how his muscles flex because of the fight. I've never seen him look so good.

"I think I made it clear that yes, he was amazing." Hannah fans her face.

"Hey! He's mine," I say, laughing and pushing her shoulder playfully.

"I think he just made that known to everyone out here, Vela dear."

I shake my head, more than a little impressed by my Intended.

"If that wasn't a keep-your-hands-off-my-girl show of force, I don't know what it was. Some men only respond to physical threats and intimidation. Words just don't work for them. I think Linc knows Rayne is one of those men."

I'm silenced by her words. They make sense, but I'm not sure how to feel. On one hand, I'm impressed and honored Linc would go to such lengths to claim me. On the other hand, I wonder if it will work. Will Rayne back off and leave me alone? Or will what just happened make him more determined?

I guess we'll have to wait and see.

I rub Jack's head mindlessly as we walk back in silence. My mind goes over and over Linc's moves until I'm burning with a need to talk to him.

"Do you mind if I go?" I ask Hannah when we reach her door.

"No, I certainly don't. You fan out that fire your guy has burning."

"I'm not sure I want to. It looks too good on him," I say, smiling. "Can I leave Jack here with you? I'll be just a minute."

"Sure! I'd love to puppysit."

Ordering Jack to stay, I turn and make my way down the street to Rick's. I almost don't know what I'm going to say to my Intended after that show.

Reaching Rick's door, I knock on it and wait impatiently.

Rick opens it and motions me inside without a word. He points to a door, and I knock on it, having learned my lesson very clearly from the one time I didn't.

"Just a minute," Linc says from inside.

I stay quiet and wait.

He opens the door as if he was expecting Rick, but then looks down when he sees me. He's drying his wet hair with a towel.

I go into some sort of shock when I notice Linc's bare chest. I cannot stop staring in awe at the physique of my Intended. Sweat or water from the shower trickles down his muscles, and I close my mouth when I realize it's hanging open. His scent is overpowering, almost as if his shirt usually contains it. Now that his shirt is off, I can't help but inhale deeply. Forcing my eyes up to meet Linc's, I blush when I see his smirk.

It reminds me so much like Rayne's trademark expression, I glance away.

"I saw you spar just now," I say softly, suddenly nervous.

He nods as he puts his arms up on the doorway and leans in toward me. "I know."

"You knew? You didn't let me distract you. That's good," I say lamely, my breath catching at his nearness.

"Distract me? You fueled me, Vela."

I look into his beautiful sapphire eyes that are glistening and shining at me. "I did?"

He leans in to whisper into my ear, "See something you like?"

I blush deeper and lean back. "I had no idea you could fight so well with a staff."

"You didn't answer my question," he says with a knowing smile.

"How could I not?" I look up at him, desire coloring my face.

"Not answer my question or how you could you not like what you see? Which question are you answering, Vela?"

Blushing to the roots of my hair, I say, "You know, Linc. Are you going to make me say it?"

"Yes."

I huff and cross my arms in front of my chest. "Fine. I really like what I saw then and what I see now. Happy?"

"Very." Leaning in quickly, he captures my arms and pulls me toward him. He tips my head up. "Does the victor get a kiss?"

I look over my shoulder. "Here?" I squeak.

He brings his lips down on mine in answer and all my fears of where Rick might be fly out of my head. I melt in Linc's arms and press into his kiss. Bringing my hands up, I circle them around his neck, relishing the feel of his wet hair. I reward his every move today with a kiss that rivals all others we've shared.

Linc growls and spins me around so that my back is on the doorjamb. He deepens our kiss, and I get lost in his arms.

I hear a throat clearing. I'm so absorbed, I don't acknowledge the noise until Linc breaks away. He looks back, and I immediately see Rick standing just behind Linc with an unhappy look.

"None of that in this house, please," Rick says with a deep frown.

I hide my face behind my hands.

"Yes, sir," Linc says, then takes one of my hands away from my red face, pulling me toward the door.

"Come back in an hour. Let me get dressed. We'll go on that picnic."

"Okay," I agree, stuffing down the humiliating experi-ence.

"Can you get some stuff together for it?"

I nod, and then with a quick goodbye, I flee. I've not been that embarrassed in a long time.

CHAPTER THIRTY-FOUR

When I return to Hannah's, Jack sniffs me thoroughly and curls around my legs.

"He was quite distraught with you gone," Hannah says, looking sympathetically down at Jack. "He cried most of the time."

Kneeling, I love on my poor baby. "He's pretty attached to me. I'll try not to leave him alone again."

Hannah nods, and I quickly tell her where I'm going. She helps me gather a few things for my picnic with Linc.

"Vela, have a good time, but please be back in time for Sally's delivery."

"Of course."

As I get ready, I have to admit I'm a little nervous about my date with Linc. I don't know why. A part of me is sure something will happen, something bad. It's an ominous feeling and I can't shake it. Maybe it's because Linc so roundly trounced Rayne. I'm expecting retaliation of some kind because I don't see Rayne taking defeat well.

Another concern is that if I'm completely alone with Linc, we might not be so good, like we're trying to be. We both want to honor God in our relationship, so I don't think we'll go further than kissing, but today proved how quickly a kiss can escalate. If Rick hadn't been there to douse the fire with his cool gaze, what else would have happened?

I resolve to talk to Linc about these things. It's best to keep my concerns in the open instead of the dark, where they can fester.

Hannah shows me where everything is so I can put together a basket of food. After I'm satisfied with the food choices, I pick it up, checking to be sure I put a canteen of water in it. Seeing there's not, I grab one and fill it, again thanking God for running water in the middle of nowhere.

Taking a deep breath and saying a prayer asking for strength to resist Linc's many charms, I leave the house with Jack at my side this time.

I'm barely outside the door when I hear my name being called. I look behind me, and I see Tonya running to catch up to me.

"Hey," she says breathlessly.

She's wearing one of my shirts, and I smile because it looks good on her.

"So, I heard all about the training exercises today." Her eyes are gleaming, and she's practically vibrating with her need to talk about my drama.

"Yea," I say, awkwardly. "It was quite the spectacle."

"Spectacle? Leon is the *only* one who can even hope to touch Rayne with the staff. It's phenomenal there's someone else who can actually beat him!" She looks at me in awe.

"Umm, yeah, I didn't even know Linc knew how to fight with a staff."

"Vela, this is awesome! If he's that good, think what else he can teach us? Especially those who have the Festan gift."

I scratch my head. She hasn't mentioned the reason Linc fought with Rayne. So, I keep quiet. I certainly don't want to be the one to start a rumor about that.

"I'm sure he'd be happy to teach everyone what he knows." I laugh half-heartedly.

"Well, if I can be his first pupil, that would be great. I mean, not with the Festan gift, but with the staff. What I wouldn't give to beat Rayne into the dirt like Linc did. I'd do anything for that pleasure." A fierce light shines in her eyes, and I wonder if she loves to hate Rayne or hates to love him. Both are interchangeable sometimes, and it seems to be that way with her and Rayne.

I also wonder if I can ever tell her what he told me the other night. When she says, "It's my dying wish to put him in his place," I think, probably not.

She just now notices my basket. "Oh, are you going on a picnic?"

I smile. "Yes, with Linc. It's our first date since we arrived."

"Oh, well, go and have fun. Sorry to take up your time. I just had to call dibs on being the first one to train with your Intended. If that's okay with you?" She suddenly steps back and looks me in the eye, like she's misstepped somehow.

"No, of course, it's fine. Please, don't think I'm some controlling, jealous girlfriend. I'm not."

"Good," she breathes with a sigh of relief. "You never know."

"Right. Well, I'd better get going."

She says goodbye, and I make my way to Rick's, knocking on the door after a fortifying breath.

Linc opens the door this time, thankfully completely clothed and ready to go. He greets Jack with a hello and a scratch behind his ears, which Jack eats up like candy.

We're soon on our way to the forest, Linc leading the way.

"Where are we going on this picnic, anyway?" I ask and hand Linc the basket when he reaches for it.

"I spotted a place when I was gathering wood for Rick's last project," Linc answers.

My heart thrums in anticipation and a little worry that we'll be way off the beaten path. I push those worries down because Linc is a complete gentleman, and he would never push me for more than I'm willing to do. I also know he feels the same way I do about saving certain things for marriage, so maybe my worries are all for nothing.

"Where did you learn how to fight like that?" I ask instead of bringing up my concerns.

He smiles and interlinks his fingers with mine. "I guess I've never told you about my history with weapons."

"No, you definitely haven't."

"Well, I'm proficient in pretty much every weapon there is. Gun, bow, knives, staff. You name the weapon, and I've probably been trained in it."

My eyebrows lift. "Wow. How long have you been training with them?"

He sighs and looks up at the trees. "Oh, I've had a weapon in my hand just about since I could walk."

"Linc, you were incredible today. I've never seen anything like that. Tonya called dibs on you training her first, by the way."

He laughs. "Oh, really? That shouldn't be a problem."

"She seems to think I'd have a problem with you training her. But, unlike some, I'm not a jealous person."

He looks at me with a smile. "Oh, really? You weren't jealous of Maria?"

"She was different. I had a right to be worried about her. She made every intention of you known."

He huffs. "I can relate."

I squeeze his hand. "Linc. You don't need to worry about Rayne. I know what today was really about."

"He needs to know I won't sit back and watch him go after my girl. I'm quite capable of beating him bloody if he tries."

I sigh. "You won't have to beat him bloody."

"Vela, you don't know that. There's only one language he understands when it comes to you."

"That's what Hannah said, too."

Linc leads us down a pretty trail through sun-dappled trees. The October air has brought color into the leaves, making them look like fire has made its home in their branches. Reds, oranges, and yellows frame my view.

We've reached a drop in the trail and Linc stops us at the edge. I'm not looking down the steep embankment, though. My eyes are on the vista. An ocean of fall colors is before me, with trees as far as the eye can see. Every shade of red and orange is represented in the sight, and I marvel at God's incredible paint pallet. I inhale deeply, and Linc steps up behind me, wrapping his arms around my middle.

"Like it?" he asks in my ear.

I lean back and say, "Mm,hmmm. I love it. It's absolutely gorgeous."

"I thought you'd like it. I've wanted to bring you here since I saw it." He squeezes me, and I place my hands on his. He nuzzles my neck, creating a path of goosebumps all over me.

Deciding I have to talk to him about my fears, I lean away from him. "Linc. I need to talk to you."

"Now?" he complains, reaching for me when I pull completely away from him. "I was just getting comfortable."

"That's what I want to talk to you about." I turn and look at him, putting my hands on his chest when he pulls me toward him. I push him gently away, needing the distance.

Fire seems to explode between us every time there's contact. I need space to think about what I want to say with a clear mind.

"Vela, what's wrong?" he asks, looking worried.

"Nothing's wrong. That's just it. Everything is so right, so perfect. It worries me."

"What could be wrong about everything being perfect?"

"It's not wrong. It's just that," I stop and look away from him, trying to get my thoughts together.

I look back, and he's looking at me, waiting. He looks painfully beautiful. I turn my head to avoid looking at him.

"Vela, you're really worrying me now."

"Sorry. I'm just so happy when I'm with you. In fact, I'm too happy." I reluctantly face him, my face burning.

He cocks his eyebrow at me. "Vela, I'm lost."

"That's it! So am I when I'm alone with you. I get lost in your arms. I almost lose myself and my intentions of being good."

"Ahh," he breathes, suddenly understanding. He leans back on his heels, crossing his arms over his chest. He smiles at me, looking relieved. "So, you're afraid I'll compromise your virtue?"

"What? No, you're a perfect gentleman. You always have been, in that respect. I'm just afraid we'll go too far one day. We seem to..."

"Make music together?" He looks at me with a soft expression.

"I guess. I've never heard that saying before."

"I have an aunt I love who used to say that perfect moments are when you make music together with someone. I had no idea what she meant until you. Now, I know exactly."

I step toward him. "Linc, you are a lethal package for me. You have the looks, the moves, the *scent*, God knows what that does to me. I just don't want to go too far and then regret it. I don't want to regret anything when it comes to you."

He reaches for me, running his hands up and down my arms. "Hey, you don't have to worry about that. I would never ask you that of you. While I can't wait until you're my wife, which I really hope one day you will be, I can wait for marriage to do those things with you." He takes a deep breath. "Trust me when I say it's not easy to make that promise. But that's one promise you can always depend on me to keep. I already told you I'd be good; do you need me to back off a little?"

Now, this is what I love about Linc. He respects me and our mutual decision. He is a gentleman, and I can trust that he will help me resist the urges he causes. He cares deeply about all things that are important to him and I'm obviously one of those things. My heart fills with love for him, and I lurch into his arms, bringing my arms around his neck.

"Is that a no?" he asks, his eyes surprised.

"It's a yes, but Linc, please kiss me."

"You're going to make my promise very hard to keep, aren't you?"

My response is pulling his head down to meet his lips with mine.

CHAPTER THIRTY-FIVE

I have a perfect afternoon with Linc. We take our time with the picnic and just enjoy each other's company now that we aren't in mortal peril. I make it back to Hannah's in plenty of time, and I'm glad I arrive early. When I walk in the door, I see that Hannah's getting the red raspberry tea ready. I study everything she does. She's meticulous as she gathers the leaves of the raspberry plant together.

"So, it's just the leaf you use?" I ask as she gathers three dried leaves and puts them in a wooden bowl.

Using a pestle, she nods and starts carefully grinding the leaves. "I can't give her too much or it will cause too many contractions and distress the baby."

Her face is set in concentration, and I allow her silence to do her next steps.

She takes a metal teapot and puts it on the burner.

"Okay, let's let that get hot and then we'll steep the tea."

"Hannah, can we use our gift to help with labor?"

She looks up and shakes her head. "I dearly wish we could. The only thing we can do is help her with the pain. Even then, I can take the edge off, but not all of it."

I slump. "Okay, well, let me know what I can do."

"I will. Let's get that water on these tea leaves."

She pours the hot water over the tea. She has a second cup waiting, which I look at curiously. After a few minutes, she takes a spoon, then holds the tea leaves back while she carefully pours the brewed tea into the empty cup.

"Okay, let's go," Hannah says and gathers the second cup in her hands, holding it protectively against her chest.

"Where's Greta, by the way?"

"She's spending the night at Betsy's. She can't bear to leave those kittens, anyway."

I order Jack to stay home and hope he doesn't howl and cry while I'm gone. But there's no way he could be there during Sally's labor. Who knows how he'd react? And I need my concentration to be on Sally and her baby, not my dog.

Come to think of it, I'm not sure how I'm going to react, for that matter.

Following Hannah down the street, I'm thankful no one stops us as we make our way to Sally's house.

We knock on the door and it's promptly opened by a man I assume is Sally's husband, Jim. His face is pinched in worry, and he ushers us in quickly.

"You have what you need to get things started?" he asks in a quiet voice.

Hannah nods toward the cup she's cradling.

We walk into the bedroom and find Sally lying on her side, her arms wrapped protectively around her large, round stomach. Ruth stands next to her bed, trying to look brave.

Ruth holds Sally up and Hannah hands her the cup telling her to only drink half of it.

"Let's see how much that does before you drink more," Hannah instructs.

Sally nods and then lays back down, strain lining her face. Jim sits on one side of her bed while Ruth claims the other.

"Now we wait," Hannah says, rubbing her hands down her pant legs. "It shouldn't take long."

After about twenty minutes, Hannah puts her hands on Sally's stomach and closes her hands as she concentrates.

She picks her head up quickly when Sally inhales deeply.

"I feel a contraction," Sally breathes, her face bright with a smile.

"It's working, thank God." Hannah says straightening. She lays a blanket over Sally and then discreetly checks her. After a moment, she rises quickly and says to everyone, "She's dilated, that's perfect. Now, let's let things progress naturally." She looks us all over. "This could take hours, so we can't get too excited."

Hannah and I spend the next couple of hours taking turns easing what labor pains we can. She also shows me what dilation looks like, with Sally's permission. I'm learning so much in this experience. I'm only too happy to help with my Gyan ability when Hannah gets tired. As Jim is a Festan and Sally a Neronian, Ruth doesn't have the Gyan healing gift, so it's up to Hannah and me to help however we can.

It's late in the night when Sally cries out from a contraction, exhaustion showing on her face. "I feel something different," she says, breathing hard.

Hannah lays her hands on Sally's stomach. When her face turns white, I lurch into action.

Laying my hand on Sally to see what Hannah sees, I gasp when I don't sense a second heartbeat. I turn panicked eyes to Hannah, who's waiting to see if I feel the same thing.

Taking one look at my face, she jumps into action. "We need to move Sally. Everyone, help us."

"What's wrong?" Jim cries.

"The baby is in distress. It could be the umbilical cord wrapped around their neck. We need to change her position to see if it will shift," Hannah says hurriedly.

The four of us guide Sally to a position on all fours when she cries out, "I need to push!"

Hannah quickly gets into position. "Push, Sally! You can do it!"

After a breathless few minutes and a cry from Sally as she bears down, Hannah holds her hands and receives the baby.

My heart holds still. Hannah's holding the tiny new infant, but something's wrong. The baby isn't crying. Even I know babies aren't happy when they come into this world. They're usually screaming.

Hannah unwraps the umbilical cord from around his neck. She was right. He was in distress. I quickly see it's a boy.

She flips him over and whacks his back with a few careful blows. When he still doesn't cry, she turns him back over and lays him on the bed.

Tears are falling down my face as I watch Hannah attempt to resuscitate the new baby. He's so small, she can't use her whole hand to pump his chest, but she does with her fingers.

Sally and Jim are sobbing in the bed, watching Hannah trying to save their son.

Hannah doesn't give up and finally, after an agonizing few minutes, a weak wail fills the air.

We all cry out in joy, and I run over to Ruth and hug her fiercely. Tears of relief pour down both our faces.

I race back over to Hannah, who's busy cutting the cord and cleaning off the brand-new baby boy. She places him in Sally's arms, who openly sobs.

"Oh God, thank you. He's beautiful," she says as Jim lays a hand over his son's head, crying himself.

Hannah steps back, and I put my arm around her shoulder and squeeze. "Hannah, you did an amazing job."

Her shoulders tremble. "We almost lost him," she says quietly, tears leaving trails down her cheeks.

"I know."

She leans her head on mine, and we watch the family coo, in awe of their new addition.

Hannah and I gather the soiled linens and towels in a pile at the door.

Jim unfolds his body from the bed and walks over to Hannah. "You saved my son's life, Hannah. There's no measure of thanks I can give." He takes her hand in his and folds it in both of his large ones. "In your honor, we're naming him after your late husband, Tom. We'll call our son, Tommy."

Hannah utters a soft cry, and more tears slip down her cheeks. She wordlessly hugs Jim for a long moment. "He would have liked that," she says into his shoulder.

After she releases him, he turns to me and says, "You both had a hand in bringing Tommy into this world. Thank you."

I blush and say, "I'm only too happy to help. Hannah is the real hero."

He looks at her and nods his head. "I won't forget this, Hannah."

She wipes her wet cheeks with one hand and puts her other hand on his shoulder. "It was by the grace of God. And you'd do the same if you could, Jim. I know that."

After a few checks on the baby and mother, we leave the happy home.

As we walk to the Hobbit House in the quiet night, I hold on to the towels we promised to wash and look up into the starry sky. "It's amazing, isn't it?"

Hannah looks at me with a smile. "Do you mean the birth? Or everything?" She motions to the entire sky.

"Everything. Creation, how God breathes life into us, and in exchange, we live our lives for him. Or those of us who believe in Him, at least. It's hard to imagine a life without God. I mean, how else could you explain tonight's miracle?"

"There are some who would say I saved little Tommy," she says softly. "But I know it was God's hands guiding mine tonight. I know that as well as I have breath. I could feel Him instructing me."

"Yes, but you're open to His guidance. That's the difference. Imagine what would have happened if you relied only on yourself tonight."

"We would have lost him," she says quietly.

By this time, we've reached home. Hannah tiredly opens the door and we're immediately greeted by Jack.

He sniffs every inch of me, and I allow him as I walk into Greta's room. I say goodnight to Hannah and fall into my bed, exhaustion quickly claiming me.

CHAPTER THIRTY-SIX

Hannah allows me to sleep in the next morning while she goes over to Sally's to check on her and the baby.

After sleeping the morning away, I find a note on the bedside table telling me to take time to relax today. When I finally haul my sleepy behind out of bed, I decide to try my hand at training today. So, I dress in workout clothes and plan to take Jack with me. He usually allows me to train, but I've never tried training with a staff, so I'm not sure how he'll react.

Greta must be at school because I'm alone in the house. I inhale a biscuit on my way out the door.

Jack's at my side when we walk over to see if Linc wants to join us at the training grounds. It's a glorious day, and I'm happy to be outside. The sun shines brightly, warming up the chilly day. There's not a cloud in sight.

A sight stops me before I get to Linc's door. Grace is painting the same house she was the other day. I walk over to her.

"Hello," I say in a cheerful tone. I hold Jack to my side, understanding he might intimidate Grace.

She jumps and looks over her shoulder at me. She scrambles back when she sees Jack.

"Oh, don't worry. He's really gentle." I hold up my hand. "Please don't leave."

Grace turns terrified eyes to Jack, then to me. She seems to war with her decision to stay or go.

I wait, hoping she'll stay.

Finally, she says, gripping her paintbrush, "I heard what you did for Sally."

Her eyes flick from Jack to me and I say sincerely, "It was my pleasure to help. But really, it was all Hannah and God. He saved Tommy through Hannah."

She smiles, and it warms her face. "I heard that, too, and I'm glad. Babies are wonderful." A wistful expression comes over her face.

"Are you looking forward to having a family already?" I ask, surprised. She's my age.

She blushes and nods quickly, looking down. "Someday."

"Well, I'm sure it'll happen. Anyone caught your eye around here?" I look around, noticing several young guys walking or working around the place.

"No, not yet," she says, blushing prettily. She twists the paintbrushes in her hand. "I want more than anything to find my Intended like you have." Her eyes shine at the thought.

My stomach clenches in worry because that possibility, especially out here, is so low. "You very well might," I tell her instead.

We both jump when Rayne walks up to us and says, "Hey. How's it going?"

How I didn't notice his approach is beyond me. Jack normally alerts me when someone is walking up to us. I was so absorbed in my conversation with Grace, I must not have noticed Jack's reaction.

"Hello," I say politely. I note that Grace doesn't say anything at all. In fact, she seems to curl into herself at Rayne's presence.

Rayne glances at her, then asks us, "You two interested in training? We're using our gifts today."

Grace ignores him and turns around to continue her painting. He doesn't acknowledge her slight and just turns to looks at me, waiting for my answer.

What happened between those two? I burn with questions and answer, "Actually, I was hoping to train today."

"Good. You ready now?"

"Give me a minute."

He nods, and with one last look at Grace's back, he leaves.

"Grace?" I ask.

She turns and when she sees Rayne leave, she breathes a sigh that looks like relief.

"Is everything okay with Rayne and you?"

She scowls. "He's not someone I like to be around."

"Why? Is he a bad guy?" I ask, needing to know more about who's pursuing me.

Her face closes off. "I really don't want to talk about him."

She turns away and I can tell she's shut down this topic. I can only hope she'll trust me enough, one day, to tell me what happened. Because it's obvious something did.

"Okay. Well, hey, can you maybe show me this field of poppies you're painting someday? I'd love to see it."

She turns her head to study me for a moment. "Yeah, I can do that. They bloom in the spring, though. But there are other places I can show you that're pretty," she says shyly.

Elation fills me. She trusts me enough to spend time with me. "Great! Most days, I follow Hannah around. But I'll ask her what day we could go."

Grace smiles timidly. "Sounds good."

"Great! Well, I'd better be going."

She says goodbye in a quiet tone, and I leave her to her painting.

Turning toward the street, I go to Linc's, happy that he answers the door and is more than willing to train with me. He says a quick goodbye to Rick, who's working outside, and we head toward the training grounds, ready to practice our gifts.

"I'm looking forward to training today. Maybe I'll get to use the staff again," Linc says with a fierce shine to his eyes.

"Will you show me how to use one?"

He smiles down at me. "Anytime, young Padawan."

Excited to learn a new skill, I lead the way to the training grounds. I'm curious because I expected to hear people practicing by now. But when I reach the area, there's no one there. Linc and I look around, and I notice an older man sitting on his front doorstep whittling something.

Nudging Linc in the side, I walk toward the man. "Excuse me?" I ask.

He turns his lined face to me, and I'm hit with two elements: earth and wind.

I'm stunned for a moment, because I've only met young people with two gifts, but it makes sense that even long ago, a mixed-element couple found love.

He turns a tired face to us and says in a gravelly voice, "You must be the new couple." He studies us for a moment, then looks back down at his creation, a dog by the looks of it. He turns a mournful gaze to Jack, but then returns to his work.

"Yes, we are. We're sorry to bother you, but do you know where the training is happening today? I know there is some going on. I just don't know where."

He rubs chips of wood off his piece and peers up at me. "You two lookin' to fight today?"

"We'll try our best," Linc says with optimism.

He nods, then studies his piece again. "I'd go myself if I wasn't feelin' so poorly."

"Are you sick? Do you need Hannah to come by?" I ask.

He winces. "No. It's nothing, but a broken heart."

"Oh," I say, not knowing what else to do. I glance at Linc, who's studying the man's carving.

"My Brutus, here, is gone and I just don't have the heart to do much of anything except make this."

"What happened to him?" My heart goes out to this man.

"I don't know. I let him out a week ago, and he hasn't come home yet." He flicks pain-filled eyes at Jack, and I squeeze Jack's neck, reminding me he's here.

"I hope he comes home soon," I say with all my heart.

He nods. "I miss him. Can't bring myself to do much of anything. My missus is gone, too. Lost 'em both now."

"I'm so sorry," I say.

"I am, too," Linc adds.

The man turns his sad eyes to Jack and asks me, "Will he let me pet him?"

I nod eagerly and bring Jack over to him. Jack sniffs the man over and then sits back on his haunches while the man puts down his carving and pets Jack's head and rubs his ears.

"What's your name?" I ask.

"Jack."

"That's his name, too," I say with enthusiasm.

"Funny," he says, his eyes lighting up a little. "I felt a kindred spirit in him right away." He continues rubbing Jack's head. "Well, if you want to join in on the conditioning, you'll need to go that way. They're out in a field where they have more room."

"Okay, thank you."

He straightens, picking his piece and knife back up from the ground. "Have fun, young'uns."

"We'll try." Linc and I leave him, and I send a prayer up that God will bring the dog back soon.

We go in the direction he pointed, and I find myself thinking back to Grace. Why did she look scared of Rayne? What happened? Did he threaten her or something?

I think maybe I should tell Linc what I've noticed, but I decide to keep it to myself for now. I don't know what happened, and there's no sense accusing Rayne without actual proof.

In the distance, I see funnels of wind and water over the tops of trees. When I point it out to Linc, I can tell he's seen it, too.

Sure we're headed in the right direction now, we make our way to the field where everyone's practicing their gifts. Once there, I can only stand and watch for a moment, mesmerized by what I'm seeing. One girl is throwing a blast of wind with one hand and is holding a small cyclone of water in the other. When her sparring partner dodges the wind, she uses both her hands to make her water cyclone bigger until it's the size of her. Before she can attack with it, her opponent fans the flame in his hand. It roars to a huge inferno, turning into what looks like a fire tornado. When he pushes his hands toward the girl, she sends her waterspout over and the two meet and dissolve in a cloud of steam. The girl laughs. She gestures toward the man she's working with, and he walks over to her, flinging his arm over her shoulder.

I can feel my mouth drop open in surprise, but I can't seem to bring myself to close it. I've never seen elements getting along together like this, other than Linc and myself. It's amazing. My eyes turn to a Festan and Gyan facing off. Much like when I had my duel with Linc, the Festan guy lobs a fireball at the Gyan girl who flings up a clod of dirt to douse it.

I'm too absorbed in the fighting to notice, but Jack pushes his way in front of me, alerting me to someone approaching.

"You made it!" Rayne calls out.

"I did." I turn to Linc. "I brought Linc with me. Sorry it took so long to get here. We got to talking with Jack for a minute."

He lifts a brow. "Your dog?"

"No!" I laugh. "The older gentleman, Jack. The one who lost his dog. He was telling me about it."

An expression crosses Rayne's face that I interpret as sadness for the old man. "It's terrible the dog hasn't come back yet."

"It is. So, who do we pair off with?"

He looks at us in surprise. "You don't want to train together?"

"Oh, yes, we can! I just didn't know how you guys normally pair people off."

This entire time, Linc has been keeping a stony eye on Rayne. When Rayne turns to him, Linc turns a cool eye to the group, not looking at him.

"We usually leave it up to you to choose your training partner. But if you don't want to train together..."

Before he can finish, Linc puts his hand on the small of my back. "We'll train together." We leave before Rayne can respond.

Not knowing what to say, I whisper, "So, I thought we would learn how to fight in a group."

Linc nods. "I did, too. I'll be right back."

He strides to an older man who's off to the side, overseeing the fighting. I watch as Linc gestures to the group as he talks to the man. After a few minutes of conversation, a shrill whistle pierces the air, and everyone stops what they're doing.

The man calls out, "We're going to try something different today. Linc here suggested it, and I think it's a great idea." He has everyone's attention at this point. "We're going to split into two groups. Let's divide this area in half and split it up that way."

He sweeps one arm to the right and the other to the left. Depending on where we stand, we obey his command. I step off to the left. The man walks down the middle, counting how many are on each side. Linc walks over and stands at my side.

"What's that man's name?" I whisper to Linc.

"Gerald."

I fold my arms and wait for Gerald's further instructions.

After moving a couple of us around, Gerald stands on a stump in the middle of the clearing. This entire field is not a natural meadow, I notice. It's been cleared of trees, with stumps littering the area.

He yells, "Now, we're going to fight against each other. Rely on those on your side. They are your allies. You will fight with your element until you've incapacitated your opponent or are about to. Stop once you're about to deliver the lethal blow, and your opponent will step out of the fight. Help one another to win. This is for bragging rights at the next bonfire."

A cheer goes up, and I turn to Linc. "They've never done this before?"

He shrugs. "I guess not. I don't know why, though."

I put my hand on his shoulder. "It's a great idea. Good job."

He smirks. "Tell me that when we've won."

"I will."

I take Jack by the collar and lead him over to the sidelines. I order him to stay and can only hope he'll obey. I shouldn't be in danger, but if he perceives that I am, he might jump in. Since this is only for practice, I don't anticipate that happening, though.

We face off, and I study our opponents. I see Rayne on the other side, and I wonder if he did that on purpose. Alice, Jennifer, and Claudette are on Rayne's side, too.

Then I look over who's in our group. Tonya and Anthony are on our side. I try to remember what everyone's elements are. It'll only be too clear in a moment, so I stop wracking my brain. All I can come up with is that Anthony is a Gyan, and I remember Tonya has the latent Gyan gift, so it's not as powerful as her primary element, wind.

I study Rayne, who's watching us all with a calculated look. I'm not sure which gift of his is more powerful: wind or water. We'll soon see.

Gerard calls out, "Now remember, especially those of you with the fire gift, we're not out here for blood or scars, so only incapacitate. On the count of three, we'll begin. One, two, three!"

On my left, Linc blasts fire and his opponent does the same. Their combined blazes collide into a great cloud of flame and smoke. I whip my head over to see who I'm facing. A small teen girl is focusing on creating a wind funnel. It's taking all her concentration, and I easily take control of roots under her feet, bringing them up and wrapping her ankles in one quick move. When she goes down, I use the end of the root to hold it against her throat. She swallows and, holding her hands out, gives up.

I turn to see who I can go up against next. Linc is busy throwing fireballs at the same opponent he had a minute ago. It's good to know that another Festan's fire can hurt Linc. The man Linc's fighting throws his arm up and sends out a rope of fire that shoots straight out. I cry out and throw up a spray of dirt to put the fire out. It works, but barely. That was too close for comfort.

I decide this man needs to be tunneled. I open the ground underneath him, and with a cry, he drops. Right before his head is covered, I close the hole at his neck so he can't escape. He yells at me in anger, but I only smile in victory.

Linc flashes me a quick thumbs up, then turns to face Alice. I'm busy with Claudette. She's throwing small globes of ice that I quickly dodge left and right. I duck when one nearly takes my head off.

"Hey!" I yell. "That could have killed me!"

"Sorry!" she yells, but she doesn't look sorry.

I'm guessing her competitive nature is coming out, and I'm going to pay for it.

I open up the dirt underneath her, but she figures out my game quickly. She jumps, avoiding the hole and steps up onto a trunk.

The roots under it are too established. I don't have the strength to move all of them to drop her in a hole. But I can use them. I dodge her ice bombs while I concentrate on bringing up a net of roots. What I don't account for is her second element. I forgot who I'm fighting, that she has two powers. It's almost not fair.

I've just ducked onto the ground, avoiding another piece of ice, when I look up to see a volley of fire coming at me.

I throw up dirt, but it's not enough. I'm going to get burned.

Before it can touch me, however, I'm stunned to see Rayne flying in the air toward me, throwing water on Claudette's flames.

In a state of disbelief, I look on as he floats on the air, avoiding bursts of water and fire in the clearing. When he reaches me, he lands and wraps me in his arms, sending out a force of combined water and air. It blasts Claudette in the chest, knocking her off her feet.

Jack's at my side, barking wildly, shielding me from anything else.

I can only look at Rayne in awe. Did I see that correctly? Did Rayne just *fly*? I look up at him, and before I can even say thank you, Linc is facing us, his arms encased in fire. His face is thunderous, and I'm suddenly afraid he's going to do something he'll regret.

"Linc!" I yell. "He was just protecting me."

My words don't faze him. He stares straight at Rayne and sneers, "Get your hands off her."

Rayne lets go of me and steps away so it's just him and Linc in their near vicinity.

I forget I'm in a competition to see who's left standing. I was defeated anyway, so I step away from the fight, dragging Jack with me.

My Intended and my recent savior circle each other, eyes pinned on one another.

Fire bursts from Linc's hands and shoots out toward Rayne, who, with one hand, shoots out a stream of water to put it out.

How is Linc going to conquer a *water* elemental? Everything he throws at Rayne can be put out.

Well, that's what I thought.

Linc produces a fire so large that the smoke fills the area he and Rayne are in. Rayne starts coughing, and Linc races over to where Rayne stands.

Before he can get there, however, Rayne does his floating thing again. He's using his wind gift to levitate himself above the smoke so he can get a clean breath of fresh air. Once high enough, he catches his breath, taking in several gulps.

Linc shoots a stream of fire into the sky, which Rayne dodges neatly. Linc's jaw clenches in frustration.

I dimly notice that the two groups fighting have stopped to watch this epic battle between the two strong Elementals.

The strain of keeping himself aloft shows on Rayne's face, but before he comes down, he sends a storm of ice onto Linc's head with both hands. Between ducking and melting most of the ice chips, Linc stands with blood trickling down his temple as Rayne drops to the ground, panting.

Linc, too, is breathing hard, and they warily watch each other. Linc reacts first and throws volley after volley of fireballs.

Rayne extinguishes them all with his water gift just as quickly.

With a roar, Linc creates a ring of fire around Rayne, which he just douses with water, sending Linc into a rage.

Sweat pouring off his face, Linc turns burning eyes to Jack, then closes his eyes.

To my utter astonishment, Jack suddenly growls dangerously at my feet. Before I can stop him, he barks viciously and takes a running leap at Rayne.

"Jack, no! Come back!"

He completely ignores me. With wide eyes, Rayne puts his hands up to fend off the attack of my furious dog. With vicious barking, Jack jumps on Rayne's chest, taking him down.

"Jack! No!" I scream, but for the first time in his life, he doesn't heed my call.

Why doesn't Rayne defend himself? I look on in horror as Jack bites down on Rayne's shoulder, and he cries out in pain.

I scream at Jack and run toward them, but suddenly realize what's happening. I spin around and run toward the real problem instead.

Linc's eyes are still closed, and his hands are out, controlling my dog.

I run into his chest and pound on him, yelling, "Release Jack now, you crazy lunatic! He'll kill him, Linc!"

My words seem to finally reach him, and he opens his eyes and looks in horror at Jack biting down on a screaming Rayne.

I shake Linc hard. "What do you think you're doing? Release Jack. Now!" I turn and see Jack release Rayne. Jack turns and walks toward me in a daze, blood dripping from his muzzle.

"Jack," I say in a broken whisper. I cannot believe Linc used Jack to do such a horrific thing. I feel violated. My beautiful dog would never be so violent unless provoked or *forced.* I turn leaking eyes to Linc and look at him in disgust.

"Vela," Linc breathes with a tortured gaze. "I'm sorry." He stammers in apology, "I, I, I didn't mean for it to go that far. I'm used to controlling more than one animal at a time. My powers are too strong for just Jack. I would never..."

I ignore his apology and run toward Rayne to heal his deep bite wound. Given by my Jack. I can't believe it.

I reach Rayne, who's moaning and holding his shoulder. He flinches when I reach him and looks for Jack with fear in his eyes.

"He's not with me. He won't hurt you again."

I turn scathing eyes to Linc, who's standing alone, his shoulders slumped and his hands at his sides.

I put my hand on Rayne's bloody shoulder and call for Anthony and Tonya. They reach us quickly and I order, "We need to be sure no major arteries were punctured. Let's all check."

I look first, and don't find anything major damaged. I turn my eyes to Anthony, and he lays his hands on the wound. When he nods at me in affirmation of what I found, I look at Tonya.

She takes a bracing breath and puts her hand out to verify what Anthony and I found. She soon nods and pulls her hand away.

"Okay, I'm going to seal his wound closed. Will you guys help if I can't do it alone?"

They both agree with grave eyes.

I close my eyes, and after a whisper of encouragement to Rayne, I concentrate. Sealing the ragged edges Jack's bite caused, I do my best to knit the wound closed. Once the bleeding has stopped, I search for ligaments I'm sure must be torn.

Hearing Rayne moan, I send in healing warmth to ease his pain. I then refocus my internal vision, searching for anything torn. I find one ragged ligament and carefully piece it together.

Suddenly exhausted, I turn tired eyes to Anthony and wordlessly move so he can take over. Between the fighting and the healing, my body feels heavy and worn out.

After a minute of checking Rayne over, Anthony leans on his haunches and says, "You did good, Vela. I don't see anything else. He should be okay."

I look down at Rayne, who's laying with his eyes closed. I put my hand on his cheek. "Rayne? Are you conscious?"

He slowly slides his eyes open and relief soars through me. I don't see his eyes glazed with pain. He does, however, look exhausted. "Vela, thank you."

"No, please don't thank me. Let me say how very sorry I am."

"Again, apologizing for something you haven't done." His eyes dart over to Linc. Gerard is talking to Linc, whose head is down as he listens.

"Please know he took complete control of my Jack. My sweet dog would never attack without me telling him to, unless he was defending me."

"I forgot Festans could do that," Rayne says tiredly. He shuts his eyes and then opens them again. "I guess this means we lost."

"In my book, you won, Rayne. You played fair. Linc didn't." I can't even look at Linc. I never would think he'd stoop to this level to beat Rayne in a fight. "What Linc did was unquestionably wrong. Why didn't you defend yourself against Jack?" I study his eyes.

Rayne's throat works like he's about to answer but stops. Finally, he looks up at me and says, "I didn't want to hurt your dog. I know how close you are to him." He then accepts Anthony and Tonya's help so he can sit up.

"You're going to feel woozy from the blood loss," Anthony says, and I nod in agreement.

"And sore," I add. "Just because I healed you doesn't mean it takes away all the discomfort. But any of us would be happy to help ease it for you. In fact, you should come see

Hannah so she can look over what I did. I want her to be sure I healed you correctly."

Linc walks up and Rayne and I stiffen and lean away from him.

"Rayne. Please allow me to apologize. I got carried away," Linc says in a grave tone.

I glare at him, and he flicks a guilty glance at me, then back to Rayne.

"I'll have to remember you can control animals," Rayne says, putting his arms around Tonya and Anthony's shoulders and coming to a stand. Before he turns to walk away, Rayne says, "We'll have a rematch one of these days."

I watch Rayne walk away slowly. Jack has been by my side, and I kneel to look him over. His eyes are glazed over, and his tongue lolls out of his mouth. When I try to wipe the blood off his mouth, he licks at me half-heartedly, then at the blood.

Turning disgusted eyes to Linc, I say, "Don't even think of speaking to me. Not for a while. What you did..."

"Was wrong, I know. I'm sorry Vels."

"Don't call me that. In fact, leave me alone for a couple of days."

I stand up, and with my hand on Jack's collar, I walk back to Hannah's, my heart sore from all that happened.

CHAPTER THIRTY-SEVEN

Andy is at Hannah's when I get there, and I fill them in on what happened at the training field. Afterwards, I half-heartedly join Hannah in the kitchen to get dinner ready.

"Vela," Andy says with a sympathetic look as he joins us in the kitchen. "Festans run around with hot blood. I'm not excusing Linc's actions, but he comes by his temper naturally. And, technically," he says, his hands raised, "he was using his gift to win that bout."

When I slam my knife down and look at him incredulously, he says quickly, "Again, I'm not saying he should have used Jack like that. But we Festans don't have much in our arsenal against water elementals."

"My beautiful dog is not a weapon, Andy," I say through gritted teeth. "And definitely not without my permission."

"I understand. But please give Linc a chance to apologize. That's all I'm asking."

I look at him. How he knows I won't accept an apology from Linc, I don't know. Looking down and resuming my chopping, I leave that as my answer.

"Andy, maybe this isn't the best night for dinner," Hannah says gently.

I wince. Because of Linc's despicable actions, Andy is missing out on another opportunity to woo Hannah. I add that to my list of things to be mad at Linc about.

Andy leaves and Greta joins us in making dinner. Her fun chatter fills the air and sooths my torn-up feelings.

We've just sat down for dinner when a frantic knocking sounds on the door.

Hannah and I jump up. She reaches the door first and finds an agitated Linc on the doorstep.

When I see who it is, I call Jack to me, and we walk into Greta's room.

"Vela, wait," Linc begs.

I shut the door, ignoring his plea.

Sitting on my borrowed bed, I fume, hoping he takes the hint and leaves immediately.

A knock has me tensing on the bed. "Vela?" Hannah asks and pokes her head in.

I glare over her shoulder and see Linc hasn't left yet.

"He has news, Vela. About your parents."

I jump off the bed. "What happened?" Running past her, I reach Linc and ask, "What have you heard? Are they okay?"

He puts his hands up. "It's not those parents, Vels, I mean Vela," he amends after my glare. "It's your birth parents."

"What? What do you mean, my birth parents?" I fist my hands at my sides, shock freezing my limbs.

Linc's eyes are full of sympathy and concern. "I was having dinner with Rick and the two men who came in from the other community." He gestures with his thumb behind him. "I brought them to tell you what they told me."

"What could they have told you about my birth parents? How do they know anything about me?"

His eyes swing between mine, and he swallows. "I told them about you. I explained the little your parents told you, and they said they know of a couple who lost their baby seventeen years ago. The mother is a Gyan, Vela. She could be your mother."

Tears spring to my eyes. I huff a frustrated breath. I want to know everything these men have to say. "And you just left them outside?" I brush past him and open the door. Sure enough, two men are standing outside, huddled in their jackets.

One is a young guy with dark hair, the other an older gentleman with lighter brown hair. Their resemblance, however, is strikingly noticeable.

"Miss?" the older man says, holding out his hand. "I'm Gene. This here is my son, Jerry. We're from the west in a settlement about twenty miles from here, called Saddleback."

I glance at the son and see he's looking at me curiously. Ignoring him, I return my gaze to Gene. "You know of a couple who lost their baby seventeen years ago?"

"I do. A little girl, with the Gyan gift and bright blonde hair." He looks at my blonde hair and I finger it unconsciously.

Suddenly aware I'm leaving them on the doorstep, I stammer an apology. "Please come in. I'm sorry for not inviting you in right away. I'm in a bit of shock."

"Understandable," Gene says.

They both walk in uncertainly and Hannah takes action. "Please come in. Have you eaten?"

As they answer that they have had dinner, I can only stand in dumb silence. Linc stands at my side and excitement fills me that I might soon learn something about my birth parents. That I might not have to even search for them. That they might have practically fallen into my lap.

Jack senses my excitement and jumps up to stand by me, pushing his nose into my hand. I pet him, happy to have something to do with my nerves.

Gene and Jerry turn to me, and Gene asks, "What do you know about your parents?"

"I don't know anything about my birth parents. Only that I was left with a note."

"What did the note say?" Gene asks.

I wrinkle my nose as I think back to what my parents told me. "I think it just said my birthday and that I'm a child of the prophecy. But I don't know what that means."

Gene takes a step toward me. "What is your birthday, Vela?"

"September 23rd."

Jerry turns a stunned expression to his dad. "That's the Autumn Equinox, Dad."

Gene nods, not taking his grey eyes off me. "Yes, it is."

"We need to bring her back to Sandy and James. They'll want to know about her. It might be *her*."

"Who are Sandy and James?" I ask in suspended disbelief that they might actually know my birth parents.

Jerry turns to me. "That's who lost their baby girl. They said that's when their daughter's birthday is. We only know it because we've been following the signs of the prophecy religiously. We think that either the mother of the Chosen Child or the Child itself will have your birthday."

"Vela," Linc's voice makes me turn dazed eyes to him. "We need to talk," he says with a serious note in his voice.

I nod dimly and before I know it, we're standing outside in the chilly air.

Linc stands close to me and says, "I know this is a lot, but I might have something to do with all of this, too. I think," he takes a bracing breath. "that I might be the Hunter that catches the Goat. I might be the Hunter and you might be the Goat. Vela, we could very well be the parents of the Chosen Child.

"Remember the prophecy? When the day and night are of equal length, the star will rise who will bear the one who will unify. That's your birthday, Vels. And under the Winter Solstice sky, the Hunter will capture the Goat. Vela, I was born during the Winter Solstice. It's too remarkable of a coincidence."

I shake my head. "I can't think about all of that right now. My birth parents, Linc, might be twenty miles away. I need to meet them." I grab onto his jacket.

He puts his hands on top of mine and says, "We'll go as soon as we can round up some supplies. We'll go to them."

Remembering what he did to Rayne and Jack, I inhale and pull my hands from under his. "I'll go, but I'm not sure it's a good idea that you do."

Turning anguished eyes to me, he says, "Vela, I can't tell you how sorry I am. What I did was inexcusable. But I'm not letting you walk into that forest without me." His eyes turn solemn. "I will be with you whether you want me there or not. And I'll do everything I can to earn your forgiveness."

Looking at him gravely, I go back in the house to talk over taking a trip to this community. I run the names Sandy and James over and over in my mind as hope rushes through me. I might meet my birth parents. That sentence just never gets old the more I think it.

CHAPTER THIRTY-EIGHT

I've gathered my things; thankful Hannah lent me her backpack. It would have been hard lugging a duffle bag on a twenty-mile hike.

"But I wanna' go with you," Greta moans and throws herself on her bed.

I've been listening all night and morning to the same phrase over and over. "You can't go. It's too long a distance for you to keep up with us big kids," I tell her, repeating myself again.

"I'm stronger than I look!" She sits up and hugs a homemade doll to her chest. "I bet I could keep up." She pouts adorably.

"I'm sorry, kiddo. Not this time. Maybe when you're older."

"But I've never been anywhere else! I wanna' meet new people, see new things!" Flopping back, she stuffs a pillow on her face and groans.

I look at her sympathetically. "I know, Greta. I'm sorry. Maybe if your mom came, but she's staying here, and she's

going to need your help around the house and at the clinic."
I walk out of the room.

There's a group of us going to this Saddleback community. Claudette and Tonya are going to visit a friend of theirs who married a guy from there. I think they're also hoping to meet someone for themselves, too. I'm doubtful anyone but Rayne will attract Tonya, though. I wish the best for her. So, I hope for her sake she does meet someone who will notice her and appreciate her for her many great attributes.

Andy's coming too. He says he wants to familiarize himself with the way to this place, so he can return there if need be. Linc, of course, is coming, even though I expressly told him I didn't want him to. And Rayne is coming. At that thought, I sigh. Apparently, he immediately signed up, but no one knows why.

I do.

I'm going and he's made it clear he wants to spend time with me. And with me mad at Linc, this is his perfect opportunity to sweep in. He knows it, I know it and I'm sure Linc knows it, too.

I shake my head at the thought. Hannah is nowhere around, so I call out to Greta, "Where's your mom?"

"She's out back," Greta answers from the room.

I open the Hobbit door and walk to the back, sure enough finding Hannah stacking firewood in her arms.

"Hey," I say and take a deep breath. "Well, I guess it's almost time."

She stops her efforts and looks at me. "Vela, as happy as I am that you might find your real parents, please be careful. There's bears and wolves out there. I worry that you not knowing how to survive in the wilds will be a big problem."

"Don't worry, I've got lots of people around me to teach me how to not get killed." I clutch my shoulder straps.

She winces. "Vela, please don't even say that."

"Sorry." I look down, shaking my head. "Look, I'm meeting up with everyone in half an hour, so I guess this is goodbye."

She puts down her load of firewood. "Come here and give me a hug, then."

I step forward, and I'm quickly enveloped in a squeeze that reminds me of my mom. Instead of breathing in lavender, however, Hannah smells delicately of pine. Blinking back tears, I say as I hug her back, "I couldn't have asked for a better friend than you."

"Ditto." She leans back and looks at me warmly. "It's all going to come together, you know."

"What do you mean?"

"You and Linc. Rayne is just a distraction. Give Linc a chance to make amends. Trust me, he's sorry."

I hang my head. "I can't. Not now. I'll think about it, though."

"You'll have time on this trip to do a lot of that."

"Yea. That's if those two don't kill each other on the way."

She huffs. "I think they've worked through their aggressions. The main problem is that they're too alike. It's preventing them from being friends."

"I think I have a lot to do with that. Which is ridiculous. I'm nothing special." I shake my head at the thought of two guys fighting over me.

She takes me by the shoulders. "That's not true. You are a beautiful soul, inside and out. Anyone with eyes can see that. Now, let's get you to where you need to go."

Greta runs around the corner and latches onto my leg. "I don't want you to go," she says tearfully.

I kneel and untangle her arms from me. "I know. I'm going to miss you, too. I'll be back soon, okay? And we'll have another day, just you and me."

She sniffs and nods, joining her mom in putting their arms around me, leading me away.

Jack follows us as we walk toward the Town Hall. That's where we're all meeting and as I walk up, I see Claudette and Tonya walk in, wearing backpacks.

This is my first time in this spacious place. I look around and immediately appreciate all the woodwork. Like the outside, fleurs-des-lis decorate the corners and the rafters. It's at least two stories tall, the ceilings arcing up.

"What do you guys use this place for?" I ask Hannah.

She looks around and says, "Oh, when we need to meet as a community and have a meeting. When it's too cold to meet outside and we want to have a get-together. Or, when we've made a bunch of things, we want to trade off and barter with each other. Since we don't use money around here, it's our currency."

"What do you trade?" I notice Linc come into the hall, and I ignore him.

"I spend most of my time healing around here, and people often gift me what I need. But I do crochet a little. So, I'll have a few things I can barter when I need something extra."

"She makes the best hats," Tonya says, walking up to us, obviously overhearing our conversation.

Claudette joins us. "Think we're leaving soon?" She fidgets with her sweater and jumps on her toes.

"That ready to go?" I ask.

Her blue eyes dance. "Yes! This is my first time going to this place, and I'm looking forward to meeting new people."

I'm painfully aware of Linc standing a few feet away, staring out the door, his look one of concentration. I wonder who he's waiting for. It's so normal for me to turn to him and ask him my question, but I force myself not to.

"Hey, by the way, sorry that I got carried away on the training field," Claudette tells me, her face apologetic.

I nod, accepting her apology. I can't help but resent her some, however. If Rayne hadn't needed to save me from her attack, Linc would never have resorted to using Jack as a weapon.

Cries go up at the door, and I turn my head to see a whiskey jack flying in. It heads directly toward me, and like before, lands neatly on my shoulder. It leans its beak into my neck, and I laugh at how ticklish it is. The bird ruffles its feathers at my shoulders, jumping when I laughed, but it resumes its place when I calm.

I turn a resigned gaze over to Linc and see he's watching with sad eyes. His hand is out, commanding this bird to be a peace offering.

I shake my head at him, and he releases the bird, which flies directly out the door, obviously wanting no part in Linc's apology.

Hannah sighs and puts her hand on my arm. "Go easy on the poor guy, Vela."

For the first time since I've known her, I'm annoyed with her. "Why should I not make him squirm a little bit? He needs to know I will not ever be okay with him using Jack the way he did without my permission."

She gives me a sad smile and looks away, obviously disagreeing with me.

"I'm sorry, Hannah. I didn't mean to snap at you. I'm just so mad at him." I glare in Linc's direction, but he's not looking at me.

"Vela, please take what I'm going to tell you to heart. Someone once told me, that not forgiving someone is like drinking poison and expecting that person to die. You'll only hurt yourself, and life is too short and precious to waste like this."

I study the ground and think for a minute. "I'll make up with him, but not here. Not now."

Hannah's eyes warm and she puts her arms around me. "I knew you were special the moment I met you."

My eyes swim with tears, and I realize how much I'm going to miss this amazing woman. "I wish you were coming," I say as I hug her back.

She lets me go and says, "I can't leave this place. You go and have a good time and good luck meeting your birth parents. I hope they're who you're looking for."

"Thanks, Hannah."

I turn my head and see Rayne heading directly to Gene and Jerry. They lean in their heads and start talking furiously. I can only look on quizzically when Jerry glances at me a couple of times.

"Is everyone here?" Tonya asks, looking over the group of us.

"I think so," Claudette says, looking around impatiently.

My gaze is pulled to the entrance when I see Grace spill in. It looks like she ran here. She's out of breath and she looks over everyone. When she sees me, she walks quickly toward me.

I walk to meet her in the middle of the hall.

She reaches me and whispers, "I need to talk to you."

"Sure. What's up?"

"Not here." She glances over and when her eyes meet Rayne's, who I notice is watching her, she looks away.

"Okay. Let's go outside." I take her arm. Jack and I walk with her out the door.

Once we're under a tree and alone, she starts, "Look, I just think you need to know that Rayne isn't all he says he is."

I flinch and look at her, confused. "Rayne and I aren't together. Linc and I..." I stop because I can't bring myself to say I'm with Linc. I'm still furious with him.

"I know," she says, and grips my arm. "You've been really nice to me. Making an effort to talk to me when there are people here who still haven't said a word to me."

I swallow my response. If she opens up a little, I'm sure others would, too. But so I can hear what she knows about Rayne, I keep my opinions to myself.

"Before you throw an Intended bond away, you should know something about Rayne. No one else knows this. He's made me stay quiet about it." She swallows and looks over her shoulder. "You know the old man, Jack?"

I nod, wondering where she's going with this.

"He had a dog who he worshipped."

"Brutus, who's missing."

Her eyes are determined as she shakes her head. "He's not missing, he's dead. Rayne won't let me tell anyone the truth because he's guilty of the whole thing."

I gasp. "What? What happened?" Fisting my hand into Jack's neck, my whole body tenses.

"I was in one of the fields, laying down in the wildflowers when I noticed buzzards flying around close to me. When I got up to investigate what they were circling, I found Brutus dead." She squeezes her eyes shut and stops for a moment. Breathing deeply, she continues after I put my hand on her arm. "Something mauled him to death after he got caught in a trap Rayne had mistakenly laid."

"Mistakenly?"

She nods. "We're really careful where we lay traps, not putting them in a place where anyone could accidentally step in one. He laid the trap somewhere any one of us could have stumbled into."

My hand covers my mouth, my eyes tearing up at the thought of the poor dog not able to free himself and dying such a horrific death. "And then he couldn't get free to defend himself when he needed to?"

She nods, her lips set in a thin line. "And Rayne should have checked that trap that day, too. He didn't, and so no one was there to save Brutus' life. He's responsible for that dog's death, and he doesn't want anyone to know about it. Then he buried him and told me not to tell anyone." Her eyes fill with a fierce light. "But I know everything."

"How did you find out about this? I mean, I know you found Brutus, but..."

"I ran into town when I found Brutus' mauled body and the first person I found was Rayne. I was hysterical and told him about Brutus. He ran back to the field with me, and while he was distraught, he told me everything.

"Then he took his body, burying him somewhere no one will find the grave. Poor Jack still thinks his dog abandoned him and ran away. He keeps waiting for him to come home." Her voice cracks and tears fill her eyes.

She sniffs and squeezes my arm. "But I wanted you to know. If he'd hide the body of that poor dog just to cover his mistake and make me stay quiet, what else is he capable of?"

I shake my head. "I don't know."

"I don't either. Listen, I heard what Linc did, and Vela, you can believe me when I say I'd trust Linc a hundred times more than I would Rayne. Linc did what he did in the open, where everyone could see him. Rayne is being a coward and hiding his mistakes and lying to old Jack. That does not make for a trustworthy man. Don't throw away what you have with Linc for someone like Rayne. Don't ever throw your Intended bond away. Ever. It's too precious of a gift."

Her eyes reach into mine, and before I can stop myself, I hug her. "I knew you'd be good for me. I just knew you were amazing."

I feel her stiffen in my hug, but she soon relaxes and pats me on the back.

"I don't know about all of that," she says, looking embarrassed.

I lean back, holding her shoulders. "No, I mean it. I know it took a lot for you to tell me this."

She shakes her head, her eyes entreating mine. "If you know what a special, precious thing an Intended bond is, why would you ever even think of not accepting it for the gift it is?"

I look down. "I do know. You have to understand something, though. My dog is as important to me as Brutus was to Jack. Linc forcing Jack to attack someone, and without even asking permission...I just can't accept it. I need to work that one out. I'm not throwing the gift of our bond away. I promise. I'm just making Linc suffer a little bit for what he did."

Her eyes soften. "I guess I can understand that. But don't make him wait too long, okay? Not for someone like Rayne."

"Are you going to tell anyone else what you told me?"

She looks away. "I should," she says solemnly. "Especially old Jack."

I nod. "Just be brave. God will give you the strength to tell who you need to tell. And Jack needs to know the truth."

"Right. Thanks."

"No, thank *you*," I say.

"Be careful out there. There are packs of wolves and bears out there."

I shudder. "I will. Thanks again." I give her a quick hug and walk away, processing the story she just told me. When I walk into the Hall, I can't help but glance at Rayne. He notices my entrance and watches me with his eyes drawn down in a scowl.

He saw me walk out with Grace, so I'm sure he suspects that his secret is out. I slide my eyes away before I can give away that Grace told me what she knows.

I look instead at Linc, who seems to be half listening to Rick. He glances at me and then holds my gaze when I don't look away from him.

I'm drawn into his cerulean eyes and my heart clenches but hurt abandons my good sense. I want to talk to him, but I also don't want to, not yet. My fingers clench into Jack's neck as I remember Jack's will being taken away from him. My eyes harden, and I turn away. I also feel terrible for old Jack. His dog is never coming back, his death hidden. I turn furious eyes to Rayne.

"Okay, everyone, listen up!" Rick says, clapping. "You need to make good time today. If you leave soon, you can get ten miles in. It won't be easy, but I think all of you are fit enough to do it. Well," he says, laughing, "We know Gene and Jerry can do it as they made it here. So, let's pray over the group so they can get a good head start."

I make my way over and stand next to Claudette and Tonya. We all huddle together and those not going with us stand around, putting their hands on our shoulders and backs.

I scent Linc's delicious smell and know he's standing right behind me. I refuse to look back at him, afraid if I do, I'll give in and let up on my punishment. But I can feel him. His body is a flame I can't ignore. He calls to me like no one else.

He puts his hand on my shoulder, and my muscles tighten under his hand. He squeezes and I can't help but melt a little.

Rick prays and I close my eyes and pray with him, asking God for strength and protection as we hike to this other commune.

Once Rick finishes, I step away as fast as I can, holding onto my belief that Linc needs to suffer.

I file after the girls as they walk out of the Hall.

Gene, Jerry, and Andy are outside waiting for us. Once we're all out, Gene calls out, "Okay, now let's stay together. If you notice someone flagging, just call out and we'll stop."

At that, we leave the community I've grown to appreciate and love in my short time here. I look back at Hannah and Greta, giving them a warm smile, which they reciprocate. I see Grace, too, who waves at me before she disappears around a corner.

I soon get into a rhythm as we walk. I'm thankful for my good hiking shoes, but soon realize I'm not in the best of shape to hike with people who are conditioned to walk ten miles in one day. I'm determined to keep up, though. I just wish my spirits were as positive as my attitude. I can't help but feel depressed that Linc and I haven't made up yet. And poor Brutus.

Linc's hiking behind me, and a part of me knows he's keeping an eye on me.

Tonya reads my mind when she asks, "Are you going to ignore him forever?"

I look up at her, surprised. "Uh, no." I glance back at Linc, who's walking alone. His eyes are down, so he doesn't notice my look. "I just need him to know what he did was wrong."

"I've never seen someone so sorry in all my life," Claudette joins in. She laughs softly so he won't hear. "If I were you, I would definitely be kissing and making up right about now."

I blush. As much as I would like that, I hold on to my decision. "I'll talk to him. Just not now. At our first stop, I will."

They both give Linc sympathetic glances, but I refuse to soften my heart toward him.

As we walk, I'm lost in my thoughts. What Andy said about Linc makes sense. Linc didn't have any other way to compete against a strong water Elemental. He used a power of his own to win the fight. But as soon as I remember my sweet Jack, his vicious nature being forced to come out against his will, I'm still hot with fury. So, I'll let Linc stew in his guilt for another couple of hours.

Despite my inner insistence on making Linc suffer, I keep glancing at him. He stays silent and anytime anyone tries to engage him in conversation, they soon give up. He glances at me, too, and every time he does, my heart flips in my chest.

Two hours into the walk, I notice Rayne has dropped back in the group. He started at the front, and I was only too happy not to talk to him.

It looks like I'll have to, however, because he's been inching closer and closer to me. I grit my teeth. What Grace revealed about him haunts my thoughts. What he did was wrong. He should have fessed up to his mistakes and admitted to what happened. I find that I can't judge too harshly, though. I've made mistakes and not told my parents. It's easier to hide in your guilt than admit to them. But old Jack deserves to know the truth. And to cover it up and make Grace stay quiet, that's too much. It's a hard situation, though, to say the least.

I'm out of breath, keeping up the grueling pace and, at one point, trip over a tree root. I find a hand at my elbow, helping me stay on my feet. Thinking it's Linc, I smile up at him. It's not Linc, though. To my disappointment, it's Rayne returning my smile.

I catch Tonya giving me a sidelong look, and I wince. It must be hard to see Rayne giving me attention like this. And for that matter, it must be hard for Linc, too.

I pull my arm away and lose my smile. "Thanks," I say in a curt tone.

"This isn't the easiest of hikes," he says conversationally, either ignoring my lack of interest or not noticing it. "I've done it a couple of times now."

"Good for you," I say and glance over my shoulder. I catch Linc giving Rayne a scathing stare before he looks away. I sigh.

"So, you think you might meet your birth parents? Is that what I heard?"

It's clear not much stays quiet in a town like Polar Bear Lodge. "Yes," I say and turn my head away from Rayne, discouraging any more conversation.

He doesn't get the hint.

"I would be pretty excited if I were you. Is it true your birthday is the Autumn Equinox?"

I huff, which is easy considering I'm breathing hard from the hiking. "Look, I'm not trying to be rude, but I can't really keep up an ongoing conversation right now." I take a deep breath after huffing. "I'm just trying to keep up."

"Do you want me to ask the others to slow down?" he offers.

I could shoot him down right now. "No! I'll keep up. Just let me concentrate, okay?"

"Okay," he reluctantly agrees. He stays next to me, and I resent his presence.

"Have I done something to offend you?"

I glare at him. He's not only ignoring what I just told him, but he's guilty of a terrible thing. I don't say anything.

"Look, if I've done something, let me make it up to you. Do you want me to carry your backpack?"

I shake my head, concentrating on my breathing, pure frustration blaring through me at his presence.

Thinking of Linc, I don't want him to think it's my choice that Rayne is walking with me. I glance back at Linc and give him a look that I hope spells out I'm sorry.

He's looking at me, and when he sees my expression, his hardens. He speeds up and soon he's walking at my other side.

Now I'm in the very uncomfortable position of having Linc to my left and Rayne to my right. Jack is off exploring ahead of me, so he can't buffer this uncomfortable position. None of us say a word, and I die a little at how tense the air is.

I breathe in my nose and out of my mouth as I keep up my trek. I try to focus on the beauty of our surroundings and not on the elephant in the forest.

The air is chilly, but with my exertion, I'm not the least bit cold. In fact, I wipe sweat from my forehead. I'm looking up at a gorgeous tree full of red and orange leaves when I trip again.

This time, instead of one hand under my elbow, I've got two. Both guys are holding me up, and I look from one to the other, not knowing who to thank first. Linc searches my eyes for a second and I'm not sure what he sees there because he drops my arm and steps away.

I'm longing to call him back, especially since Rayne hasn't let go of me yet.

"Vela? Are you okay?" Rayne asks, his handsome face set in concerned lines.

"I'm fine," I say quickly. "Thank you." Then I look at Linc, who's watching me with sad eyes. "Thank you," I say softly. I'm about to say more when a huge roar fills the air.

CHAPTER THIRTY-NINE

M y heart stutters, then stops, as I look around to see where that horrible noise came from. I'm not the only one.

I hear someone crying out. Claudette's panic-filled eyes is looking beyond our trail into the distance, and I follow her gaze.

To my horror, I see something I'd hoped I'd never see. A huge white bear stands up on its hind feet and sends out a roar that chills my bones and makes my heart stop beating. It's the grizzly-and-polar-bear hybrid. The grolar bear Rayne mentioned. It's easily a thousand pounds sporting dirty white fur. And it's here.

"Do we run?" someone asks.

I immediately look for Jack. He takes one look at the massive bear and runs away in the opposite direction. Smart dog.

Linc is immediately next to me, holding my arm. "Vela, we might have to fight that thing. If we do, I want you to run."

"What? No! I won't leave you alone to fight that."

He's insistent, and he gets in my face. "When I say run, you run, Vela," he yells.

I turn my terrified eyes back to the bear. It's on all fours now and it's sniffing the air and swaying, like it hasn't decided to attack us or not.

I pray it doesn't.

Gene and Jerry, who are at the front, start making loud noises. They yell at us to do the same. I manage to bring my voice to a shout as we bark loud noises at the irritated bear, hoping to scare it away.

It swings its head back and forth, and I'm sure it will run away. Instead, it charges.

I scream.

"Vela, run!" Linc pushes me toward Rayne. "Fly her out of here," he orders a stunned Rayne.

I'm shoved into Rayne's arms and pushed away from the trail. I look over my shoulder and see fire and wind rushing at the enraged white bear. Andy and Jerry are alternating attacks.

It stops for a moment before it bellows out a roar that shakes the trees. I watch helplessly as Linc charges toward it with twin ropes of fire and whips them around the bear's neck.

"Linc, no!" I fight against Rayne's hold as I try to run back to him, but I can't get free.

Linc barely hangs on as the bear swings from side to side, screaming its rage. Gene and Andy add to Linc's weapons with fire ropes of their own, directing others to attack with their own gifts.

The bear lunges up on its hind legs and all three lose hold of their ropes. They fall to the ground. The monstrous bear drops to its feet and charges again.

It's like the bear is immune to fire, but I know it's just because it's so massive. The ropes aren't enough to disable him. Even from here, I can smell the burned fur.

My heart stutters when the bear nearly reaches Gene, who hasn't recovered yet. He scrambles backward in the dirt, but he's in its sights and is way too close to him. Reaching back with its huge paw, it prepares to strike at Gene when Claudette hurtles an ice spear at its shoulder, making the bear roar in fury.

That gives Gene the ability to run away, and the bear lurches toward Claudette, who runs away screaming. It's giving her chase, and I fight Rayne's hold with all that I have.

"I have to help!" I scream in Rayne's face.

He gives me a grim look and refuses to let me budge.

I hear an anguished scream and turn to see the bear swat at Claudette's back. She goes down.

"No!" I scream and cry into Rayne's shoulder at my utter helplessness.

Someone, Jerry, I think, starts a cyclone. Leaves and sticks swirl around the area as the wind spins. He adds fire to the cyclone, making for a deadly weapon. I shake Rayne's shoulder. "You can help him, you idiot. Let me go!"

Indecision wars in his eyes.

Before the cyclone can reach the bear, it lurches past the firestorm and races toward Linc and Tonya. Linc sends a stream of fire straight from his hands, but the bear just charges through it. I see Linc running up an incline, then climbs a tree, taking safety in its branches.

The bear chases him to the tree and starts pushing on the trunk, trying to get him down. Linc closes his eyes, and I know he's trying to find an animal to help defend him. I look around, wondering what he senses that I can't see.

Suddenly, birds come flying from every direction.

Gene and Tonya both duck under the onslaught of wings. The small, fast birds swarm the bear, one in particular, attacking the bear's eyes. It looks like my friend, the whiskey jack. Its pecking seems to blind the bear, and it falls back crashing into the partially uprooted tree.

The tree sways, slowly teetering at a sharp angle when Linc, realizing he's not finding safety in the tree anymore, jumps out. He runs off to where I can't see him. The birds disperse without Linc's commands, and the bear gives chase with a roar.

Gene, Jerry, Andy, and Tonya race after the bear.

I beat Rayne's shoulder and scream at him, "Let me go! I will never forgive you for this. I need to help them!"

"No, Vela. You need to stay safe. It's imperative you are safe no matter what. You could be..." he stops himself, but I see his throat working like he wants to finish.

"What? Rayne, I could be what?"

He shakes his head and refuses to answer.

I look at him with incredulity. "I am nothing, Rayne. If Linc is hurt, I will never forgive you. Do you hear me? Never!"

"It's worth it. You're worth it."

I slump in despair, unable to budge in Rayne's steel grip.

Just when I think I've seen the last of them and Rayne relaxes his grip on me, everyone that disappeared with the bear reappears, coming around the bend, screaming.

"Run, ruuuun!" Linc screams at Rayne and me with wild eyes.

Rayne's arm squeezes my side, and he pulls me roughly off the trail, running, dragging me along with him. We run and run. I'm not sure which way we're going, only that it's away from the grolar bear. I push bushes to the side, making a trail for us. I hear crashing behind us, and I don't know if it's the bear or my friends.

Rayne, without consulting me, suddenly slings us off an edge of the trail I didn't notice. I scream and plummet down an embankment, holding onto Rayne for dear life. He grunts and I feel an up shift of air underneath us pushing and slowing our descent.

I grab onto his neck and hide my face in his shoulder. Rayne's entire body is tense and trembles with the effort he's exerting. We're falling, but not as fast. I'm confused for a moment because I feel the familiar warmth, like I'm using my Gyan gift. How could I when I'm falling?

I brace myself for hitting the ground. I have no idea if we'll survive the fall. And worse, I don't know if the others behind us are going to survive the enraged bear.

Rayne and I crash onto the ground, my leg smashing against some rocks. I feel a rip in my knee, and I scream in pain. My side, too, hit hard, and the pain takes my breath away.

I turn my face into the leaves and moan, breathing erratically. I'm alive, but I'm hurt badly.

"Rayne?" I ask and try to control my sobs.

"I'm here," he says, exhaustion in his voice.

"Where are we?" I ask, looking around and up. My breath catches at the impossible drop we just made. We must have fallen ten stories. We've landed in some kind of ravine. There's a sheer cliff face on both sides of us.

"I don't know. Somewhere off the trail."

"Can we go back?" I gasp as I sit up and hold my aching side and leg. "We have to see if everyone is okay." I hiss at the pain.

"We're not going back that way. We can't," Rayne says gravely and looks around.

"There are vines growing all up those walls, Rayne. We can climb."

He scans his eyes over my leg. "You're not climbing anything, Vela. You can't heal yourself, and I certainly can't. We're going to have to get back another way."

My hope drops, and I slump over, completely overwhelmed. "What about everyone else? How will we know if they're okay?"

"We're going to have to wait until we get home to find out news. We can't go back the way we came, Vela."

I turn burning eyes to him. "This is your fault, Rayne. I could have stayed and helped. *You* could have helped defeat that bear. Now I'm stuck here with you. You *coward.*"

His eyes blaze, and he leans toward me. "You don't know what you're saying. If you knew what I did, you'd do the same."

"What? What could you possibly know about me that I don't?"

He slams his hands down on the ground, one on each side of me. "You are the Child, Vela Ashcroft. The Chosen Child we've all been waiting for. That's why I had to save you. *You* are meant to save our world."

I look at him with wide eyes, and my heart stops beating in my chest. It can't be true. I don't believe it. There is no way I am meant to save anything.

"I'm just a girl," I say weakly.

"You're not. You're *The Girl.* Vela, our world needs you."

Rayne

Free Book!

Receive a free novella, Operation Kane, from the Terra, Torch, and Tempest world if you join my newsletter!

Elia will do anything to get her best friend's older brother to notice she's a woman now, even become a spy.

Dive into this world of Elementals, unrequited love, and the power of hope. Enjoy the best friend's older brother, forbidden love, fake dating, and friends-to-lovers tropes in this powerful story of faith and young love.

Go to: www.sofiasimpson.com to find this charming novella. Connect with me there if you'd like to have me on your podcast.

And if you enjoyed this book, please leave a review on Amazon, Bookbub or Goodreads, or if you're especially generous, all three! It means more to us authors than you know.

Fill your rooms with the delicious scents of my book candles!

Vela, Honey Butter Rolls
Linc, Roasted Marshmallows
Rayne, Evergreen and Ash

Go to:

https://linktr.ee/sofiasimpsonauthor

Acknowledgements

How could I not acknowledge the one Person who gives me inspiration on a daily basis? Jesus is my Best Friend and Source of every creative thought I've had.

My hunny, you have been so patient with me on this crazy journey, supporting me in all the areas I've ventured. Listened to my many joys and woes, encouraging me all the way. I love you more than my heart can say.

Nicky, if it wasn't for you, I probably wouldn't have a podcast. You suggest great guests and then help me schedule them in. You also have the most encouraging voice of reason for when things get hard. But you're also my biggest cheerleader for when things are good! Thank you baby, I love you.

Matthew, you're such a good listener. It helps me to talk through things and you have the kindest ear, you just let me rant or rave, whichever mood I'm in. I love you!

Milana, how many books of mine do you have to buy before you read one of them? LOL! You are one of my biggest supporters, thank you for believing so much in me! Love you, Minnie Mouse!

Jessica Gwyn, you are the best editor I've ever worked with. Your suggestions made this book a hundred times better and more readable. And thank you for helping me launch this book! Your talents astound me! Thank you for all you've done for this book.

Jenny, you know how near and dear to my heart you are. You've talked me through many a problem, in my writing journey and personally. I could not have written this book without your support. And you are a genius with newsletters, have I told you that lately? Thank you for your friendship, it is highly valued.

Darcy, I could not have written this book without you. The many plot holes you talked me through and character questions you answered are endless. Thank you for helping me stretch my wings in being the best writer I can be. I wouldn't be the writer I am without you!

Dana, if I ever am in need of a cheerleader, I call you. You
have a way of turning any upside-down day right side up
again. Thank you for encouraging me through this crazy
world of writing, I won't forget that you were one of my first
fans!

Heidi, if ever I need a marketing guru, I call you. You have
been invaluable in friendship to me and in my career of being
an author. In every way, you have encouraged me. Thank you.
I can only hope I've done some of the same for you. I've been
blessed to know you, ever since I found out another author
attended my church! I don't regret showing up on your
doorstep that morning, AT ALL!

My Lakeland Writer's Group and Word Weaver friends, each
of you have had a hand in turning my writing from awful to
what it is now, hopefully good! I have found so much
confidence in my writing thanks to all of your advice and
help in overcoming my many bad writing habits. Thank you
from the bottom of my heart!

Mom and Dad, your prayers keep me going every day.
Knowing you're praying not only for me but my boys and
family helps me through so many tough days. Thank you for
your love and prayers.

And to my Readers, especially Charlotte, you make this
dream of writing a possibility. Thank you for your many
encouraging words and devotion to my stories, knowing you
need the next part of the story. It keeps me writing!

And to the writing community of Instagram. I just read the
acknowledgements of Christopher Paolini in his latest book,
and he literally had three pages devoted to thanking the
editors, marketing people, publicists and everyone else
responsible for putting his book out into the world. As I
don't have those resources, I am thankful that I have you. I
was able to market my book through your pages and
accounts, and I couldn't be more thankful for all of your
support.